PANDEMIC!

- McRoberts stumbled over grotesquely disfigured bodies, clutching his mask. He had to reach a telephone. Suddenly McTavish was there, his face encrusted with black pustules, clutching at McRoberts mask, exposing him to the deadly anthrax spores . . .

- Trevor, aged 12, was late getting home to Strumford. He pedaled quickly towards the darkened village, aware that something was amiss, but never suspecting that his parents and friends, all his neighbors, were dead . . .

- The family stepped off the boat onto another shore. They were safe at last. But the angry crowd greeted them with hysterical shouts, showering them with bullets. How dare they come here, carrying their dread disease . . .

MAN'S ERROR HAD DISPERSED THE DEADLY ANTHRAX SPORES ACROSS THE COUNTRY. SOON THEY WOULD SPREAD THROUGHOUT THE WORLD. THIS IS THE HORRIFYING STORY OF WHAT HAPPENS WHEN AN EXPERIMENT IN BIOLOGICAL WARFARE BACKFIRES, CLAIMING ITS CREATORS AS VICTIMS . . .

The Anthrax Mutation

(Original title: Project Dracula)

ALAN SCOTT

PYRAMID BOOKS NEW YORK

THE ANTHRAX MUTATION
(Original title: Project Dracula)

A PYRAMID BOOK

Copyright © Alan Scott 1971

Pyramid edition published April 1976

ISBN 0-515-03949-7

Printed in the United States of America

Pyramid Books are published by Pyramid Publications (Harcourt Brace Jovanovich). Its trademarks, consisting of the "Pyramid" and the portrayal of a pyramid, are registered in the United States Patent Office.

Pyramid Publications
(Harcourt Brace Jovanovich)
757 Third Avenue, New York, N.Y. 10017

ACKNOWLEDGEMENTS

I would firstly like to express my thanks to Elizabeth Compton who has pioneered the fight against chemical and biological weapon research in this country. Her advice and criticism have guided me along the uncomfortable study of gas and germ warfare. I must also express my gratitude to many people who have contributed in their own personal way towards making The Anthrax Mutation the book it is. I especially wish to acknowledge the patience and assistance of my students, Nigel and John, who have endured more my typing than my teaching, and to Thomas Anderson for his invaluable technical assistance.

This book is in no way directed at one specific person or enterprise, and where specific names of companies or people have been used, this in no way implies that they would become involved in any eventuality as described in this story. Unless specifically mentioned, any similarity to persons living or dead, or to any company, is unintentional.

I have relied upon several sources of information in the writing of this book and I name a few of them as references for any reader who may wish to explore further the realms and implications of chemical and biological research. Under this heading and those of specific chemical and biological agents the "Encyclopaedia Britannica" offers concise explanations. "Chemical and Biological Warfare, America's Hidden Arsenal" by Seymour M. Hersh (MacGibbon and Key, 1968) offers a broader understanding of American and international involvement in such research while "We All Fall Down" by Robin Clarke (Pelican, 1969) traces the history and current development of gas and germ warfare and includes informative tables in its Appendix. Government information services, the Ministry of Defense and the individual military services will release no pertinent information to any private person.

CONTENTS

PROLOGUE

The Fort Detrick Research Station is perhaps the largest in the world. Its sole purpose is to provide a testing and developing center for biological weapons which could be used in an attack against hostile countries or in the defense of the United States. The station produces many of the mutated forms of biological agents and is continually creating improved viruses, bacteria and other micro-organic substances. As early as during World War II, Detrick developed a way of concentrating twenty-four thousand, nine hundred billion Brucella organisms into an ounce of ordinary paste. Its current research involves the development of organisms which cause tularemia, Rocky Mountain Spotted Fever, Q-Fever, encephalo-myelitis, brucellosis, plague and anthrax. Detrick is also concerned with the various methods in which these substances can be disseminated for maximum effect.

Because the American government feels that research in these areas is vital to the defense of the country, we have the greatest facilities found anywhere in the world for cultivation and investigation of biological weapons. However, we still enjoy a close liaison with our allies in developing these arsenals; for our mistakes and the mistakes of our allies contribute towards international experimentation which increases the defense of the free world; since mutual exchanges of information save both money and thousands of man hours of intensive research. England in particular is very much involved in this inter-change of information. The research base at Porton in Wiltshire is to Great Britain what Detrick is to America. But many times our mutual discoveries are kept secret for months, sometimes for ever. Naturally, neither the United States nor Great Britain wish to let each other know exactly who's got what or what each is currently developing. It has happened that a country will take up a project which America gave up as unsatisfactory and carry it further or develop it to suit its particular needs. This is what England was doing, but keeping it a closely guarded secret, so secret in fact that only the Dwarf Hill Microbiological Establishment in Cornwall knew the full details. But somewhere along the ultra-security block something slipped and Detrick got wind of it. Because my job was Liaison Officer among the international weapons research centers, I was sent from Fort Detrick to try to uncover what mysterious project the English had dug up from the grave of American rejects. We had no real information other that the scheme dealt with a time-delay delivery of highly potent anthrax bacillus. My colleagues who joined me on the expedition had no idea of which plant was working on the project, nor had I. We were invited to tour each of the bases on the precept that it was the periodic comparison-of-notes visit that we make and reciprocate. None of us had any real idea of what to look for and most probably anything we did discover would be by chance. We had done this sort of thing many times before, though, and we knew the ways of getting around security precautions and reticent military officials. One of us might come up with the answer in his individual inspection and we would all return home, having thanked the British government profusely for a charming and enlightening visit, and having expressed the hope that we could soon see some of their men visiting us. It was all very formal, cordial and downright phoney.

Exactly what did happen after we landed in England

and how the discovery of what the British were up to was made is chronicled here. It is ironic that we came to England to discover what secrets they kept, and in the end we had to surrender one of our most tightly guarded biological defense weapons in order to save England from herself.

SECTION ONE: THE INVASION

Saturday, 10th October

I

The Captain was impatient. He paced the white tiled corridor, glared at his watch, turned on his heels, and stomped back to the office. "Anything from the gate?" he asked sourly.

"Nothing yet, Sir. Who is it this time?"

"Bloody Yanks, that's who. You'd think they know enough without having to come snooping around here."

"Yes, Sir," the Private acknowledged meekly. A bell rang. The Private looked up from the switchboard. "It's them, sir."

The Captain strode off in the direction of the main entrance, mumbling anti-Americanisms. Last week it had been anti-Germanisms (Hadn't they done enough in the last War?) and the week before that he had been ordered to bone up on his French so as to converse more easily with a contingent of—in his words—Frogs. Bloody annoying, he was thinking. Won't let us get on with things. He knew of a thousand reasons not to let foreigners come trapsing around the plant, security being one of his priorities, and England another.

"Look sharp, Corporal," he snapped bad naturedly at a wooden crate on two legs. "And what in hell is that full of?"

"Bats, Sir," replied something from behind, below or beneath. "For Section Three."

"Bats?"

"Yes, Sir. And they're rather heavy, Sir."

"Get on with it then. And mind none of them have any teeth."

13

The Corporal turned slightly. "Teeth, Sir?"

"Bats—you know. Blood and vampires."

The Corporal stared at the crate which nestled uncomfortably close to his neck. He stretched his arms out and scurried around the corner towards Section Three.

The Captain grinned. "Bats. What next?" He reached the main entrance in time to see a car pull up. As he had done so many times before, he quick-stepped up to the door and swung it open. "Captain Andrew McRoberts, Sir," he saluted crisply.

Colonel Wyers returned the salute from his seat. "Captain, this is Major Glen Thomas from the Fort Detrick group. Major Thomas, meet my unofficial first mate. Captain McRoberts will take you over the base." As he heaved himself from the car, he turned to the Captain and nodded imperceptibly. "I won't delay you. Meet you in the mess in an hour."

Major Thomas swung across the seat and stepped out. He wanted to stretch, but he reserved the pleasure for another time. Instead, he glanced about him and watched the car roar away much like a child on his first day at boarding school. "How do you do, Captain," he smiled at length. "I suppose I'm wearing out the visitors' mat."

The Captain glanced up. "How's that, Sir?"

"I understand you've been having sort of a mini UN going on up here."

"It's not been easy, Sir," he admitted as they walked up the steps and passed through the glass doors into the spotless corridor. "These lads find visitors disturbing."

"And you?" Thomas said casually.

"It's security, Major. And it's the work. Damned funny business, all this. Top secret, hush-hush. Why the lads feel they're fenced in—even in the town. Then you lot come marching about the place—well I'm sure your boys have the same problems." He stopped at the Security

Desk and pushed across a folded card. The guard glanced at the pass, looked up at the Major, and pushed a button on the panel in front of him. Major Thomas heard a slight hiss and another set of glass doors opened automatically.

"We're a bit tighter than you," Thomas began, noticing a sign which was directing them towards Section Two. "No one but the very special."

"Smart fellows. Wish we could be as strict." The Captain pushed open a door ominously labelled "Danger, Neuro-Cerebral Toxicants" and nodded at a group of men in white coats and plastic gloves. "This is Section Two. We process much of the nerve gases here before sending them on for mass production—stockpiling. Sort of the final filter."

Major Thomas stared over the shoulders of the researchers who were totally absorbed in their labors—a maze of test tubes, burners and glass pipes. "Do you develop the gas or just refine?"

"A little of both," someone offered without glancing up.

Their attention was focused on a large glass bulb which was turning a crimson, fading, and trying a different color. The explanation continued. "The raw gases come to us for separation into the toxic agents. Sarin, GB, VX and all that. We process only in very small amounts. Porton handles all the big stuff."

There were some guinea pigs and rabbits munching lettuce in their cages. Major Thomas sidled over and tapped one of the glass panes. The guinea pig wasn't interested. "How many of these do you get through?"

One of the scientists looked up. "Quite a few. We have to test each new batch before sending it on." He grinned. "Shouldn't want anyone killed with bad gas."

"Very humorous," his colleague snapped, leaving the table on which the bulb continued its exploration of the color spectrum. "We test new batches because we don't want any unknown effects creeping in—effects we don't already know about. Here," he said, lifting a rabbit from its cage. "We're going to put some of that gas in the bulb through its paces. It seems a bit unstable at the moment."

The Major followed the scientist over to the table on which sat the rabbit apparently unconcerned about his questionable future as he ruminated on the remains of his lettuce.

"We use a two cc solution of about the same proportion as one might expect to find in the field. The VX gas is rather effective in that it throws the nervous system into chaos—but I'm sure you're well up on all this."

The Major raised his eyebrows uncommittingly. He watched the rabbit's courier of death plunge the hypodermic into its side.

"Almost immediately you will notice the body begin to convulse. Next paralysis sets in until the rabbit can no longer breathe. We've found that in most cases there is a general constriction of the organs and muscles including the erection of the male reproductive organ and a secretion from the tear and salivary glands. Though heart rate is considerably retarded, death comes from paralysis of the lungs—sort of a cross between drowning and suffocation."

The Captain was still staring at the rabbits and guinea pigs who nestled safely in their cages. He had seen it all too often to be even callously interested. But Major Thomas watched carefully as the rabbit struggled to fill his paralysed lungs and at the same time choked to death on his own saliva.

"We find that GB has much the same effect," Thomas began. "Though its persistence is far less than VX. We prefer inhalation or ingestion rather than injection."

"Yes, I've read your papers on that. About some chaps who wandered into the testing area or something . . ."

Thomas heard this one before. "And Martin and Cockayne? Didn't they work here?"

The researcher grinned without taking his eyes from the dead rabbit. "Accidents have been known to happen, I daresay. This sort of thing can get pretty sticky—especially if the public get on to it."

"I can't recall any of our men here meeting up with any accidents," mumbled the Captain as he pushed away from the cages. "And I've been here since we opened."

It was an obvious effort. The researcher looked up at Thomas and smiled knowingly. "No, not a single case. Must have been somewhere else. We have all the safety devices, you know. We hold a very respectable record."

"And you don't stockpile any of this stuff?" the Major asked.

"In very small quantities," the Captain replied. "We've got more than usual here this week as we've only just completed testing several batches, but most of it will be shipped out tomorrow. Porton carries the stocks, but you must realize that each of our plants works independently of one another. Very little information passes between us unless it's of vital importance. The Ministry feels it's better that way—security and all. Really, we hardly know anything of what the other plants are developing—all that's left up to London." He led him out of Section Two and passed through another set of automatic doors into Section Three. There was a sentry sitting before the large metal gates which barred the way into the inner laboratory. He rose as the Captain approached.

"Aren't those two little red marks on your neck, Corporal?" McRoberts asked.

"Yes, Sir," he replied uneasily. "One of them blighters bit me."

The Captain laughed. "Hope he didn't get too much." He turned to the Major. "Private joke, what?"

Thomas nodded and glanced across the room to a

17

group of technicians who were bent over a map of Great Britain, pegged out with red and black flags. The Captain noted his interest. "Damned if I know what's going on in here, but it's got something to do with bats."

"Bats?" he said casually.

"That's what I said. Flying mice type bats. I saw a crate of them coming in here this morning. Typical Section Three. Purely experimental biological delivery. If there's a way of dispersing horrible little creepy-crawlies without anyone knowing it, this is where the idea will come from. The whole place is run by a monster named McTavish—a Scot. Genius at the macabre."

Thomas was thinking. "We used bats back in forty-four or was it forty-two? Some of our boys thought of strapping tiny incendiary bombs to their bottoms and dropping them over Japan."

"Did it work?"

"Oh, the bright ones managed it all right, figuring the bats would find the nearest oriental nook and cranny in some Jap factory, but when they tested the thing out in New Mexico, some of the pests escaped and burnt down two million dollars worth of hangar and the General's car to boot."

"Gave up, eh?" The Captain enjoyed America's failures.

"They never gave up in those days. Another group took over the project and decided to freeze the bats into a sort of hibernation, drop them from airplanes and hope to God they thawed out and flew away before they hit the ground."

"And?"

"Some say New Mexico lay under six feet of frozen bats for a week before the Army could scrape them all up. It didn't take them long to thaw out once they hit the ground, but after falling twenty thousand feet even a pyromaniacal bat can't fly with every bone in its body busted."

"Then you gave up."

"Yea. We invented the atom bomb instead. Much more reliable."

"Well, I hope McTavish hasn't come up with a sequel," the Captain replied, shaking McTavish's hand. "This is Major Thomas from America. I think you'd better explain what it is you're up to else the Major might sue for copyright infringement." He drew a bit closer and whispered. "You'd better mind Corporal Frimley out there—he's been bitten by one of your pets."

McTavish who had been considering this in all seriousness glanced up.

"Keep a wooden stake handy."

"Away with you, McRoberts," he frowned, waving him off. "Haven't we enough to do without your humor to add to our troubles? Now, Major Thomas, did I hear you are working with bats, too?"

"No, Sir," he drawled. "We gave all that up after the war."

McTavish looked hurt. He thought again. "Which one?"

"One what?"

"War."

"Why the Second, of course."

"I thought it might have been Vietnam you were speaking of," he replied hopefully. "You're making the best of that one, eh?"

"How do you mean?" He stared into the mischievous whiskered face.

"Using the defoliation agents. We'd like to get a hold of some of your findings on that I might tell you."

"I think we're making some reports for your Ministry last I heard."

"That's good to hear. Save us mucking about in the New Forest."

"How's that?"

"Just a joke we have."

"You fellows seem to be full of jokes," he said unsuredly.

"Major," he began, leading him towards a corner of the room. "If you work on this stuff too long, it gets to you. I keep my lads smiling as much as I can. Keeps them from taking their work too seriously."

"Don't you find that a bit risky?"

"Major, within the four walls of this room are enough biological agents to eliminate man from the face of this earth some ten thousand times over—given optimum conditions, of course. That is where the risk is."

Thomas nodded. How many had Detrick? Then he became aware of squeaking noises from somewhere near.

"This is our latest project. It's one of the Ministry's brain waves. We've code named it Project Dracula. Rather good, don't you think?"

"The project or the name?"

"Oh, the project's mad. It's the name we like."

Thomas shook his head. He peered through a double glazed window, but saw only darkness. McTavish turned to an assistant and nodded. Immediately, the darkness was turned to day and Thomas choked involuntarily. A sea of something black rose before him and settled slowly onto several tiers stretched across a small room behind the glass. He began to discern rows of hundreds of bats, hanging upsidedown as their night was abruptly ended. Most were but a few inches long, but some hung down as much as two or three inches below their mates. He was transfixed by the macabre scene and McTavish relished his surprise.

"There are fifteen hundred bats in there and each one has been fitted with a time-delay capsule. We have managed to copy some of your ideas—the very ones you mentioned to Captain McRoberts. We've micro-encapsulated bacillus anthracis and tied it to their bottoms, as you say. Those bats are living on rarified oxygen at the moment, and when we expose them to normal atmospheric conditions, a slow oxidation takes place in the encapsulation material. Roughly, it takes ten hours for the capsule to decompose sufficiently enough to expose the bat to the anthrax. After initial exposure, it should take three or four minutes to bring him to earth and thus spread his delights over the surrounding area." He seemed pleased.

"Unbelievable. It's crazy."

The Captain, standing far enough away to remain unnoticed, heard the plan and agreed. It was madness.

"Unbelievable, possibly. Crazy, no. The bacillus is a hybird variety—extremely potent. We have stepped up the infective power and raw strength to such an extent that the toxicity factor is something like fifty four times the normal. Exposure to it through simple contact will result in death within a few hours. Respiratory contact will kill in two hours. Mind you, our experimentation is restricted to the lower animals, but humans are as equally susceptible."

"But why anthrax?" he persisted.

"It's a common enough disease. The English often get it from their precious roses—from the bone meal. But any bacteria is itinerant—it loves to spread itself around. It likes people, too. Oh, yes, these bacterium are extremely sociable. They'd be very good companions were it not for their danger. And they have long lives. Normal anthrax can survive in the wild for several years. Our variety can withstand strong ultra-violet rays for ten, maybe fifteen years. And this stuff multiplies like mad. If on the average one spore divides in half every fifteen minutes, in twelve hours there'd be millions of them. If it develops in the body, well, you haven't got a chance.

21

Imagine the mass panic when this stuff gets loose. No doctor in any country has enough antibiotic in his surgery to treat more than a few cases at most, and hospitals could only treat the vast minority who were lucky enough to realize they were infected in time to be injected. Even if only a few of the bats got loose, the general alarm among the public would cause complete chaos."

The Captain stared hopelessly at McTavish.

"How long have you been developing this idea?" Thomas asked.

McTavish signalled for the lights to be turned off. Immediately, there arose a flurry of wings. "Not too long. We developed the anthrax in its potent form several months ago, but dispersing it was the problem. Then the Ministry came up with this idea—we're the only plant working on it."

"And you plan to let these things go somewhere?"

"We plan to release them right here," he replied, watching the last crate of bats being shunted into the preparation room. He struck the wall. "Behind this cage area is a wire enclosure with an assortment of buildings which any bat might expect to find in an average country. We're going to let them out tomorrow morning just before sunrise. That should give them enough time to settle where they will, and then the atmosphere will do the rest. When the capsules decompose sometime tomorrow afternoon, we'll be able to see exactly what happens."

"What about the village—won't your anthrax run wild?" He felt in his pocket for a cigarette, then remembered he had given them up two days ago. He cursed. He'd buy some first chance he got. "And who's going to be there to see if the anthrax works?"

"The entire surrounds will be hosed down hourly with another of our creations. The only known antidote for this particular variety. We plan to keep the area completely neutralized for at least a week while we poke about in the enclosure. After that, we open the flood gates and let the disinfecting agents wash out the whole area. Should be quite safe, thanks to your boys, McRoberts."

McRoberts wasn't listening. He was gazing at his watch in vain effort to move the minute hand a bit faster. He never did like having his men risk exposure to the various diseases Section Two dreamed up, nor to the experiments created by Section Three. But he had his orders. He sighed as the minute hand crawled over to two and he turned towards the Major. "I think we'd better make for the mess if we're to catch the Colonel."

Thomas looked away from the cage for the first time.

"Well, Major Thomas", began McTavish, following him out. "I hope our little efforts here have impressed you."

"I never thought you fellows would dare anything like this," he admitted slowly. "It's so goddam risky."

McTavish shrugged. "Times are changing, Major. And you can take some of the blame for all this—it's your influence."

The Major twirled his cap in his hands. "Yea, our influence."

"Well, good-bye. I'll let you have some details on Project Dracula when it's over."

The Captain frowned. Security was bothering him again.

McTavish grinned and pushed his shoulder. He glanced at the Major. "McRoberts here is worried again. Go on, take him to the mess before you get an ulcer. I'll see you at tea and you can tell me off."

McRoberts forced a smile. "The Colonel will be expecting us."

"Yes, yes," the Major replied. "Thank you Mr. McTavish. I would be very interested in hearing about this."

23

"I bet you would," the Captain mumbled to himself. "McTavish, I hope one of those bats fancies your hairy neck. Serve you right."

McTavish wrinkled his forehead. He glanced at the glass doors behind the gates where Corporal Frimley sat. "Frimley," he shouted. "Frimley, have you seen the medic yet?"

Frimley stood up and peered through the gates. "No, Sir. I thought I'd wait until dinner."

"Well don't bloody wait until dinner. I want to know what he says."

"You don't really think it's true?" Frimley whimpered to the Captain. "I mean about what you said."

"No, Frimley. McTavish is having you on again. Just see the medic and tell him he made a pass at you."

Frimley smiled, frowned, scratched his head and sat down.

The Colonel was by himself at a small table in a corner of the canteen. He was drinking a cup of coffee as Major Thomas sat opposite him and McRoberts marched off. He signalled to an orderly for more coffee. "Have you seen enough?"

The Major placed his cap on the table. "Very impressive, very impressive. I'm a bit surprised by your Project Dracula, but I suppose we've done worse."

"We work towards the same goal, Major, regardless of our individual aims," he replied flatly.

"The total annihilation of the human race." He grinned, but he didn't think it was funny. "You know, we tried an experiment not long ago—we tried to estimate the overkill rate of our stockpiles and had the boys from IBM rig out a computer program on it. Took them about four weeks and a computer half the size of this room. We had all the top brass in to see what the results would be. Here were these mathematical wizards racing around the computer, punching cards and pushing buttons and looking very pleased with their efforts, and there were the generals and colonels and majors and scientists all eagerly waiting to see what the overkill rate would be. You could see their tongues hanging out. Well, it took the computer about a minute and a half to come up with the answer." He paused. "And you know what the answer was?"

The Colonel raised his eyebrows and shook his head.

"A hum, a few clicks and clacks and then the goddam thing short-circuited. Smoke was everywhere. It's impossible to estimate—even for an automated Einstein."

"You don't approve of this?"

"Not entirely. I was on the experimental end at one time. I remember my first briefings when we were working on botulinum. I was told that the purpose of my work was to develop a biological that could not be treated effectively with antibiotics or other drugs, and that the disease should not be one which people might have a natural immunity to. This was the principle of germ warfare. I was given a little table in a little room with lots of little tubes and bottles and jars and several types of botulinum. After a while I separated the proteins into their groups and found the most effective ones—A and B. Working with a friend, we estimated the lethal dose of type A at somewhere around ten hundred millionths of a gramme, and we were a few hundred millionths off anyway. Feeding this into the computer, it told us one ounce could kill fifty million people. Then Tom—the fellow working with me—broke a rule and ate a sandwich he had brought into the laboratory. He was dead in a few minutes. The botulinum toxins had infected his food. It scared me, then. It scared the hell out of me, Colonel. But they thought I was still valuable and so now I'm the Liaison Officer."

The Colonel looked into his empty cup and seemed

perturbed. He found the orderly and signalled him for more coffee. He looked happier.

"I've learned a lot in going around from country to country. You have a nice civilized place here, but think of some backward little country who's struggling like hell for recognition. You get some petty little Hitler seizing power and he digs up some small-time chemist from around the corner and gives him a handful of nasty bugs, a few pots and pans, some old jam jars and maybe a burner or two. Pretty soon he comes up with either some God awful germ that even he hasn't the faintest clue how bad it is and hasn't the guts to test it, or he tells one of his assistants to take a whiff of this jar and he promptly drops dead. If the chemist has had the presence of mind to remember just how he perfected whatever it was that killed his friend, he has just developed his country's first chemical or biological weapons system. The newly seated leader gets power happy because he has a jar of bugs he can't see, and then I've got to go snooping around to see what it's all about. If the discovery is threatening enough, we recognize the country and keep him from throwing his jar across the border."

"Surely, it is not as bad as that."

He laughed. "Colonel Wyers, you remember the Batlavian uprising last year? Schelsznik took over the revolutionary government and announced his army had uncovered a weapon so powerful that it was a threat to the entire Eastern world? Well, we smuggled three of our boys in to find out what this weapon was. Schelsznik had been taken for a ride by his peoples' government— the biggest threat he posed to the world was the common cold. Just an ordinary virus. But how were we to know?" He felt his pockets again. Wyers offered him a cigarette. "But tell me how your villagers down there feel—don't they mind you being so near?"

"We are entirely self-contained. They have no contact

with us other than in the pubs. Really, they know surprisingly little of what we do. Occasionally, word leaks out about something or other, but the people in Stumford are a tolerant lot."

"I see," Thomas replied, stifling a cough. His head began to spin slightly at the smoke.

"The plant generates its own electricity, purifies its drinking water, disposes of its own sewage and chemical waste, does its own catering and even grows its own produce. We have an auxiliary system in an emergency which can take over any function should any one or all of the main systems go. Did you notice the generator in Section Three? The controls were next to the bats' cage. That runs on bottled gas and we store enough fuel to last up to three months. There are a hundred and eighty miles of electrified fencing surrounding us, radar surveillance, guard dog patrols and two hundred men involved in aerial, ground and general security."

Thomas began to think about the rabbit.

"No one gets in without clearance from London. No one gets clearance from London without a damned severe check. Once at the front gate, no one gets any further without a check from internal security." He grinned. "I remember once we had some MP from Bagshot stuck in here for two days before London cleared him out. Some foul-up at the Ministry. Haven't had another MP since—I think word got around that we planned it."

Thomas thought of the bats. He envisioned one escaping and landing in Trafalgar Square or Piccadilly.

"You look troubled, Major. Something I said?"

"Nothing like that, Colonel. I was just thinking about what could happen if one of your bats decided to do some independent research on its own."

"Oh," he laughed. "Impossible. The outside cage has double fencing. The inside fence is made of quarter inch square wire netting and the outside net carries ten

thousand volts. If any bat managed to eat his way
through the inner net, he'd end up cooked on the outer.
And the indoor cage, well," he smiled, "like the rest of
the building the walls are made of six inch thick reinforced concrete—and the only exit the bats have is
through the hydraulic hatch. I shouldn't think a bat
could push that open, do you?"

"No, of course not," he mumbled thoughtfully. He was
thinking of how a milligramme of hydrocyanic acid crept
through twelve feet of earth and cement and contaminated the local water supply. He was tiring of the formalities. He thought he might even be tiring of the war
game. He wanted to settle down somewhere and write
his memoirs, slinging a few bricks at officialdom which
forever guaranteed that what might happen never could
and usually did. Was it time to get out? Impulsively, he
looked at his watch.

"Tell me, Major. Where are you staying?"

"At a pub in Chesterly. I leave for London tomorrow
to meet up with the rest of our bunch before going home.
I think we're supposed to have a conference with Sir
Something Willets."

"Sir Joseph Willets, you mean. Yes, damn fine man.
Probably the only minister who isn't corrupted by his
own government."

"Very few of them left, huh? You're lucky you've got
even a few left hanging around. We haven't got one
honest politician in Washington—not since Kennedy anyway." He shook his head and stubbed his cigarette out in
the tin Players' ashtray. Inside he began to simmer, and
he thought maybe now he'd get it off his chest.
Obviously, this Colonel wasn't about to inform Washington he was going around the twist—not knowing what he
did. "It's a damn game to every one of them. They
promise their voters paradise and they give 'em hell. And
these goodwill tours we have to make—like this one. I get

a memo that says I'm to fly to England to visit some of your research outposts and a week later I'm here, leaving my own work uncompleted in the States. You fellows give us the red carpet, show us what you want us to see and we go off smiling. It's a game, isn't it Colonel?"

"It's a game," he smiled obligingly. "And I think you're getting tired of playing it if I may say. All those microscopic creepy-crawlies getting under your skin, what? I know what it's like. I've been dodging Whitehall, too. And nobody likes bureaucracy like the Ministry. Still, like you say, it's a game." He paused to offer another cigarette. "Now you consider this research we're doing. We haven't got a few hundred thousand million to spend on developing nuclear weapons like you chaps—and once you've got the bomb, well, everyone else has it. One bomb is the same as the rest. Granted, yours may be a bit bigger than theirs, and maybe you've got a rocket which can deliver the punch a few milli-seconds faster, but there's not much challenge in that. Besides," he whispered, leaning across the table, "you fellows get to put your bombs on our soil just so long as you get first go at pushing the button. But we get the protection.

"Anyway, look at this research. There are millions of ways of mutating these organisms, of developing gases, of dispersal methods. No one else but the country working on the stuff knows exactly what they've got—and an enemy can't possibly dream up antidotes for germs they've never seen. Look at this plant for example—we're the only station in England who's commissioned to develop this bat idea. If it works well, we'll still be the only base that knows all the ins and outs. And there's something else. You're the only chap who knows we're doing it. You now know more than the blighters in London who gave us the job. You seem surprised?" He sipped his coffee. "We're all in this together, Major. You came over here to uncover our secrets. We know that. So do you know that we know. It's that ruddy game again. Guesswork, clues, leads—everything adds up. Put the pieces together and it doesn't take Sherlock Holmes to deduce the elementary. So we show you our little project. You aren't about to cable Moscow, and we're not about to use Project Dracula against the Americans. Equally, you aren't about to take over the idea. It was yours once and if you fellows saw any future in it, you would've made the most of it. Now we're got it. Bats—so bloody what, you ask. So why not pigeons or falcons or budgies? It's just an idea using the best of what nature can give us. We keep it in the family, eh? This policy of reciprocation and all that. Blow the gaff and we blow you." He smiled again, and it was friendly. "The game Major. Your move."

He shrugged and stared at the ashtray. In his mind he saw an enormous chess board with Detrick on one side and Dwarf Hill on the other. He had thought himself either clever or lucky to uncover Project Dracula. Now he knew it was neither. The British had deliberately hung the bait in front of his nose. The results of the project would be very valuable to Detrick—just as the results of defoliage in Vietnam would save McTavish from stomping around the New Forest. International blackmail in a most subtle way.

"We all have our little projects—lovely little creatures so mutated and cultured that they can destroy us and everybody else in a few minutes. Just as deadly as your bombs but a damnsite cheaper and without the mess. It's us little countries' way of keeping in the running with you big boys. We don't know all of what you're up to any more than you know about us, and we keep just enough secrets to keep you fellows interested. Maybe one fine morning we'll all wake up dead," and he stared Thomas in the eye, "but by God we'll take some other bastards with us if we go."

Thomas thought about his absolute sincerity. "You really think you'll ever use this stuff?"

"Oh, come now, man," he laughed. "Look at your men in Asia. Perfect opportunity to test defoliants—and they're only the appetizers. Stripped the ruddy forests bare and destroyed the rice crops. Trouble was you didn't reckon how fast everything grows there. And then there're the harassing agents, CS gas and so on. How much of that have you sprayed around the paddies? Oh, we use it too. Bloody Irish uprising saw to that. Unfortunately, some old dear in Devon caught on and had half the men from Porton in Belfast making sure nobody suffered long term effects. Just our luck a handful of people decided to die that week, and every death was blamed on us. Messed up our research nicely. Not as lucky as you—running Vietnam and all. No problem to get the information out of there."

Thomas didn't like comparing notes, at least not on who made the most of whatever chances there were. He made an obvious effort to calculate the time. His head began to throb and the two cigarettes has given him a foul feeling. "I really think I should be pushing off. I have to ring London."

"Certainly, Major. Let one of my men run you back." He caught sight of the orderly and signalled for his car to be brought around. "I hope we've been of some help to you. Maybe some day I'll get one of those memos and see you at Detrick. It's about time I got a trip overseas. I like that place, Detrick. Damn fine research going on there. Only wish we had the facilities."

"Oh, I don't think you're doing so badly here," he replied, pushing himself from the comfort of his chair. "We have some pretty wild things going on there, too."

"You wait until the results of Project Dracula come out. I'll see if I can't smuggle some figures out to you.

Might find you working on the same thing some day, what?"

"Sure," he smiled. "Anyway, thanks for the tour. I'll see that your boys in London get a letter—compliments to the staff and how interesting it all was."

"And you got exactly what you came for, eh? You cynical bastard," he laughed. "You know the ropes, don't you?"

"Most of them. Form five, Code Reference C-118: Correspondence relating to overseas inquiries."

They left the canteen and made for the front gate. Thomas noticed Frimley had been transferred from Section Three to the Main Entrance. He smiled as the Major passed. "Enjoy the visit, Sir?"

"Yes, thank you, Corporal. How's the wound?"

"Ruddy horrible, Sir. I feel all weak—like all me blood's been drained away."

"What's all this then, Frimley?" Wyers demanded loudly. "Blood all gone?"

"Nothing really, Sir. One of those things from Section Three bit me."

"What things—you mean McTavish?"

"Might just of well of been. One of the bats."

"Never mind, Corporal. You can always get a transfusion."

"Very kind of you, Sir." He pulled open the door. "Shall I escort the Major to the car?"

"No, Corporal. I'll take him. Stand easy."

He saluted, "Yes, Sir."

"One of our younger chaps," Wyers began. "The youngest, I think. Must have a damn fine record if they're going to give a twenty year old a post up here. Must be in the family." He pulled the car door open and nodded as the Major shook his hand. "Give my best to Sir Joseph, will you?"

"Shall do. Thank you very much, Colonel. I hope to see you Stateside."

The Colonel slammed the door and the car swung away down the narrow road towards the checkpoint.

"Where to, Major?" the driver asked.

"Fox and Pheasant, Chesterly, Lieutenant."

"Lootenant," he laughed. "Haven't been called that in a long time. I forgot you Americans have a different name for everything."

"I always thought it was you guys who changed it all."

"Yes. But we were here first, remember? Did you enjoy your rounds?"

"Rounds?" He leant back into the heavy leather upholstery and gazed out at the miles of electrified fencing.

"Rounds, Sir. You know—the visit."

"Oh, yes, very much indeed. I found it quite interesting."

"Did you see our zoo, Sir?" At the gate he handed over a pink slip of paper and passed through. "All those rotten black things. It's all over about poor Frimley. He hasn't been half given the fright of his life. Got old McTavish looking out the corner of his eye, too."

"I thought you fellows were supposed to be so damned keen on security."

"We are. All of us know who's coming, what they look like and how much they're being told. No secrets let out of the bag, eh?"

"No, no loose cats, Lieutenant. I guess that's a pretty good way as any."

The driver grew silent and the Major was content to look upon the sea pounding against the coast a few hundred feet below. Travelling downhill, they turned sharply into Stumford where he could just make out the buildings of the research base perched high above the village. He wondered just what did the people think of it all—whether they gave a damn, but it was obvious that they weren't interested in him or in the official car, at least they paid no attention. It seemed to the Major that Dwarf Hill was invisible to the people, that familiarity had smoothed over any rough edges which may have been present in the village when the military took over the hill. But it was a small village, insignificant in any contribution to the country and any ill-feelings or presentiments the townsfolk bore would be meaningless. They had chosen the site well. The Army knew what it was doing even if Stumford didn't. The Major smiled. In America they had erected chemical and biological research bases wherever they damn well pleased. Detrick was in the middle of a small city. If anyone dared squawk, they were promptly sat upon by Washington. The United States Government had a swift and effective way of keeping people quiet. Back taxes, shop licenses, fines, minor offenses—everyday people were prone to everyday mistakes. But in the face of the government, these mistakes were exactly what they needed. It was a kind of blackmail, but what is blackmail in the face of National Security? How refined and civilized England seemed as he sat there in the Bentley and watched the English seaside countryside pass gently by. He thought it incredible that he had just left one of the most sinister and machiavellian creations of current society, carefully tucked away from the public scrutiny. War and the bomb and deadly micro-organisms seemed so far away.

Stumford. 19:15 Hours

Captain McRoberts was drinking alone tonight, primarily because McTavish was working late with his bats. He looked over the regulars at the Nag's Head, but saw no one with whom he could engage in an argument—for that was exactly what he wanted most. It had been a rotten day. Having foreigners poking about was bad enough, but when the orders came through that a Major Glen Thomas was to have free run of the place and be witness to the biggest thing Dwarf Hill had ever developed, it was just too bloody much for him. As he settled back against the bar and sloshed the beer around in his pint, he cursed the Ministry for using the plant as a showpiece and cursed the yank for coming. Thank God, he thought, that there wouldn't be any more special visits for several weeks and even they might be cancelled if Project Dracula were a particular success. This made him speculate and he began to hope the ugly black creatures might cooperate enough to prolong the experiments. He'd wish everyone of the blighters a fate worse than McTavish if they didn't.

It was a stirring at the door which first drew him from his speculation. Someone was pointing towards a dog which seemed to have managed a few too many when his master's attention was elsewhere, but then he noticed something else about it, something which froze the blood in his veins. With a shaking hand he deposited his glass on the counter and pushed away the stool, ignoring the thump as it fell to the floor. Dazed and unbelieving, he elbowed through several of those who had gathered around the animal and stopped a few feet away. His skin had turned white and clammy and his eyes were large with fear as he turned around to face the onlookers.

"Get back," he choked in a measured tone. "Get back or you'll all be killed."

The dog stopped whimpering and collapsed. It trembled convulsively, twitched its legs and head, and died. But its forelegs and neck seemed unusually swollen, its eyes were glazed and even to those who knew nothing of what it was, the animal's death seemed evil and frightening. The Captain turned again from the dog and faced the crowd who had by now become uneasily quiet. He forced himself to keep calm—not to sound panicked, but it was no good. Even he was trembling and unsure under the realization of what this was.

"Get back. I warn you—get back away from here."

The people stared back at him and a few shuffled towards the rear of the pub.

"Look!" someone screamed. "My God, what is it?"

The Captain whirled about. He watched as a man staggered from the doorway, clutching his throat. His neck and forearms were enormous purplish lumps, covered in swelling pustules some of which had burst open and dribbled a black slime along the puffy flesh. His eyes were wild, crazed and before he crashed to the floor, his fingernails ripped open the infected flesh around his throat and dark pus covered his already stained shirt and jacket. He trembled once, opened his mouth as if to scream, jerked crazily to one side and passed out, probably dead.

Two women had already fainted and someone was being sick in the corner. The Captain couldn't tear his gaze away from the grotesque figure and stood frozen to the floor while around him the customers fled in panic. Some trampled the dog underfoot in their flight, others elbowed the Captain back and forth until he found himself up against the doorframe, staring into the night. He was mumbling something.

"Stop, come back. You mustn't go. Please come back." But even if anyone could hear him, no one was about to stop. Then he noticed a dim glow from somewhere near the hilltop. Others too had noticed it and were watching it from the street. "It's on fire," he announced suddenly. "My God, the bloody thing's on fire." He began to run, but before he crossed the street he saw a huge fireball light the sky and moments later a thunderous explosion ripped through the village, shattering windows and blowing open locked doors. Bits of debris began to fall about the street and people scattered for shelter. McRoberts knew what would happen next. He had been told what to do if it did happen. Years of training, of instinct, took command and he forced his eyes away from the inferno and pushed himself in a frenzied run towards his car, shoving aside the people and stumbling over the curb. He snatched something from under the front seat and ran back to the pub. Quickly he tore open the felco zip and pulled at the thin plastic coverall. In a moment he was safely covered in its milky-white screen and he slipped his gas mask over his head. He wondered about the wind and he tried to discern a tree not far away, but he saw it was too late. At the far end of town a group of people collapsed almost as one. They convulsed, clawing at their lungs and twitching uncontrollably. Almost immediately people around him began gasping, trembling and falling to the pavement. He pushed past them, across the street. He knew there was a telephone kiosk around the next corner—or the one after it—and he must reach it. He felt dying men and women clutching, tearing at his legs and ankles, and half-crazed with fear and panic, he kicked them away. He felt tears trickling down his cheeks and the lens of his mask fogged. He rubbed his sleeve over the glass, but the mist was on the inside. Sweat rolled across his forehead over the top of his mask and down the sides of his face beneath the plastic hood. He could hear hundreds of muffled cries. He saw the street as one seething mass of fallen people, convulsing and wretching. He saw others tumble out of doorways, or fall from windows as they looked out to see what was happening.

Nearing the first corner, he caught sight of two young boys emerging from a hallway. He leapt over the pavement and threw himself into them, pushing them back into the house. A light beamed above them as they lay together on the floor, scrambling to get free of each other's grip. The Captain was first up. He held both boys to the floor, but he had been too late. He saw their faces grimace almost at the same moment as they struggled to fill their lungs. One was trying to claw at his throat as if ripping open his trachea would let in more air. Then he lost control of his hands and they flopped uselessly at his side. Tears dribbled down their terror-stricken faces, and saliva drooled from their mouths. They made sickening choking sobs, unable to cough and bring up the saliva which was pouring into their lungs. In a moment the Captain felt no resistance to his hold on the boys. They were dead. As he tried to raise himself he noticed a bulge in their trousers and he suddenly felt sick. He wanted to wretch—he could feel it building up inside him, but he forced himself to swallow it down and staggered to the door. Outside was another boy lying on the curb in a broken lump. He had fallen from somewhere above and he looked imploringly at the Captain, his eyes begging for mercy. He twitched once and died.

Now there were few people left standing. In the grotesque light of orange street lamps, hundreds of bodies lay scattered about the high street of the small village. Some hung from windows, others lay across the bonnets of cars or slumped over the steering wheel. For a few moments the Captain was paralyzed by the scene. The whole village was dead in the street. He heard a baby crying from somewhere—it seemed to gurgle once or twice, then silence. He glanced up and from the end of the street he saw headlamps of a car appear, coming from the base. He watched it scream around the corner, skidding into the wall of a shop and rebounding off. McRoberts figured it must have been doing seventy when it slammed into the first group of bodies which lay on the street. The car carried on, bumping and skidding over the next lot until it reached the entrance of the pub where some bodies lay one on top of another. Hitting one of these piles, it swerved into a van and burst into flames. In the light he managed to recognize Frimley who was struggling to get free of the mangled car, his mask and garment ripped away. As he fell clear of the wreckage, another explosion rocked the van and fire engulfed the car, Frimley and several bodies which had been squashed between the two vehicles. Frimley wriggled briefly and McRoberts wondered which killed him first, the fire or the gas which had destroyed everything else.

The Captain turned away and stumbled around the next corner. The kiosk was only a few yards away and he spotted a body lying on the floor. Carefully, he rolled it over and wrenched the receiver from its frozen grasp. He banged down the rest until he heard a dialing tone. His hands trembled as he fought to dial 999, misdialing the second nine. He started again, but got fouled up in a cross-line. The receiver went dead as he banged down the rest. Frantically, he tapped the rest again until the tone returned. He tried again and got through.

"Fire, police or ambulance," repeated the voice.

"Fire—no police. Hurry."

"Connecting you, Sir."

McRoberts tried to wipe some of the sweat from his forehead, parring his mask. He straightened it. "Come on, damn you," he pleaded. "For God's sake, hurry up."

"Police, here."

It was difficult to hear through the hood. He pressed the receiver closer. "Hello, police, Captain Andrew McRoberts from Dwarf Hill—"

"Who?"

"The government base at Stumford, damn it."

"I'm sorry, you'll have to speak clearer—"

"There's been an explosion—everybody's been killed."

"You'll have to speak up, Sir. I'm not hearing you at all well."

"I've got a bloody mask on!" Suddenly he felt a hand on his shoulder. He whirled around in surprise and fear. McTavish stood before him, his free hand swollen and blackened beyond recognition. His face was distorted with pustules and blood dribbled from his mouth. His mask hung useless about his neck and as he raised his disfigured hand from McRoberts' shoulder, he slipped, ripping away the Captain's own mask.

"Save us," McTavish cried, "It's all over."

McRoberts gasped, choked and fought to free himself of McTavish's grip, but his hand was tightly fixed about the mask. McRoberts' own hands lost control, his lungs grew tight and his eyes watered.

"Police here," repeated the receiver. "What's going on there?"

McRoberts tried to speak, but choked again. He felt dizzy and nauseous and he knew it was over for him. He could feel his body twitch and his lungs refuse to function. Saliva was trickling down his throat. He was on top of McTavish who lay sprawled across the other body. His hand clutched at McTavish's hair and pulled upwards. He lunged forward once, then fell back, staring straight up at the moon and a hundred million stars.

The receiver clicked dead.

Chesterly: 19:30 Hours

Dwarf Hill Microbiological Establishment was built on the hill overlooking Stumford because the Ministry felt it was safer placed above populated areas. The architects had little knowledge of chemical and biological weapons research, but they did know that gas is lighter than air, and in the unlikely event of a leakage the poisonous vapors would rise harmlessly upwards and be carried out to sea by the prevailing winds. They didn't count on the fact that nerve gas is specifically designed to 'sink' and spread over a wide area. When the Ministry touched upon this point, the fact that the walls of Dwarf Hill were constructed of reinforced concrete and the base was equipped with every known safety device over-ruled any sense of peril. What they didn't count on were several hundred cubic feet of propane gas exploding in its bunker under Section Three; the ensuing explosions of hydrogen, oxygen and nitrogen stored in small but potentially dangerous amounts for research use in gas development. The force of the initial blast in a confined area was enough to blow through six feet of concrete and steel, and as the maximum width of any one wall at Dwarf Hill was several inches, there was nothing left standing after the explosion for over a thousand feet around. When the gigantic fireball had burnt itself out, only bits of scattered debris smoldered uneasily atop the hill.

The townspeople of Chesterly had a clear view of the blast, some had even noticed the flickering immediately prior to the blast as the village was on another hill almost level with the base. By now everyone had left their homes to see the slowly dying remains of Dwarf Hill and to speculate among themselves what had happened. The fire brigade had tried to contact Stumford police station to see if assistance was required, but at first it was thought that as Dwarf Hill has its own appliances and Stumford could easily assist, no further action should be taken even if the police didn't answer the phone. However, when repeated calls failed to bring an answer, the Fire Marshall rang the police in Chesterly who were equally perplexed by the lack of communication. They dispatched a patrol car which was in the area, but it made it to within only a half mile of Stumford before it careened into a tree: the occupants were dead before they hit.

The villagers were in the beginning content to watch the fireworks from the town, but when the fire died down, some decided to investigate on their own. Major Thomas, equally interested in the excitement, failed to realize that it was the research base which was on fire until he overheard the gossip among the people. His first thought was that the explosion was connected with some sort of research—they often burned off large quantities of gas at Detrick, but when he noticed the fire brigade steering their appliances into the street, he began to worry. Any fire or explosion, no matter how small, was dangerous in a chemical and biological center, and this one wasn't small. He wandered towards the police Inspector, watching the first car leave the village to witness the excitement in Stumford.

"Anybody know what's going on? Thomas asked casually."

"Looks as if Dwarf Hill isn't there anymore," suggested the Inspector solemnly. "Though I guess it's not as bad as all that or we would have been alerted."

The Fire Marshall approached. "They've got their own equipment—seems to be under control whatever it was."

"But what if there's a leak?" Thomas asked.

"A leak?" replied the Inspector.

"The gas."

"Oh, we wouldn't know anything about that. Whatever they do up there is a mystery to us."

The first car was just making the turn into the short hill near Stumford. They could see its headlights quite clearly in the distance. Suddenly without warning it swerved crazily to the right, plunging over the embankment and rolling down the hillside. When it came to rest at the bottom, it burst into flames. A shout went up among the villagers, and the Fire Marshall made a move towards his engines.

Thomas grasped his arm. "Wait a minute. I wouldn't go down there if I were you."

"Why the blazes not, man?" he exclaimed indignantly. "Maybe you don't care about burning cars in your country, but we do here!"

"Watch the next car before you do anything," he suggested calmly.

They peered into the darkness as the following car emerged from the woods and approached the hill, not realizing that the car ahead of them had just crashed. It made the turn and proceeded on.

"Now can I let my men go?" the Fire Marshall asked.

"Just wait a minute." Thomas repeated.

"He's not braking," whispered the Inspector. "Look his brake lights aren't on." The car gathered speed down the hill, swerved against the feeble guard rail, and bounced off. When it reached the bottom of the road, it smashed squarely into the first house on the bend.

"My God," gasped the Marshall. "What's going on in that village?"

"What I feared might be happening," replied Thomas coldly. "Every man, woman and child in that village is probably already dead."

"Dead?" shouted the Marshall. "Now I know you're mad."

"Hang on, Syd," said the Inspector. "Remember we couldn't raise the nick?"

"When the plant blew up, it must have spread some form of gas over the village—probably VX or sarin. And you'll find that Stumford isn't the only town to get hit if there's a wind."

"Just exactly what are you on about, Mister . . ." began the Inspector.

"Thomas, Major Glen Thomas from the United States. I work for a chemical and biological research center in

Maryland. I just came from Dwarf Hill this afternoon and I can tell you that the gas they were developing up there is enough to wipe out London let alone Stumford." He stubbed out a cigarette with his shoe. "If the explosion blew open the canisters, that gas would spread out every which way and just wait for the wind—unless it settled first. It's designed to do that, otherwise it wouldn't be any good."

The Inspector looked perplexed. "Good? Good for what?"

"Never mind," he replied curtly. "It doesn't matter now. You've got to get these people off the streets. Tell them to go into their basements."

"We don't have basements in this country," the Marshall explained heatedly. "They all start on the ground level."

"Then tell them to lay on the floor and cover their mouths with something—a wet handkerchief would do. I don't suppose you have any masks up here?"

"Masks?" queried the Inspector. "Gas masks?"

"Any mask."

"Major, we thought the war was over a long time ago."

The Marshall turned to one of his men. "Get me the loud hailer—and get the engines back inside."

"And for God's sake don't let anyone else go near Stumford," said the Major, nodding towards the doomed village.

"Inspector," cried one woman, racing towards them. "What are you going to do? My son's in that car!"

The crowd followed her, waited for the answer.

"I'm afraid there's nothing we can do, Mrs. Frost. Please go home—we'll do all we can later." He felt like a fool.

"What's wrong down there?" shouted a man from behind. "Why did those cars crash?"

"We don't know yet," said Thomas. "You must go home."

"Who are you?" shouted several at Thomas, suspicious at a foreigner's presence.

"Well, crash or no crash I'm going to see what's going on," shouted someone. "My daughter's down there."

Thomas shouted after him. "If you go down into that town, you'll be dead before you're halfway there."

The gathering crowd grew suddenly silent.

The Inspector frowned at the Major. The Marshall thrust the loud hailer into his hands. "You tell them what you told us. You seem to be the only one who knows what it's all about."

Thomas took the hailer and stared unsurely at it. "Listen to me, all of you. Some of you perhaps know that Dwarf Hill was involved in research into chemical and biological warfare agents. I believe some of the chemical agents known as nerve gas have escaped. If what I believe is true, then the people in Stumford never stood a chance. You saw for yourself what happened to those cars—the people in them were probably dead before they crashed."

"Can this gas spread to us?" someone shouted.

The crowd stirred.

"Not necessarily." He raised his hand. "Most of it has probably blown out to sea, but there is the chance that some of the gas in Stumford could blow towards Chesterly."

The people began shouting amongst themselves. One woman was screaming about her two sons in Stumford, another knew her daughter had gone to the village with a friend. Others had family or relations there. Those most affected stood in stunned silence, questioning whether to believe this horrible story.

"Now listen," Thomas cried. "If you all do as I say, there is nothing to worry about. Go to your homes. Shut all the doors and windows and find the room with the least access to the outside—a hallway or bathroom."

"My toilet's outside," someone shouted angrily.

"So's mine," added another.

"Then use your hallway. Any room will do. Just stay put and cover your faces with wet handkerchiefs."

"For how long?"

"Until someone tells you it's safe to come out. Now go home—you're just endangering yourselves and your families by staying out here."

The crowd slowly, almost reluctantly began to disperse. There were mumblings of leaving Chesterly and driving inland. Others thought it was all a load of rubbish and wanted to see Stumford for themselves, but the police were already setting up roadblocks, and the Inspector had ordered his men to hustle the villagers indoors. The Fire Marshall told his men to go home. "There's nothing more we can do," he said.

Thomas found the Inspector as the Desk Sergeant approached.

"Sir, we can't seem to pick up Delta Two on the car radio," the Sergeant explained.

The Inspector turned to him. "Never mind. Keep trying to raise Stumford."

"Can you get me through to London?" Thomas asked.

"What for?"

"I think I should contact your Ministry."

"Which one?"

"Ministry of Defense. There's a fellow there by the name of Chardwell or Chatwell or something. I saw him when we arrived."

"We can get through all right, but—"

"Hold it a second," he interrupted. "Isn't that a light out there?"

The Inspector peered into the darkness. He spotted a

dim red light flickering along the road towards Stumford. "It looks like a bicycle tail-lamp."

Thomas glanced around. "Does that thing work?"

"What, the motorcycle?"

"Yea. I'll never reach him in time by car. Can I cut through the woods?"

"The woods? There's a stream going through that woods—you'll never make it."

"Want to bet?" he called, running towards the Triumph police bike. "You just get London on the phone, but don't say anything unless I don't come back. I'll try to catch whoever it is before it's too late."

"I'll have a car follow you on the road," he shouted, but his words were lost as Thomas leapt on the kick start and the engine thundered to life. Quickly he adjusted himself to the English controls—he felt for the clutch and brake and touched the gear pedal with his foot.

"Here," shouted someone who suddenly appeared next to him. "The lights." He leant across the handlebars and flipped a switch. Two powerful beams bore through the darkness. "Follow the road to the fork. Cut along the footpath."

Thomas nodded and opened the throttle. His foot snapped the bike into gear and he eased off on the clutch. The bike shuddered, slowed, then bit into the road and lurched forward. Thomas hadn't been on a bike for over ten years, but he managed to get the general idea of the controls once again. He was revving too high in first before he realized his speed, and bore down on the gear pedal sharply. He let out the clutch again and burst forward in second. Third was easy and in a moment he had shot past the roadblock at over sixty. The wind scratched at his face and forced him to squeeze his eyes nearly shut in order to see ahead, but he managed to pick out the green post indicating the footpath. He eased off the throttle and downshifted. The bike lurched and settled into second. The smooth surface of the road changed to slippery gravel, then to grass and clumps of earth as he bounced and skidded over the rough woodland. Several times he stuck his leg out sharply to stop from turning over, revving hard to pull out of the skid. A tree flew past him on his right and he swerved hard, barely regaining his balance. He had to slow down. His reflexes were not up to it. He brought the bike to a halt and peered again into the dark. He caught sight of the bike. He was at right angles to it, riding perpendicular to the road. The hill couldn't be more than a few hundred feet ahead of the cyclist. He shouted and flashed his lights. The cyclist stopped, then pushed on. Quickly, Thomas bolted away again. He crashed through second and brought the bike up to fifty. Suddenly his headlights picked up the stream. It was at least ten feet across. There were trees bordering the opposite edge. If he tried to jump it he'd end up a mangled heap on the other side. He veered right and raced along the edge, sending rocks and twigs scuttling. He noticed an opening about thirty feet on. He pulled away from the stream, rode a hundred feet on, turned and revved his engine. The rear wheel spun into the soft earth, bit and threw the front wheel off the ground. Thomas caught his balance and leant forward. The stream was coming on fast. As he felt the front wheel shoot off the edge, he stood straight up in the saddle, bending his waist so that his head was nearly over the front numberplate. As quickly as it had left the ground, it plunged into the other side, throwing Thomas forward and scrapping his chest on the gas tank. The rear wheel hadn't quite made it and screamed as it fought to gain hold on the bank. He eased off on the throttle, dropped the gear and accelerated again. It worked. The bike lunged forward and shot out unexpectedly into the road not thirty yards from the crest of the hill. The cyclist was about fifty feet away in the direction of Chesterly. It had paid no attention to the frantic efforts of this motorcyclist, but pedalled on. Thomas waved his arm. Suddenly he saw the figure collapse over his handlebars, the bike swerved off the road, and the rider disappeared into a ditch. Thomas dropped his machine into first gear and roared down the last forty feet, letting the bike slip out from under him as he leapt off.

Staring into the almost total darkness of the ditch, he could barely discern the prostrate cyclist who was gasping heavily. Thomas glanced around him and realized how near Stumford he was. He felt his pockets for what he knew was his only chance. He withdrew the pencil-like object, whipped off its cap, and plunged it into his thigh. That done, he leaned into the ditch, holding onto a fallen branch with his free hand. His other hand worked its way beneath the cyclist.

"Just try to keep still," he whispered between clenched teeth. "Lie still and let me do the work."

But Thomas felt the gas reaching him. It had penetrated his clothes and slithered into his lungs. His grasp was weakening. He could neither lift the cyclist nor hold the branch firm enough. Sweat poured from his forehead, and his lips trembled convulsively. He knew he couldn't hold on any longer and let himself fall into the ditch. He stopped to rest and looked down at the figure next to him. Whoever he was, he was crying softly.

"Keep it up," Thomas choked. "Keep crying. But don't move."

He wiped the tears from his own eyes and swallowed hard to rid his mouth of the excess saliva. His head was clearing slightly. Once again he tried for the branch. His hand missed first time, but caught it on the second. The muscles in his arms were barely controllable. He forced himself, willed himself, to pull while he tried with equal

49

force to convince the other arm to grasp the cyclist. But the effort forced the dizziness back, his eyes refused to focus on what he was doing. He shook his head and tried to breathe harder, concentrating only on the hand that would pull him free of the ditch. He managed to get halfway up. His feet dug into the side, but a clump of earth gave way and he lost his balance. Still fighting to keep hold of the branch, he commanded his feet to anchor themselves. Every inch upwards counted and every lost inch meant more time exposed to the deadly effects of the gas. The cyclist couldn't survive much longer, even if the concentration was weaker this far from the village. His fingers clawed viciously into the branch. His mind was losing control. There seemed little hope left. His strength and will were fading.

Suddenly he felt another hand pulling upwards. He raised his head and tried to focus.

"Hold on to the boy," a voice was shouting. "We'll get you out."

Thomas closed his eyes. With the little strength he had left, he gripped the cyclist's waist and held tight. Somehow in some incredible way, they were hoisted free of the ditch and bundled into a car parked just beyond the motorcycle. He was barely conscious when a mask was pushed into his lap and he heard a vague voice instructing him to put it on. He shook his head drunkenly and looked at the boy beside him. "What about him," he slurred.

"We only found three—he'll have to chance it."

He felt the car quickly reverse, then surge forward towards Chesterly. At the same time he leant over the seat and pushed the mask against the cyclist's face, pressing in his chest as he did so. "Breathe," he mumbled. "Breathe." He heard the strangled sobs grow stronger.

"You can forget the mask, now, Major," said the

driver, glancing over his shoulder and slowing the car down. "We're clear of the danger."

Thomas struggled upwards to look out. He rolled down the window and stuck his head out. Slowly, the burning sensation left his throat, his eyes cleared and his own breathing became more rhythmic. Vaguely, he picked out two men sitting in the front seat dressed in strange white suits. "How," he gasped. "How did you fellows get here?"

"Inspector Morris told us to hop down here and see if we could help. We borrowed these masks and suits from the brigade. Lucky break for you."

"Yeah," he grinned. "Damn lucky."

"Well, we're back. The Inspector has London waiting for you. Want me to hold it off till you're a bit stronger?"

"No," he replied, pushing open the door moments before the car drew up in front of the station. "Bring the boy in and lay him on something flat. Got any oxygen or something?"

"We don't, but the brigade has. Ted, run over and pick up a bottle. Here, you'd better let me give you a hand."

As the Major stumbled from the car he stripped off his jacket, shirt and trousers as the two policemen scrambled out of their isolation suits and grabbed Thomas' arms. "You're still not up to it, Sir."

"I'm all right. Just strip the boy and get him into oxygen." He pushed away from the officers and made for the station. The Inspector spotted him and ran down the steps to help him. Two other policemen ran to help the boy.

"Christ, man, you look horrible," said the Inspector. 'I've got Chadwell on the line, but—"

"I'm all right, Inspector," Thomas insisted. "Just find me some clothes."

"Take these here," he replied, snatching a uniform which hung on a peg behind the front desk. "You can take the call from the desk."

"Hello, Mr. Chadwell?" shouted Thomas as he fought to dress himself.

"This is Chadwell here. What's going on up there?"

Thomas shook his head. He must think clearly. "Dwarf Hill's exploded. Stumford is wiped out. There's gas everywhere. You'd better get some of your men up here right away—gotta get this area sealed off."

"What are you talking about? Who is this?"

"You remember me—Major Thomas from the Detrick group."

"Oh, yes, Major. Saw you in London. Now what's all this you say—Dwarf Hill has exploded?"

"Exploded—blown up. It just isn't there anymore. But worse than that, nerve gas has spread all over the area."

"You must be joking, Major. Must be a mistake. Dwarf Hill can't simply blow up. It's designed not to. There must be a mistake."

"Do you call a few hundred dead people a mistake?" he choked heatedly, his own words searing his throat. "I've seen what's happened. I've just come from outside Stumford and if one of your police here hadn't pulled me out, I'd be dead, too. This isn't any joke, Chadwell."

"Hang on a minute, will you?"

Thomas heard mumblings, something about raising Dwarf Hill on the telephone. His fingers fumbled with the buttons on his shirt.

Chadwell came back to the phone. "I can't seem to get an answer," he said vaguely. "You'd better give me the Inspector."

Thomas held out the receiver. "He doesn't seem to believe me. You'd better tell him."

"Morris here. What the Major says is quite true. Stumford's gone, Sir—at least the people are. I saw two cars smash themselves up even before they reached the place. Well, no, I've not actually been into Stumford. Well all I can say is that something bloody strange is going on and it isn't safe around here. Two of my men just pulled the Major out of a ditch not half a mile from Stumford. There's something in there and I just hope whatever it is stays there."

There was a pause. Thomas looked up and shook his head. "Damn fool."

The Inspector nodded.

"There's something amiss, all right," Chadwell announced. "We can't seem to raise Dwarf Hill on the security line, either."

"Of course you can't," snapped the Inspector. "It's bloody well blown sky-high. We saw the explosion from here—there's nothing left standing."

"All right, Inspector Morris. I'll get someone on to it straight away. But I'm sure you'll find it all a mistake— a small fire or something. These research places just don't blow up like that. If I can't raise them in another hour, I'll pop up there myself. Good-night, Inspector."

The Major snatched the phone. "Hello, Chadwell? Look, I don't know what you're playing at, but I do know there's something more than a little fire. Little fires don't scatter brick buildings all over the place."

"Now see here—"

"You see here, Chadwell. I may not be exactly in my rights to say this, but you better do something more than make a personal visit up here. I know nerve gas when I get hit by it, and I also know that Stumford is wiped out. You forget I work with this stuff."

"But—"

"Then for the sake of your people you better get the Army up here to seal off the area. If anyone decides their son or daughter is late coming home and goes to investigate, they're gonna end up just like the rest of them—dead. That gas just doesn't walk away."

"Let me get this straight, Thomas. You think that Dwarf Hill has exploded and released an unknown quantity of nerve gas. You also believe that the village of Stumford has been affected. You yourself have experienced a poisoning of some sort or other. The Inspector says he saw something like an explosion. And on this you want me to send in the army?"

"Have you got any better suggestions? I'm not exactly an amateur at this sort of thing."

Chadwell paused. He seemed to be talking to someone. "All right, Major. I'll have a detachment sent to Stumford at first light. I suppose I better instruct them to wear masks and isolation garments, eh?"

"If you want them to come back, you'd better."

"And I'll be down there as soon as I can get away in the morning. Meanwhile, you better have Inspector Morris set up some roadblocks around the village. And don't let the press get onto this. I don't want any publicity until I know exactly what's going on."

"Naturally," Thomas replied sourly. "The safest thing in that case is just to send them into Stumford to see for themselves, huh?"

"Pardon?"

"Never mind. I'll be here at the police station when you arrive. And you'd better not see Stumford first—*you* might not come out, either."

"Yes, Major. And Major—you appreciate that if this is a mistake, your country will have to assume full responsibility."

"I'm not worried about that. It's no mistake. I'd stake my reputation on that."

"Major?"

"Yes, Chadwell."

"You have. Good-night."

Thomas rang off and turned to the Inspector. "God, if he's responsible for the defense of this country . . ."

The Inspector made to answer, but the Desk Sergeant interrupted him. "The boy, Sir. He's coming round."

Morris glanced at Thomas. "You'd better see to him. You seem to know all about it."

"Anybody know who he is?" he asked, walking towards the front of the station where the boy lay on a blanket thrown across the floor, and covered with a policeman's coat.

"He's a lad from Deignby," the Sergeant replied. "Must have been meeting his mate in Stumford."

As the Major leant over the boy, he suddenly realized how stiff his muscles felt, how every nerve cried painfully from exposure. He had to steady himself against the wall, but declined help from Morris. "My first time," he smiled weakly. "Never really been so close to that stuff before. Do you think one of your men could get my case? It's in my room at the pub. The grey one on the bed— it's got some pain killer in it."

Morris nodded at the Desk Sergeant who left immediately. "Not to rub anything in, but now you know what the blazes you're throwing around. Not very pleasant is it?"

The Major glared at him. His face softened and he smiled again. "No, not very pleasant." He looked down at the boy who was barely conscious and he looked about him. "Do you think we could carry him onto the enquiry desk? More light up there."

"Tomkins, Wendover, carry him over. Easy now!" The Inspector picked up the blanket and laid it across the desk. Wendover slipped off his jacket, folded it carefully, and placed it under the boy's head.

Several of the policemen gathered around to watch.

They were apparently stunned by what they saw for they could only stand and stare at the pale flesh and quivering body. They felt helpless for they knew they could do nothing—whatever was hurting the child was beyond their knowledge. When the Major put a gentle hand on the boy's wrist, the policemen looked up at him, expressionless. Some were no doubt thinking that this prostrate figure could be their own son. Thomas returned their piercing gaze for a moment. "Could you give me some light?"

Inspector Morris seemed to wake up. "Come on, lads. Hop it. There's more than enough work to do and I want some extra patrols laid on. McKinley, take Watts and Anderson with you and re-schedule the patrols."

"Yes, Sir," McKinley replied awkwardly. He paused. "Will he be all right—the boy, Sir?"

The Major sighed. He nodded—more to himself than to McKinley. "I think so. He's still alive anyway."

Slowly the lad's eyes flicked, squeezed shut and opened slightly. He turned his head, winced and suddenly tried to raise himself. The Duty Officer put his hand on his shoulder and eased him down. "Easy on, lad," he said kindly. "You best not be moving for awhile."

Thomas observed the boy's movements—obviously, he was in much pain, and his breath came in hiccough-like gasps. His body twitched erratically every few moments, his right arm trembled continuously. Undoubtedly he was feeling the effects far more than himself, and with far less understanding of what was causing his suffering. As he grasped his wrist and placed his free hand on his forehead, the boy turned his head and peered up through bleary eyes.

"Am I going to be all right?" he asked in complete uncertainty.

"You'll be right as rain before you know it," the Sergeant said. "Won't he, Major?"

"Yes," he said slowly. "Of course he will be." He looked about for his bag when he saw that the Duty Sergeant had returned. Morris handed it to him, and he quickly withdrew a small metal case. From it he took a syringe and needle and drew two ccs of a cloudy serum. "Lie still until your head clears. This will make you feel better." He looked towards the Sergeant. "Hold his arm tight just above the elbow, will you?" The lad looked up at him. Thomas smiled assuringly, and the boy managed a faint smile back. "This won't hurt. You'll just feel a slight burning sensation in your arm." He eased the needle against the skin in the boy's forearm until it burst through the flesh and penetrated the vein. It was over in a moment.

"What's your name, laddie?" Morris asked.

"Trevor, Sir," he whispered, again trying to push himself up. "Trevor Brecon. I was late for me mum and dad—in Stumford. They won't be half mad." He became aware of the trembling in his right arm and he watched it curiously.

At the mention of Stumford, the Inspector looked sharply at Thomas who was fiddling with his hypodermic "We'll have to keep him here, you know," he began quietly.

"Yes, you will. He'll need a lot of attention. He's had a bad dose of that gas. And Chadwell's coming along—he'll scream blue murder if you let him loose."

"All we've got are the cells. They'll have to do." He paused. "How bad is he?"

"He's had enough nerve gas to knock hell out of his nervous system. His body's lost a lot of the control it normally has. I just hope it hasn't affected the sympathetic nerves."

"The who?"

"The nerves controlling involuntary movement—digestion and so on."

57

"What about me mum and dad—can't I go home now?" Trevor cried, sensing the gravity of the whispered discussion. "Mum'll be dead worried if I don't."

The Sergeant ruffled the boy's hair. "You'll just rest here for a while and we'll sort things out for you. I'm sure the Inspector will send a car around if you think it'll help." He glanced at the Major. "Think we can move him now?"

Inspector Morris stepped forward. "Put him in the end cell for the moment."

"Think you can walk?" Thomas asked, helping him slip down from the desk. "Feel a bit dizzy, eh?"

He nodded shakily.

"Take his arms," Morris suggested as the Sergeant and Duty Officer moved to help him. "And leave the door open. One of you stay outside—just in case he needs anything." He looked at Thomas. "What about it?"

"It's gonna be rough," he replied, boosting himself onto the desk. "He'll have to know." He paused to look at the clock. "Anyone know his age?"

"Oh, about thirteen. I've seen him around here once or twice. Goes to the secondary modern in Deignby. Nice enough kid."

"Local orphanage for him, I suppose."

"Or relatives. Tell me, how is it you managed to stay alive in that ditch—and why is the boy's arm trembling so?"

"I used atropene. Counteracts the effects of nerve gas. It's just lucky that I didn't change my coat this afternoon or I wouldn't have been carrying it. It's the only thing we know of that has any effect on VX."

"VX?"

"If that's what I think it is. VX is a type of nerve gas —one of the deadliest. Dwarf Hill had just finished storing a batch of it before shipping it on to Porton. As for the boy's hand, it could be an effect of the nervous damage from the gas, or it could be brain damage. It's difficult to tell until he's been thoroughly examined. He'll need very special treatment, you know."

"Where does he get this treatment—in a hospital?"

"Only place I know of is at Detrick. There's a special center there for nerve gas and biological weapons contamination. I suppose Porton has one."

"Not that I've heard, but that isn't really my department." He thought. "Do you think any of that gas will reach *us*?"

"I hope not, Inspector. If the wind stays as it is, most of the gas'll stay where it is. If it changes, well, odds are we'll never know about it."

Morris sighed, looking at his watch. He wasn't looking forward to the morrow.

"I want to give that boy a shower."

Morris frowned again.

"A good hot shower'll get rid of the traces of this stuff. Obviously our clothes were contaminated."

"There's a staff shower in the cell block. You can use that. I'll have the Sergeant see to some clothes for the boy. I think his kid's about the same size."

He nodded. "I suppose I better start, then. The sooner we finish up, the sooner we can get some sleep. I think it's gonna be a long day tomorrow."

"So do I, Major," he replied tiredly. "So do I."

SECTION TWO: DETECTION AND THE OFFENSIVE

Sunday, 11th October

II

Mr. and Mrs. Bream puttered about the kitchen while Michael, their only son, played outdoors with the puppy. It was a typical Sunday. Breakfast was on the stove, Mr. Bream was toying with the knot of his tie and Michael would be late again in getting ready for church. Mr. Bream looked away from the mirror.

"Hear the radio this morning?" he asked.

"No more than usual," his wife replied. "Why?"

"Been an explosion at some secret Army base in Devon. They've cordoned off the whole area and won't let anyone know what's happened. Announcer said that nerve gas or something had spread all over the place—hundreds killed and all that."

"Typical, isn't it," she remarked, handing him a plate of eggs. "If you fool around with that stuff, one day it's bound to blow up in your face." She pushed open the window. "Michael, come in get your breakfast."

Mr. Bream shook his head. "That ruddy dog and him are inseparable lately. Take him to church if he could. I don't know why we haven't gotten him one before."

"Because he wasn't old enough, that's why. He's only just old enough now, and that's stretching it a bit."

The door pushed open and Michael appeared with an armful of puppy. "Dad, there's something wrong with Nip. He's all weak and trembling."

"Bring him here," he sighed, turning from his already less than warm eggs. "There now, Nipper, what's the trouble?"

Nipper looked up through hazy eyes.

"What's wrong with him, Ed?" his wife asked.

"Don't really know. His nose is warm so I'd say he's got a cold from somewhere. Never mind. We'll see how he is after church—maybe run him down to the vet. Put him in his basket, Michael, and come eat your breakfast. You've got choir this morning, remember."

"Can't I stay with him?" he pleaded wistfully, staring through strands of floppy hair. "It won't hurt to miss choir just this once."

"It wouldn't if you didn't have a solo," his mother said flatly and without much room for bargaining. "It would sound pretty funny when it came to your part. Besides, puppies are just like babies—sick one minute and a pain in the neck the next. You'll see."

The boy wasn't satisfied, but he had no choice. Carefully, he lay the animal in his basket and knelt beside him, stroking his fur. The pup whimpered.

"You know," Mrs. Bream whispered to her husband, "I really do think there's something wrong with Nip."

"Well, whatever it is, it'll have to wait till after church. Mind you, he's just had his injections so it could easily be that what's causing the trouble."

She turned to her son. "Eat your breakfast, Michael. You'll need something in your tum if your going to sing."

"Not for me, thanks. I'll have it when I get back if it's OK."

"Please yourself. But you'd better get dressed quickly. We've got to be at the church in twenty minutes."

Michael looked down at the puppy. He rose unsteadily, grasped the doorknob for support and shook his head.

"You all right, son?"

"I think so, Dad. Feel a bit dizzy, that's all.

"Well, no matter," Mrs. Bream said hastily. "If you won't eat, you won't feel well."

The bells for morning service were pealing sharply for those who were late when the Breams parked their car next to the dozens of others. Father Morgan was scurrying about, hurrying people inside, but he stopped when he spied Michael.

"Come on, lad," he urged. "Mr. Stuart will be looking for you. You know how he is about punctuality, especially if you've got a solo."

"Yes, Sir," he replied unhappily, and walked off.

"I do hope he sings well enough today, Father," Mrs. Bream was saying. "His puppy's ill and he's taking it pretty poorly."

"I noticed something was wrong," he said kindly. "But I'll have a word with him before the service. Will you excuse me?"

"Of course," she nodded, and Father Morgan walked off after Michael.

The dizzy spells were coming back, waves of dizziness with red dots flashing in his eyes. His fingers trembled and he was having difficulty in pulling the gown over his head. He braced his legs against the bench and tried to wriggle into the white cotton robe, but the dizziness overcame him and he tottered backwards threatening to crash to the floor.

"Hang on there!" cried Father Morgan, jumping to catch him. "You'll have to do better than that. Hitting the old Communal wine, eh?"

"I'm sorry Father. I slipped," Michael whispered shakily. "I don't feel very well this morning."

"I know. Your mum mentioned that Nip was feeling a bit under the weather."

"I hope he's all right. I wouldn't have come today if I hadn't that solo."

"I shouldn't worry too much, Michael," he began, sitting the boy on the bench. He straightened his ribbon. "But if you really want to go home again I think Ralph can take your place."

Michael looked up. Father Morgan looked fuzzy. "No, it's all right. I'll sing—but can I skip Communion?"

"Certainly, my boy," he grinned. He glanced furtively about, then whispered in his ear. "Sometimes I wish I could skip Communion, too. But you'd better hurry now. I think Mr. Stuart is coming after you."

"Bream?" called a voice from the passage.

Father Morgan ducked behind the pillar. He had a michievous grin on his face as he glanced at Michael.

"Bream? Where are you? Are you in there?" He emerged from the archway in his flowing gown. "So here you are. Come along or you'll hold up the procession."

"Yes, Sir," the boy replied wearily.

"I held him up, Mr. Stuart," said Father Morgan, poking his head around the pillar.

"Oh, sorry, Father. I didn't realize your were here," he said quickly.

Father Morgan held up his hand. "Quite all right. But go easy on Michael today. His puppy's sick."

"Nothing like a good bit of singing to clear an aching heart, eh Michael?" he called out, hustling him towards the front of the church.

His reply was lost in the echoes above as Father Morgan himself hastened off.

The choir had finished the *Venite* when Father Morgan arose and walked to the pulpit. Michael was trying to focus on various objects without much success.

"Here beginneth the Twelfth Chapter of the Book of Ecclesiastes." He opened the text. Michael blinked several times and looked at his hands. They were shaking. " 'Remember now thy Creator in the days of thy youth, while the evil days come not, nor the years draw nigh, when thou shalt say, I have no pleasure in them;' "

Michael began to sense a tingling in his hands.

" 'While the sun, or the light, or the moon, or the stars, be not darkened, nor the clouds return after the rain: In the days when the keepers of the house shall tremble, and the strong men shall bow themselves, and the grinders cease because they are few, and those that look out of the windows be darkened.' "

Ralph nudged Michael and grinned. He was about to whisper something when he spied Mr. Stuart's eyes bearing down on him. Michael blinked and shook his head.

" 'And the doors shall be shut in the streets, when the sound of the grinding is low, and he shall rise up at the voice of the bird, and all the daughters of music shall be brought low; Also *when* they shall be afraid of *that which is* high, and *fears shall be* in the way, and the almond tree shall flourish, and the grasshopper shall be a burden, and desire shall fail;' "

Ralph noticed something. He was looking at Michael's hands trembling. They seemed darker than his. Nerves, he thought.

" 'Because man goeth to his long home, and the mourners go about the streets; Or ever the silver cord be loosed, or the golden bowl be broken, or the pitcher be broken at the fountain, or the wheel broken at the cistern. Then shall the dust return to the earth as it was: and the spirit shall return unto God who gave it.' Here endeth the First Lesson."

As Father Morgan folded the text and returned slowly to his seat, the choir rose. Michael was the last to stand, and his eyes were quite unable to focus on anything. His hands were trembling and his right arm felt sore, throbbing, tingling. He shook his head. His lungs felt tight. He thought he must be more nervous than usual. The organ was playing. He looked up and tried to make out Mr. Stuart, but he appeared only as an indefinite figure amidst clouds of mist. He could barely see the raised arm: it was nothing more than a blur. He closed his eyes tightly. When he opened them, the hand was still a blur. He squinted. It seemed a little better. The hand was coming down. He took a breath and clenched his shaking fists.

"Oh be joyful in the Lord, all ye lands."

The choir sung the next lines. He had gotten through the first line. It sounded all right. Could have been a bit stronger. But then this wretched dizziness was growing worse. He fought it off. His lines were coming up again.

"Be ye sure that the Lord he is God."

And another short break. More of a strain that time, but no one noticed, he hoped. He found his hands were clutching the railing. Sweat was making the surface slippery. His lungs felt tighter. The pain in his arm was worse.

"O go your way into his gates with thanksgiving, and into his courts with praise."

His lungs were too tight. He couldn't get enough breath. He had to gasp on the last word. Was Mr. Stuart looking at him? He felt sweat trickling down his sides. He licked his lips and pushed back moist strands of hair which covered his eyes. The dizziness lunged through him. He glanced quickly around to see if anyone had noticed, but Ralph only looked back at him and smiled. He winked. Another breath.

"For the Lord is gracious, his mercy is everlasting."

One more line to go. His head was spinning. He could no longer see Mr. Stuart. The organ music sounded strange and far away. Out of tune. He put back a feeble hand to his forehead. He was teetering back and forth. Someone from behind grasped his shoulder gently, firmly. He mustn't fall. He gripped the railing, but the pain in his right arm shot through him and he winced. He couldn't feel the grip in his left arm, either. His knees were weak. He glanced down to see the floor, but it rose and fell in oceanic currents. His vision was failing him. Everything was blurry. He could only hear the choir faintly. His final lines were coming up. He breathed in. His mouth was dry. He gasped.

"Glory be to the Father."

It was hardly a whisper

"And to the Son."

Ralph was squeezing his wrist. He was whispering something. He tried to turn his head. He must finish.

"And to the Holy Ghost."

It was over. He could hear the choir finishing the lines. But what was Ralph saying? What was Mr. Stuart saying? He tried to focus on Mr. Stuart, but even his flowing vestments were blurred and unrecognizable. His grip on the railing was loosening. The pain in his arm was growing unbearable. He could feel tears trickling down his cheeks and his lungs tightened still more. He had to gasp to breathe. He was trembling all over. His whole body began to shudder. The whole church was trembling. The altar was swimming about in front of him. The Cross lunged towards him, then swam away. He put his hand out to touch it, to hold it, to stop the swaying. But is was no good. He felt himself slipping into the waves of swimming fragments, and he was frightened. He looked up, looked at Ralph, at Mr. Stuart. He was falling. It was no good. His eyes turned imploringly upon the Cross. He felt the cold damp of the stone floor. He could see a great figure before him dressed in flowing white garments. He cried out. But no one heard him. He was dead.

The congregation mumbled. Some stood up. Father Morgan walked hastily to the boy and knelt down. Mr. Stuart vaulted over the railings and one of the choristers pushed through to the front. Father Morgan looked up. He faltered. "I think the child is, is dead, Dr. Hughes."

Mr. Stuart motioned for the choir to sit as he walked to the pulpit. Mr. and Mrs. Bream were rushing up the aisle. "Please remain seated," he called. "The lad's just had a faint. Happens to the best of us. I think we'll take up the collection now, Mr. Todd."

Mrs. Bream was at her son's side. "What's wrong with him?" she cried, herself rather faint.

"I don't know yet," Dr. Hughes replied. "But could you wait..."

"Yes, yes," began Father Morgan. "Come to my study. Dr. Hughes will see that Michael is all right."

"But—" tried Mrs. Bream.

"Come along," said Mr. Bream, putting his arm around her shoulders. "It'll be better this way."

Dr. Hughes looked after them. Mr. Bream turned. Dr. Hughes shook his head slightly. He felt for the boy's pulse once again. As he lifted the arm slightly off the floor, Michael's sleeve slipped back. Dr. Hughes shuddered impulsively. There was a large black pustule, surrounded by darkening blood. Slowly he lowered the arm and drew back the sleeve. Father Morgan appeared again.

"Have we got a stretcher anywhere?" the Doctor asked in a whisper.

"Yes," he replied. "Somewhere."

"Try to find it. And I think you better call for an ambulance and the police. Tell them to come as quietly as they can—no sirens. We'll meet them in your study."

"Is there any, I mean is he..."

67

"I'm afraid so. He's beyond any help from us."

Father Morgan crossed himself. "God rest his soul, the poor child."

"We must get the choir away from here," the Doctor insisted. "But they must go near no one. I'll get Fred to take them to the Rectory while you make the calls."

"What about the congregation?"

"I'll talk to them when I've got the choir away from here."

Father Morgan nodded slowly. He looked down at Michael. He sighed, and his sigh shuddered in his chest. "What on earth caused it? He was so young."

"There's no question about what caused it, Father. I'm worried about how he got it."

"What is it, then?"

"Anthrax."

"Anthrax? How the devil . . ."

"Kneel down here." Dr. Hughes lifted the sleeve. "Look."

Father Morgan winced. "It's horrible. It's unbelievable. The poor child."

"I'd say this is a very special type of anthrax. It's killed him in a very short time."

"How can you tell?"

"This is a very severe reaction. Had he caught it yesterday, he would have been far too ill to sing in the choir today. No, my guess is this is a very special strain. Now you'd better make those calls. And hurry."

Father Morgan looked down at Michael. He closed his eyes and whispered something. Slowly he removed his cross and chain and laid it over the boy.

Dr. Hughes glanced up at the choir. Ralph was trying to blink. He shook his head and blinked again. Dr. Hughes approached him. "Are you all right, Ralph?"

"Dizzy, that's all." He held his hands out in front of him. "And my hands are tingling sort of."

Chesterly. 10:45 Hours

"And you're certain that the explosion came *after* the fire?" Chadwell asked. "It couldn't have been a bomb or something?"

"Look, Chadwell," Thomas replied, angrily banging his fist on the iron railing outside the police station. "There are dozens of witnesses who saw that fire. There's no easy way out of this one—your microbiological plant caught fire and blew. That's that."

"Well, of course we shan't know anything really until after the inquiry. I'm sure the Ministry will want to know all about this as soon as possible."

"And what about the people in Stumford? What are you going to do about them?"

"That is a problem, isn't it? I suppose the Army will have to deal with them—can't just leave them lying about."

"What I meant was what about the survivors?"

"What survivors?" Chadwell tapped his pipe on the rail.

"For one there's a thirteen year old boy in there whose parents and family were in Stumford last night. What about him?

"Oh, I'm certain the villagers will look after him until the authorities can take over. We do have homes for these sort of children, you know."

"I'm sure that will be of great consolation to the boy. You do realize that he's suffering pretty badly?"

"Suffering? Suffering from what?"

"From nerve gas, damn it. He's the one I pulled out of a ditch last night."

He paused and puzzled over his pipe. "Another problem. If he's been exposed to the gas—if that's what it was—the Ministry will want a look see. I don't think they'd like him running about knowing what he does."

"Firstly, Chadwell, I can't really see him doing much running about in his present condition, and secondly he doesn't know anything yet. He doesn't even know what hit him—nor that his parents are dead."

"I suppose it's better that way. We'll let this go through the normal channels. I'm sure—"

"What I would like to know is when are you going to have the boy treated properly? The most I could do was jab him with oxime to help him feel better, but he's going to need a complete check-up. Christ knows what that gas may have done to his system."

"Did you say oxime, Major?"

"I did. Oxime P_2S."

"But that's a top secret antidote. How did you get hold of it?"

"We have all sorts of ways of getting hold of your 'top secrets'—just as I suppose you get on to ours."

He grunted. "Not very professional, I must say."

"So go on—what about treatment?"

"What treatment, man? What *are* you on about?"

"Look, Chadwell, that boy must have a proper diagnosis and early therapy if he's going to pull out of danger. He's already suffered nerve damage to his epidermis and he's got a right hand that won't stop shaking. It could be brain damage you know."

"Well, we'll pack him off to Great Ormond Street. They deal with kids all the time."

"Not this sort of kid, they don't. Doesn't your Porton have a special center? What happens when your researchers get exposed?"

"Nothing I suppose. I've never heard of such a place— if it does exist." He scratched his head. "No, I've never heard of anything like it."

"Then I'll have him sent to Detrick. They can deal with it right now." He turned to enter the station.

"See here, Major Thomas, I really cannot see how any of this is your affair. I mean, this is our problem and not the Americans'."

"Perhaps you would rather I left, huh? Perhaps you would like that boy in there to die like all the rest only a lot slower and a hell of a lot more painfully?"

Chadwell hesitated. "Well, this whole thing will have to be kept rather hush-hush, you know. We mustn't let the public know of what's happened. If that's possible." He eyed the rows of newspapermen who lined the barricades on the edge of the village. His stomach sank further when he saw a BBC outside broadcasting unit arrive and immediately begin setting up their cameras. "You will of course respect the Official Secrets Act. I'm sure you can appreciate—"

"Chadwell," the Major began coldly, "can you tell me exactly what was going on at Dwarf Hill?"

He laughed. "Even if I did know, I couldn't tell you—certainly not after what's happened."

"Exactly—you don't know. If Captain McRoberts was at all right, the personnel working in that plant are the only ones who knew precisely what they were doing. And they're all dead."

"And who is this McRoberts?"

"He worked at Dwarf Hill. God knows what's left of *him*."

"Well, I doubt what you say is true, but even if it were, where does that leave us?"

"I was told just before I left yesterday that I probably knew more about what was going on in that plant than your boys in London did. Work was so secret and specialized that only when they came up with the results

71

would the information be passed on. Apparently that's a policy among your research laboratories."

"My dear fellow, that's highly unlikely. More near impossible, I'd say."

"Did you know that they were developing the micro-encapsulation of a highly virulent anthrax bacteria?"

"No, I can't say that I did. But I'm sure London has the fullest details on what was going on."

Inspector Morris plodded wearily down the steps of the police station and approached the two arguing figures. His hopes of some rest before the onslaught from London had been shattered during the night when proof of the disaster reached the Ministry. By four o'clock troops had begun to arrive and establish roadblocks and barricades, and he had been told to empty Chesterly of its inhabitants by six. When that had been accomplished, Chadwell had arrived, and there had been no time for rest since. As he surveyed the village, he knew it would be a long time before he could even think of a kip.

"Excuse me, Mr. Chadwell, but Major Thomas is wanted in the station," he said. "Can you spare him a moment?"

"Certainly. I think I'll go too. Want to get on to Head in London. See exactly what was going on before the bang."

As he strode confidently off, the Major shouted after him. "You might see what this Project Dracula's all about or if there's any record of deliveries of bats."

"Bats?" Chadwell spouted, turning abruptly about.

"Flying mice-type bats. If they can't tell you anything, maybe I can."

"Sounds a bit melodramatic to me. I think you and I better have a talk about all this. I'm sure London will want to see you before your return."

"Return?" said the Major, walking towards him with the Inspector.

"To America of course. I thought you and your lot were going back tomorrow."

"Don't know yet," he replied casually. "Maybe I'll stick around and see how things go. That is if you have no objections."

"It won't be up to me," he replied disappearing into the station.

The Inspector pulled at the Major's sleeve. "It's that boy of yours. He getting pretty restless in there and he seems to be in a lot of pain. I figured you might be able to handle him—I daren't let any of the other lads tell him anything."

"Christ, I don't know what to say. Why doesn't Chadwell tell him?"

"You don't really mean that?"

He flipped his cap from his head and banged it against his knee. "No, I don't mean it. But I don't know what to say to the kid. How do you tell him his parents are lying in Stumford dead as doornails, and he'll be just as dead if he doesn't get treatment?"

"Gently, that's how you tell him. Didn't you ever have anyone close to you—I mean who maybe died?"

"Yeah, my wife."

Morris seemed ashamed. He shook his head and tried to count the pebbles on the steps of the station. "I'm sorry."

"Forget it. I didn't mean it that way. That was a few years ago. It's over. But I see what you mean." He sighed and replaced his cap. "Yeah, I'll tell him."

"You mentioned this treatment he must have . . ."

"Well, he should have a proper diagnosis. I know that some of his nervous systems have been affected, but which ones and how bad only an expert could tell. All I can do is keep him on oxime until he gets help."

"Oxime?"

"Don't you start. Oxime—it's a drug which helps counteract the effects of gas poisoning. But Chadwell doesn't know of any place that can treat him. No ordinary doctor would know where to begin."

"What do you think we should do?"

"We?"

"He's your problem, Major. You rescued him and it seems you're the only one who knows what to do. I'll do whatever I can to cut red tape, but it won't be much."

"Well, the only place I know of that handles cases like his is at Detrick. But I doubt the Ministry is going to let him simply fly out of their hands. No doubt their scientists want to have a poke and a prod. It's not often people get exposed to this stuff."

"Thank God. Look, I'll see what can be done. You see to the boy."

"What about Chadwell? Aren't we supposed to be hush-hush—nobody's to know what happened?"

They climbed the steps to the station. "Just tell the boy what you think is best—what he needs to know."

"What if he asks about tomorrow, about what's going to happen to him?"

"Well, Major. Right now his life is in your hands. You decide what his tomorrow's are going to be. Whatever you decide I'll try damned hard to put through. I don't like to see him suffering any more than you." Morris looked at the Sergeant who nodded. "He's in the same cell. You know where it is?"

"Yeah. And look, keep Chadwell out of my hair, will you? At least let me finish with the kid first."

"I'll do my best."

"Down here, Sir," the Sergeant offered, leading him through the narrow passage. "Here we are, cell fifteen." He knocked on the partially opened door. "All right if we come in, laddie?"

"If you want," replied a stronger voice than the Major remembered. "Need the key?"

"Not unless you've managed to lock it from the inside," the Sergeant grinned. "You've got a visitor. I'll leave you to it. Maybe this fellow can answer some of your questions."

"Thank you, Sergeant," Thomas replied, shutting the door behind him. It clanked shut and he laughed. "Hope someone's got the key. Not used to the inside of these places."

"Me neither," he said, pushing up his pillow. "Filled with sawdust, this. Ever slept with a pillow full of sawdust?" Trevor tried to grin, but shut his eyes in pain.

"No, can't say that I have." Thomas looked down at the boy. Wouldn't have passed for twelve in America, he figured. He was thin, pale and with a lock of wispy hair which partially hid his eyes. His face had character, though, with a definite hint of mischief. Underneath, he must be all English. The very fact that this was an *English* boy held some kind of mystery for the Major like it did for all Americans, and the mystery was deepened by the fact he would in all probability be the lad's keeper for some time yet. Thomas would have found dealing with an American kid difficult in these circumstances, but at least he could predict yanks—he was used to them. It was silly, he thought, that English kids should be any different, but his generation had been brought up in respect and admiration for the British (didn't they *beat* kids in their schools?), and while Thomas felt he could predict grown-ups, he hadn't the slightest idea how this young boy would react or behave. He scratched his head and picked out a crack in the wall.

"You ride a motorbike pretty well," Trevor began, breaking an uncomfortable silence and eager to uncover some information.

"Yeah," he scoffed "From my early days in the Army. We couldn't get killed in Vietnam in those days so we had to find other ways of doing it. I chose motorcycling."

Trevor knew little of Vietnam, but he knew it was some kind of trade mark among all Americans.

"May I sit down?"

Trevor tried to move his legs, but his reactions were slowed. Thomas helped him.

"What's your name, then—better start with that."

The bed creaked under his heavy frame.

"Didn't the coppers tell you?" he sighed uneasily.

"I'm very bad at names. I know your first name," he announced proudly. "Trevor."

"And my surname's Brecon. Haven't got a middle name. And I live in Deignby and I want to go home. Can you tell me what's going on, or aren't you allowed to either?"

"No I'm not allowed to either. But I'll tell you what I can. Just keep it between us, huh?"

"Then what's happened in Stumford—why can't I go home?"

He sighed. He hoped it wouldn't be this direct "It's a bit of a long story, Trevor." He removed his cap and twirled it between his knees. "And not a very nice one." He looked at him. "I think you'll have to have a lot of courage."

"It's about Mum and Dad, isn't it?"

He paused before he nodded. "And about others."

Trevor stared beyond him. "Are they dead? Is that why nobody'll tell me anything?"

"Yes, Trevor. Your mother and father and everyone else in Stumford." He saw tears well up in the boy's eyes and he waited for it to come. He had a sudden desire to help him, to comfort him, but how did he comfort a child who's just lost his family? He raised his arm to put about the lad's trembling shoulders when he turned over and buried his head in the rough pillow.

"Why?" he sobbed. "What happened to them?"

"They, well—"

The door opened. The Sergeant stepped hesitantly inside. "Begging your pardon, Sir, but Mr. Chadwell wants to see you straight away. I know you weren't to be disturbed, but he says it's rather important—urgent."

"That's all right, Sergeant," the Major replied quietly. He looked down at the boy. "I'll be back soon, son. If, if you want anything, there'll be someone just outside." He gave him a reassuring squeeze on his shoulder and arose. He heard Chadwell and the Inspector coming down the hallway, evidently engaged in an argument.

"Damn it, Morris, I don't care who it is—I told Thomas he's not to give out information to anyone." He peered around the door to the cell. "There you are, Major." He noticed the boy. "Oh, sorry, old man. May I have a word with you?" He watched him slowly withdraw from the bed, and—with an obvious effort to control his temper—came into the corridor. "Now see here Major Thomas, you fail to realize that we're dealing with a case of National security—you simply can't go round telling people what's happened." He nodded towards the cell. "Even if what has transpired involves people personally. I know the lad lost his family and relatives, but can you imagine what might happen if any of this leaked out?"

Thomas' hands were white as he glared at the Inspector who shrugged his shoulders from behind Chadwell's back.

"How much *have* you told him?"

"I told him, Chadwell, that his parents were dead and so were a hell of a lot of other people in Stumford."

"Is that all?" he asked cautiously.

"That's all."

He looked relieved. "Well, I daresay that isn't news. I thought you might have told him more."

"I would have if you hadn't come—what would you have me say, that his mother and father have gone on a long vacation and can't be traced?"

"Oh, forget all this, for heaven's sake," Morris cried. "There's enough bother about without you two having a go at each other."

"Quite right," Chadwell announced emphatically. "Major, I apologize. Can't be too careful, you know. Anyway London wants you to tell me all you know about what was going on at Dwarf Hill. They, ah, well, they don't seem to know all I had hoped they did."

"Then McRoberts was right—you don't know from nothing what was going on up there."

"Well, I shouldn't go so far as to say that. Let's just say that we don't have all the information we'd like to have in our possession."

"You can use my office," said the Inspector, leading the way out. "I'll see that Dr. Phipps has a look at the boy. Give him a sedative or something."

"Thank you, Inspector. And don't let the boy out of the station, will you? Not until we're sure he won't say anything."

Thomas boiled inside. His head was throbbing with fury when he plopped himself in the chair on the other side of the Inspector's desk where Chadwell sat rifling through a file of papers.

"You mentioned this Project Dracula and something about a consignment of bats. Could you elaborate?"

Thomas chose his words carefully. "Dwarf Hill was working on a wild idea code-named Project Dracula."

"Yes, yes. I gathered that. Exactly what was this idea?"

"Some of your fellows in London had the idea of

micro-encapsulating a high potency strain of anthrax bacillus in a time delay device and attaching the whole thing to hundreds of bats. Presumably, the bats would be able to fly undetected and unseen and eventually be brought to ground when contaminated by the anthrax. I think the whole thing was based on something we experimented with before the end of the last war."

"So you have tried this as well." He never glanced up, but continued writing.

"Only we used incendiary bombs. It never succeeded of course, but probably one of your boys was reading some history book and hit on the idea."

"Carry on, Major."

Chadwell's quiet unflappable voice, his thin glasses and portly figure reminded Thomas of the psychiatrist who had examined him years before—for security reasons. He cringed at the recollection, and hated Chadwell all the more. He continued his explanation. "The operation was to begin this morning just before sunrise. They had rigged up a special netting around the phoney village they had built. After the bats were released, the plan was for the time delay mechanism to expose them to the anthrax at various intervals. The men would calculate how effective the device was, where the bats were brought down and where they nested—if any tried to. The basic objective would have been to determine area of contamination, virulence . . ." He shrugged. "Time and so on."

"Brilliant idea, what?" Chadwell seemed to have forgotten the explosion. He was intrigued by the experiment. "Strike at night totally undetected and spread uncurable anthrax all over the bloody place. Pity we'll never know the results."

"Won't we?" Thomas mused.

"Not if the Base has blown up like everyone says it has."

"You better goddam hope so. I'd hate to think what would happen if any of those things got loose. They *were* prepared, you know. They were fitted with the device."

"Impossible, dear boy. Nothing could escape. It was just unlucky that the nerve gas leaked out over Stumford. If that's what it is."

Thomas glanced upwards. "I suppose it's just going to be unlucky if a few of those bats blow over London."

He laughed. "I don't mind admitting that would be a bit of bad luck for us. It's going to be hard enough explaining our way out of this one."

"I don't suppose that bad luck of yours would affect a few million people."

"Oh, come now, Major. If that explosion was as bad as you seem to think it was, surely nothing could survive."

"Mr. Chadwell, have you ever seen the actual effects of an explosion—I mean, what an explosion can do?"

"I don't quite follow . . ."

"You know that if your gas stove explodes in your face, usually the windows and sometimes the walls blow out."

He nodded thoughtfully.

"And if your wife, say, was coming in the door when you blew up the stove, how she would probably be blown back a few hundred feet or so?"

He nodded thoughtfully again.

"Well, picture in your mind about a thousand bats settling down for a nice night's sleep when Bang! The floor blows up and blasts the ceiling several hundred feet high. Now, not every bat is going to get blown up as well. A few will die from concussion, flying debris will remove a few more and maybe the heat will roast those who aren't quick enough, but," he paused, leaving Chadwell hanging, "but there will be quite a number of lucky ones who manage to get loose. Like you wife standing in the doorway, they'll be *blown* clear of danger."

"But you mentioned something about a netting," he replied as if guessing the answer to a riddle.

"Do you honestly believe that if the explosion was strong enough to level a six-inch thick concrete building, it wouldn't be powerful enough to snap the wire on a miserable *net?*"

"Good point, Major. Your theory is unsettling. But I hardly understand how anything could survive that. Besides, if any did get away from the blast, they'd be dead by now anyway. Didn't you say the capsules would melt or something?"

"Dead they would be, Mr. Chadwell, but where?"

"Well, Major, I'll be honest with you," he began, leaning across the table. "We have more than enough to cope with right now here in Chesterly without worrying about itinerant bats. But what you say is important so I'll notify London when I make my report. I can't honestly see them warning people over television and radio not to touch any dead bats they might find in their back gardens, now, can you?"

"I know," sighed Thomas, raising his hand. "Mass panic."

"Panic nothing," Chadwell exclaimed. "They'd think it was a bunch of rubbish!"

For the first time in his life Thomas felt utterly defeated. He couldn't help hating the British and their damned stiff upper lips. He mused to himself that the stiff upper lips of a few million people might be attached to rather stiff bodies if this fellow from London didn't get off his pompous ass and do something. Wearily, he looked up and sighed. "Have you heard enough?"

"For the moment, yes, thank you."

The Major began to rise.

"Oh, before you go, London has said that you should feel free to stay in England until this thing is over. In fact, the Home Secretary would be very grateful indeed to have you helping in the inquiry."

"Oh would he. Well, Mr. Chadwell, you tell your bully boys in London that I shall be most pleased indeed to help you with your inquiry provided I get a little more say in what's going on. And you can also tell them to remember that I'm the only one who knows exactly what Dwarf Hill was up to when your so-called bang banged."

"I'll convey your sentiments when I ring," he answered drily. "And one more thing. Do you know the name of the gas which may have affected you?"

"May have my ass. It did. And I think is was VX or sarin. The effects were similar to the same stuff we use."

"Oh, that's another thing. Do you think you could let me have a report on precisely what effects the gas had on you? I think Porton would be very interested."

"Yes, and I'll have Trevor write one, too. I think he'd be delighted to assist you. Give him something to do while he's thinking about his mother and father."

Chadwell hadn't looked up from his file. "Trevor?"

"The boy in the cell."

"Oh, of course. Yes, well thank you very much, Major. I'll see you later, I daresay."

"Yes," he thought to himself. "I daresay you will." And he slammed the door behind him.

"Glen," called the Inspector who had by now decided that first names would perhaps relax the formalities insisted on by London. "Glad you're through in there. Listen, Dr. Phipps has seen the lad in there and you're quite right."

"About what?" he asked, leaning on the inquiry desk and fumbling for his cigarettes.

"About the effects. He's never seen anything like it. Couldn't begin to offer help. Except he says that the lad needs someone now. Someone to look after him for awhile—you know, take his mind off things. I'd try to find one of his mates in the village, but the Army's evacuating everyone for miles around. And since Mr. Chadwell's sort of impounded the boy, well, I thought of you."

"Christ, that's just when I need now. I've just heard enough crap from Chadwell to keep the wheat country in manure for a year. What I need is a drink—not a son."

The Inspector hesitated. "He asked for you." He searched for the right words. "I can't assign any of my men—they just haven't got the time or experience. Except maybe McKinley, but he's too worried about his wife and kids. I've still got Chesterly to run and what with the whole British Army trapsing around and half the world's supply of reporters trying to weasle in, my hands are tied. Say you'll do what you can—and you can still have that drink."

He stared at Morris. Unconsciously, he knew he wanted to help the boy. Somewhere something told him that he was in part responsible for the death of the parents and for the boy's pain—responsible for the deaths of hundreds of parents. He wanted himself to be comforted: to be told that it had nothing to do with him; that the research in England and America was unconnected; that his hands were clean. But no one would comfort him. No one would say what he wanted to hear because he knew it wasn't true. He *was* responsible. He was a small but vital part of what had killed hundreds of innocent people. He knew he must help the child. It was his only chance to assuage a painful conscience. Still staring at the Inspector, he said, "He asked for me, did he?"

83

He nodded. "You're the only one who's been honest with him."

"Now all I gotta do is be honest with myself."

"Feeling the weight a bit, eh? Maybe you feel like your predecessors did when they dropped the Bomb on Japan. It's in all of us old enough to have fought in the War. I wiped out a few square miles of German cities in the War. How many people died thanks to me? How many kids were mangled, or burnt or buried? Someday we all meet up with our past—our work." He paused to rest his hand on the desk. "Go on. Face a result of your work. Face the boy and help him make something of his life. You were old enough to carry on when your wife died, but *he's* only a child. Right now his future looks about as bright as those four cell walls. He'll have to start again, and I think you might like to help him try. That's why I thought of you—it's a chance for you both."

Thomas searched the floor. "It's the treatment. He needs treatment."

Morris felt helpless. He was out of his depth.

"I figure Trevor's received a mild dose. He seemed better this morning, but it'll take months before his body's fully recovered. It'll take the best care anyone can give. He'll need cerebral taps—like having a goddam knife twisted in your back. He'll need hydrotherapy and physiotherapy and masses of recuperative serum. If he's not kept on drugs, there'll be times when he's in agony —when every muscle fights conscious control, when his head will ache so bad it'll make migraine seem enjoyable. And there's the chance he's suffered brain damage. I doubt it looking at him, but there's that arm." He paused. "You're not kidding when you said he'll have to start again. That's what that poor devil's up against. I can't help thinking he'd be better off if the gas had wiped him out, too."

"And you, Major—wiped you out, too?"

He shook his head and rubbed his sweating forehead. "It'd be easier wouldn't it? It just . . ." He struggled for words. "It kills me to see a kid hurt like that—knowing what he's going to have to face before he's better."

"And he'd get his treatment at Detrick?"

"Only if your country asks for it."

"You think they will?"

"No. I remember reading about cases you had—in this country. We were asked by the families of these men who had suffered exposure—we were asked to help cure them. But we couldn't. We couldn't unless the government made the request official. And they wouldn't. Oh, I don't know. What a goddam mess this whole thing is."

"Well, you better make up your mind what you're going to do," Morris replied more firmly than before. "If you refuse the kid help, you more than anyone know how long he's got. If you don't take him with you, you'll be his executioner. Don't you think life is something for the boy to decide? Do you think he *wants* to live? To be cured? Or does he want to suffer a slow and painful death? If the government won't help him, don't you think he's worth fighting for on your own?"

Thomas pondered the situation. He knew what was ahead at Detrick if he took the kid home. He knew he would be a part of it—the cure. The cure. He wondered if he could face it.

"He'll be a reminder, Glen. He'll always remind you of what you and men like you can do. But maybe that'll bring you closer together." He shrugged. "I don't know. I don't know a lot of things. But I'm usually a pretty good judge of character. Of people. You've got a lot of heart, and Trevor's a fine lad."

Thomas took out another cigarette. He thought he must try to give them up again. "Will I represent what killed his parents? Is that the reminder?"

"No," he replied slowly. "He's too numb to blame anyone or anything. He's lonely and frightened. If you can help him feel happier—forget a little of his grief, it'll be your interest in him that he'll remember. Your love, if you like. You haven't got a son, have you?"

He shook his head. He would have had if . . .

"Ordinarily I wouldn't mess about in this sort of thing —it's not my business. But I can see the hurt. I can see that you feel somewhat to blame, or that you're involved in some way. At least I think so. And I can see how Trevor is hurt. That doesn't take much. Put the two together. Sometimes it works."

Thomas looked up. He smiled. "I wish we had more cops like you." It was the only thing he could think of.

Morris put his hand on the Major's shoulder. "It's not me, Glen. It's all of us. Maybe there's too little emotion in this world, too little caring. It's easy to look the other way." He paused. "Will you do it?"

"Yeah," he sighed heavily, plunging his cigarette in the ashtray. "I'll do it. I suppose it's about time I took my head out of the sand."

They began walking towards the cells.

"You know, I think we all must be like ostriches—the ones who work on this stuff. We're really afraid of what we're doing. But we bury our heads and do it anyway. McRoberts called it our job. I'm almost glad this happened, but I wish to hell all those people hadn't died."

"And you will take him to America—see that he's all right?"

"Yeah, I'll take him. After all, if he's my son or something, I don't need your government's request, do I?"

Chadwell emerged from the Inspector's office, waved to them and made for the desk.

"All that moron's worried about is the press," Thomas

mumbled. "Stick a camera in his face and he'll have heart failure."

"That's another reason why I think you should look after the boy."

Thomas turned his head.

"Chadwell's going to see to it that Trevor is as far away from the outside world as he can get him until this blows over. He's already mentioned to me about sending him to Great Ormond Street. If he's with you, he stands a chance of getting out of here without being locked in an isolation ward in London."

They were in the cell block. "I wouldn't let that bastard have the satisfaction of it," Thomas swore. He stopped outside the cell. "Well, here goes."

The Inspector gripped his shoulder and nodded.

Thomas walked in. The lad was laying on his back. Hesitantly, he sat on the edge of the bed with unaccustomed hands he gently pushed back the wet strands of hair from the boy's eyes. He took a handkerchief from his pocket and held it out. "Feel any better?"

Trevor took the handkerchief, but only to grip it in his trembling hands. "What happens now? he choked.

"Happens?" he repeated softly.

"To me."

"That's a rough question, son," He recalled the Inspector's words. Of anyone in this world he was the only friend that boy had at the moment. "How old are you, Trevor? Thirteen?"

He nodded, fighting hard to keep back the tears.

"You're getting on, then?"

He nodded again.

Thomas took a deep breath and stared at the floor. "I suppose you mean where are you going."

Trevor closed his eyes.

"Well, you're not going to a home or anything like that if that's what you're thinking. I mean, well, no one's going to send you away." He felt lost. His words sounded empty, out of place. "I thought maybe we could move out of here together. I mean, well—" but Trevor cried out and flung himself over, burying his head in the pillow. Thomas turned him back and pulled him close. He could feel wet cheeks on his neck, and his own chest vibrated with the shuddering sobs of the boy's. He pushed Trevor's hair back in gentle strokes, and gripped his neck assuringly.

"Don't leave me alone," he whispered through his choking cries. "Please don't leave me alone."

"I won't, son," he replied. "I won't."

Stumford. 14:30 Hours

Major Thomas had never seen anything like it. Not in pictures, nor in life. Everywhere bodies were scattered like human debris; bodies fallen without purpose or direction. He looked at the Inspector and Chadwell who was tisktisking behind his mask as he scribbled hasty notes.

"I simply cannot understand how all this could have happened," Chadwell said as he glanced from his pad to the gruesome scene before him. "I mean it just wasn't supposed to happen."

"You sound disturbed, Mr. Chadwell," the Major replied. "Perhaps what you needed was some first hand experience."

"It's terrible, Major. We shall most probably have to redesign every single plant—the public will demand it."

"The public outcry will call for the closure of your bases—not their reconstruction," Thomas smiled, hidden behind his mask. "Yep, you'll have plenty to explain."

"I thought you were *involved* in this research—not against it."

"Perhaps we could all confine our research to just one station in the middle of nowhere."

"*Our* research?"

"You do realize that the implications of this disaster will be world-wide? Nobody working on this sort of thing will come away unscathed. I should think the UN might even have a say for all the good it'll do."

"You're a very difficult person, Major," Chadwell said angrily. "You come to our country to inquire of our research, then leave with the idea of confining everyone's work. I shouldn't think your people will be very pleased with your attitude."

"In America, Mr. Chadwell, when we don't like something we say so."

"Yes, very undisciplined lot you are. But that's going to get neither of us anywhere." He began picking his way across the bodies, shaking his head and jotting his observations.

The Inspector was walking towards the pub. There were some people he recognized, some he had often seen, but never knew by name. There were children he had often stopped to talk with, whom he had picked up for minor offences. The scene would have sickened him were it not for the disbelief and lack of comprehension. It could have been a set on a macabre stage ready for the principle character to appear. But the principle character had appeared, and its name was death. Invisible and unknown, it had played out its role and disappeared.

Something caught his eye and he called out. "Hello, what's this? Major? You better have a look."

Thomas found his way across and stared into the dim light and musky odor. "Looks like an animal. You wait out here. I'll have a look." Carefully he stepped through the narrow doorway and knelt down. "It's a dog. Looks pretty messed up. Must have been trampled on or something." He was searching the floor for a stick to turn the animal over when he saw the man. He froze, and the Inspector saw his face turn pale behind the mask and protective hood. His eyes enlarged with fear, and for the first time in many years he felt his stomach lurch with surprise and shock. Nothing he had ever seen in a laboratory resembled the sickeningly disfigured man who sat against the wall before him. His hands were quivering uncontrollably as he looked slowly up at Morris and pointed to the corpse. "Take a look," he gasped. "But not too close."

Morris stepped in and shone a torch against the wall. The puffy face and arms bloated beyond recognition, covered in blackened pustules and dried blood stared back at him. He wanted to be sick, but he found himself unable to tear away from the haunted stare, the expression of terror and pain. At length he managed, "You, you know what this is?"

He nodded. "You'd better get our friend in here."

The Inspector backed slowly away into the door. He turned abruptly and peered out. "Chadwell? Chadwell, come here. There's something the Major wants you to see."

"What have you found—not something new I hope," he called back, moving quickly towards the pub.

"I don't know what it is, but you'd better take a deep breath before you go in there."

"More bodies, I suppose," he said, cilmbing the step.

"No, just one."

"Well, what is it?" He noticed the dog. "Oh, that's bad luck. Is this what you wanted to show me. He does look rather—"

"Not the dog, Chadwell," said the Major through clenched teeth. *"Him!"*

Chadwell followed the Major's pointed finger until he spotted the figure. His notebook dropped from his hand and in his retreat backwards he tripped over the dog. Thomas caught him and stood up.

"That isn't gas poisoning." said Thomas. "That is anthrax."

"Anthrax," he whispered. He hesitated, and when he spoke again his voice carried the weight of realization. The impossible had—for Mr. Chadwell—become reality and it was more the shock of this than possible National infection that made him repeat simply, "Anthrax."

"Anthrax. Look at those lesions," directed Thomas.

"I must get on to London straight away. I shall take the land rover. Are you coming?"

Thomas pushed him out the door. "No. I want to look around. There may be more of this. It could be spreading all over."

"Be careful, Major," he warned and the Major thought for a moment that he meant it sincerely. "That is horribly dangerous."

"I know, Mr. Chadwell. I know it very well. By now you and I and the Inspector are contaminated with it. When you get to Chesterly get rid of that isolation gear. Burn it. Make one mistake with it and you'll end up like that man in there. Got it?"

He nodded. "I think so. Can I send anything down to you?"

"Send down a jeep to get us. Then order everyone out of Chesterly. I mean everyone—the Army, the lot. And clear this area for ten miles. Complete evacuation. This stuff is so powerful it could spread everywhere in hours. The more carriers there are about, the bigger the chance of a pandemic."

"Major?" began the Inspector slowly as Chadwell made for the rover. "If this is anthrax, if anthrax is spreading . . ."

"It's spreading from those bats they were working on."
He kicked a stone and listened to it rattle along the pavement until it came to rest outside a doorway. Thomas
reached where it had stopped and glanced idly into the
hallway. "Look," he said, pointing. "There. Just a
couple of kids, Inspector. They couldn't be more than
eleven or twelve. Look at their expressions."

Morris shook his head. The total devastation of human
life was to him incomprehensible. A bomb, an entire
city burnt to the ground, an earthquake, these were
explainable. They just happened. They were acceptable
as part of life. But this. A village whose architecture was
untouched, but whose inhabitants would simply lay
about the streets until they decayed, returned to dust.
These boys who lay at his feet, unmarked, but pale and
cold. What earthly explanation could there be for this?
As a copper, he knew he had seen many atrocities, but
nothing of this magnitude had ever come his way. He
couldn't think of any human being alive who would even
contemplate such disorder. The Inspector—for all his
years as a policeman—was succumbing to shock. His
mind, like an over-loaded powerpoint, was fusing.

"Inspector, down here," Thomas called, pulling him
from his confusion.

"A phone box—so what?" he asked dully.

"That's McRoberts—the guy at the base."

"But how—"

"I don't know, but let's have a look," he replied,
already running down the cul-de-sac. "It's McRoberts,
all right," he announced when the Inspector had caught
up. "And there's McTavish under him."

"He's got it as well."

"Yea, he sure has. Listen, we better get some antidote
for this stuff. If it's as contagious as Dwarf Hill makes it

out to be, we could be catching it now. And if Chadwell's soldiers come traipsing around here, they won't last long either."

"Where do we get the vaccine?"

"Penicillin, aureomycin, streptomycin—any of those will do. Dr. Phipps should have some."

Morris was tottering uneasily. "One of them must have been calling for help."

Thomas looked back. "Pity he didn't make it—he might have saved a lot more of them."

"Might have," Morris whispered, falling against the side of the call box.

"You feeling all right?"

"It's all this, Major. It's beyond me." He pushed up. "Come on. I need a drink."

Chadwell was waiting for them when the jeep drew up sharply outside the police station. He looked worried, something that Thomas had not yet seen him capable of —he was pacing across the steps and wringing his hands. As Thomas emerged from the jeep, Chadwell pulled him near by the collar and whispered, "Trouble. I fear the worst has happened."

The Major brushed his hand away. "I thought there might be."

"I've heard from London that there's another case of this anthrax. In Beckington—about a hundred and fifty miles from here. Some boy in a church choir. I'm leaving in about an hour. I think you should come."

"What's the trouble, then?" asked the Inspector, stepping around the side of the rover.

"More of that anthrax," Thomas replied. "I figured there might be." He turned back to Chadwell. "What's going to happen to this place?"

"It's been taken out of my hands. The Ministry's sending down their experts on all this and they're moving in troops to evacuate."

"Well, I better come. There won't be anything for me to do here. What will you do, Inspector?"

He shrugged. "It's still my town—what's left of it." He glanced around him. "Looks like the Army's moved everyone out except us."

"I'm taking Trevor with me," said Thomas, waiting for Chadwell's reaction.

"I think it's best," Morris added. "We can't hold him in there much longer. It's cruel."

"Hold who? What's cruel?" he snapped, totally unprepared for this new problem.

"The boy. He's going with me."

"Do you really think that's wise? I don't think the Ministry would want him involved anymore than he already is."

"That boy goes with me. Damn your Ministry. Right now he's a frightened and lonely kid and I'm not leaving him here."

The last thing Chadwell was bothered about was this child. It was an additional burden. He had too many already. "I wasn't intending to leave the boy here, Major. I've made arrangements for him to be transferred to Great Ormond Street Children's Hospital this afternoon. He's being sent for examination first—at Porton. When they're through with him, they'll see he's well cared for in London."

"You're a bastard, Chadwell," Thomas leered. "Do you know what they'll do to him at Porton? Do you know why they want him there?"

Chadwell flapped the lid of his tobacco pouch nervously. He had rarely been challenged like this before.

"Do you know?"

"No, not exactly."

"Well, I'll goddam tell you what they'll do. They'll use

him as a guinea pig. They'll stick needles in him and take out flesh and blood and bone marrow. And when they're through, then they'll send what's left for Ormond Street to deal with. Are you so goddam cold that you'd let that happen to an innocent boy?"

"Major, I hardly think—"

"That's just it. You hardly think. You haven't thought one damned minute since you came down here. No, there was no chance Dwarf Hill could have exploded. No, there was no chance that nerve gas could have wiped out a few hundred people, and no, there was still less chance that those bats could have escaped. What did you say? Ah, yes. You said that the people would think of it as rubbish. Do you still think so after having seen Stumford? You goddam fool, Chadwell. You've mucked about here and done nothing but hinder us. You refused to believe any of us. But by God, Chadwell, if you think for one goddam minute I'm letting you send that boy into certain torture and Christ knows what kind of death, then you're very much mistaken. That boy is coming with me. He's not leaving my side. And if you or your bloody Ministers try to take him, I'll blow this whole affair so wide open, you won't know your ass from first base. Tell your superiors that, Mr. Chadwell. And tell them to get lost."

Chadwell waffled incoherently. He had been wounded. Thomas grabbed his chance. Fighting his fury he said, "Besides all this, you must see that the kid is a security risk. It'd be much safer for you and your government if I kept an eye on him." He nodded in the direction of the swarm of newspapermen and television crews. "They look pretty bloodthirsty to me."

"Well, I suppose you may be right. Can't say I like the idea, but you have left me little choice, haven't you."

"I meant it that way."

"If that's settled, I'll ring London and tell them we'll be leaving soon. I'll, ah, I'll cancel the arrangements for the boy."

"You do that," Thomas replied coldly.

"Which car will you be using?" asked the Inspector.

"I'll use mine," Chadwell said uneasily almost expecting another tirade from the Major. "London's arranged to have an escort meet us halfway and they'll be looking out for my reg . . ."

"I could have one of my men drive you if you like."

Chadwell thought. "No. I think we'll manage." He glanced quickly at the Major, then climbed the steps and vanished into the station.

"I say," began the Inspector. "You gave him a proper bollicking. You're lucky he let you win."

"Let me win?" Thomas cried in astonishment. "Why I'll wring his—"

"Major, remember that you're in England. He is a representative of the English government. As pompous and pigheaded as he is, it's his orders that count. I'm on you side all the way, but mind how you go with him."

Thomas relaxed. "Yea, well, it's better I got it out. I probably would have killed him otherwise. Sending that kid to Porton—some nerve he's got."

"He didn't know, Glen. He doesn't know about any of this. He's just a civil servant. He's doing his job."

"Yes, I guess so. We got 'em, too."

"I guess this is it then. You'll probably be too busy to let me know how things go, but if you get a chance give me a ring or something."

"I'll keep you posted, don't worry," he grinned. "This isn't war, you know. I'll be back when it's blown over."

"It'll be bloody war in London I can tell you. If this anthrax scare is really true, this country's in for the biggest shaking since Hitler."

"I'm afraid it is true. I can't think of it not breaking out if those bats are loose. Some poor devil is gonna walk right over one—most likely what this kid's done in Buckingham or Beckingham or whatever."

The Duty Sergeant hastened down the steps and approached them. "Message for you, Sir. From London."

"Thank you," Thomas replied.

"And Sergeant, can you bring the boy around?" asked the Inspector. "And see if you can't find an extra change of clothes for him and the Major. God knows where you'll find it, but have a look."

"Yes, Sir."

"I shouldn't worry about the clothes, Sergeant," said Thomas as he read the message. "We can pick some up on the way—or in London." He frowned.

"Bad news?" asked Morris.

He handed him the message. The Sergeant disappeared. "'Case of suspected anthrax bacillus infection in Beckington confirmed at 15:15 Hours. Am sending Special Branch Murray to rendezvous Beckington. Have instructed Whitehall wait your report. Signed, Sir Joseph Willetts.' Doesn't sound good, does it?"

"At least they're going direct to me. Maybe we'll cut throught this goddam red-tape after all. But I don't like the sound of this anthrax."

"Could it be an isolated case?"

"Christ, don't you start! Chadwell's probably assuring London that it's the only possible case and that everything's gonna turn out fine."

"He's had a rough shock, you know. I'd try to see this thing his way for a while if I were you. Maybe give him another chance—and you want to protect Trevor as well."

"Your judge of character again, huh?"

"My judge of character. I may be wrong, but with things as they are, you can't lose anything."

The Sergeant was leading Trevor from the station. He seemed to squint in the bright sun, but he managed a smile when he saw the Major. He raised his hand as if to wave and limped stiffly over.

"Not much color in you yet, kid," Thomas announced.

"They're all like that around here," explained Morris. "All television and not enough fresh air."

"Are we going somewhere?" Trevor asked, rubbing his right hand which had begun to tremble again.

"Yes, my boy," Thomas began, ruffling his hair. "We are going away. But first we all have to get a jab from Dr. Phipps if he's around."

The Inspector looked up.

"Can you ask Phipps for a few shots of aureomycin? One for Chadwell, you, me and Trevor—just in case. It's not that we're infected for sure, but there's no telling with this hybrid stuff."

"I'll see if I can find him." Morris walked off in the direction of Dr. Phipp's surgery.

"That isn't an injection, is it?" Trevor asked.

"That, Trevor, is an injection." He glanced at the door to the Inspector's office. It was still tightly shut. "Why don't we sit here. Better than waiting in the car."

Thomas eased himself onto the cold stone steps and watched Trevor try to guide himself down with the railing. His body must be badly affected, he thought. It must have taken him a hell of a lot of concentration to force his muscles to obey. Trevor picked up a pebble and twiddled it idly in his left hand.

"Major, how it is I didn't die?"

He hesitated, but he thought it best to tell the truth. It was a straight forward question. "You mean from the gas?"

He nodded.

"Probably because you caught the tail end of it. The spread must have been stopped by the hill. If you had gone any further, well, that would have been it."

"Have you been into Stumford?"

Again he hesitated. "Yes, this afternoon."

"Was everyone dead?"

"I'm afraid so, Trevor. But they never felt a thing, I promise you." He lied. He hated himself for it.

"Did they feel like I did?"

He thought quickly. "No, most likely not. You caught just enough to make you very sick. The dose they got would have killed them instantly."

"They didn't suffer?"

Major Thomas stopped him. He put his hands on his shoulders and looked into his eyes. "Trevor, whoever was in that village last night died quickly and painlessly. The gas is very deadly. They didn't suffer."

The boy stared back at him for a moment, then stood up and looked away. "What will happen now?"

"We're going to Beckington. There's something there I've got to investigate. Then we're going to London."

"Won't Mr. Chadwell mind? I heard him talking earlier on. He said he didn't want me along. He said they were going to send me to some hospital."

Thomas cursed Chadwell. "You're going with me, Trevor. Nobody is going to send you away. *I* am going to take care of you until *you* decide what you want to do. Believe me?" He arose and put his hand on his shoulder.

Trevor shrugged off the hand and started walking. Thomas began to follow him, but stopped. He watched him shuffle slowly on and decided to let him go. It would be his last time near home, and perhaps he knew it.

The Major was sitting on the steps when Chadwell

appeared half an hour later. Under his arm was an over-stuffed folder of papers and maps, and he carried his bowler and umbrella in the other hand. He looked hot and tired when he sat down next to him.

'Still waiting for the boy?" he asked quietly.

"No, he's up there," replied the Major, pointing to a small figure at the other end of town. "He's not very well."

"Humph, I can't say that I blame him, poor devil. It was pretty awful down there, wasn't it?"

Thomas took out his cigarettes and offered him one. He declined and fumbled for his pipe.

"They seemed so strange—I mean lying there without any marks or anything."

"That's the beauty of gas poisoning—it leave everything intact. No mess to clean up except the bodies."

"Really, what a horrible way to fight a war."

"Seeing the light, are we?"

"I never thought—"

"You never do until you see it. Anyway, we'll have more than enough to do in London."

Chadwell hesitated. He filled his pipe and lit it in great puffs of smoke. "Major?"

"Huh?"

"I'm, well, I'm sorry I've been such a bloody fool. It has been so much of a, of a shock. All this. I, well, I never meant to hurt the boy."

"There are some things that are important to different people. You just never opened yourself up enough to see how much Trevor has suffered—and will suffer."

"You mean his treatment?"

"Yes, his treatment."

"Morris told me about it. I'm sorry."

"So am I."

"He's a brave lad. He's obviously come through a lot already."

"He's got a long way to go, Mr. Chadwell."

"But he's got a good friend to go with him."

Thomas turned and peered into the deep greyish eyes of Mr. Chadwell. He was never very good at carrying a grudge. He smiled. "Well, I better get Trevor if we're going." He stood up and stretched.

"Major?"

"Yeah?"

"Nothing. Forget it. Only I'm glad you're on our side."

Thomas began walking off. Chadwell looked after him and slowly shook his head. He watched the erect frame of the Major's body carry him deliberately along the deserted road until he reached the boy when he put his long arm around the small shoulders and started to walk his charge further down the street before turning around. For a moment they talked, and before returning, Thomas hoisted Trevor onto his shoulders. Chadwell remembered Dickens. He remembered a lot of things he wanted to forget. But he forced himself to relax and put the past and present out of his mind. Somehow all the trouble seemed far away. The sun and smell of leafy air, the boy and the man growing slowly larger as they approached, the unusual peace in the village—it all seemed too perfect, but it was pleasant while it lasted. Chadwell knew what would happen when they reached London. The Ministry would demand all the first-hand information they could get, and right now only he and the Major could supply that. The Major was right. It was a damned messy business. No wonder he had felt the way he did.

The Inspector sighed heavily as the car pulled away. He would miss Thomas, he thought, as he turned to look upon his empty town.

"Have they gone, Sir?" shouted the Sergeant, running down the steps.

He turned around. "Yes, Parker. They've gone. Why?"

He held out a slip of paper. "Another message, Sir. For the Major."

"Have you read it?"

"Yes, Sir. I took it down."

"And?"

"Another report. Another case of anthrax."

"Where's it at?"

"Somewhere outside Cardiff—in the Rhonda."

He sighed again. "Well, I guess Major Thomas has enough to think about before he gets this one. Thank you, Parker."

"Shall I send it on to Beckington?"

"Yes, do that. They should be there in a couple of hours."

"Yes, Sir."

The Inspector took the message, stared at it a moment, then crumpled it up and stuffed it into his pocket. He started walking back to the station.

"Anything wrong, Sir?"

He stopped and looked at the Sergeant. "Parker, I'm afraid everything's wrong. I don't think we've seen the end of all this. I don't even think we've seen the beginning."

Beckington. 17:30 Hours

The sun was considering the western horizon and dim shadows crept across the road as Chadwell's car drew near Beckington. Ponderous clouds threatened from the North and Thomas mumbled something about rain. It had been a long and uncomfortable journey for each of them, each thinking of the uncertain future and what their roles might be in that uncertainty. Thomas longed to estimate the possible consequences of an outbreak of anthrax, a pandemic, but he forced himself to be optimistic—that only isolated cases would cause a minor flap and in a few days the whole thing would be over and he could return home.

Trevor had slept much of the way. He had nestled down in the rear seat with his head buried in the Major's lap. His body demanded rest. It needed time to compensate for the nervous damage, to diagnose and treat itself as only the human body can. But the roar of the two motorcycles who had escorted them nearly three quarters of the way woke him from his sleep, and he peered out of the window for an explanation.

"Looks bad," Chadwell announced, looking over the seat. "The Army's already moved in."

A military policeman stopped the car and leaned inside the window. Chadwell withdrew his identity card. "Yes, Sir. They're expecting you at the church. You can just see it there."

Chadwell nodded and drove on. "Major, see the fellow on the steps?"

Thomas searched for the figure.

"That's Murray. One of the best, but you'd never think it to meet him." He pulled the car alongside the pavement and switched off. "He'll have all the details."

Chadwell looked down at Trevor.

"You wait here," Thomas said, reaching into his trouser pocket.

"Can I get some sweets?"

"I don't know what the hell sweets are, but here's ten shillings for some candy. And take this. It's my ID. If you run into any trouble, show this and say you're with me And," he began, halting him in his race for the door handle, "go easy."

"Thanks," he replied. "I won't be long."

"And if that pain comes back, you get straight back to me."

Trevor nodded and grinned. He was off.

"Hello," shouted a police officer suddenly. "Where's he going? And what's he doing here?"

"It's all right, Constable. He's with me," Thomas explained from the car.

"Er, sorry old man," Chadwell whispered over the seat. "That's a Detective Inspector—not a constable."

"Then what's he doing in uniform?"

"How should I know? What are you doing in uniform?"

Thomas stared down at the dark blue trousers and pale blue shirt. "I can't help that," he muttered, pushing open the door. "It's the only thing Morris could find and you know it."

The Inspector eyed him disdainfully.

Thomas bowed politely. "Sorry."

"And who might you be?" he demanded, rocking forward on his heels.

Chadwell interceded. "He's with me, Inspector. We're the party from Stumford." He held out his identity card.

"That doesn't explain your friend's uniform."

"Oh, for Christ's sakes," Thomas exploded. "Look, Detective Constable or whatever you are, I've just come from a police station in Chesterly. They lent me some clothes."

"Inspector," called someone from behind. "Inspector, what seems to be the trouble?"

Thomas turned around. He thought he saw the man who Chadwell had described as Murray. He was tall like himself, but exceptionally thin, confident in his stride and certain in every movement as he hastened towards them. He thought there would be very little that slipped past this newcomer—the prominent features of his face and glint in his eyes warned of that. He looked the type

Thomas would like, and he prayed he was as deadly realistic as he appeared.

The Inspector didn't seem to approve of this latest addition. Murray pulled a slim wallet from his pocket and let it flap open in his face. "Inspector, buzz off." He turned to Chadwell when the chastened figure was far enough away. "Hate those bloody sods. Think they run the world."

Chadwell smiled. At last he had an ally. "Major Thomas, this is Ian Murray."

"You're the one from the States, eh?" he said affably, extending his hand. "Yes, I've been hearing a lot about you."

"Pleased to meet you."

"Well, you won't be. I'm your escort from now on. London's been calling out your name up and down the corridors of Whitehall all morning. "Who let him in?" and "Who is he?" and "How does *he* know so much?" You're in it, all right."

"My luck, huh?"

"Where the hell did you pick him up, anyway?" Murray demanded of Chadwell. "This isn't your department."

"He just happens to know a lot of what we don't seem to. And it is my department. You just stick to being his bodyguard."

"Well, Major. I've had my orders. Just don't try to run away."

"I won't. But watch out I don't hide in the Embassy."

"They won't let you near it," he sneered. "But we can discuss your escape plans later. I'd better tell you two what's going on. We haven't much time. There was this youngster singing in the choir at morning service when halfway through some hymn or something he collapsed. The local doctor diagnosed anthrax. Not just any anthrax, mind you but one of our sacred government's special varieties so I gather. Luckily, someone had the sense to keep everyone shut up inside. They're vaccinating them now. Christ, half of bloody Porton's down here."

Chadwell glanced at Thomas.

Murray led them up the steps of the church. As they passed through the arches, they could see the parishioners still gathered together while nurses moved swiftly about the aisles with trolleys of syringes and serum. Murray signalled to one of the white-coated medics who grinned and wheeled a trolley towards them.

"Roll up your sleeves, please gentlemen," he ordered "Guaranteed painless. I'm getting quite good at it."

"What do you mean "good at it"?" Chadwell mumbled. "Haven't you done this before?"

"No," he replied flatly. "It's just that there was a rush on and they grabbed the first chaps in sight."

"Don't feel bad, Chadwell," said Murray, rubbing his own arm. "This is Dr. Luther Wilks from Porton—the brass in all this."

"I take it you were going to see the boy?" Wilks began, smothering Chadwell's arm in ether. "Not very pretty. He won't last long."

"Last long?" cried Thomas, rolling up his sleeve. "I thought he was dead."

"The first kid is—the one who collapsed. But there's another one. I think he was sitting next to the other boy. We've got him in the Rector's study."

Chadwell winced. "Can you do anything for him?"

Wilks hesitated while he let the syringe drain into his arm. "We've made him as comfortable as possible—drugs and all that, but it's too far advanced. I've never known anything so quick acting."

"I'd better have a look," said Thomas. "We may have to get used to this."

"What about your friend?" Chadwell remembered. "Can't let him go roaming around with that stuff on the loose."

"What friend?" snapped Murray. "I was told there's only two of you."

Chadwell let Thomas fish himself out of this one. "He's a boy who I decided to keep with us. His folks were killed in Stumford when all that gas broke loose. He's had a bad dose himself so I want to keep an eye on him."

Wilks looked up from the Major's arm. "So you're the one who's taken him. We were told he was coming to us."

"Well he isn't. Ouch—Christ, you aren't used to this, are you?"

"I'm a research scientist—not a doctor. Just be thankful we've got enough of this stuff to go round."

"Yeah," Murray began quietly. "This is the last of it. Two bottles left. I hope there isn't much more of your anthrax going about."

"I doubt it," Chadwell prophesied.

"You've got two more to deal with anyway," Murray said. "But they'll have to muddle through on their own."

"*Two* more?"

"Didn't you get the message?"

"We got one this afternoon—that's all."

"Two more sightings. One in the Rhonda Valley near Cardiff and one in Bognor Regis, or somewhere down there. They've had a confirmation on the Welch sighting already."

"Oh, boy," Thomas sighed. "They've broken out."

"You think so?" Chadwell plied weakly.

"Sounds it, doesn't it?"

"What about your boy?" Wilks thought. "Can we have a look at him?"

"No," replied Thomas curtly. "He's had enough

already. Anymore and you'll be sure to scare the hell out of him."

Wilks looked hurt. "We *might* be able to help him, you know."

"Have you got a neuropathic synthesiser?"

Chadwell looked at Murray.

"No," Wilks said slowly. "We don't often—"

"I know. You don't often treat cases like this. But we do. And no one's going to lay a finger on so much as a hair on his head until I have my men check him out," He recalled Morris' words. "If that's all right with you."

Wilks shrugged. "I suppose we've got enough problems without sticking needles in this boy of yours. Still . . ."

"Exactly what's wrong with him?" Murray asked.

"Just exposed to nerve gas. That's enough," Thomas answered, rolling down his sleeve.

"Poor kid. Wonder he's still alive."

"You can thank the Major for that," Chadwell explained. "Now he's sort of adopted him."

"He'll be a lot poorer if he catches this bloody anthrax," Wilks said. "You better go after him, Ian. Major, tell him what he looks like."

"He was headed for the nearest candy store. About thirteen—good looking boy. He was wearing jeans and a red and blue sweater. He's got an oversized police shirt on and he limps. His right hand tends to quiver, too. That should single him out."

"I could find him in Piccadilly in the rush hour with that description," Murray decided. "Doesn't matter, though. All the other kids in town are locked up in the nick."

Thomas looked at him. "Is that what you do in this country—just put everyone in the police station when there's a panic on?"

Murray stared at Chadwell for the answer. "It's quite

all right. The Major's just got the wrong impression of things, that's all."

"Right, well, I'll go look for this boy. Wilks will want to give him an injection, too. Won't you Wilks?"

"With the Major's permission."

"Just don't do anything else."

"I'd better show you the anthrax case, first. Follow me."

Thomas turned to Chadwell. "This can't go on without telling the public. You've got to warn them sometime."

Chadwell sniffed. "I'm afraid that's not up to us. London will make the necessary decisions when it feels it's best. We just have to wait and take orders."

"In here, gentlemen," interrupted Wilks, pushing open the door to the Rectory.

Thomas looked in. A team of doctors stood around the vicar's desk which had been converted into a makeshift bed with cushions from the pews. He could make out the figure of a young boy behind them. He walked over. Wilks followed.

"This is Major Thomas. He'd like to have a look at the child."

"Well," began one of the medics, pulling off his gloves. "He can take my place. I've got to ring Porton about this. You better come too, Halliday."

Another doctor nodded and together they left through a side door. Wilks decided that he was needed outside and excused himself. Chadwell dared go no further than his position at the door.

"Look here," one of the two remaining doctors said. "The right arm. This boy was standing on the left of the one who died. You can see where the infection has set in."

Thomas peered at the arm. It had begun to swell and turn the characteristic purple. Two black spots threatened to burst through the skin which was drawn tight over the muscles.

"We've got him on morphine, but I doubt he can last much longer."

"Is he conscious?"

"Barely. You can try to talk to him if you like. I'm going out for a break. I've seen enough of this for one day. Coming, John?"

John seemed reluctant to follow. "I want to have another look at the other kid. We've got to find out more about this stuff." He seemed surprised. "It's so bloody powerful."

John walked to the side door and turned around. "Major, when you're through with that fellow, the other one's in here. A bit worse."

Thomas nodded. He knelt down beside the boy and stared into his face. He breathing was slowed. He pushed the hair out of the lad's eyes and waited for a response. He didn't stir. He couldn't make any sense out of it. In a church of all places. He noticed the boy's choir robes laying on a chair in the corner.

"His name's Ralph," Chadwell said from the doorway.

At the mention of his name, Ralph opened his eyes and made a conscious effort to focus on the Major. He stared expressionless as if his body were incapable of movement, but Thomas saw the fingers of his left hand slowly open and close.

"Ralph?"

The boy tried to move his lips, but they were dried and the very effort of separating them seemed too much. Thomas glanced around for some water. He saw a flannel in a basin and pulled it nearer. He wrung the cloth and dabbed his lips. Ralph smiled faintly.

"How is Michael?" he asked.

Thomas glanced at Chadwell. He shrugged.

"He's all right, Ralph," Thomas said.

"I thought he was sick when I saw him," he whispered.

"Sick?"

"He looked funny. Kind of dizzy sort of."

"Is that how you feel?"

He shook his head. "I don't feel anything."

"Can I get you anything?"

"Me mum and dad if they're here."

Thomas looked up at Chadwell again. He shook his head and frowned.

"Find 'em," he ordered roughly.

Chadwell disappeared.

"Why can't I feel anything?"

"Cause you've been given something so you don't feel anything."

He closed his eyes again. Thomas waited for a few minutes until he saw Chadwell appear at the door. He nodded.

"This is Mr. and Mrs. Toryshot," Chadwell said when the Major came to his side.

"How do you do. Your son would like to see you. But he's—"

"He's not going to live," Mr. Toryshot answered. "We know. We could see that in their faces. Can we see him?"

"Yes, of course. But try not to go too near. I know you've been vaccinated, but it's still a risk."

Mr. Toryshot looked up at him. He spoke softly without malice or feeling. "He is our only son, Sir. We've built our life around him. It doesn't matter to us if there's a risk. He's our son."

Thomas nodded. "I'm sorry."

Ralph opened his eyes again and peered up at his mother.

"Hello, Ralph," she said.

He lifted his left hand. She held it.

"Mum," he whispered as tears crept from his eyes.

"It's all right, Ralph. Lie still and everything will be all right."

Chadwell and Thomas looked on from the door. Chadwell's throat felt tight.

"You'll be late for the milking," Ralph whispered again. "Don't wait about for me."

"We don't mind, Ralph," his mother choked, fighting to keep her voice even. "Jack can do it."

He closed his eyes. She felt his hand grasp hers tightly. She looked towards the Major.

"Find out where that kid lived and get me some police or the Army or somebody. We'll strip that house to pieces if we have to." Thomas had just finished examining Michael. It had gone unnoticed to the others, but he had found scratches of some kind on the boy's arm. To him it meant an animal, and when he learned of the dog, he knew that the anthrax must have come from him. It was the only way Michael could have exposed himself to the disease—his parents would have remembered if there was anything about a bat in the house. If the dog got loose in the village, he would spread it to other dogs, and to people. That is if the dog was not dead himself which was more than likely. Thomas knew now what he feared most had happened. If one bat had reached Beckington and had already claimed two lives, if another bat had been found in Wales and in some other city, the odds were that they'd find a hell of a lot more. And they'd better find them before a lot of innocent people did.

"They'll have a car ready in ten minutes," Chadwell said from behind. "The house isn't far away."

"Good. The sooner the better."

"And Murray found your boy. Wilks has him now."

"He'll like that."

"And this came for you," he said slowly, handing him

a folded slip of paper. "Murray was right. They want you in London this evening."

He opened the message and read.

"All of us—Murray, you and me. They're laying on a helicopter at half nine."

"When?"

"Nine thirty."

"That'll still give us just enough time to check this house out."

As they walked towards the front arches Chadwell pointed out Trevor and Wilks. Thomas felt relieved. Wilks had done no more than what he promised.

"Another one for the record, huh?"

"Yeah," Trevor replied, rubbing his arm. "Some record. How many more of these do I get?"

"None until someone dreams up a better antidote." He led him out of the church and down the steps. The clouds had moved nearer and a stiff wind rustled about them. "We're going to London tonight. Flying in by helicopter. How does that sound?"

"Good, I guess. I've never flown before."

"There, you see. Things aren't as bad as they seem." He glanced around. Chadwell was talking to Murray while they waited for the car. "Come on, I'll show you some of the Army stuff. They've moved in quite a few things already."

"Missile launchers and stuff?"

"No, not missile launchers. Trucks and jeeps and things."

"Oh," he replied. "Here, you better take this. It's your pass. I didn't need it."

"Thanks. Mr. Murray found you all right, huh?"

"Yeah, he found me. Never did get any sweets. Everything's shut up."

"Sunday night, what do you expect?"

"We had a shop in Deignby that opened until nine on

Sunday nights. Me mum used to run out of fags and . . ." But he trailed off in silence.

"Major?" Murray called out, running up to them. "Phew, not in very good shape any more. Sorry about this, but I've got to stick with you from now on. Ministry's orders. Until we know what's happened, anyway."

"You a bodyguard?" Trevor asked, kicking a stone.

"Sort of." They began walking back. "How do you get on with our Mr. Terrence?"

"Terrence?" repeated Thomas.

"Chadwell."

"Not too well but getting better."

"Still heavy on the great government, is he? Don't blame him. It's the blighters up top that cause the real trouble. These smaller chaps like Chadwell are scared silly of the bigger boys. They daren't make a move without official approval. When anything out of the ordinary happens, well, they're lost. They just clam up like an oyster and swear everything'll be all right in the end. They're trained to. Nothing British can go wrong. Right now Chadwell's trying to see things your way. He could've enforced the order on the boy—he's got the authority to. He could have done a lot of things, but he's coming over to your side. You wait and see."

"So I've been told once before."

"I don't like Chadwell either," Trevor added. "Want a sweet?"

"Mr. Chadwell to you," said the Major, taking a semi-melted chocolate from a scrunched up bag. "I thought you couldn't get any."

"I couldn't. Mr. Murray gave them to me."

"Yeah, and you're not to repeat anything we say here, got it?" he ordered sharply. "If you're going to come along with us, you've got to do as you're told."

"I won't say anything," he replied softly, somewhat indignant that his friend thought he might.

Thomas glanced at Murray who shook his head. They walked on in silence until they joined Chadwell at the church and piled into one of the two police cars. The Major thought about what Murray had said, and a little of the contempt he had felt for this man faded. He had known that Chadwell was deeply affected by Ralph's death—he had seen it in his eyes. Maybe he was coming round. Maybe he might actually be of some help. Who could tell? Who could tell anything the way things were going? He thought of the future and he wondered how the hell the government was going to sort out this one. It was going to take some rather careful planning, thinking and explaining to climb out of the hole with any respect left, and if Murray's prophecy was true, he'd be right in the middle of it.

"This is the house," said the Inspector. "Number Thirty-four."

Thomas stared at Number Thirty-four it was no different from the row of houses which bordered it to the right and left, in front of it and behind, yet each of them, Chadwell, Murray, the Superintendent, Trevor and the Major and several constables felt the evil that lurked somewhere nearby. Whatever caused the death of the boy who once lived here, it was ugly and frightening, even to Thomas who had long since learned to live with the unseen and unpredictable. It was perhaps a fear of the unknown, or of what they might uncover inside—of microscopic bacteria which could stalk them invisibly and kill in so brief a time that cure seemed impossible—it was this that held them back.

Finally, the Superintendent broke the silence. "You best have the lad wait here. No telling what we'll find in there."

"Stay near the gate," ordered Thomas, "We won't be

long." He looked at Murray who shrugged his shoulders and pushed open the wooden gate.

"After you, Major. It's your baby."

"See if you can spot anything under those shrubs," Thomas said, approaching the front door. "And maybe one of your constables can look around the back."

"There's nothing out here," Murray announced somewhat relieved when he had seen that the others failed to turn anything up. "Try the inside."

"Let me," said the Superintendent. "This one ought to do it." He tried the key, listened for the click and pushed open the door. "There, thought it might".

All but three of the policemen followed him in. It was easy to decide that nothing had hidden in the kitchen, nor was there any sign of a sick puppy and they advanced slowly into the drawing room.

"Damned if there's anything here," said Chadwell, lifting the occasional cushion and poking among a pile of magazines. "Just what are we supposed to find?"

"A bat maybe," replied Thomas. "Or a dead dog. Or maybe nothing."

"There's something here," said Murray, bending over a spot on the carpet.

"I wouldn't do that," snapped Thomas, pulling his hand from a moist patch near the fire. "Never can tell what it is." He took a slide of glass from his breast pocket and pulled it across the fibres. "Anybody got a light?"

Murray turned his gas lighter up and held it away from him as he struck the flint. "Never did trust these bloody things. Had one explode in my face not long ago."

"Blood," Thomas announced, peering through the slide.

"Blood?" cried the Superintendent. "Blood from what?"

116

"The dog I would think. He's got to be around here somewhere."

Chadwell glanced uneasily around him. He felt as if he were a character in a horror film, and the time had come for the villain to attack.

"There's more of those spots out here," called one of the constables from the hallway. "I think so anyway."

"Just don't touch it," said Thomas, marching into the passage with his glass. "Blood again. Look, it leads up the stairs."

They followed the path of spots up each stair with their eyes, wondering who would take the initiative, but Thomas pushed past the constable and slowly climbed, warning the others to keep well clear of the patches. "If it's anthrax, it'll be in that blood."

"There's more of it up here," said Murray, following close behind the Major. "Where's the bloody light switch?"

"It's back here," replied the Superintendent from the bottom of the stairs.

Thomas blinked when the lights overhead flicked on. He could see the trail of spots clearly and they lead into a room off the passage. He waited until each of the others had reached the top of the stairs before he pointed a torch along the path of spots.

"What if it's still alive?" Chadwell asked. "I mean wouldn't it attack or something?"

"The dog?" said Thomas. "I doubt he's alive. And if he is, he won't have enough strength to bare his teeth."

"You better hope so," said Murray. "Cause I ain't going in there first."

"I'll go," the Superintendent offered, pushing through to the front.

"Nobody's going in there first except me. I work with this sort of stuff."

"Always did say the Yanks had guts," Murray smiled unashamedly. "I like to see what I'm fighting."

"You will," Thomas replied, easing open the door. "In a minute." He peered into the room and in the dim light he could just make out the figure of a small animal on the bed. "He's in here all right." He stamped his foot. The figure didn't move. Slowly, the beam from his torch shone along the floor, crept up the side of the bed. "There it is," he sighed. "It's anthrax all right."

Murray flipped on the light switch. He grimaced and Chadwell looked away.

"Christ," the Superintendent swore.

The puppy looked much the same as the dog in Stumford: it's neck was grotesquely enlarged and blackened blood dribbled from its mouth.

"There's your culprit," said Thomas, moving no closer. "That's what gave the boy anthrax. Now we've got to find what gave it to the pup."

Suddenly, they heard footsteps creaking up the stairs. It was Trevor. "Major," he wheezed, fighting to catch his breath. "Major," we've found it."

"Stop him," Thomas shouted at the Superintendent. "Keep him outside."

"Major," he repeated. "We've found a bat. It's all puffy and horrible."

"Where?" he exclaimed. "In the garden?"

"Yeah, Constable Dobbs found it under a bush. He says he thinks the dog may have eaten half of it."

"So do I," he replied, following him down the stairs. He turned to the Superintendent. "You better have the area closed off. Get the Army in to cordon off the house. Better have the whole street checked. If there's one, there may be more."

"What about this anthrax?"

"Have your men vaccinated by the fellow in the church. You'll all need shots if you've been this close."

118

"We haven't much time, Major," Murray reminded him. "That helicopter'll be flying in any time now."

"Just let me see this bat and we'll go. There's nothing more to do until we can figure out how to decontaminate everything."

"This way," Trevor was saying from the kitchen door. "It's out here."

"That's one of them, all right," began Thomas. "You can see the metal band where the capsule was strapped."

"What do we do now?" asked the Superintendent.

"Nothing. There isn't a thing we can do. Not until I see your friends in London. My knowledge of all this stops here—what the hell you guys are going to do is out of my jurisdiction."

"That's what you think," Murray mumbled.

"Well, what do you usually do when something like this happens?" the Superintendent persisted.

"I couldn't tell you—it doesn't *usually* happen. This anthrax isn't ordinary stuff. It's a hybrid strain and what affects it is known only to the few who were at Dwarf Hill."

"Fat lot of good that'll do," replied Murray.

"Surely London will know what . . ."

"I hope so, Superintendent. Because if they don't, there's going to be anthrax all over this country in a few short days. It doesn't take long for this stuff to get hold."

"What a mess," he sighed. "What a hell of a mess."

London. 19:45 Hours

Chadwell and Thomas sat in silence. Beyond them in the room that was securely locked were assembled the Heads of the Ministry of Defense, the armed forces and the experts from Porton. It would not be long before the Major would be asked to address the gathering, but

somehow his mind refused to co-operate. He had to concentrate—he had to formulate a speech, a plan, something, but it was of no use to even try. Alone, facing a
nervous Chadwell, recalling what he had seen and the
dim prospects of the immediate future, he wanted
desperately to flee from it all. Behind those doors, he
thought, lurked the details of the horrors of what had
happened to England in the past twenty-four hours.
Reports would be coming in of more bats, of the
death count in Stumford and its surrounds. He tried to
guess how many more would die before the whole mess
was cleared up. And just how would it be cleared up? No
doubt that question will be put to him. How does one
look for several hundred bats scattered across the
country? What measures should be taken to protect the
people? He tried to think of an answer, some sensible
idea, some practical solution, and his mind drifted away
again. He spotted a newspaper on the desk. The head-
line speculated on the Dwaft Hill disaster, and he had
heard that the BBC had hauled some Army Officer over
the coals on the six o'clock news. Many of the closely
guarded secrets had been spilled. It wouldn't be long
before the round-the-world repercussions rolled in. International relations would be shaken loose; France—too
near British soil to be really safe—would be demanding
the most intimate information about the anthrax-ridden
bats—just in case one or two of them elected the Eiffel
Tower as a prospective residence. Top Secret information would have to be released, England's ridiculous
brain-child would be thrown open to public scrutiny and
no doubt would be the target of international ridicule.
To anyone but research scientists, the idea of even using
bats would crack the soberest face. He envisioned what
America would be open to if ever a similar accident occurred. And how much of the blame could be attributed
to the good ole USA? Surely, the papers would speculate

on his presence at the Base, and the fact that the damned thing exploded only a few hours after his departure would be the object of editorial conjecture for weeks. He shuddered at the thought. There was just too much to consider and he was too tired. He leaned back in his chair and closed his eyes.

Chadwell looked up. "I suppose we share similar thoughts, Major."

"And what might they be?"

He filled his pipe from a deflated pouch. He hated trips to the country—no shop sold his blend. He dug at the shrivelled remains of tobacco, praying he might get at least half a pipe. "That the country is in trouble."

He sniggered. "In trouble?"

He replied slowly. "I've been an old fool."

"What is it you fellows say, there's no fool like an old fool."

He cocked his head.

"Oh, forget it, Chadwell. We're all fools sometimes. Sometimes we pick the worst moments to show it. Trouble is, it's your country and you've got a lot more to worry about, huh?"

He seemed to be pleading. "But I was *told* so often that these plants were impregnable. Nothing is supposed to go wrong. At least not what did at Dwarf Hill. It just seemed impossible to believe it could happen."

"So thought the Captain of the Titanic as he ploughed happily through an iceberg. And," he continued stretching, "maybe she wouldn't have sunk if that frozen thing hadn't been there, but it was and she did."

Chadwell leant forward. "Major, I've been thinking. Has the idea of sabotage ever crossed your mind?"

"I think just about everything has crossed my mind," he laughed. "You told me these stations are so closely guarded that even your *own* men have trouble getting in. Yet you admit that there is a possibility of sabotage.

121

But who? The Russians? Never. Nothing to gain. Perhaps a smaller country with a big grudge. Perhaps an inside job. No, I don't think it was sabotage. It was simply some accident within the Base. You mix the wrong gases together, or they leak and combine or someone drops a match in the wrong place . . . It could have been anything."

"Except sabotage."

"Except sabotage—unless it was one of your own."

"Major," he cried. "Really."

"Oh, get off it, Chadwell. It's been know to happen. There are Benedict Arnolds even among the British."

The door suddenly opened. "Gentlemen," began a soft but too deliberate voice. "This way, please."

They arose and entered. Chadwell felt like he was being called before the headmaster. Thomas was too tired to worry. Muffled by the thick carpets and heavy drapes, the door clicked silently shut behind them. Thomas took a moment to reconnoitre. The walls were papered in a deep burgundy print; the enormous table was mahogany, and the whole room depicted a Victorian dinner party without the cutlery rather than a high level conference. At any moment he expected a butler to come sweeping in and announce that dinner was served. He was unaccustomed to these surroundings, and he felt ill at ease and unsure. It was so much unlike the films where the finely dressed general marched in and immediately took command of the situation. *He* would have liked to retreat.

"Major Thomas, I am Sir Joseph Willets," began an impeccably attired gentleman, distingushing himself from the other impeccably attired gentlemen only in that he rose from his chair. "Will you and Mr. Chadwell please sit here." He gave them a polite silence until they were seated. "Gentlemen, it is these two who hold the answers to many of our questions, and it is Major Thomas who holds the key to what really was going on at Dwarf Hill. No doubt we have many questions to ask, so I think we should waste no time."

Thomas breathed in deeply and reached for the box of cigarettes. He had a choice, and he took a Senior Service—whatever the hell that was. Chadwell had his lighter belching fire before he had time to get it in his mouth, and when the first few drags had taken effect, he eyed his new colleagues as Sir Joseph introduced them. He didn't like the manner of Colonel Combs from the Army, nor Lord Tenningly. Admiral William Downing-Wright seemed far away, General Percival Davies was clearly bored, and the only alert figures who appeared at all interested in the proceedings were Air Vice Marshal Coff and Dr. Marsh from Porton. There were two men from MI5 in case Chadwell's idea of sabotage panned out, and a Sir Something Penn from the Ministry of Defense. He'd never remember one from the other and he knew it. But his time was up. He was being called upon to speak. He hesitated only a moment, rose, and cast his gaze around the table. "I think before I make any statement on what has happened, I want to first express my own feelings as one who has been engaged in this sort of work for some time. What has happened in your country could easily have happened in America—or in any country developing these weapons. Because of this and the enormous peril this accident has placed the general public in, I am less inclined to believe so stubbornly in the beneficialities of my work. I think we must all give serious thought to reconsidering our positions on this type of warfare, and when this disaster is over, we must each of us examine just how important a role chemical and biological warfare plays in the defense of humanity. After what both Mr. Chadwell and I have seen, I am convinced that this is not the way to win a war—any war—no matter what are the stakes."

He paused and hoped this broke some of the ice.

"Major?" asked Colonel Combs. "Just what do you consider our first priority?"

"The public. They must be warned."

"Then what?"

"Protect the people. We have to find out the best way of keeping the people away from these bats."

"I agree with the Major," Combs announced. "And I would like to deploy some troops at key points around the country just in case there's a panic on."

"And treating this stuff?" asked Dr. Marsh.

"Dwarf Hill had some kind of disinfectant developed which they were going to hose down the test area with. If Porton could make enough of this, it would be a start."

"But we haven't got any," Marsh said simply.

Thomas frowned. "What do you mean, you haven't got any?"

"It was McTavish's formula. He developed it along with his mutation of the anthrax."

"So there is no known way to curb the spread of the anthrax," asked Sir Joseph, "or to cure it."

Marsh began again. "We can cure it if we catch the patient in time. But the stocks of anti-anthrax serum strong enough to cure this variety are nearly used up now. It would take days to replenish our supplies, and Christ knows how long to make enough for the whole country."

"Excuse me," said Thomas, "but wouldn't any anti-biotic do?"

Marsh thought. "Only if it was given in time. And there's no certainty in that, either."

Sir Joseph had pushed a button on the table. A messenger entered sharply, took a folded slip of paper from him and departed. He nodded for the Major to continue.

"It's clear that there is every chance of an epidemic breaking out in a very short time. This bacteria will spread like lightning among people and animals. I think the first thing we should concentrate on is the defense against a possible pandemic."

Combs smiled. This is exactly what he had considered. It was exactly what he wanted to hear. "I think we should establish a perimeter around the maximum distance these bats could fly. Presumably, this distance would be greatly influenced by the time capsules—if that's what they are." He flapped a handful of papers in his hand. Thomas nodded. "After all, these bats can only fly for so long before either the sun brings them down or the anthrax."

"We must remember," the Major began, "that the microencapsulation was an experiment and we can only hope that the delay mechanism has worked effectively. If the unit fails to operate or is at all retarded—there could still be bats flying about as yet unaffected."

"Do you know the sequence of the mechanisms?" asked Sir Joseph.

"No, Sir, I don't. I was told about ten hours."

Sir Joseph pushed his button again. Another messenger entered. "Get Sir Godfrey on the phone. No, better yet, send a car round for him. Tell him it's an emergency—top priority. Ask him to bring over all the information he can scrape together on bats—especially their flying habits." The messenger nodded and left. "Sir Godfrey is the best chap we've got in natural science. He should give us all we need to know on the distances these creatures are capable of."

Combs had been scribbling some figures. He stood up and walked to a large wall map of the British Isles. Taking up the pointer, he said, "I would like to establish six bases along the perimeter line which will later be determined. Supposing that these bats will fly no further than two hundred miles in any one direction and taking Dwarf Hill as the center and extending the radius for two hundred miles, we could assume for the moment that the rough boundaries would be Caernarvon, Wolverhampton, London, Southend, Dover and Bognor Regis. I believe we already have a report on Bognor Regis?"

Sir Joseph nodded.

"These Safe Bases, let us say, would be separate command posts for the dispersal of troops. They could work inland towards Dwarf Hill and thus form a huge converging net."

"With what end in mind, Colonel?" asked Penn.

"Presuming we choose a disinfectant as the best weapon, both land troops and air support could ensure maximum coverage." He rested his pointer on the floor.

"It's a good idea," began General Davies. "If your perimeter theory is operable."

Admiral Downing-Wright had been silent. He was wondering about the sea. He was thinking of France if the maximum flying distance was indeed two hundred miles. "Gentlemen, suppose some of these bats have landed in the Channel or reached the Continent—we have not yet considered these possibilities."

"Shouldn't the French authorities be informed?" asked one of the MI5 men.

"No," Sir Joseph replied flatly. "I would say that the risk to international relations is far too great to merit frightening the French at this time. Let's wait a while."

"Once the news of this gets out," said Lord Tenningly, "there won't be any international relations. We're going to have one hell of a lot of questions that want answering."

"I'm afraid that the government has its head on the chopping block as it is, gentlemen," replied Sir Joseph. "We don't need to lower the axe until the last minute. There is obviously no way out of this one no matter what we say or do. No doubt in the eyes of the public we're the blighters responsible for all this—one village wiped out and masses of disease-carrying bats wandering about the place. No one's about to let this go by sympathetically. I'm quite sure that some of these bats have found their way to the Continent—probably sunning themselves on the Riviera right now, but we must stall for time. The PM is coming down from Edinburgh and the Royal Family are being gathered together at Windsor—we may need the Queen. I've ordered several men from Porton to join Dr. Marsh here, and I've scheduled a meeting with everyone for midnight. I've also asked for the Commissioner of Police and the Heads of the Fire Brigade to be present. Our responsibility at this time is to the country, and when we have something concrete to say to the public other than an explanation of what has happened so far, then we'll notify the Continental authorities. I've also asked for a television spot so we'll have to prepare something for that."

"I could have some of my men flown over from the States," Thomas offered. "They might have a few ideas on how to fight this thing."

"I fear I shall have to await the PM's arrival before I can accept your offer, Major, but I think you might alert your government to the dangers of this situation. Under the strictest confidence, of course. I think we might also require the assistance of your military stationed in England."

Thomas nodded.

"Perhaps you could organize something after the television announcement."

He nodded again.

Combs had an idea. "I suppose we could rely upon NATO." He left his map and sat down.

"That would be dangerous," Sir Joseph answered. "Firstly, we would be forced to reveal the exact nature

127

of our difficulties to European sources and, secondly, this is a domestic problem presumably the fault of our government. Might be sticky under the treaty terms." He paused to look at his watch and check it against the large grandfather clock which faced him. "I would like to adjourn this meeting so that each of you can go over your notes and prepare everything for the midnight conference. We shall use Room 101 and please be assembled by half eleven. Mr. Chadwell, I shall leave it to you to act as go between with Comcent and I want you to arrange a link-up with the conference room. Major, perhaps you and Dr. Marsh will find a quiet corner and get some statement ready for this television announcement."

"I'll take the Major to Room 20 if it's free," said Marsh.

"About the only one that is at the moment. And gentlemen I need not emphasize the security. Scramble all outgoing calls through Comcent. I want no more information leaking out of here than what appears on television. And avoid the front entrance. The place is crawling with reporters. I dare not order the building shut else they'll know there is a big flap on."

Amidst the mumblings of the retreating military and government officials, Combs grabbed General Davies and tried to convince him of the genius of his plans. Sir Joseph disappeared into his study to locate the PM while Dr. Marsh and the Major found Room 20. Admiral Downing-Wright headed for Comcent, the communications center, to order an immediate plot of all his ships within a thousand miles of British waters. Chadwell scurried off behind him to reserve his seat in the massive link-up room and sort out a direct lead to the conference room. When he had settled comfortably near the control desk, he relaxed and turned his head to look out upon London through the misty window. Outside a gentle rain had begun to fall, and a slight mist crept about the city.

"This is BBC One. And now in place of our regularly scheduled program there is an urgent message from the Ministry of Defense. This broadcast will be carried on BBC Two, the Independent Television Authority and on Radios One, Two, Three and Four."

Sir Joseph appeared on the screen. His voice introduced himself over four radio bands, and he announced to the public the dangers which faced them. Major Thomas and Dr. Marsh had prepared a carefully worded text, not too much of the gruesome facts, but enough to impress upon sixty million people that they were in a hell of a mess. Sir Joseph explained the problem, how it arose and what the dangerous anthrax could do. He told everyone of treatment centers being set up in every police station in England and Wales. He told them to keep well away from bats. He prayed that among this mass of humanity would linger the sense to remain calm. "The government is doing everything possible to locate these bats," he said. "At the same time we are mounting operations to control outbreaks and decontaminate infected areas. The military is taking much of the responsibility for this work, and I would ask that you give them your fullest co-operation. In some areas the military may have to assume temporary command of land or buildings, but please remember that this is for your own protection. The soldiers are there to help you.

"We shall keep you informed both day and night. We urge you to co-operate and to help yourselves and your neighbors. If you suspect the disease has spread to any area, to any person or family, contact the police by dialing nine, nine, nine. If you have special queries, you can ring your local police station.

"The Prime Minister will address the Nation on this entire problem tomorrow morning at eight fifteen. Immediately before his broadcast, the Ministry of Defense will be on television and radio to inform you of further developments. Until then, please remember what we have said here tonight. Remain calm, follow the instructions given you, and remain indoors."

When it was clear that Sir Joseph had nothing more to say the announcer appeared and said, "This special broadcast has been carried on both television networks and on radio. For those of you who may have missed any part of it, we are repeating it immediately."

Sir Joseph arose stiffly and looked at Major Thomas and Dr. Marsh. He shook his head and sighed, glancing at his watch. "The bomb has dropped, gentlemen. God only knows what is going on out there now."

"It went very well, I thought," said Marsh. "I shouldn't think there'll be much panic."

Major Thomas was thinking about Chadwell's remark —how the people might regard the whole thing as utter rubbish. "Suppose you were a family man," he began, leaning against the window frame. "You had a wife and kids. Someone tells you there is something outside, something almost invisible yet as deadly as anything they'll ever come across. Like plague or radioactivity. Like gas. You can't see it, can't smell it, can't feel it, yet it could destroy you in minutes or hours while you sleep. That's the problem, Dr. Marsh—that's what you want to worry about. It's fear. It's fear of the unknown, sort of like walking down a lane at night. You create the fear—you build it up in your mind. It's like walking down that lane and there's no light and you're convinced there's someone following you. Then you reach some sort of light or another traveller and you feel safe. But for those people out there, there is no light," he said, pulling open the curtain. "Not the kind that'll help calm those people. And there is no friend to meet along the way, and home is as dangerous and frightening as that dark lane. That's what you must combat first before you go marching across England throwing disinfectant everywhere. Unfortunately, fear has a habit of accumulating in people. It might reach mass panic if you're unlucky. But it's gonna be fed by the newspapers, by the TV, by the radio and by people who feel damned indignant about being restricted. After all, whose fault was it that the Base blew up? Certainly not their's. And you can't pawn it off on them that it wasn't anybody's fault, either. They don't want to hear that. They're gonna be mad and they're gonna be scared. Most people are going to die—it's inevitable. There could be an epidemic like we discussed. The police, doctors, the soldiers who fight this stuff can be infected. We just don't know what's going to happen—the whole experiment was and still is totally unpredictable. People will put up with their fears only just so long and then instinctively they're gonna fight back—like being backed into a corner. And that is where the real danger lies. Gather a few men together and only one of them has to carry the anthrax bacteria before it spreads to others."

"Just what are you getting at, Major?" asked Sir Joseph. "What do you want us to do?"

"Be damn sure of every step you make before making it. Every mistake the government makes now will make things a thousand times worse. God help everyone if there's a panic."

"Not to add to the melodrama," said Marsh, "but we've got the Continent to think of next. France'll be on the hot line in minutes and after that we'll have a United Nations in Comcent unless we get a general release out."

"Hold them until morning—we have to," Sir Joseph replied, wringing his hands. "At least until the PM arrives."

"If you'll excuse me," began the Major, suddenly remembering his own duties. "I'll see what my people can arrange. I'll go through the Embassy—sure to get quick results that way."

"Major," called Sir Joseph. "Keep it as quiet as you can."

He nodded and withdrew.

"Quite a man," said Marsh, pulling open the curtain and gazing out on a misty London.

"Emotional. Too emotional. I'm wondering if he is the man we seem to think he is."

"Give him a chance. Think of what he's been through already. And this isn't exactly home to him, either."

He shrugged. "I guess we're all getting pretty keyed up. We've got precisely six hours to prepare a comprehensive outline of what we plan to do as a government and as a country. Our own people will want to know a lot more by morning, and the Continent will be screaming bloody murder if they aren't happy with the way we handle this."

"Well, in that case I'll get my men sorted out. They should be here by now."

"Yes, sort something out." He watched Marsh disappear and sighed heavily. The television crew were closing down in the next room and he heard their muffled footsteps. He walked to the window and peered out. His own reflection seemed far away, and so did London. Christ, he thought, what was going on out there?

Chadwell was falling asleep. The hum of hundreds of circuits to every point in the world, the rhythmic clickety-clack of the teleprinters and the continuous flow of hushed voices were lulling him into another world and he was damned happy to be there. His head bobbed, his chin found his chest and he breathed heavily.

"Mr. Chadwell? A message through. From British Rail."

Chadwell looked up drowsily as if reluctant to return from his world. He focused on a uniform clutching a slip of paper. "What is it?"

"Edinburgh to London Express has crashed, Sir."

"So what? I've got enough worries with bats—not flip-ing train crashes."

"But this is bats, Sir. And the PM. The engineer was pulled from the cab suffering from what the police think is anthrax—all black and puffy."

Chadwell snatched the paper and read through it. "Get me all the information you can," he snapped. "And what time is it?"

"Nearly midnight, Sir."

"Well, make it damned quick, lad. I've got to get this message through to the conference."

The messenger hustled off, Chadwell stretched and accepted another cup of coffee from a Wren Officer. She looked at him and smiled. "Rough night, Sir?"

"Going to be Lieutenant."

She looked around and, seeing no one near, whispered, "I've checked on the boy for you. You can tell Major Thomas that Murray's got him safely tucked in at Brown's."

"How is he?"

"Not too well, I'm afraid. I think it's all caught up with him what with the Major away and all this activity. At least Murray says so. He's going to stay with him until his relief comes. I think Sir Joseph wants him at the con-ference."

"I'll tell the Major when I see him. That's kind of you to do that, Lieutenant—I mean with things as they are."

She put her hand on his shoulder. "If it means some-thing to this Major fellow, I'm glad to. I wouldn't want to be in his shoes for all the tea at Lyons."

The messenger appeared again. "I can't get much more, Sir, but what there is is here. We've got Paris coming through, though, and the other lines are filling up. We've had to divert."

"Any more bats?" he asked, gathering together his papers.

"Two more, Sir. Unconfirmed,, but one is in Wolverhampton and the other near Watford."

"Watford? Hertfordshire?"

"Yes, Sir. Looks like London's next."

"Christ, what bloody next? Bats coming down like rain and the PM in a train crash. Now who's going to take over?"

"I don't know," replied the Lieutenant. "But if I were you I'd get those reports to Sir Joseph PDQ."

"Yes," he nodded hastily. "Yes."

Room 101 or the Great Hall as it was sometimes called was standing room only. The men from Porton, the military, a representative from the American Embassy, police and those who had attended the earlier conference were stretching the limits of the room. Colonel Combs was still fully occupied with maps, having discovered an enormous wall chart of the British Isles and somehow having also found several workmen to stick it up. Sir Godfrey Toddler was sorting out masses of notes and photographs in one corner while various Heads of the Ministry, military, police and fire brigades settled themselves uncomfortably in the front row chairs. Sir Joseph was preparing his initial address to the assemblage when Chadwell burst in from a side door.

"From Comcent," he spouted to Sir Joseph. "Rather bad news." He thrust the paper into his hands.

Major Thomas caught Chadwell's attention and signalled him over.

"You look worried, Chadwell."

He sat down wearily in a chair Thomas had saved for him. "I am. London's next, old man, and the PM's just gotten it. The London-Edinburgh Express crashed at speed and the engineer's got anthrax. They pulled—"

"Gentlemen," began Sir Joseph. "If I may have your attention, please."

He waited for the dozen of whispers to fade. There was a cough, some sighed wearily glancing at their watches, and others crumpled their hastily scrawled notes. It was too late at night or too early in the morning for most, and many had left grumpy wives behind.

"You have been summoned here on a matter of the gravest importance. No doubt you have heard the news and many of you have already been briefed by your respective Heads. I have here another message which makes our job that much more difficult. The train on which the PM was travelling has crashed and the authorities suspect anthrax is responsible. Wolverhampton and Watford have had two unconfirmed sightings—one each, that is, and I fear the Watford sighting puts the bats to within twenty miles of London.

"Our job tonight—regardless of these new developments—is to find a way of combating the disease before it gets a foothold in the country. I dare not think how badly the people will be hit before we can bring this killer down. It has already claimed the lives of two young boys, and I may say that they died in a church. This disease know no boundaries, gentlemen. It has no feeling for whom it kills or how. Our second responsibility is to other countries who may be directly or indirectly affected by the spread of the disease or by the bats themselves. We must consider what the international implications are, and we must be ready to assure our European allies that every possible precaution will be taken to inhibit further spread of anthrax." He paused. "We are facing the greatest single threat to our country since the plague. At no time in our history has an enemy invaded England so swiftly and completely as have these bats, and for the most part undetected. It is all the more unfortunate that this enemy has come from our own soil, our own research, and those who will die will do so because of our mistakes. We must, therefore, formulate a plan of attack. We must devise a way of locating these bats, of curbing further spread of infection and of cleansing our country completely. We shall draw upon the resources of our own Nation and those abroad who are willing to help. We shall call back from over-seas duty all military personnel if necessary. We shall put every soldier in the field and every pilot in the air. We shall spare no expense. Because we can't. I must now say in conclusion that in the absence of the PM I have been instructed to assume control of these operations until the PM can appear personally.

"I would now like to ask Sir Godfrey to take over. I am sure our first objective is to learn as much about these creatures as we can."

Sir Godfrey glanced up at the mention of his name, collected his papers and charts, and strode briskly to the front table. Sir Joseph took his seat next to the Major and Chadwell.

Toddler removed his spectacles and pushed an unruly lock of hair from his eyes. "We are dealing with a bat which is very common to all parts of the country. No doubt all of you have at one time or another seen such a bat. Under normal conditions we can predict the creature's method of flight, its approximate length and pattern of flight and where it might conceivably seek shelter. But bats are different from any other species of flying animal in that they rely upon a form of sonar for guidance. What influence this time mechanism will have on their guidance system, and indeed what influence the disease will have once it has contaminated the bat will greatly influence the known predictions. I do not wish to appear pessimistic or alarmist, but we must be aware of what we are dealing with." He replaced his spectacles and peered down at his papers. He looked up again. "I have been able to compute some quick estimates based on the latest sightings in Wolverhampton and Watford. These, combined with the other sightings, already begin to form a kind of pattern—a three quarter circle. The maximum distance yet known is about two hundred miles. This in itself is a great distance for any ordinary bat to fly. In fact, it is almost unheard of, but we must consider the time mechanism which has possibly thrown the creature off balance. I should like to put forward the hypothesis that these bats were treated with a stimulant prior to their release. If the experiment were to take place in the morning, the technicians at Dwarf Hill could have easily injected many of the bats with artificial stimulants in an exercise to determine to what degree length of flight could be extended. This would then account for the great distance so far covered."

Admiral Downing-Wright arose. "Excuse me, Sir Godfrey, but if what you say is true, and it looks quite possible, is it not proper to suppose that there are bats floating around in the Channel at this time?"

"More than possible. And I would estimate that a certain portion of these creatures has reached France and possibly beyond."

The Admiral scrawled a hasty message and had a courier run it to Comcent. At the same time the Foreign Secretary caught Sir Joseph and they withdrew from the room.

"However, my job tonight is to give you facts and figures." He held up a large picture. "This is your culprit. The order of Chiroptera. The wing span is approximately seven inches, sometimes greater. The wing itself is composed of a membrane stretched between the bones of its four fingers along its body to the tail. The method of flight is entirely dependent upon sounds which the bat emits as it flies."

Sir Reginald Penn stood up. "Have bats ever been known to attack?"

"I presume you mean attack humans. Certain species will attack, but the British variety has rarely been known to molest humans. However, under the influence of the anthrax bacteria who can say what the variations of behaviour might be."

"What do you feel is the absolute maximum any of these bats could fly before being brought down—or coming down voluntarily?" asked one of the scientists from Porton.

"That is a difficult question." He replaced his chart on the table. "Entirely dependent upon the weather, period of darkness, whether or not the time mechanism has worked, what affect has the mechanism had upon the sonar, and of course whether or not an artificial stimulant has been used. However, for practical reasons I should estimate that a two hundred mile radius of flight would be maximum. One must remember that these bats will not fly straight, but weave and settle as they wish. Some will double back while others may carry straight on."

Another Porton scientist arose. "Where would the bats most likely settle?"

"In barns, caves, lofts—all the traditional lodgings of bats. That's if they survive to reach such a place."

Major Thomas looked up. "We discovered a dead bat in Beckington earlier this afternoon in the back garden of a house. I think if the bats are contaminated in flight, they'll drop anywhere."

"Naturally, if the creature is forced to land, he will be indiscriminate." He glanced around the room. There seemed to be no further questions. "If there are no questions, I would simply like to add that we do not know how many have escaped. There is not now and probably never will be any way of determining the number of bats, so selective decontamination is virtually impossible. What you gentlemen must work on is an idea which will disinfect vast areas of the country. Without detailed knowledge of the behaviour patterns of bats infected with anthrax, without the knowledge of how many are or were flying about, well, precise calculations are impossible. I leave you with it, gentlemen. I believe Colonel Combs has requested to speak next . . ."

Colonel Combs needed little introduction among those who worked at Whitehall. His enormous frame and companion swagger stick had hounded the halls of government buildings for years—ever since his change of position from the military to military politics, and subsequent change of attitude. He was the Paisley of the armed services, and he was out to put himself as Number One regardless. The disaster had been playing right into his hands, and he knew if he could lick the problem of decontamination, Whitehall and Parliament would be his. His eager stride which carried him swiftly to the front of the Hall seemed too eager to Major Thomas, too much like the politicians in the White House and Congress. He felt uneasy in the hands of this overanxious hero, and he was not alone in his fear. Combs' voice boomed out as his swagger stick thumped against his monstrous map. "I should like to put forward my plan of attack. My idea ties in well with what Sir Godfrey has established about the habits of these creatures. I want to organize a perimeter line using Harlech, Wolverhampton, Bedford, Southend, Dover and Bognor Regis (the latter of which barely survived the Colonel's thumping stick) as what I shall call Safe Bases. Troops and supplies will be built up around these Bases and the area behind the perimeter line will be known as the Safe Zone, or non-contaminated. By stretching a line of men, machines and aircraft along the perimeter, the greatest possible area within the perimeter could be treated. It would mean a mass convergence, ever decreasing in size as the troops worked towards Lands End." He missed Lands End altogether and punched a hole in Swansea. It went unnoticed.

Chadwell sighed and he began to realize that Combs was pushing everyone else out of the Club and assuming complete control. Major Thomas objected. "Colonel, do you not think that this plan—however effective—will take a great deal of valuable time?"

"Time, Sir?"

"Time. How long will it take to establish your men?"

"With the means at our disposal I should say we could deploy men and machines at each of the Safe Bases within twenty four hours."

The Major continued. "What about the time you would require to reach Lands End?"

"I estimate seven to ten days doing a thorough job."

There arose a general stirring among the gathering and Sir Joseph reappeared.

"To expedite the actual operation, we could also position men at Lands End who would work towards the others. This might cut the time by a half. Not more."

Murry—who had just entered and pushed into a seat near the Major—was puzzled. "How would you treat the contamination?"

"Dr. Perry Marsh has found a powerful disinfectant formula which destroys the bacillus of anthrax. This could be mass produced by one or two of the major chemical companies and be ready for us in two days."

"What about immunization?" Murray suggested.

"Impossible," sang out Marsh from behind. "Anthrax is a disease reasonably unknown in this country. Natural immunity is impossible and mass innoculation is also out. We just haven't got the supplies."

Combs was pleased that Marsh had unknowingly

given his plan a boost. He was indignant that even a few speculated on the success of his genius.

Admiral Downing-Wright sounded bored when he addressed the Colonel, but he knew he had to defend his ships or Combs would have them as well. "My men are on standby at the moment. We could if necessary disinfect the beaches and coastal waterways at the same time as the ground and air forces are mounting their attack."

Sir Joseph arose. "I think I should say here that the Foreign Secretary is talking with Paris at the moment. In view of the rising situation we must inform the Continental authorities of the danger. Furthermore, the PM is still missing."

Lord Tenningly asked if each sighting might not be treated individually, moving in to disinfect large areas only when there is a suspected outbreak.

"Here, here," someone shouted from the assembly.

Combs smiled. "As Sir Godfrey said earlier, selective contamination is out of the question. Before we can give the all-clear, we must be sure that every bat has been found and destroyed. Only tactics which I have described would in any way guarantee this."

Sir Joseph walked to the front of the room. "I must agree with the Colonel. Whatever method we employ must guarantee safety from any further outbreak. Our trade, our industry and our people will depend on it."

Dr. Marsh spoke. "We have little time to discuss how to tackle this problem; however, my colleagues and I feel that the Colonel's idea is the best. The disinfectant which we have formulated will serve as the greatest surety against continued outbreaks. If the application is widespread, and if it is controlled, there need exist little worry about the disinfectant's influence on people, animals or plant life. Any other method could not guarantee the comprehensiveness of mass disinfecting."

"Has the disinfectant been developed—has anyone tested it?" asked Lord Tenningly.

"Not yet. We have it in formula, and I believe one of the chemical companies is working on a sample now."

"I should like to have this matter in the hands of Colonel Combs and Dr. Marsh," Sir Joseph began. "Could we not have them use Room 131?" A guard nodded from the doorway. "If you gentlemen could take this time to get a more definite plan on paper, we'll carry on with things here."

Colonel Combs seemed pleased enough with the idea and signalled for his staff to vacate the Hall. Dr. Marsh gathered his team and was followed out by Admiral Downing-Wright and the Air Vice Marshall.

Sir Joseph began again when the door had shut behind them. "Together with the Foreign Secretary and in the absence of the Prime Minister, I have drawn up the following measures. The Queen has declared that a State of Emergency now exists and I'm afraid we have overridden Parliamentary approval in view of the critical situation. England, Scotland and Wales are to be quarantined. All ports and air terminals will be closed to the public. No foreign vessels will be permitted to land unless it is an emergency, and no vessels will leave the country either by land or sea or air. The Royal Family has been taken to Balmoral until the danger is over. Parliament will remain in session and all MPs will find accommodation in London. Rail services are to be cut to a minimum and travel by the public restricted to only the essential. All postal services are suspended. I should also think that if the Colonel's plans are accepted, there will be further quarantine restrictions imposed along this perimeter line. These orders are effective immediately, and Comcent is alerting those responsible for enforcing these restrictions at this moment. I have prepared a general statement for the press which is also being copied for release.

"Our next step is to prepare a report for the television and radio for this morning's broadcast. I shall of course have to stand in for the PM, but I shall require your assistance in deciding how much should be released as general information. I feel, however, that we have little alternative but to reveal most of what has happened, and the plans which are now being formulated. I expect that other countries who might be contaminated will rely upon us for suggestions."

A courier entered the room and looked about. He recognized Chadwell and found his way over. "Message for Major Thomas, Sir."

Chadwell had been struggling to stay awake. He looked first at the messenger and then at Major Thomas. "It's for you."

The Major unfolded the paper, nodding as he read. "It's from the Embassy. Washington is willing to do whatever possible to help. If the PM or Sir Joseph makes a formal appeal, I can request whatever assistance we decide is needed."

Murray nodded approvingly. "If this disinfecting lark goes through, I think you might supply us with a few thousand bottles of Dettol and several million mops. Christ knows where Combs thinks all that disinfectant's coming from. I use a whole bottle just to clean my bathroom floor."

Chadwell huffed. "If you aimed a bit straighter, you wouldn't need so much."

"You better tell Sir Joseph that the Yanks are coming," said Murray. "After the formal appeal of course."

The Major heaved himself from his chair and walked up the aisle to the table. He lay the message down without interrupting Sir Joseph and returned to his seat. Sir Joseph stopped speaking long enough to glance at the note, and nodded towards the Major.

"I nearly forgot," began Chadwell. "That message reminded me. I'm supposed to tell you that Murray said that Trevor is resting, but a bit done in."

"That's good, Chadwell," Murray spouted. "We've got the world's biggest communication center and you can't even tell the Major what's happened to his kid. The Lieutenant said she gave you the message hours ago."

"She did. I forgot. You know as valuable as the lad is, Mr. Murray, the PM still comes first."

"Yeah, yeah. Never mind. You know, Major, the best thing for the boy right now is if you're around. Can't you get away for awhile?"

"Does it look like it?"

Murray shook his head.

Chadwell was mumbling again. "Why don't you bring him over here? Put him in Comcent Quarters."

Murray scoffed. "With security as it is you wouldn't get him past the doorstep. Who's going to let a thirteen year old boy march around communications?"

"Even if I requested it?" asked the Major.

"Hang on," Murray replied slowly. "There's a special suite of rooms upstairs—reserved for the big wigs and all that. Sir Joseph could authorize it—medical reasons or some such lie."

"Marsh wants a report on the gas effects," Charwell offered sleepily. "And you know how Wilks wanted the kid. Say the lad knows all about it and he's doing his term paper on it."

Murray stood up. "I'll see what I can do. If it's all right, I'll have one of my men pick him up first thing in the morning and bring him over. I'll let you know which room he's in."

Thomas watched as Murray squeezed out of the stuffy room. A thick pall of smoke was clinging to the ceiling and he felt ill. He looked at the weary figure of Sir Joseph who was trying to organize a statement, but since Colonel Combs had left, the conference had broken up into smaller groups who were discussing the problem amongst themselves. Every so often a messenger from Comcent would appear with a folded message and Sir Joseph read the news with growing despair. The urge to escape spread over the Major again, and he longed for some fresh air. The room was growing smaller, the faces further away, and Charwell was nearly asleep. He poked him in the ribs. "Wake up, Charwell. How about a stroll?"

"Can't," he replied simply. "The building's sealed. No one in without a pass and no one out—pass or no pass. The downstairs looks like Selfridges on the day before Christmas."

"What about a cup of coffee—or tea?"

Chadwell opened his eyes and sat up. He glanced about the room. Sir Joseph had stopped talking and was making his way towards them. "Hello," he said tiredly. "We're taking a break until two. Like a drink?"

The Major smiled. "Exactly what I'd like. A drink and some fresh air."

"Come to my office. You too, Chadwell. Might as well get as far away from this as the building permits. Won't have another break until four or five I should think."

Murray appeared suddenly. "It's arranged. The boy will be brought here by ambulance this morning at nine. He'll be in Room 300 A—that's the room next to the one we've given you, Major. I've had a guard laid on so no one gets near him except you."

They were walking out the side door and into the corridor. "What's all this, then?" Sir Joseph asked. "What machiavellian schemes have you been dreaming up?"

"You've just arranged for the Major's boy to sleep here tomorrow, Sir Joseph," Murray explained. "You wouldn't want them separated, now, would you?"

"His boy? I thought you were single, Major."

"I am. My wife died a few years ago. This boy is the one from Stumford—he got a bad dose of the gas but somehow managed to pull through."

"How did you come by him, then?"

Chadwell answered. "He saved him, Sir. At the risk of his own life I may say. The lad's parents were killed in Stumford so the local police thought it would be best if the Major sort of adopted him pro temps."

"Jolly good of you, Major," Sir Joseph replied, opening the door to his office. "But I fail to see what I have to do with the boy's residence here."

"You've authorized it," Murray replied. "Through me."

"Nice to have someone to do the thinking for you, isn't it, Major? Drink?"

"Whiskey if you have it. Straight."

"Chadwell?"

"Sherry, please. Medium dry."

"And Murray, you have the same as the Major. Neat."

Murray smiled.

Major Thomas pulled back the curtains from the window and pushed open the pane. He looked out and breathed in the damp night air. Rain still fell in a slow autumnal drizzle, and the lights towards Trafalgar Square were blurred and confused. Below, a little traffic stirred, and only the occasional stroller interrupted the night. He thought of Trevor, and the hotel in which he was asleep. Adopt him pro temps? He figured he might make it longer if things worked out. But would this youngster like America—could he adjust? What about school—weren't the English so far ahead of Americans in education? And could Detrick cure him completely? He was almost enjoying these questions. It gave him relief from the fears of the moment.

"Your drink, Major," Murray proffered, pushing to get his head outside the window. "That's what I need—fresh London air and booze. One deep breath of that muck and it's the same as twenty fags. Too much of this and your liver turns into a gherkin. What the hell's the point of living, Major?"

"Right now I say to hell with it all. Damned if you do, damned if you don't. Devil and the deep blue sea." He paused and swallowed half the contents of the glass in one swig. "I wonder what a few hundred passengers at the airports and docks are feeling right now."

"You mean with the quarantine and all. They're thinking how the hell are they going to get to wherever they were going before you know who did you know what. This is one time I'm glad I'm not going on holiday."

Major Thomas glanced up at the sky, at the millions of droplets rushing towards him. He felt the fine spray licking his face and dribbling off his chin. It felt good, clean. He looked at Murray and grinned.

London Heathrow Airport. 12:50 Hours

Speedbird Golf Alpha had stopped at the end of the runway. George Lucas, a passenger in the first class compartment, tightened his seat belt and looked nervously out at the two starboard turbo-jet engines throbbing heavily in anticipation of take-off. The bats had frightened him silly and the prospects of meeting up with some contaminated creature be it man or beast had driven him to literal flight. Quickly, he had booked on

BOAC Flight 914 to New York, grabbed what few material objects he felt necessary for his continued survival and belted to the airport. Now it was just a matter of seconds before London was a memory, fading away into the misty rain at five hundred miles an hour.

"Good evening, Ladies and Gentlemen. This is your Captain speaking. Before taking off, I would like to welcome you aboard BOAC Flight 914 and hope that you have a pleasant flight. I shall be talking to you at various times throughout the flight, and—" His voice clicked off. Lucas glanced up. In a moment it returned. "Ladies and Gentlemen I regret that we have an order to return to the central boarding area so we shall have to delay your departure for a short time. I would ask that you remain seated and keep your seat belts fastened until we come to a complete stop. Again, I apologize for the delay, but I expect that we shall be cleared for take-off shortly."

George Lucas had a strong suspicion as to what this "short delay was all about, and he had a stronger suspicion that it wasn't going to be short. He unbuckled his seat belt and pushed through the passenger sitting next to him.

"I'm sorry, Sir," said an obliging stewardess coming from the galley, "but you'll—"

"Never mind that. I've got to see the Captain," he snapped as beads of perspiration trickled down his cheeks. He pulled at the knot of his tie and tried to push past.

"If you'll just sit down, I'm sure the Capt—"

"No! I've got to see him now. You don't know what's going on out there. I do."

Another stewardess appeared from behind and tried to coax him back.

"No," he repeated, pushing forward. "I've got to see the Captain. You don't understand."

"Now then, what's all this?" called a steward, rushing forward. "Come along, Sir, we'll be back—"

Suddenly George Lucas flailed out and sent the steward crashing backwards into a passenger's seat. At the same moment he lunged forward and pushed open the door to the cockpit. "Get this plane off the ground or you'll never see the sky again," he snarled viciously. "I'm not going back there and neither are you."

The stewardess found her way past the galley and pushed in from behind. "I'm sorry, Captain, but he just—"

"It's all right, Joan. See to the other passengers."

"Call from Control," began the co-pilot. "They want to know what's delaying us."

"Tell your Control to clear you for take-off. I've got a six inch blade here that says we're leaving now."

The Captain glanced at the co-pilot. "Ask Control for clearance."

In a moment he replied, "We're quarantined, Sir. We can't take off. The whole ruddy airport's quarantined."

The Captain turned to Lucas. "You heard, mate. No go."

"Look, *mate*, I flew more missions in the War than you got fingers and toes between you. Either you take this crate up or I do. You got a few passengers back there to think of, so which do you think they'd rather have flying this thing?"

The Captain flushed. "Look, old man, you just can't take this craft off whenever you like. There's laws about hijacking, you know. Now why don't you go back inside and we'll forget the whole thing, huh?"

"There's a few thousand bats lying around out there," he retorted in a hot sweat. "And every one of them's got enough poison to kill a bleedin' army. I'll take my chances up there." Before the Captain could respond, Lucas slammed his left arm against his face and drew

149

the four throttles towards him, bracing himself against the arm of the Captain's chair. The engines thundered to life and belched arcs of red-orange flames as the fuel poured into the turbines. The thrust veered the craft starboard, and Lucas battled to reduce the thrust in the port engines. As the co-pilot fought against Lucas' attempts the plane spun wildly port, evened up, leered again to starboard and sped towards the boarding area, cutting across the grass strips alongside the tarmac. The Captain regained a sitting position while Lucas stuggled with the co-pilot. Someone hit the hydraulic brakes. The plane shuddered slightly, tipped forward and again began to spin and skid along the slippery runway. There was only one chance left to stop the giant aircraft before it careened into the central area. The Captain elbowed Lucas backwards against the navigator who had banged his head against the banks of switches and was gushing blood from a gash on his forehead. At the same time he reached out and reversed the pitch of the turbines. There was a shattering roar as the engines reversed pitch at high revs and as the Captain fought to hold himself back, he caught sight of another plane cutting in front of him. The intercepting plane opened its port engines in an attempt to turn, but the wing swung wide and crashed through the cockpit of 914. From the Control Tower the collision blinded the operators. Several thousand gallons of aviation fuel exploded and both planes were engulfed in an ocean of flames moments before the Tower windows blew inwards and sent shrapnel crashing into the boarding area.

Whitehall. 1:30 Hours

Sir Joseph and the Major returned to the Great Hall with Chadwell and Murray shortly after one. As they sat around the head table, Lord Tenningly and Ian McHugh from MI5 joined them.

"Any news of the PM, Sir?" McHugh asked, pulling out a chair.

He shook his head. "Nothing. They're still digging through the wreckage. It's supposed to be quite a mess."

"This problem," began Lord Tenningly, "is something rather unique, is it not? We have here what a hostile country might expect to suffer if we were to use just these weapons. But unfortunately it is not a hostile country. It is our own. It is our people who are dying, and it is the government who will suffer most. I see no way out of this."

Sir Joseph seemed perturbed. "With all respect, Lord Tenningly, our commitments at this time are to saving the people, not the party."

He removed his glasses and wiped his forehead. "I know that. I just feel that we're responsible for all this. We sponsored the research. It was a government station. It's hopeless."

"We all feel pretty hopeless," began Thomas. "But we can't stop now. After all, it is the government's responsibility as you say, so you can't let the people suffer. And it's the people who are going to suffer—not you."

Murray was fed up. "For Christ's sake, man, we have every resource at our disposal to save the country from further contamination so let's use it. If we go round feeling sorry for ourselves, God knows what's going to happen to the public. You said you feel the government's responsible so by God it's going to be the government who's going to make amends—and not just to our own people. What about the foreign powers? We've got exactly seven hours to have our plan of action ready and it better be bloody well good."

"Six hours," Chadwell whispered.

"What's Combs up to?" Tenningly asked.

"He's drawn up a workable plan for disinfecting the contaminated areas. Provided his theory is correct, it should work," Sir Joseph explained. "The Foreign Secretary is finishing with the statement for the Continent and we've got our press boys getting the publicity sorted out. Obviously, Combs' work is the most vital so he's been given every possible support."

"You realize of course," said Tenningly, "that we're playing right into Combs' hands. He'll really make a meal of this and I'm not even sure I trust him. He's power hungry."

"You have anyone else better qualified?" Sir Joseph retorted heatedly. "Anyway, it doesn't really matter. Major Thomas has contacted his men in the United States and they're ready to do whatever they can. I understand there's quite a bit they can do."

"Like what?" asked Tenningly.

"We always have had greater resources for experimentation," Thomas began, "so naturally we have accidents—deliberate or otherwise, and these give us the opportunity to find cures, preventatives and so on. Though we've never had anything like this happen— thank God—we have a special research unit which is responsible for having plans ready to counteract any accidental leakage of the chemicals or biologicals. I've already requested their advice, and I should have something by noon tomorrow—or today as it happens to be. Naturally, my government is prepared to supply whatever equipment is necessary to put whatever scheme they draw up into the field, but they'll need your official request."

"That's hopeful," replied Tenningly sourly. "I knew it would come to this."

"If I may," Thomas continued, "I would like to help whereever I can. I know I'm not in the best position—

being American—but I have had quite a bit of experience with biological weapons and I can act as a go-between with Washington."

"That goes without saying, Major," replied Sir Joseph. "You've already been of invaluable assistance and we shall be indeed grateful for whatever advice you can give."

A courier entered and handed Sir Joseph a message. He left quickly. Sir Joseph looked at the others before he wearily broke the seal on the envelope like he had dozens of others during the night. He looked at the Major. "If it's got a seal on it, it's bad news." He glanced through the message. "There's been a rather serious incident at London Airport. Two jets have collided in the central area and the whole place is in chaos."

"Not due to bats, I hope," said Tenningly.

"Nothing yet to indicate it. Apparently a Boeing 707 was returning to the boarding area when it went beserk and crashed into a VC 10 which was maneuvering out of its way. Both had full tanks."

"My God," Chadwell sighed. "What a hell of a thing to happen."

"Yeah," Tenningly muttered. "And I'm wondering when it's going to end."

"That's up to us," replied Sir Joseph. He looked at his watch. "The summary report should be ready soon. We've only a few minutes before the conference."

"Well, I'm going to make the most of those minutes," said Murray. "Anybody want a drink?"

The major stood up and stretched. "If you're buying."

"Don't look at me—it's Sir Joseph's booze. You don't mind, do you, Sir?"

"Not so long as you're both back by two. And sober."

"As a judge, Sir Joseph. Come on. We got time for at least two quick ones."

153

Stumford. 1:50 Hours

The two figures crept stealthily forward, dodging behind trees and bushes whenever they felt they were being watched. It was great fun—the real thing—and they had proved how good they really were. They had slipped past two roadblocks and avoided three Army patrols. Now they were near Stumford and they could see for themselves what all the flap was about.

"I told you we could do it," said one of the adventurers. "It must really be something big with the Army here and all."

"I don't like it. I want to go home. It's late and Mum'll be doing her nut."

"Aw, stop moaning. We got this far. It's just over the ridge." He stopped behind a rock. "Tell you what. We'll sneak into the village, have a quick look, and then head for home. All right?"

"Yeah, but let's go. I'm tired."

The obvious leader of this expedition pressed on. He spotted the road not far away and considered whether or not to try it. He decided against it. Too many patrols. Instead, he cut alongside and found cover behind a hedge.

"There—you see. Stumford. I told you."

"But I can't see anything. It's too dark."

"Dad said there was an Army Base here what blew up. The one on the hill. They were making some top secret weapon—like a ray gun. If we get through the village and up that hill, we might find something. You know— a clue or something."

"You said we were going home after we saw Stumford. Well, I don't see anything and I'm going home."

"Hang on, Paul. Just let's see why they closed the village. There's got to be some reason. Dad said it was mighty suspicious."

"And my mum said to stay away from here. She said it was dangerous."

"Aw, everything's dangerous to her. You wait here. I'll go and have a look."

"Give me the torch, then."

"How can I see anything if you've got the torch."

"What was that?"

"What?"

'Over there. A stick crackled or something."

Paul snatched the flashlight and pointed the beam in the direction he heard the sound. There didn't seem to be anything there, but the crackling came again. He suddenly felt scared. "I'm going home, Jim. I'm not staying around here. We can come back tomorrow."

Jim began to agree. He made a move when he spotted something—something moving slowly and deliberately.

"Give me the torch," he whispered. "Don't move."

Paul felt for his hand and pushed the torch into it.

Jim took careful aim at the intruder before switching the light on. He aimed at the head, found the button and pushed. They both froze for a split second. It was a monster. It was some horrible creature. This was the weapon. No wonder they had closed the village and were keeping everything away. Jim was the first to move and he made for the road. Paul scrambled after him and they heard the monster clawing its way behind. Jim wanted to reach the village—there must be somebody still in Stumford and even being caught by the Army was preferable to being torn to shreds by the thing that was after them.

They reached the road. Chesterly was at least a mile the other way while Stumford was just down the hill. Jim glanced behind him and waited for Paul to catch up.

They stood on the roadside and listened. It was still after them. It was tearing about in the woods. Jim took one final look around and bolted for the village down the hill. Paul didn't wait to follow. They raced along the road, passed the sign and started down the hill. They could see the outline of the houses. Safety seemed not far away. They reached the bottom of the hill and turned the corner. Jim screamed once and froze. Not twenty feet ahead were six more of the monsters standing around a jeep they had obviously just attacked. Paul grabbed his arm and they turned to run back up the hill. They heard the monsters calling after them and only ran faster. They were near the crest of the hill when the other creature appeared. Jim grabbed Paul's arm and they fled into the woods. Paul tripped over a branch and brought both of them crashing to the ground. Jim looked up and shook his head. He felt suddenly strange. His muscles were going all funny. His eyes were watering and he couldn't breathe. Paul was clutching his throat and rolling about. Jim coughed, struggled to stand, made it halfway to his feet, turned and collapsed, kicking his feet at nothing and quivering all over. His face rubbed in the dirt and he was barely conscious of an agonizing stiffness in his trousers. In a few seconds he was unconscious. In a few more seconds both Jim and his mate were dead.

"Over here," shouted the Sergeant. "There they are."

A powerful beam sliced through the darkness and underbrush. Four soldiers in heavy isolation gear and gas masks trudged slowly through the woods, impeded by the garments and wary not to trip.

"Poor blighters," said one of them. "Why the hell didn't they stop?"

"Why the hell were they here in the first place?" demanded the Sergeant.

"One thing's sure," began the fourth soldier who wore

a large red cross on his sleeve. "They won't be walking out. Come on, we better get them down to HQ."

"The Captain's going to be mad as hell when he hears about this."

"So's London when they hear about it," replied the Sergeant, heaving one of the bodies across his shoulder. "No one is supposed to get through. And a couple of kids manage to beat the British Army. How's that going to sound?"

The first soldier was still shaking his head and wondering why they hadn't stopped when they saw him.

Whitehall. 14:56 Hours

The messages from Comcent were piled high on the edge of the table. Lord Tenningly was sifting through them and jotting down notes. Dr. Marsh was standing in a corner in deep discussion with a technician from ICI who looked terrified at being called to such a formal gathering. Chadwell, Murray and the Major were half asleep in the front row, waiting for the conference to begin. Murray mumbled remarks about how many glasses they were missing every time five minutes passed, but neither Chadwell nor the Major heard. When Dr. Marsh nodded towards Sir Joseph, he wearily arose from his seat and walked to the head table.

He gazed upon the rows of chairs and waited for the murmurings to fade. "Gentlemen, I would like to resume this meeting. Lord Tenningly, will you review the present situation?"

There was a rustling of papers and creaking of chairs as those assembled settled down for the long night. Murray looked at Thomas and nodded. Quietly, they left through the side door and disappeared into Sir Joseph's study. "He should take about ten minutes—then we'll go back in," Murray explained, pouring out two glasses of whiskey.

"I gather you know what he's going to say."

"No matter what happens in this country, he says the same thing. He's just like Dovell—the PM. We must mount our defenses, we must sacrifice, we must all pull together—and he sits there drinking his wine or sailing his yachts while the rest of the country suffers. Personally, Major, there are two people in the world I hate most. One of them is Dovell. The other one is your President. I hate politics. I hate politicians."

"Diplomatically, I can't agree with you, but I would off the record—about our President, I mean. I don't really know much about your PM.

"Yeah, well, cheers."

Thomas lifted his glass. "Cheers." He looked about the room. "Still raining out?"

Murray opened the curtain. "Worse. At least it'll keep the people inside."

They were silent for a few minutes as each gazed out. The rain was falling harder and they could hear it striking the window.

Lord Tenningly was summing up his summing up. ". . . It is not yet known what has caused the collision at Heathrow, but so far over three hundred passengers and ground support men have been killed. I have also been given a rough estimate of those killed at Stumford. So far over nine hundred and fifty men, women and children have been counted. Troops are still combing the area immediately around Stumford and tomorrow they will be inspecting the housing estates where more are thought to be dead. Whatever hit that village, we now have some idea of its effectiveness.

"This is the picture at the moment. What further reports come in will be—"

Admiral Downing-Wright stood up, clutching a slip of

yellow paper. "Lord Tenningly, I regret to add that I have just learned of another sighting. One of my ships, the "Victoria," has discovered two bats on the deck. Already, three men are beyond help. The Air Force is flying out medical assistance now."

"Thank you, Admiral," he replied sullenly. "I think that is all I have to say. Perhaps Colonel Combs and Dr. Marsh could take over . . ."

As the Colonel and Dr. Marsh approached the table, another message arrived. Lord Tenningly read it, folded it again and sighed. He glanced at Sir Joseph and shook his head.

"The most important part of tonight's work," began Dr. Marsh, "is establishing a plan of attack. Colonel Combs has already deployed troops in the Safe Zone Bases and I have managed to get a report from Imperial Chemical on the disinfectant to be used. Mr. Nigel Spence has been good enough to come along and I shall now let him explain the structure of this chemical."

Nigel Spence arose from his seat and walked nervously forward. He seemed unprepared and ill at ease. Only an hour before he had been standing over a table full of test-tubes at ICI, very safe and comfortable in his work. Suddenly he had been ripped from his security and thrown into the den of government lions. His voice began uncertainly and his hands fumbled with a folder of papers. "As most of you know, disinfectant is made up of phenol, cresols and xylenes. Phenol is a colorless, hygroscopic crystalline solid which is commonly called carbolic acid. In its raw form phenol is highly poisonous and blisters the skin on contact. The cresols and xylenes are benzene hydrocarbons which come from common coal tar. It is the mixing of these compounds which produces the ordinary household disinfectant. Simply, when one compound is increased or decreased, or diluted, a safe proportion of each is reached. Though the disinfectant thus formed is deadly to germs, it is relatively harmless to humans."

"And to think I had always thought that stuff was glorified soap," Murray commented drily to the Major. "The wonders of science."

Sir Joseph frowned at him.

"We are now faced with decontaminating vast areas of the countryside, streets, houses, buildings, forests and so on. Also, the bacillus which must be destroyed is a hybrid variety—it is stronger and more resistent than one would normally come across. At this moment my colleagues are working on a suitable formula which will destroy the anthrax bacillus, but because of its exceptional potency, the resulting molecular combination of phenol, cresols and xylenes will have to be of greater strength. Unavoidably, this will have some effect on vegetation, insect, animal and bird life and even on humans. However, we cannot say at this time precisely what this effect will be. I can say now that its strength will be such that there will be a great loss of plant and animal life and a subsequent shake-up in the ecology of the country. Those responsible for administering this disinfectant will have to ensure that whenever possible animals have been evacuated from the area. I think Colonel Combs is in charge of that?" He glanced around and seemed relieved when the bulky form of the Colonel strode majestically forward.

"We are moving swiftly," he grinned. His swagger stick found the map immediately. "I have ordered all available troops to converge on their nearest respective Safe Bases. In addition I have several standby forces at the ready. As it now seems that London may well be next, all available troops have been ordered to assemble at zero six hundred hours in Hyde Park."

Murray glanced heavenwards. The Major seemed intent on what the Colonel was saying, and Chadwell had finally fallen asleep.

"When the disinfectant is prepared, I hope to have every tanker available, both civilian and military, ready to transport the stuff to the Safe Bases. There the men will transfer it to pumpers and begin the disinfecting operation in conjunction with the local fire brigade who can use their own pumpers."

"If I may make a suggestion," said the Major. "I could have back pumps sent over which the soldiers can use in the field. Our Forest Service uses them in fighting fires in the back country."

"That would be of great assistance, Major," he boomed. "I trust this can be arranged."

Sir Joseph nodded wearily.

"Good. These back pumps should allow the men greater freedom—mobility—less reliance upon the fire brigades."

The fire marshalls huffed indignantly.

"Initially, we shall concentrate our ground offensive on those areas which are known to be contaminated. Then the Air Force will spray the sparsely populated areas. We have investigated the possibilities of using aerosols, but Dr. Marsh and the Meteorological Office have decided that conditions would be unfavorable."

Murray's imagination envisioned hundreds of pilots leaning out of their cockpits with tins of aerosol sprays while they whizzed along the rooftops. He grinned to himself. Chadwell began to snore quietly.

"When the troops move into the areas already sprayed by the Air Force, the flyers will use a dilute solution on the preceding areas. Just to be sure."

"How many gallons of disinfectant are you planning to use?" shouted someone from the rear.

"As many as it takes to destroy this disease," he retorted confidently. "Mr. Spence has made a provisional estimate of a gallon of disinfectant to fifty gallons of water. It is impossible to say how many gallons of water we'll use as nothing like this has ever been presented to us—but the disinfectant companies will produce as much as we need for as long as we need it." He glanced across the table at Nigel Spence. He dared do nothing but nod in hasty agreement.

Sir Joseph arose. "Colonel, might I take over at this point?"

The Colonel bowed politely, thumped his stick beneath his armpit and marched off the floor. Spence scurried for his chair.

"Gentlemen, I know it is very late and we are all tired. I would like to break up the meeting until six thirty when I shall have breakfast served in here for any of you who wish it. In the meantime the top floor of this building has been converted into what can only be described as a rather crowded hostel. We shall resume discussions here at eight forty-five immediately following the broadcast. I do this only because I feel all of us will need whatever rest we can get and as many of the difficulties in dealing with this problem have been overcome, there is no need to stretch ourselves more than necessary. Thank you."

Many stood up eagerly, long ready for bed. Others continued to talk among themselves while Sir Joseph gathered the Major, Murray and Lord Tenningly together. By the time they had seated themselves around the head table, the room was empty. Chadwell was snoring quietly. He was one of the few who actually looked content.

"Major," began Sir Joseph, "you and Murray will share the room put aside for you and the boy. I would like you down here by six so we can go over the broadcast statements. Lord Tenningly will give the initial address, and I may have to conclude."

"I've got most of what I need," said Lord Tenningly, shaking a pile of papers straight. "I'll get these notes into some readable form."

"Major, I would suggest that you get some rest. Tomorrow will be the roughest day and I shall need you. I am hoping you will be able to get some time away to see your young friend, but with you acting as go-between with the American government, your presence here will be most valuable."

Murray arose. "Come on, Major Tom. We've got time for exactly three hours sleep."

"I wish I could be of more help tonight, but—"

"We shall need all the help you can muster up tomorrow."

He looked down at Sir Joseph. "Good night, then, Sir. I'll do my best."

"I know you will, Major. I am very grateful. Now get some sleep."

Murray hastened him out. "Give what you want, old man, but don't overdo it. No one does around here—it isn't normal."

Sir Joseph turned to Lord Tenningly. "We better get these statements finalized."

Tenningly sighed as he frowned upon the masses of notes. "Let's review everything we've got to date. I've got a few more sightings around here somewhere." He rifled through his papers until he found what he was looking for. Behind him the cleaning staff had already begun to straighten the room, and the cool air from the open windows felt good to each of them. Chadwell was left to sleep undisturbed. Sir Joseph glanced out through the rain. It sounded restful, and he was very, very tired.

Whitehall. 08:10 Hours

"This morning I greet you with the worst news since our predecessors were forced to declare that England was at war. In many ways I, too, must make this declaration in the absence of the Prime Minister. England has been invaded by an unknown number of disease-carrying bats capable of inflicting heavy casualties among both civilians and the military. It is very difficult for me to have to admit that this enemy has emerged from within our own country. You are all aware by this time of the critical situation with which we as a country are faced. I therefore call upon you to bring together a desire to help destroy this menace. It is a time when all the resources of the country will be tapped, and it is a time for you all to call upon yourselves and your own resources to protect yourself and your families."

Sir Joseph leaned forward and adjusted the volume. With the Major and Murray he watched Lord Tenningly address the Nation and he was thankful that it had been decided his own appearance wasn't necessary. The minutes ticked slowly by, and he was happy to see Tenningly finally begin his closing statement. It was typical.

"This, then, is the situation as it stands at the moment. We must prepare for the worst, and pray for the best. We must all—everyone of us—pull together to fight this enemy which has invaded our country. We are getting help and advice from highly experienced sources and we are taking every step to ensure a quick end to this menace. With your co-operation casualties will be kept to a minimum, and the military will be able to arrest the spread of the disease before it can do any great damage." He stared into the camera. "Thank you."

Sir Joseph switched off the set. "We know the rest,"

he sighed. "Seventeen cases so far, and I bet Comcent has a few more already."

"What about the Continent?" Murray asked. "France has reported three cases and East Germany is screaming deliberate aggression."

"Naturally," replied the Major drily. "Moscow'll be shouting that half a dozen bats have arrived in the Kremlin."

"There goes the Common Market," Sir Joseph whispered.

"Surely the countries will accept this for what it is," the Major offered, "After all, you're getting the worst of it."

"Ah, yes," he replied. "But any country looking for an excuse to poke holes in our government policy has it on a silver platter."

"Including the opposition," Murray said.

"And they're the bastards who started all this," Sir Joseph said without thinking. He didn't like to swear.

Murray toyed with his watch strap until he remembered the time. He looked at the Major who was staring idly into space. "Your friend will be arriving any time now."

Sir Joseph glanced up. "Yes, by all means, take the Major downstairs. I should think they'll be using the security entrance."

Murray rose. "It'll do you good to see each other. I had a call from Mac this morning, but I didn't want to mention anything to you straight away. He's not very well, Major. Wouldn't eat breakfast and still seems rather close to tears most of the time."

"I don't suppose I could take him for a walk?"

Sir Joseph was thinking. "Look, Major. I'll book you out of here for an hour. Use the security entrance— Murray'll show you when he takes you down. Leave at nine fifteen and be back no later than ten ten. If you aren't, we automatically start looking."

"What about things here?"

"I don't think things'll really start hopping much before lunch. I've called an assembly for one fifteen so you'll have plenty of time to prepare whatever you want. When you get back, stay with the boy. Murray can let you know when you're wanted."

The phone rang. Sir Joseph answered it, mumbled an acknowledgement and rang off. "He's downstairs now."

Belfast Avenue, Slough, Bucks. 09:00 Hours

"Bloody bats and anthrax and Christ knows what," Mr. Monks swore heatedly. "Bleedin' marvellous, isn't it? Last night a whole village wiped out, and to-day the bloody government is telling us we're at war again. All because of some flipping experiment Lord Whatever-his-name-is dreamed up." He leant forward and switched off his telly. "Still, I suppose this means I get some time off. Damned if I'm going marching around the trading estate with them creatures dropping down everywhere. Mind you, I'll get me wages—work or no work. Let the bloody government pay for it—they started it, didn't they?"

Mrs. Monks hastened back into the kitchen. "I don't like it, Fred," she said nervously. "It scares me, all these bats laying about the place and all. What if Sally finds one? She won't know to stay away, will she?"

"Then don't let her outside. You heard what they said."

"Ha!" she cried. "You try stopping her. You don't have to mind her all day like I do. You don't know what she's like."

"Yeah, well it looks like I'm going to have plenty of

time to find out, doesn't it? Maybe get to know me own daughter again."

Mrs. Monks reappeared with more tea. "Do you think we're in a danger area?"

"So bloody what if we are? According to that newscaster there was a bat found in the bleeding High Street last night. Wonder what poor sod found that one?"

Mrs. Monks handed her husband his tea and moved towards the window. She was visibly shaken even before Sally entered clutching her teddy.

"Here's my darling," cried her father, holding out his arms. "Come to Daddy."

"I don't feel well, mummy," she whimpered, clutching her already squashed teddy harder. "I feel funny."

Mrs. Monks' jittery hands turned to shaking blobs as she stared from Sally to her husband to the telly and back to Sally. Slowly her cup dribbled tea over the side until it crashed to the floor.

"I feel sick, mummy." She took a hesitant step towards her mother. She backed against the window. The little girl began to cry, and she took another step forward. Mrs. Monks began to sidle along the edge of the wall, her eyes wide with terror.

"Get away," she whispered between clenched teeth. "Don't come near me."

The little girl cried louder. Mrs. Monks moved further along until she reached the corner.

"But mummy, please mummy . . ."..

"Stay away!" she screamed hysterically. "Don't come any closer." She was crying, sobbing, covering her face.

Mr. Monks leapt up and grabbed Sally. He looked from his daughter to his wife. "For God's sake, what's the matter with you?"

"I don't want to die," his wife cried, falling into a heap on the floor. "Please, I don't want to die. Not that way."

Mr. Monks walked away with his daughter. He shook his head and swore.

"I have a tummy ache, Daddy," the little girl was saying. "What's wrong with mummy?"

Whitehall. 09:00 Hours

Major Thomas followed Murray down the corridor which led to the security entrance. He felt chilled by the pale green walls and exposed pipes deep below the building. It was cold and impersonal. It was just like security. He looked at Murray who nodded in the direction they were going. "He's just around the corner. Should be at least."

As they turned the corner, the Major saw Trevor. He looked pale and lonely; his head was bowed sullenly and his right hand still trembled. When the guard spoke to him he only shook his head.

"Hi," said the Major. "Waiting for me?"

"No one'll let me move," he replied. "Where am I?"

Thomas grinned at the guard. "Top secret." He put his arm around the lad's shoulders and led him towards the lift. He could feel him trembling uncontrollably. He would have to find some more oxime. "Aren't you going to say hello to Mr. Murray?"

He looked up at Murray and tried to smile. "Where are we going?"

"This will be your home for awhile," Murray explained, holding open the doors to the lift. "We thought you might like to be near friends."

Trevor stared at the panel of glowing lights. A green lamp flashed and moments later the doors swung open.

"Fourth floor," Murray began. "All out."

"How do you like your accommodation?" Thomas asked. "Better than that old hotel, huh?"

"Yes, I guess so."

"Well, follow me and I'll show you to your suite," Murray announced, flowing his arms about and bowing. "Nothing but the best for our young subjects."

"Does it have a telly?"

"Color telly if I know this place."

The Major glanced at Murray. He was worried. No doubt the television would be saturated with the warnings and newsmen's latest discoveries. "How about a record player and all the pop stuff or whatever you call it."

"I don't mind. Have to do something, don't I?"

Murray opened the door to the rooms. "After you."

Trevor entered. He looked about, spotted the heavily quilted bed among the expensive furnishings which meant nothing to him and sank down on the mattress. He hung his legs over the side and held his hand.

"Like it?" asked Murray.

He didn't answer. Thomas thought he saw tears coming. He turned to Murray.

"I'll, ah, I'll see what Sir Joseph is up to," he said. I'll come back when he wants you." He made to leave. "Oh, and if you do go for a walk, be sure to be back by ten ten. Sir Joseph wasn't joking when he said they'll be after you."

"Thanks," he replied softly, closing the door.

"Major," he whispered, just before it clicked shut. "He'll be all right."

He nodded. He stood by the door a moment, then padded silently across the thick carpet and sat alongside Trevor. The boy hung his head and sniffed.

"Better try this again, huh?" he said, offering his handkerchief. "We seem to get through quite a lot of these, eh?"

Trevor stared at the officer. He wiped his eyes with his sleeve.

"Feeling a bit rough, huh?"

He nodded without lifting his eyes from the floor.

"It's pretty rough for a lot of people out there."

"The bats?" he choked.

"The bats—and anthrax. It's coming down everywhere it seems."

"Is that why you brought me down here?"

"Partly, I guess. I thought you might like some company."

He tried to smile without looking up.

The Major gently swung Trevor's legs onto the bed. "Why don't you lie down for a spell. Might make you feel better."

"You won't leave, will you?"

"Do you want me to?"

Trevor looked up at him. The fringe of his hair was damp. He shook his head.

"Thinking of your mum and dad, huh?"

He nodded. "And everything inside me hurts?"

"I think I know how you feel—about your folks, I mean. I lost my father when I was fourteen. I lost someone very dear to me a couple of years ago."

He looked up at him.

"My wife. She was killed in an accident. We'd been married eight years."

"My dad's first wife was killed in a car crash," he whispered.

Thomas hesitated. "Trevor, would you like to go to America with me?"

"With you?"

"With me. To the United States."

He stared up at the ceiling. The Major studied him. His blonde hair was matted and uncut and flopped over his forehead. A splodge of mud or chocolate smeared his cheek. Somewhere, something touched him, and he knew he was growing fond of the lonesome boy.

He hated to see the suffering and agony he knew he himself had suffered. He felt the loneliness and despair. He could see it in the lad's face, in his quivering lip and trembling shoulders. He watched as Trevor wiped his eyes.

"I'll be leaving when all this is over. Maybe you'd like to come with me. I've got some friends in America who can cure this pain you have."

He rolled onto his side and faced the wall, picking at a piece of wallpaper with his finger. "Will you be coming back?"

"Sometime, I expect. It's not cheap to fly over here, you know. Even with that pregnant plane they got."

"I won't see you again unless I go with you?"

"No, I don't expect you will." He paused and put his hand on his shoulder. "I'd like you to come, you know. That is if you'd like to come."

He kept picking at the wall. Tears began to stain the pale blue bedcover.

"Listen to me, Trevor. You're going to get a lot of people who'll be telling you to buck up and that you've got to start putting back the pieces and begin again. I got it from all sides when Ann died. It's not what you want to hear, I know, but they're right. Try to think about what's ahead of you in the next few years. If you think there's a place for me in those years, you come to America with me. If you'd rather fight it out here in your own country, I'll understand how you feel. And I guess we can arrange to have you treated here so you're healthy again. But don't let things get you down too far, eh? You know, your mom and dad loved you very much and they would want you to grow up happy. If they were around now, they'd do everything they could to help you. But now someone else has to carry on where they left off. I've never had a son—I would have if Ann hadn't been killed, but we could sort of combine our

losses and try it, huh?" He forced a laugh. "I don't suppose for a minute I'm making much of a job of it now,
but I do want you to know that there is someone around
when you need, when you need to turn to somebody—
even if it is a grumpy old Army Major."

"I guess I'll have to go with you," he choked, trying
hard to hold back the tears and face him. His tense
muscles were relaxing.

"No, Trevor," he replied, taking hold of his shoulders.
."You don't have to go. I'm sure there are friends here
who would take good care of you, but if you want to
come, I'll be glad to make room for you."

"Can I see my mates again before we go?"

The Major closed his eyes and smiled. "Sure you can,
son. You can see all your mates, and maybe someday we
could invite a couple of them to America. How would
you like that?

"They'd like that, I guess."

He ruffled his hair. "Yea, I guess they would, wouldn't
they?"

Trevor wiped his face again. His sleeve was soaking.
He looked sheepishly at the Major and grinned.

"Do you think you'd like to take a walk?"

He wrinkled his forehead. "Yeah, kind of."

"I've got us a free pass out of this jail if you'd like
to come now. We've been given an hour's leave of
absence."

Trevor tried to take a deep breath as he sat up. The
Major put his hands under his shoulders and lifted him,
laughing and pulling him close. "You can tell who's out
of shape now!"

"I thought all you Army blokes were so keen on
muscles."

He held him away. "When you get to be a Major you
let everyone else do the dirty work. Come on, give your
face a wash and we'll go."

172

Monday. 10:00 Hours

"To-day throughout the country, on roads and highways, in the air and on the water, troops of the Army, Air Force and Navy are converging at specially designated areas. In Caernarvon—scene of the Investiture not long ago—men and machines have replaced the ceremonial aurora. From there to Colwyn Bay to Chester, along the A41 to Wolverhampton, to Birmingham, on the A45 to Northampton and Bedford, through Hertford, Chelmsford and on to Southend, over three hundred miles of roads, men from the British and American forces are taking up their positions. More troops have gathered at Luton, Gatwick and Heathrow Air Terminals and at other smaller airports once open to the public. Ports and railway stations have been taken over, and the country is under a net of total quarantine. In London Hyde Park resembles a battlefield as men from London barracks meet and encamp. It is a strange mixture of Horseguards, Household Calvary, Grenadiers and the Scots and Irish Guards and of other regulars drafted in from miles around.

"Cities within the vast perimeter established by the government are quiet, seemingly desolate and empty—ominous without the Monday morning rush. Birmingham, Bristol and London appear lifeless, less crowded than are the shopping districts on a Sunday. People throughout England and Wales have imposed their own quarantine as they wait and watch. Already the government has postponed their latest statement over two hours while they finalize their plans, but from the movements of the military, the shutdown of transport services and the strict quarantine, it is clear that they are taking no chances."

The newscaster looked up, pressed a tiny earphone closer and listened. "We have just heard that the statement by Lord Tenningly, is now scheduled for ten fifteen. That's in," he glanced at his watch, "just over ten minutes." He rifled through some papers. "To recap the situation as it now stands, England, Scotland and Wales have been placed under a State of Emergency and quarantined. No person or craft, either boat or plane, may land or depart. A further internal quarantine exists stretching from Caernarvon to Southend and Dover. Along this route the military are taking up positions, concentrating on the larger towns and cities. It is not yet known the precise purpose behind these maneuvers, but no doubt it will be explained in the government's statement."

He rifled some more papers. "Unofficial observers near the stricken village of Stumford in Devonshire now place the total death toll at one thousand, including those areas adjacent. Reports of infected bats both confirmed and unconfirmed now total twenty-four, and there have been at least eleven deaths known to occur as a direct result of anthrax contamination. The sightings have been in Ilfracombe, Barnstaple and Crediton, Devonshire; Pontypridd near Cardiff, South Wales; Sharpness and Cheltenham, Gloucestershire; Worcester and Redditch, Worcestershire; Wolverhampton and Warwick; Beckington near the Salisbury Plain; Christchurch, Bognor Regis and Cowes on the Isle of Wight, and around London the sightings have been confirmed in Thatcham near Newbury, Camberly, Horsham, Dorking, Croydon, Slough and Watford. So far this morning there have been five additional sightings and it is anticipated that to-day will carry the highest number of sightings as the bats will by this time have been brought down by the automatic timing mechanism.

"There is as yet no report on the condition of the Prime Minister who was last night pulled from the wreckage of the Edinburgh Express. Rescue operations there have been hampered severely by the presence of suspected anthrax, and there are still many people trapped in the crash. Lord Tenningly has unofficially taken over in the absence of the Prime Minister, and it is understood that Sir Joseph Willets has reconvened Parliament on a stand-by basis." He glanced off-screen, nodded and turned to the camera. "Now follows a broadcast by Lord Tenningly from the Ministry of Defense, Whitehall, scene of the command operations. This message will be carried by all television networks and radio."

The familiar face which the people had begun to associate with trouble, hardship and loss appeared again.

Salisbury Plain, 10:15 Hours

If someone had estimated the percentage of the public who were aware of the Dwarf Hill incident and the resulting plague of bats, they would have had to take into consideration the very few who still lived without telephone, television or radio, or whose residence was such that outside communication was limited. There would be a small number of homes scattered about the Highlands of Scotland, but these people were well clear of the danger area. Other similar homes in remote areas would equally be fairly safe from the bats. Therefore, the government could rest assured in the knowledge that the vast majority of England, Wales and Scotland were fully aware of the situation. There were, however, a few but very important exceptions.

Ten Scouts from the 46th Troop, Paddington, along with their leader had left early Saturday morning for an expedition into the Salisbury Plain and they weren't planning on returning until Tuesday morning. Reaching their campsite by Saturday night and well away from the reach of the outside world, they had pitched camp and dedicated themselves to putting into practice the theory they had learnt in London.

"Take the stones," instructed Scout Leader David Madigan, "and lay them flat so no animal knocks them over. Lay them in a straight line and put the biggest in the direction you're going. There. If you make this marking every five hundred feet or so, you can never get lost."

"What if it's foggy?" Simon asked, staring around at the emptiness of the place.

"Then you don't go out hiking. If you're already out and it gets foggy, what do you do?" He glanced around for a show of hands. "Peter?"

"Stay put or else you'll go around in circles."

"Right. Now who's been keeping track of our direction? Tony?"

"We've been traveling due north, Sir. About three miles from camp."

Madigan checked his compass. "Full marks. It's easy to get lost out here so the compass is your most precious companion." He was praying his still worked.

"What's this, Sir?" Martin asked, poking at the ground with his shoe.

"It's a bird, idiot," Madigan announced without walking over to investigate himself. "And it looks dead."

"But it doesn't look like a bird, Sir."

"Why not? Have you seen every kind of bird there is?"

"No, Sir. But birds have feathers."

Madigan decided he better make the best of it. "Well come on. Bring it over here. Let's have a look at this featherless bird."

Martin picked it up between his thumb and index finger and held it away. "Doesn't look half horrible."

"So do you when you're dead. Bring it here."

The Scouts gathered around Martin as he deposited his

discovery at the Leader's feet. "There, Sir. That's no bird."

"Course it's not a bird," Madigan said as if he had known all along. "It's a bat. Must be a special one, too. Do you all see the metal band on its leg? This means he's been banded by some ornithological society so that its movements can be traced. Here, if we take down the number of the band, the owners can usually be traced. Simon, read it out."

Simon knelt down and poked it with his finger. "It's all stiff, Sir."

"Couldn't be dead long, then."

Simon lifted the hind foot of the bat and tried to read the inscription on the band. "There's no numbers on it, Sir."

"Then what is on it. There must be something. People just don't stick bands on bats for nothing."

"It says Minuvdef."

"Martin, you read it. Spell it out."

Martin squinted at the band. "M-i-n space o-f space D-e-f. Min of Def—that's what it says."

"Min of death," repeated Simon. "That's what I said."

"Min of Def?" Madigan puzzled. "Ministry of Defense. Of course. Well, must be a spy or something."

A few of the Scouts giggled.

"The bat from MI5, what? Well, we can ring up the Ministry of Defense when we get back to London and tell them we found one of their bats lying around."

"There's something else, Sir," Peter began, having looked around for more bats. "It's a pill or something."

Madigan looked at the capsule-like object Peter had discovered. He squeezed it and nothing happened. "Here, see if you can cut it, Simon."

Simon gladly withdrew his knife, placed the tin capsule on one of the directional stones and smashed it open with his knife.

177

"I said cut it, you fool. Now, what's in it?"

"Powder," he announced, rubbing some in his fingers. "Must be a pill."

"Who ever heard of a metal pill?" The leader frowned, wondering what to do about these discoveries. "Well, we can tell the Ministry that we found their bat and a suspicious pill full of powder. Let's go."

"Sir?"

"Yes, Martin."

"Maybe it was a special bat that was smuggling in heroin or something. You know, the pill was attached to it."

"Why, Martin, would the Ministry of Defense try to smuggle in heroin? If they want heroin, I'm sure they can get it without having to resort to smuggling."

Martin shrugged. He liked the idea. It gave him something to think about while 'Sir' waffled on about natural studies, rock formations and how to survive in the wilds of Salisbury Plain.

Whitehall. 10:30 Hours

Murray stood up from his chair, Major Thomas and Chadwell were still listening to Lord Tenningly's address. Murray looked across Sir Joseph's desk into the liquor locker; he smiled—there was yet another bottle unopened. He poured three glasses, and though he knew Chadwell hated whiskey, handed them out and took his over to the window and leant against the curtain.

"Why doesn't he shut up?" he mumbled. He smiled, shook his head. He frowned. "Why the bloodly hell doesn't he shut up?" he shouted suddenly, throwing his glass angrily against the door. "Damn it, he makes me sick."

Chadwell didn't look up. "Easy on, old man, or they'll have you put away. He's only doing his best."

"And a fat lot of good that's going to do a lot of people. What good's it doing anyone? What good's it going to do for those kids?"

Thomas glanced around the side of his chair. "They knew what they were doing was wrong, Murray. Christ, they had the area sealed off—their parents must have told them Stumford was off limits."

"Damn it, Major—should it be off limits? Those kids were just curious. And now look—they're dead as the rest of them. And *he* just babbles on about sticking together through all of this."

"Let him be," Chadwell said. "He's just got a touch of what we all get around here at sometime or another. You should have seen the guilty faces when that coal tip collapsed. "Who's fault was that?" everyone asked."

Murray sagged into Sir Joseph's chair. He looked up at the chandelier. "Sorry. He just gets on my wick—that's all."

Thomas stared at him. "Want another drink?"

He pushed away from the desk. "Thanks all the same, but I might do something I'd regret."

"Like resigning," offered Chadwell. "Or a leave of absence. Say you're a confirmed alcoholic. And you know I hate this stuff."

"Chadwell, why don't you go to hell?"

There was a tinkle of glass. The door opened and Sir Joseph was looking at the stain on the carpet.

Murray rose from the chair and leaned against the wall. "My fault."

"Slipped," said the Major.

"Like hell it did," Murray admitted. "I threw it."

"I hope it felt good," Sir Joseph replied, closing the door. "Only you've left a scratch."

"I'll mend it myself."

"How's his Lordship doing?" Sir Joseph asked, ignoring his offer and slipping into one of the vacant chairs in front of the television.

"Might reassure the people a little," Chadwell replied. "But it's nothing we haven't heard before."

"How's it going outside?" Thomas asked.

"As one might expect. The military are moving well, but there's a delay in the disinfectant. Something about too much phenol and too little something else. Apparently the test batch burned a hole in some chap's arm when they put it through its paces. By the way, you'll be leaving tonight," Sir Joseph finished, turning to the Major.

"Where to?"

"Comcent got a message from your Detrick group. They're flying over a transport with a bunch of your men. They want you to rendezvous at Ruislip and fill them in."

"Know what they're bringing?"

"Very little so I understand, but two other transports are due in just after them with your back-pumps and some other equipment." He paused. "I suppose you'll be wanting to take the boy with you."

He rubbed his chin. "Any other ideas?"

"One."

"Yeah?"

"I've got a house in Stake Poges not far from the airfield. My wife would be glad to look after him for awhile. Might be better if he's kept away from all this."

He stared at the television before nodding in agreement. "Yea, it would be good for him."

"Getting quite close to the lad, aren't you?"

"We have something in common."

"Shall I ring my wife then?"

"If you think it wouldn't put her out. He's still a bit shaky."

"I'll drive him up this afternoon when I go. No, better yet, I'll drive you to the base and then take the boy on. Give you two a chance to talk things over a bit more before he goes. Maybe make him feel better—oh, and Dr. Marsh has given this to me. He said you'd know what it was." Sir Joseph withdrew a small plastic box from his pocket and handed it to the Major.

Thomas seemed surprised at the least. "Where did you get this from?"

"Dr. Marsh," he repeated. "He said he'd let you have it if no questions were asked."

Murray was intrigued. Whatever it was had shocked Thomas visibly. "What is it?"

"It's a special serum for Detrick," Thomas mumbled, fondling the box. "It's *supposed* to be highly classified."

Sir Joseph enjoyed the Major's surprise.

"What's so special about it?" Murray persisted.

"It's a cholinesterase stimulant."

Murray raised his eyebrows.

"Trevor's body is restricted in its production of acetycholinesterase. That's an enzyme used in nerve signal transmission. If his body cannot produce enough of this enzyme, he builds up a surplus of cholinesterase which would eventually kill him if it isn't neutralised. That's how people die when they come into contact with nerve gas. Luckily, Trevor's system can still produce enough acetycholinesterase to neutralise much of the cholinesterase, but not enough to stop the continual pain he's in."

Murray wasn't sure he got the last bit right, but he nodded in sensible agreement.

"This stimulant here," Thomas continued, "is a much more sophisticated version of the stuff I gave him in

Chesterly—your oxime. This will last much longer with much better effects."

Chadwell peeped around the corner of his chair. "Of all the cheek, Major. You were quite ready to use our oxime—which you shouldn't have had in the first place."

"And you've got ours. Still, it will be used in a good cause."

Murray touched the side of his nose. "What do you think they pay us for? Probably got a few more secrets stashed away somewhere, too."

"I was sure I'd have to ask Detrick to send some over." He pocketed the case.

"Say," Murray began, leaning against the desk. "You wouldn't want to adopt me I suppose. I could do with a trip to America."

"Who's adopting?" demanded Thomas. "I just want this stuff for the kid."

"I did. It's as obvious as the nose on your great ugly face. I mean, you're not going to leave him to rot in this country, are you?"

Chadwell turned to Sir Joseph. "I'm afraid Paddy over there has developed a sudden streak of disloyalty."

"I'm as loyal as the next bloke. I just don't like the idea of sharing my pension with some itinerant bat."

A new face appeared on the television. It was the newscaster. Chadwell leaned forward and switched off.

The room grew silent. Major Thomas yawned and glanced at his watch. "Any chance of some coffee?"

Sir Joseph nodded at Murray. "And bring in some biscuits—not those stale horrible things either." He turned back to the Major. "How is the boy this morning?"

"A bit lost, I guess. I probably pushed the idea of his going to America too soon."

"Nonsense. Something else for him to think about."

"Quite a lot to think about, I'd say," said Chadwell. "What are you going to do once you've got him there?"

"Haven't really given it much thought yet," he lied. "Get him fixed up at Detrick then send him to school, to college. I don't even know what interests him."

"Football. Got plenty of that in America?" Chadwell continued. "Give him a football and that's what he'll be interested in."

"Keep him out of politics and the civil service and he'll do all right," Sir Joseph mused. "And the Army."

"The Army is right," Thomas agreed, sitting on the edge of the desk. "Not the way it is today."

"I had a son once, you know," Sir Joseph began, playing with the end of his pencil. "I made him go into the Army when he was fifteen. Cadets and all that. I thought maybe it might toughen him up a bit."

"Did he like it?"

"Oh, he put on a good show, all right. To please me more than anything else. Inside he was hating it. Wanted to be a doctor. I told him he had plenty of time to study medicine when he got out." He smiled. "I was younger then. I had just become MP for Croyden—you remember, Chadwell? But one day he grew careless. He was on the training field. He and his mates were supposed to be looking for unexploded shells. One of them—no one ever knew who—tossed a few rocks around and, boom! No more son. One other boy was killed, one blinded. The other lost both legs." He stared at his pencil, blinked and shook his head. "You try to forget it, but it keeps coming back. Even after thirty years it still hurts."

Murray pushed open the door. "That was lucky—trolley was just down the corridor." He laid the tray on the desk and looked at the sombre faces. "Well, isn't anybody going to have anything?"

Southampton Waters. 11:00 Hours

"Permission to dock is definitely refused, Sir. We are instructed to turn about and hold in the Channel."

The Commander frowned and stared over the bridge. He caught sight of some passengers on the Quarter Deck. "Get those people off there," he snapped angrily.

"Aye, aye, Sir," replied the Signal Officer and disappeared out the side door.

The Commander turned to his Navigation Officer and seeing no one at hand mumbled, "I've got two thousand passengers on this ship and I'm supposed to hang about in the channel. What the blazes is going on out there?"

"Shall I send a signal, Sir?"

"Signal? What Signal?"

"That we're turning about. We can't just sit here, Sir."

"Damn it, boy, I know that. Yes, send your blasted signal. And tell them we can't last it out more than twenty-four hours."

The Signal Officer returned, took the message and hopped it down to the communications room. "Elizabeth Two, over."

"Go ahead, Elizabeth Two."

"Message received. We are turning about. Will report our holding co-ordinates when ready. And the Commander requests permission to dock within twenty-four hours. Over."

"Message received, Elizabeth Two. Over and out."

As the giant ship swung about, the Commander's voice boomed out through every tannoy in the ship. High above, just beyond the gleaming single funnel, a few people noticed a black speck fluttering unsuredly. It reeled to port, flew back to starboard and dropped lower. A sea gull, most thought, and they turned away to listen to the Commander. The black speck grew larger still, stopped fluttering, dropped, fluttered once or twice again, and fell. Some who saw it thought it had missed the ship. Others thought it landed near the funnel. There was little interest. Instead was another day at sea. Slowly, ever so slowly, the Isle of Wight slipped past them and soon that too was a forgotten speck.

The Perimeter. 12:00 Hours

Harlech had been given up as a Safe Base and in its place soldiers built up at Caernarvon Castle. It was the same across the country. In the larger cities troops encamped in parks and playing fields, and along the perimeter track the roads were blocked by troop transports, half-tracks and supply trucks. Commanding Officers were left to decide where exactly to best organize their men between the Safe Bases, and frequently cows, pigs and sheep found themselves sharing quarters with several hundred soldiers. Few of the men knew what the deployment was all about—many regarded it as a tactical exercise, and even the COs were a bit vague on their instructions sent down by Whitehall. They had been issued with hastily drawn maps which indicated the perimeter track and told to set up along the thin red line. Various regiments were assigned so many miles of track to cover, and when it was found that the track was too sparsely covered to be of practical use, extra detachments were sent in. It was planned that every mile of the three hundred odd miles of track could be evenly guarded, but whatever areas were too awkward or inaccessible would be watched by air support. The idea seemed to be working well, at least in troop deployment. There were easily enough men for the job, and as the perimeter followed the paths of main roadways, it was the easiest tactical exercise the soldiers had yet encountered. Drivers were told simply to reach such-and-such a town by midday where the COs would direct them to their actual base. Where there were not towns or very small villages, the men pitched tents in surrounding fields, most of which had only just been hayed. The plan went quickly and smoothly even if the skepticism was mounting.

It was intentionally planned that another line of troops would guard the perimeter track to maintain the internal quarantine as well as assist with decontamination exercises. This line was established as near to the main perimeter track as roads would permit, but as the country roads were few and far between, the quarantine perimeter was often several miles from the points at which the main support troops camped. Colonel Combs had hoped this would be the case. He wanted as little discussion among the men as possible as their private speculation might easily breed fear and mistrust. Citizens would be eager to talk with single sentries posted along the quarantine track, and from them the sentries would learn more of the outbreak. But people would be far less inclined to go marching into a military camp with only the idea of idle chit-chat. Combs knew that fighting an enemy as undetectable and deadly as the anthrax could spread as much panic and unrest among the soldiers as it might among the public.

By nightfall the perimeter track was complete. The country was divided in half.

Coastal Waters. 14:30 Hours

There were few troops stationed at Holyhead as the main spearhead for Wales was encamped at Caernarvon. There was very little these soldiers could do, therefore, to prevent a small scale exodus via the Irish Sea. Many local villagers and many from as far East as Somerset had taken to the water in the hope of avoiding contamination. It was too early for the military to have closed roadways within the perimeter, they hadn't even begun their trek towards Lands End. So families with boats and trailers headed West, towards the Welsh coast, as well as some who dared the Channel, thinking France was the safest country at the moment. The Navy caught most and forced them to return, but even had many of them crept through undetected, France was in no mood to allow anyone near her shores. She was having exactly the same problems as England, and it wasn't long before the French Navy surrounded her coastline and small escort boats from the French Navy were taking the English back to the Royal Naval Patrols, and the Royal Navy escorted curious French boaters back to their shores. Not since Normandy had there been such chaos in the Channel.

As the hope of flight by water grew, however, the Channel was awash with small family craft, trying first to avoid the English patrols, then the French and vice versa. Those who made it through found they daren't dock for fear of being caught by Customs and police patrols, and many simply gave up and turned about voluntarily. A few managed to look on the bright side and chalked it up to a good day's outing in miserable weather—with the added thrill of dodging Navy patrol vessels. The more persistent often greeted each other whom they had begun to recognize in their repeated efforts to reach one another's country, and some stopped long enough to share a drink and exchange information. For the most part what was originally planned as a last ditch effort to escape turned into a comic fiasco which even the Navies looked upon as rather humorous.

The picture was very much different in the Irish Sea. Royal Navy Patrols were scarce and it was little trouble to get within hailing distance of the Irish coast. But the people of Northern Ireland were frightened: though no bats had yet reached their shores, they were afraid that the English might bring the disease with them. When the first wave of British families struggled ashore and the local peasants learned of their arrival, they set up their own barriers against the invaders. At first content with shouting abuses and scaring the boats away with stones, sticks and clumps of earth, their fear gave way to more hostile precautions when the boats arrived more frequently and more persistently. By the time the police—many of whom turned a blind eye to the less dangerous enforcement of the villagers' private quarantine—had realized that a small army was gathering along the coastal waters, the first fatality had occurred.

A small single engined outboard had been fighting the sea for several hours and the occupants were cold and wet. As it bobbed its way shoreward, several villagers gathered to warn it off in the accepted method, but the engine's unsteady staccato muted any verbal warnings. When the craft struggled to within a hundred yards of shore, the locals sent up a barrage of sticks and stones, bottles and anything else near at hand. But the boat pushed onward. Realizing, however, that they were hardly welcome, a young woman stood up in the boat, clutching her baby and shouted. The father was leaning forward in the bow with his hands cupped about his lips in a vain effort to explain their plight. Their son manned the engine, trying desperately to force more speed out of her before the petrol was consumed. Now, within a couple of hundred feet of shore, the villagers grew angry and resentful. One grabbed his shotgun, aimed, and pulled both triggers simultaneously. The mother and child were peppered with shot and blown overboard by the blast. The father's face was perforated with a dozen holes as he fell backwards and landed face up on the floorboards. The terrified boy leapt forward, waving his arms frantically, but before he could utter a word, another roar from ashore blew him back ten feet across the water, his right arm and shoulder ripped clean away.

News of the shooting spread quickly along the coast. The elimination of one family seemed to justify the elimination of others. They were enemies. They carried with them a deadly killer and so they had to be destroyed. The rocks and abusive language gave way to volleys of shotgun blasts. Youngsters lined the shore with .22's and pellet rifles. Families in smaller crafts were wiped out in a single round and other boats simply blew up. It became a game. There was even a point system. Slowly, the police came round to the troubled situation and began to inform the Navy.

Whitehall. 16:00 Hours

Colonel Combs, Admiral Downing-Wright and Air Marshall Coff stood around a large table map decorated with red lines and tiny colored flags. Combs was especially pleased. It reminded him of the War Office, and the feeling of battle; of pitting wits against the enemy. It stimulated his imagination. Little did he care that the tiny flags he poked about with his stick were troops of men who were rapidly growing tired of playing the pawns on the chessboard of Great Britain. Combs had reshuffled the Bases, and put them back again when air reconaissance advised him that the original Bases were better. The perimeter line had been adjusted again and again, sometimes only because Comb's recollection of the scenery appealed to him more than the practicality of deployment.

"This then," he began, "is the situation at present. Most of the roads are occupied as planned. Ships of the Navy are positioned in the Channel here, here and here, and ten patrol vessels have been diverted to the Irish Sea. The Air Force are now flying spraying aircraft in dummy runs. I should think we'll be ready by nightfall."

"We'll be ready," said Coff. "But will the disinfectant?"

"I don't know, really," he replied offhandedly. "There are three companies working on it now, but last reports have it that they were no closer to neutralizing the phenol. Should have left it up to Porton."

The door opened. "The teleprinters are ready, Sir. Can we rig up now?"

Colonel Combs looked away from his maps. "Yes, certainly. And have you my phones yet?"

"We hope to have them working by six, Sir."

"Good," He returned to his maps. "I've had communications duplicate their receiving printers in here so we have the progress reports as soon as they come in. Saves Chadwell running back and forth. The phones will give us linkups with our field operations. Damned if I'm running into Comcent every time I want to know what's going on."

Admiral Downing-Wright was wondering who was in charge of his ships when Sir Joseph pushed in behind the workmen.

"There you are, Colonel Combs. Lord Tenningly wants a plot on your map of the sightings and your troop deployment by five. He's coming round in half an hour for a conference." He looked at Coff. "He wants you to arrange for him to survey the perimeter track at first light tomorrow."

"Where from?"

"Heathrow, I think. That's if they've got that mess cleared up. We're waiting for clearance now."

Colonel Combs was searching a drawer beneath the table. "I'll need some more markers. Can you get me some?"

Sir Joseph nodded. "I'll have Martin send some up. Get what you want off him."

Chadwell suddenly appeared looking pale and worried. Murray followed him in. "More trouble, Sir. Lots of it."

"Bats?"

"Bats and a massacre in the Irish Sea."

"A what in the Irish Sea?"

"A massacre. People—murdered. Shot dead."

Sir Joseph turned to the Admiral. "I thought you had that area sorted out."

"We had—or so I thought," he replied, leaning over the map. "Combs had placed eight destroyer markers in the Irish Sea Zone, and I had twenty patrol boats in the Channel keeping our people from France. Then I find out that Combs' markers were in theory—not in actual position."

Combs blushed. It was rare for him to err.

"I've sent some ships in there, though, so whatever happened should be dealt with by now."

"Then what's all this about murder?" Sir Joseph asked.

"They're firing on anyone who comes near the shore." Chadwell explained. "There're boats and bodies all over the place."

Colonel Combs stared at Coff. "You better get some air support in there. Try to head them back or something."

"Aren't the police doing anything?"

"They are now, but it's a bit late."

Murray was shaking his head. "Whole bloody country's gone mad."

Sir Joseph glanced at the map. "Colonel Combs, I want a detachment of your own men flown to Ireland. Whip them off the line if you have to."

"We've still got some regiments in Belfast. I'll start with them." He looked at the two remaining blocks in his hand, shook them, and dumped them in the Irish Sea.

"That's not all," Chadwell spouted, moving nearer the map. "It's the perimeter track."

"What's wrong with it?" Combs demanded indignantly. "Not good enough or something?"

"Comcent has just had two sightings. One here at Wrexham and one at Wellingborough, here. That one at Wrexham put your perimeter about thirty miles below the mark."

"Are they sure?" asked Sir Joseph. "Has anyone confirmed it?"

"The Wrexham sighting is confirmed. No report on the other one."

Sir Joseph stared at Combs who was looking mournfully at his map. He frowned. "That means pushing Caernavon out to Llandudno and raising the line to Flint."

"And what if another bat decides that's not high enough?" asked Murray. "Exactly how far can you push this line?"

"As far as we need to," Combs snapped. "Unless you've thought of something else."

"I have—or at least a modification."

Combs glowered at him. It better be good. "Well, we're all waiting."

Murray moved closer to the map. He looked over it carefully. "Can I have some markers?"

"We haven't any more," the Colonel replied.

"Then I'll use these," he said picking up a handful of perimeter markers. Combs looked ready to burst. Murray began placing the markers where the bats had been found nearest the line. "If you see, gentlemen, these bats have begun to form a sort of a pattern. They have somehow homed in on London and Birmingham—with a few scattered exceptions. If they were somehow programmed or guided to seek out large cities—or if they prefer large cities for some reason known only to them—

192

then this is where your concentration of men should be."

"Conjecture," the Colonel retorted. "Pure guesswork."

"Then what is this red line, Colonel?"

"Damned careful planning, that's what it is. It's based on Sir Godfrey's findings. He says these bats will land anywhere as soon as that time mechanism goes off."

Murray continued. "If we assume that all of these time mechanisms have worked and therefore all the bats which have escaped are down, it is merely a question of time before each is discovered. Even if my guess that these bats are homing in on cities is wrong, the bulk of the sightings thus far have been in the populated areas. Naturally—where there is a greater concentration of people, there are going to be more discoveries. If we wait another day or so, we're going to know exactly where the greatest number lies. At least we can assume where they are. If they wander above your perimeter line, you can send in more troops as needed."

"I thought we decided against this sector by sector attack," said the Admiral. "I prefer the Colonel's idea."

"No one is suggesting a sector search and destroy. I am trying to say wait until we know where these things are before you chaps go hell bent for leather across the country. Suppose, just suppose, you get halfway through your march and a bat turns up beyond your perimeter. You're going to have to retrace your steps and begin all over again."

"Nonsense," said the Colonel. "We'll just send a detachment of men back up and treat that particular area."

"Wouldn't it be simpler to wait a day or two before your men are too firmly encamped? You have to wait for the disinfectant, anyway."

"The disinfectant could be ready at any time. We could commence operations tonight if we had the stuff."

Chadwell interrupted. "Why not have two lines—two perimeters?"

"*Two* perimeters?" asked Combs incredulously.

"One roughly where it is now, and another say halfway in. Better yet, stagger your men in say fifty mile lines."

"Mr. Chadwell," Combs began patiently. "We are speaking of the British Army not the combined Allied forces. It's hard enough stretching the perimeter line without having two."

Murray thought. "Suppose we do both. Suppose we have one perimeter of broken arcs about fifty to a hundred miles apart. Look, set a perimeter of fifty miles across from Caernarvon or Flint. Set the next fifty mile perimeter from Montgomery to Kidderminister. Then one above Birmingham and another above Wellingborough. Then one at Southend working towards London, and one in the Buckinghamshire to Surrey area working towards Lands End. As the perimeter troops from behind reach the areas cleared by those ahead, they can be airlifted to the front—sort of leap frogging as it were."

"Sounds reasonable," Sir Joseph decided, looking down at Murray's explanation. "This way the troops could back track if necessary if a bat were found behind the lines."

"What about it, Colonel?" Chadwell asked. "It wouldn't take too much to re-organize your men."

"I say it sounds good," said the Admiral, poking some of the markers about. "If this idea of the bats homing in on cities is correct, the troops would be in a much better position to concentrate their attack."

The Colonel sighed in disapproval. "It's going to stretch our men, but I'll try it. I'll arrange a meeting with the Heads of Staff in an hour."

"Don't forget Lord Tenningly," Sir Joseph reminded him as he walked towards the door. "I'll stall for as much time as you need."

Murray looked at Chadwell and grinned. "Let's find the Major."

The slow drizzle which had begun to fall the previous night had changed to a heavy rain and the wind around Trafalgar Square whipped Lord Nelson and his lions. Groups of pigeons huddled beneath the statues and none took notice of the occasional passerby. Umbrellas were blown away as the wind grew stronger and from the North came reports of gales, of heavier rainfalls and severe weather. Along the perimeter track the troops took shelter in the farms and homes near their bases as rain and wind lashed their hastily erected camps. But it was just a storm, thought the Major from his vantage overlooking Whitehall, and it would soon pass. He took one final look at the pavements awash with rain, at the few people who struggled against the elements, and returned to Sir Joseph's desk. Chewing the end of his pen, he thumbed through the afternoon's work. He had plotted the perimeter area, estimated the manpower involved, charted the land to be disinfected, found out how much would be dealt with by ground forces and how much by air, and put it all together. From it he drew one conclusion, that the plan could not possibly work. There were twenty-seven confirmed sightings of bats and for this the military were going to cover an area half the size of England and most of Wales. And there was this ever increasing pattern Murray had mentioned. He glanced at another pile of papers, copies from Comcent. France was under quarantine and Germany was screaming murder over one bat. There were undertones of economic disaster if England was stuck for the bill—for the vast quantities of disinfectant and man-power France had already begun to assemble. He smiled inwardly when he heard that East Germany had cordoned off fifty square miles of land encircling the only bat to tread on her soil—she was in a state of panic. Moscow had already issued a statement decrying the careless use of chemical and biological research and Washington had countered it with an ineffectual these-things-must-happen. He admitted to himself that there was little else any government could say in defense of the disaster, but he felt that America could have offered something a bit better.

He laid down his pen and took up reading his notes again. His mind wandered. Michael and Ralph and the choir robes flashed across his vision—and the puppy. Other nameless, faceless people with blackened arms and necks, swelling pustules and dried blood, appeared. He could see youngsters writhing in pain while parents looked on in terror and shock. He saw children standing over their parents who lay stricken on floors and streets while all around hundreds of bats swarmed, fell, rose again and fled. Another face appeared. The Captain was crawling towards him, his arms and face puffing up like enormous black balloons. His hands were out-stretched as if to grab him. Then he saw a gas—a cloud of mist descending upon Stumford. He saw the villagers running about and convulsing helplessly on the streets. He wanted to help, warn them, but his voice was gone. The mist grew heavier and the people faded. He turned away and saw a bicycle. It was travelling towards the mist. He ran, but his feet were like elastic. His legs were numb and useless. He saw a face, a boy, and his heart beat faster. He was crawling and shouting. He began to choke. He called again, but he was coughing too much. He flailed about as if in a quagmire, and he was sinking, and the bicycle was nearly into the mist. He was shouting again, and suddenly he could run. He ran faster after the bicycle, calling, screaming, waving, and still the rider rode on. He felt something on his shoulder and he whipped around.

"Bad dreams, Major?" asked Sir Joseph. "I expect I'll have mine soon enough."

He sat up and wiped his forehead.

"Here," said Murray, pushing a glass towards him. "Drink this."

The Major swallowed, felt the burning in his throat and stomach. He shook his head. "Like a little boy, huh?"

"Like all of us," Sir Joseph replied. "I've got some news to cheer you up. This storm has forced your men down at Manchester and they won't make Ruislip until tomorrow morning. I'm taking you and the lad up to my place for the night and I'll drop you at the Base on my way into London in the morning. Give you a chance to rest up—forget about all this for awhile if you can."

"That's about the best news I've had since this whole damn business began. Christ, you know it's just like a nightmare. I was dreaming about all these people—and the kids we saw in Beckington. Then you wake up, and you're still in the middle of it all."

Murray finished pouring out the glasses and refilled the Major's. "You're lucky. You can call it a day if you like. We're stuck with it."

"Lucky, Murray?" He shook his head and stared at the blotter. "If I could pull out of this thing now, I'd be the first one in line. We're all in this together, ole buddy, and in it to the end."

"You're bloody mad, but I always suspected it in you Yanks. Anyway, I've put my brainwave before the committee in there like I said I would and we've changed the plan."

He looked up.

"They found two more bats. Both just outside Combs' famous perry track and that knocked a hole in the old bucket. I figured it would be better to stagger the perimeter and move things around a bit. Here, picture a row of sound waves crossing the country from Northwest to Southeast. Chop the waves up, throw out a few, and you've got my idea. That way the troops have forward and rear lines and can back-track a lot easier if more of these little dears are found behind them."

"So the disinfectant idea is still go?"

"You don't sound encouraged."

"I'm not," he said flatly. "There's something about disinfecting a few thousand square miles of England that rings of something like ridiculous." He raised his hand as if prepared to stop an objection. "Now don't get me wrong, but there's got to be a better way."

"Well, first you've got to think of one—then you've got to convince iron pants in there that it's better than his perimeter."

"Custer's last stand."

"What?"

"Forget it," Thomas replied, pushing himself away from the desk. "Is it still raining?"

"Raining?" Murray laughed. "If those bats had webbed feet, they'd be swimming out of the country. And it's supposed to get worse. If this disinfectant comes through tonight, they figure they'll have to change the dilution formula."

Sir Joseph, pulling some papers from his safe and stuffing them into an overfilled case, turned from what he was doing. "The chaps at Met seem to think it's going to be bad at the perimeter—flooding and all that. I won't envy those lads tomorrow if they have to move out."

"They're used to it by now," Murray said. "Combs has been shuffling them about all day."

"Have they perfected the brew?" asked Thomas.

"If you mean have they managed to weaken the disinfectant so that it doesn't burn a hole in half of England, no," Murray replied, shaking his empty glass. "And if they weaken it, it won't be strong enough. Apparently this hybrid bacillus is a bit tougher than they reckoned on."

"Our boys at Detrick have got something which they think may well blow the lid off this disinfectant idea. Right now it's in the form of a dust and if they prove it won't harm humans, well there's your answer." He looked up at Murray. "That is if you haven't swiped it already."

Sir Joseph stood up from the safe. "You mean you've got something already developed?"

"Not already. We've been working on anti-bacterial crop dusting for some years. Some bright spark figured if it works on plants, why not develop it further and see if humans and animals can be dusted in the same way."

"And they've got it?" he asked eagerly.

"We've got it, but whether or not they'll let you have it is another problem."

"Why didn't you mention this before, Major?" he persisted, picking up the telephone. "It might change everything."

"Put the phone down, Sir Joseph," he replied slowly. "There's one minor problem. As I said, this is a rather secret development—as far as we know this idea of ours is ours alone. It's a highly effective way of treating millions of acres of land and it is deadly simple—and cheap once perfected. But it's taken Detrick about five years to develop the idea far enough to extend to people."

He still held the phone. "Yes, yes. But why can't it be used now?"

"The formula which we would use is basic—the dust that is. But it is classified. Add to it a highly specialized anti-anthrax compound and even if we did manage to create the right formula, I think Washington would still refuse to release it. If someone got a handful of it as it was falling, the formula could easily be traced and bang goes a few million dollars of research. Whoever gets it will develop something similar, maybe something that neutralizes our dust and all we'll have is a few billion tons of worthless powder. That's the trouble."

"But surely if you've got the answer to this problem, your government will be willing to use it. I mean think of the people.

"Oh for Christ's sake," Murray snapped, "stop being so naïve."

"Hang on, Murray," said the Major. "I've been trying to think of a possible way out. If we can make it sound like you've invented this stuff instead of us, we might be able to persuade the Pentagon to release it. Besides, if I know the top brass like I think I do, they'll be itching to try this stuff out in the field."

"Do you think it can be arranged?"

"Look, give me a line to General Stockport at Detrick —scramble it. I'll need about half an hour with him and a hell of a lot of luck. But if you can promise to take the rap if this stuff knocks off a million of your people along with the bats, and say you developed it all on your own, then I think there's a chance."

Sir Joseph nodded. "Murray, get Comcent to open a line to Detrick—absolute priority. I'll get on to Tenningly straight away."

"Then you'll accept the responsibility?"

"The government will accept anything in the state it's in now. Just get as much of that dust as you can."

"I'll stock up on Pledge," said Murray from the door.

"You're mad," replied Chadwell, pushing past him into the study. "What's he saying now?"

"A bad joke," said Sir Joseph somewhat angry. "I've got a job for you, Chadwell." He looked at the Major from the doorway. "I'll leave you to it. Good luck."

Thomas smiled as encouragingly as he dared and sat back to wait for the phone to ring.

Perimeter. 16:45 Hours

"Perimeter Delta to Perimeter Lima. Over."

"Perimeter Lima. Over."

"We're losing hold here. The wind's made a right mess of the field and I can't keep the men in the trucks much longer. Over."

"Hold on, Delta. I have a message for you. You are to move Base to Flint. Repeat Flint. Perimeter Bravo will rendezvous at nineteen hundred hours. Over."

"Roger, Lima. Any idea how long we're going to be out in this? Over."

"No idea, Delta, but don't make any holiday plans."

"Roger, Lima. Out."

"Tango Romeo One to Perimeter Charlie. I am at two zero zero feet. Visibility one five zero. Am returning to Base. Over."

"Roger, Tango Romeo One. Shall instruct Tango Two and Three to do the same. Out."

"Helicopter Three Eight Fox Trot to Lima One, Over."

"Lima One. Come in Three Eight Fox Trot."

"Look, MacPhearson, I can't hold this thing up much longer. I got seventy-five knots kicking my backside and this rain's pushing hard to get inside. Over."

"Roger, Three Eight Fox Trot. You'll have to take her over to Birmingham. Inform Perimeter Control of your position. Over."

"Helicopter Three Eight Fox Trot out."

"Perimeter Control to all Bases. Stand by for orders to redeploy. Repeat, stand by for orders to redeploy. New areas will be allocated within twenty minutes. Assemble your men and break camp. Perimeter Control out."

"Birmingham Tower to all surveillance aircraft. The perimeter track is being broken. Return to either Birmingham or Manchester. Out."

"Helicopter Three Eight Fox Trot to Birmingham Tower. Over."

"Birmingham Tower. Over."

"Can't find this wind, Birmingham. Am setting down at Ditton Priors—I think. Over."

"Roger, Helicopter Three Eight Fox Trot. Contact us when you're down. Good luck. Over and out."

"Perimeter Control to Comcent. Over."

"This is Comcent. Go ahead Perimeter Control."

"We are standing by for redeployment orders, but all planes are down. The weather is getting worse out here—can't you chaps hold things off until tomorrow? Over."

"Colonel Combs is with Staff now. I doubt whether you'll get your hold. Over."

"We can't expect the men to set up field camps tonight. Over."

"Hold on, Perimeter. Orders coming through. You are to stay put tonight, repeat, stay put. Combs will issue further orders at zero eight hundred hours. Keep warm up there. Over and out."

"Perimeter Control to all Bases. Cancel orders to redeploy. Stand down your men. Perimeter Control out."

"Birmingham Tower to Helicopter Three Eight Fox Trot. Over."

"Helicopter Three Eight Fox Trot. What do you want?"

"Repeat your landing position. Over."

"Repeat my what?"

"Repeat your landing co-ordinates."

"I'm setting down at Ditton Priors—or so this ruddy map says. How am I supposed to know where I'm coming down in this weather?"

"Birmingham Tower to Helicopter Three Eight Fox Trot. Your position of Ditton Priors has no landing field. Over."

"I know that, Tower. I'm taking my chances. Three Eight Fox Trot out."

"Air Force Delta Charlie Bravo, this is Manchester Tower. This will be a PPI continuous descent approach."

"Roger."

"For identification turn Left heading one six zero degrees."

"Roger. One six zero degrees."

"Charlie Bravo is identified five miles West of Manchester."

"Roger. Five miles."

"Charlie Bravo your position seven miles South West of Manchester."

"Roger. Seven South West."

"Position nine miles South West turn Left heading zero seven zero degrees for base leg."

"Roger. Turning heading zero seven zero."

"Position ten miles base leg turn Left heading zero two five degrees to close with finals."

"Roger. Zero two five."

"Turn Left onto three four zero degrees, final approach, range eight miles."

"Roger. Range is eight miles."

"Range coming up to six miles, check wheels down and locked."

"Roger. My wheels are down."

"Five and a half miles—stand by to commence descent to maintain three degrees glide path—five miles, begin your descent. You should now be leaving one six zero zero feet. Do not acknowledge further instructions."

"Roger. Down the line."

"Slightly to the right of center line turn Left five

degrees. Two and a half miles from touch down on the center line you should be passing eight zero zero feet. Two miles from touch down—should be passing six five zero feet, check your critical height. Surface wind two four zero degrees, forty knots. Range one mile. Approach completed—radar out."

The first of the American transports had landed.

Whitehall. 17:00 Hours

Sir Joseph sat back in his chair and breathed deeply. He felt relieved. He felt something was finally being done which might possibly put an end to this disaster; and he admitted that it was due to the Americans. He hated to admit it. He hated the feeling which until now had driven him deeper and deeper into despair as Colonel Combs paraded about the corridors of Whitehall, scattering the British Army half way round the country. He hated most the feeling of helplessness, knowing that the people were dying and there was nothing he could do. So he contented himself with admitting that once more the Yanks were coming to the rescue, and something was being done to help the crippled Nation. He had confidence in the Yanks—he knew they were cool, calculating, and under the veneer of neurotic power lay a network of deadly efficient men. The Americans were coming. Aircraft, dust clouds and military scientists. It was a tough bargain, one which jeopardized the already chastened government and gave the Americans the upper hand, but he knew the sanity of Whitehall and the lives of a few score million people lay in the balance. England takes the blame if the project fails—what England would be left—and if the project succeeded well, they bloody well expected it to succeed. The one stumbling block which he saw was Combs: he would be politely but irrevocably told to take a running jump while several top brass from Detrick assumed control of his carefully constructed operations room. How would he take it? How sure was he that Combs was more interested in his future than the lives of the subjects? Another gamble to be reckoned for.

The glimmer of light *was* shining brighter, but at what cost? How far down had England been driven when it relied upon America to save its tattered neck? He shrugged his shoulders in reply. What did it matter—it was too late for that. His life in politics was nearing an end. The party was nearing its end. Maybe even England was nearing her end. Even if she wasn't, the party was finished. Already the Opposition were tabling motions to censor the party, and the people would waste no time in hanging the whole bloody Parliament if conditions worsened much more. The Yanks were about to save the country from another bungling attempt to save herself. But his job was easier now: the government had accepted the offer, tomorrow the American Officers would assume command, and all he would have to do is to sit back and watch. If it worked, he got the credit. If it failed, well, no one would be around to blame him. He swirled the remnants of his drink and looked towards the door. It was the Major.

"OK if we come in?"

He rose. "Certainly. I've been enjoying the security of American salvation."

Thomas pushed open the door and Trevor walked in before him. He seemed shy amidst the splendour of Whitehall, but he tried to conceal it.

"Well, well, you do look the new man," Sir Joseph pronounced. "New jacket, clean shirt, pressed trousers and polished shoes. And I do like your tie. Is this what you got this morning?"

Sheepishly he glanced up. "Not me—the Major."

"Well, someone's got good taste. Murray had said you'd been on a spree."

The Anthrax Mutation

"Murray?" said Thomas, startled. "He wasn't with us."

"Not that you saw, Major. It's his job, remember?"

"Like spies and all that," said Trevor, looking about the room. "Is that what Mr. Murray is?"

"A lot more than spies, my friend," Sir Joseph replied kindly "Would you like something to drink before we go?"

"Yes, thanks."

"And you, Major—the usual?"

He nodded. "Trevor can have a Coke."

"Already the master, eh?" he grinned, handing out the drinks. "I see that injection worked very well."

"Not half," said Trevor. "It's just this trembling in my hand that won't stop."

"I'm sure that will pass in time," Sir Joseph assured him.

"I understand that my men are coming in tomorrow night," the Major began. "The second support."

"Cheers. Yes, scheduled to touch down at Ruislip at fifteen hundred, I believe." He paused. "And you, Trevor, what are your plans?"

He looked at the Major.

"I haven't really told him anything yet."

"Well, how would you like to come to my home for awhile—until the Major finishes with his work."

He glanced from the Major to Sir Joseph. "I guess I would—if the Major will let me."

Thomas cuffed him on the neck. "Sure you can. That's what we had planned all along. It'll be a lot better than sitting around here all day. Besides, you'll have Mrs. Willets to look after you."

"That's my wife. Jolly good cook, you know. And there's plenty of land to roam—I mean, well, when all this is over."

"Will the Major be coming with us?"

"I'm going to be right next door to you at the air-base," he replied. "And if Sir Joseph will have me, I'll probably be spending most nights with you unless we're posted out."

"Tell me, Trevor, what are you interested in?"

"Football mostly—and I like swimming."

"How about school—what did you like best there?"

"History and English I guess. I wasn't much good at either. I like PE the best."

"Did you ever study electronics?"

"No, that's in the fifth year. We had biology."

"How would you like to see some electronics now? We have a communications center here known as Comcent and it's about the biggest mess of gadgets you'll ever come across. We're rather proud of it."

"I don't mind. I don't know much about it."

"Well," he said, looking at the Major. "I'll ring down for the car and then we'll push off for Comcent. There's someone there who'll tell you all about it."

Trevor shook his glass from side to side. He watched Sir Joseph push a button on his desk and order someone to have his car made ready. He wished he could do something like that. He thought of how good it would be to be able to push a button and have someone bring whatever you liked. He wondered if they had such things in America.

"Right, then. You follow me, Trevor", began Sir Joseph, his hand across his shoulders.

They entered the long carpeted corridor and passed the many conference rooms, most of which hummed and crackled with activity.

"I'm sure the Americans have something much bigger, but we're pretty pleased with what we can do."

"Can you call New York from here?" Trevor asked as they passed beneath a small archway, turning right and carrying on along another corridor.

'We can obtain radio contact with any part of the world — on land, sea or air — within seconds. If you had an aunt living in Sydney, we could ring her right this minute."

They approached the Comcent checkpoint. A sentry looked disapprovingly at the boy, but Sir Joseph ignored him and passed through the doors. Trevor's eyes suddenly lit up. "Cor," he cried, "I never thought it would be like this!"

"Good afternoon, Sir Joseph," said a voice from behind. "And who is this — a new recruit?"

"Hello, Lieutenant. This is Trevor Brecon."

The Lieutenant, the same who had informed Chadwell of the lad's condition the night before, shook his hand, "I've heard a lot about you from Mr. Chadwell. And you must be the Major everyone's talking about."

"Pleased to meet you, Lieutenant. I hope what they say is good."

"So far. Mind you, Major, professional pride around here doesn't include foreigners." She smiled and the Major liked her. "And you've come to inspect Comcent, Trevor?

He grinned. "I thought it would just be a lot of telephones."

"Well, you come with me and I'll show you it's not just a lot of telephones." She nodded at Sir Joseph and led Trevor off through another set of doors. They could see them through the long glass panelling which surrounded the bulk of the communications network.

Sir Joseph looked after her and then turned slowly to the Major. "There's a fine bit of woman, there, Glen— if I may call you that. She's kept this place going for some time and hasn't lost any of her charm. Kind, generous—she's everything you'd want and she wastes it locked up in this, this pregnant computer."

"I don't know. She seems happy enough." He leaned

against the doorframe and watched her bend over Trevor's shoulders as he fiddled with a set of dials.

"Not happy. Dedicated. Most of the men and women here are. Have to be."

"Is she married?"

"Was. Her husband was killed in a nasty air crash in the RAF. She came here shortly after that and has been here ever since. That was four years ago. She should be getting away from all this."

"She's good with the boy."

They saw her smile at Trevor who was laughing at what was coming through a set of earphones. Together they pushed buttons, stared at a whirling radar screen and pushed more buttons. She put her ear close to his to hear what was being said and together they grinned.

"Just what the boy needs, Glen. See how happy he is. He's forgotten everything for a few moments."

The Major pushed himself from the wall. "Now just a minute, Sir Joseph. First I end up with this adopted son and now you're planning my marriage."

"I'm only thinking of you all," he smiled without looking at him. "You might do well to take a couple of memories back home—good memories."

The Major was interrupted before he could reply. The sentry entered and said the car was waiting.

Point of No Return. 17:15 Hours GMT

Air France had managed to persuade the authorities to let some of its overseas flights depart despite the quarantine. Orly had been packed and overflowing and since passengers would be *leaving* Paris rather than entering, it could do no harm to reduce some of the burden on the airport authorities. One of the first flights out was a New York bound 707 with a full complement of passengers and crew. Most of the travellers were Americans, but a few French, German and Swiss had managed to squeeze onto the passenger list with the hope of avoiding possible contamination. As dangerous as the bats were and however strong the disease they carried, even the best of them could never reach America.

Three hours into the flight the airplane crossed the point of no return. It was then the first six passengers became delirious and a noticeable swelling on their arms and necks appeared. The crew were powerless to act. They were powerless to allay other passengers' fears. Within an hour everyone knew they were doomed, and the most the cabin staff could hope for was to bring the plane down safely at Montreal and perhaps save those least affected. But the disease was their better and just thirty-five minutes from the coast of Newfoundland the 707 fell from the skies and was lost forever in the depths of the Atlantic. What the pilot never knew was that not one of his passengers was alive when he could no longer fight the agony in his arms. What no one could know was that no one was alive when the sea opened up to swallow the dead.

Hillingdon, Middlesex. 17:45 Hours

Sir Joseph's car had reached the roundabout where the turning to Ruislip swept off to their right when the radiophone buzzed. He seemed reluctant to answer. Trevor, like the Major, followed his gaze to the phone.

"Sir Joseph here."

"Comcent, Sir Joseph. We have an unofficial report of anthrax at Wexham Hospital near Slough. Can you have Major Thomas investigate and confirm?"

"We're on our way. I know the hospital. You can tell them to expect us in fifteen minutes."

The phone clicked dead.

"More trouble?" asked the Major as he watched Sir Joseph slowly replace the receiver.

"Suspected anthrax case." He pushed a button on his armrest as he picked up a small microphone. "Randall, straight across the Denham Roundabout and head for Wexham Hospital. Put on your lights and make this a fast one, eh?"

Randall nodded from behind the glass partition. They felt the smooth acceleration of the Bentley thrust them gently back in their seats and the steep hill leading from one roundabout to another evened out. Quickly they crossed at Denham, swung past the next roundabout towards Slough and past Black Park and the film studios.

Sir Joseph awoke from his thoughts and turned to the Major. "Must be a case just in. First for Wexham."

"Doesn't Slough already have a confirmation?"

He shrugged. "There're other hospitals. Any of them could have handled it."

"Do you think we'll see a lot of bats around here?" asked Trevor, deciding whether he wanted to or would rather not.

"Not if you do as you're told," the Major replied, rubbing his charge's neck. "Those bats are as deadly as anything you'll ever come across. And that injection doesn't last forever."

Trevor grew silent again and poked his finger at the radiophone, drew a pattern on the spotless plastic body, then sat back and toyed with his fingernails. Sir Joseph returned to his own worries until they reached the Stoke Road, turned into Stoke Green and pulled up sharply at the hospital.

"Keep the lad with you, Randall," Sir Joseph ordered as he pulled open the door. "Take him for a sweet or something."

"You better leave this to me," Thomas said. "If it's anthrax, it's not going to be pretty to watch."

211

They had reached the hospital steps. "I intend to. But I want to be around when you make your confirmation—Comcent's expecting it. Your boys have asked for a minute by minute plot so they can figure out how much dust they'll need to bring over."

A doctor saw them as they approached Casualty. "Are you the team from London?"

"This gentleman will help you," Sir Joseph replied.

"This way, please. You'll have to hurry."

"I'll wait out here, Glen. Good luck."

The Major nodded before he followed the doctor through a maze of curtains, down a short corridor and into a small room. There was another door beyond at which he stopped. He looked at the red banner, ran his fingers through grey strands of hair and looked at Thomas. "It's a child, Sir. Young boy. We have the antidote ready as soon as you confirm it, but if it's what we suspect, my guess is we're too late."

"I'll do whatever I can," he said simply, wondering why the hell it always had to be over-adventurous boys who managed to contract the disease. He put his hand on the door to enter. The doctor stopped him.

"You have seen this sort of thing before?"

"I diagnosed the same thing two days ago—another boy. I've seen it before."

The doctor seemed satisfied and pushed open the door. A nurse sitting at the bedside arose. She moved quickly into the corner as Thomas walked silently to the foot of the bed. Another kid, he thought. Another kid who couldn't be more than twelve and draped in white sheets. He lay still, but he saw tears running down his cheeks as he rolled his head slowly from side to side, crying softly to himself. His long brown hair was matted and moist and clung to his fevered forehead, and Thomas noticed that when he tried to move his arm, it had been strapped to the bed.

"How long has he been in here?"

"Ambulance picked him up at four twenty-eight. His mother rung. We think he found it somewhere in the park."

"What park?" he asked, tapping the metal frame of the bed.

"Baylis Park—about two miles from here. It's a big place where the lads play football. There's a swimming pool there as well."

"Have you informed the police?"

"They know the boy was brought in, yes."

"What about closing the park?"

"I couldn't tell you about that. I suppose they'll rope it off when we give them a confirmation."

"Then you better tell them to move," he snapped, angered by this risky delay. "If it is what you suspect, Doctor, this whole damned place of yours is going to be crowded with kids."

The doctor stared at the boy.

"Well, move, man! I can handle things here—that's what you called me up for isn't it?"

"Nurse, see that he gets what he needs," he replied hastening from the room. "And call me if anything happens."

Thomas moved to the bedside. Sister looked at him. He smiled. "I'm Major Thomas. Can you give me a hand here?"

She returned the smile and crossed to the opposite side of the bed. "I'm afraid they tend to be a bit slow around here."

He looked up.

"The doctors, I mean. They always play it careful."

"Pick up your side of the sheet and lift it—slowly. Yes, I've noticed that."

The boy's eyes opened very slightly. He tried to focus and when he found he could distinguish two hazy figures, he tried to sit up. The binding on his arm hurt and he winced.

Thomas gripped his shoulder gently. "Easy, son. Lie still and we'll get these handcuffs off." Carefully he unbuckled the strap and as he lifted the left arm free, he noticed the tell-tale bluish-black swelling had begun immediately below the elbow. With infinite care his fingers ran over the swelling, pressing softly until he determined the extent of the infection. His fingers moved upwards to examine the lad's neck and shoulders, under his arm and in the lymphatics. Finally, he took both the boy's hands and held them in his own. "Can you grip my hands?" he asked.

Satisfied with his findings, he turned to Sister who was still holding the sheet. He motioned for her to remove it entirely and as she did, he unbuckled the clasp of the lad's belt, popped open the snap on his faded jeans and slid them over his legs. The boy was only vaguely aware of his presence, but in his semi-consciousness he felt the pain in his arm and the fever in his body.

Once again Thomas began a methodical examination, his first and he prayed his last. He probed the ankles, the slender calf and below the knee. There was no swelling—anthrax rarely attacked the lower limbs. A good sign. He felt deep into the thighs, the sartorius, adductor and vastus muscles, and below the gluteus medius and maximus. This done, he advanced to the abdomen, searching below the inter-costal arch, down to the sartorius again and iliopsoas. There was nothing. The infection was still localized. There was a chance to pull the lad through. He knelt down, remembered Ralph, and whispered, "Can you tell me where it hurts most?"

The boy tried to turn his head. "Me arm," he choked. He tried to raise it to show the Major, but the pain knifed through him and it fell useless.

"How about anywhere else—your tummy or your legs?"

Stiffly he shook his head.

Thomas pushed himself back slightly and glanced around. He was looking for an ashtray. There was none. Though the implication was definitely "No Smoking," he ignored the unwritten notice and struck a match to his cigarette. Suddenly he realized how good it felt, and how long he had been without one. "You had better tell the good doctor to bring the antibiotic," he said at length. When Sister had gone, he returned to the boy. "Can you tell me what happened to you?"

Without opening his eyes he mumbled softly, "I was swimming. Then I began to feel funny." He stopped. He hoped it was enough.

"How long had you been swimming?"

"All day. I brought me lunch."

"Was anyone else feeling funny?"

He thought, and shook his head.

"And you never left the poolside—you were around the water all day?"

He nodded.

Sister re-entered quietly and let the door close behind her.

Thomas stood up and rested his hand on the boy's shoulder. "Don't worry, son. The doctor will be here again soon and he'll fix you up."

"We have the mother outside," began the nurse. "Shall I order an injection for her?"

Thomas nodded. "And for anyone else who's been in contact with the boy. That includes you and the doctor."

She smiled. "We've had ours. Just to be safe."

He turned back to the boy and ruffled his hair. "You've gotten yourself into a right old pickle, haven't you?"

He tried to turn his head again. "A pickle?"

"Yeah, a pickle. A mess."

215

The doctor suddenly appeared with the syringe. Thomas rolled the boy onto his side, slid the side of his pants down, and looked away as the doctor wiped the skin in ether and plunged the needle deep into the muscles. He felt the boy jerk.

"He'll be all right now," said the doctor. "I'll have the wound dressed now that we know what it is."

"I'll do that. I know how it should be done."

"Well, tell Sister what you need and she'll see that you get it. If you'll excuse me, I must make my report."

Sister wheeled a trolley near the bedside. "This should do." She paused, curious. "You seem to know quite a bit about all this—your job?"

"Military research mostly. It just happened that I was here when the trouble began. I'm not a doctor if that's what you mean."

"No, I could see that. I mean the way you looked at the boy. You're feeling sorry for him. It hurts you to see him hurt."

Thomas frowned. "It's not that I'm entirely innocent of what's happened to him."

"He'll be all right. Unless the infection spreads, he'll be well enough in a week or so. You'll see."

"Know about this, huh?"

She handed him the dressings. "I know Dr. Stead is good." She found her scissors and handed them over. "By the way, I'm Sister Charlotte and this is John. We really haven't been introduced yet."

"I'm Major Thomas—or did I tell you?"

"Your friend out there seems rather impatient. Is he from the military?"

"Sir Joseph—no, the government. Here, give me a hand with this."

"Ointment first?"

"Yes, just on the swelling. Easy now, John."

The boy winced.

"That's fine. Now, I'll support the arm while you stick the pad over the ointment. A little higher. Good. You might want to lance that pustule in a day or so. Help drain out the poison."

"The gauze?"

"Around the pad."

John was crying softly.

"I guess most of the staff will be inoculated as well," said the Major.

"They're doing it now. It'll cause chaos when the night shift comes on. I think they're planning on doing most of the patients, too."

"Not much longer, John. Just keep your arm steady. You relax and let me hold it."

"But it hurts," he cried.

"It won't be much longer," Sister Charlotte replied, handing the Major a syringe. "You know how to do this?"

"What is it—morphine?"

"Yes. I'll tape it up if you jab him."

"There," he announced when he had finished. "I bet that feels better."

He shook his head.

"He'll be asleep soon," said Sister Charlotte. "He'll probably be going through the worst of the fever tonight. Might just as well go through it asleep."

The doctor looked in. "Everything all right?"

"Fine," replied Thomas. "I told the Sister here she might lance the wound tomorrow if it's any better."

He nodded. "I've told Sir Joseph the situation. And he gave me his number so I shall ring you when there's any news on the boy."

"Thanks. I'd like to know."

"Yes," he smiled. "Well, good luck on the front lines, eh?" He swung the door shut and left.

"Front lines?" inquired the Sister.

"You might say I deal with this stuff direct."

She cocked her head with a safety pin between her teeth.

"You know what the boy's got? It's springing up pretty much everywhere."

"I heard about this anthrax and the bats and so on— but we don't get much time for all the news in here. Most of it comes from the patients." She pinned the end of the dressing and lay the arm down.

"The less you know the better off you are."

"Shall we cover him?"

"Have you got one of those hospital gowns?"

She went to the dresser and pulled open a drawer. "One of these?"

He nodded. "Yes, that'll do nicely. Come on, John, time to wake up again."

John was feeling too much the effects of the drug to care much what was going on and he let himself be hoisted up long enough to have his pants removed, and draped in the baggy gown. His eyes were still closed tight when the Major laid him down again and pulled the sheet and blanket up to his neck.

The Major continued explaining. "It's simply that a war research station lost a few of its experiments and they're beginning to find them."

"The bats?" she replied, picking up the loose dressings. "Not very nice, is it?"

"That's why Heathrow has been closed?"

"And every other air terminal. You should listen more." He smiled. "Some people think it's kind of exciting."

"Not if they saw John here, they wouldn't," she replied flatly.

He finished tucking in the sheet. "You don't seem very surprised."

"Why should I? You aren't surprised by bombs exploding and guns going off six inches from your head—I'm not surprised by this. Call it professional callousness." She wrapped the leftover dressing around her finger and pulled it off.

"Twentieth century Florence Nightingale."

"If dear old Florence could see what goes on today, she'd soon snuff her little candle out."

He laughed. "Progress."

"Well, that's that done. I guess we can leave little John to rest. He'll be pretty miserable the next few days, poor nipper. I suppose we can expect to get a few more in like him."

"If what's happened that I think may have, this place will be crawling with kids soon," he said, holding open the door for her. "This anthrax has come from the swimming pool. Every kid who was in there will be infected."

"I don't mind it so much when older people get involved in all this, but it's the kids that bother me. Never have a fighting chance."

"Maybe John will. I hope so."

"So do I," she sighed.

They grew silent as they walked through Casualty and into the corridor. Sir Joseph noticed them and hastened over.

"Is he all right, then?"

"Should be," the Major replied. "He seems to be in competent hands."

Sister Charlotte smiled. "Dr. Stead is very good with children."

"I wasn't referring to the good doctor. Anyone can jam a needle in."

"I must go," she blushed. "I'll let you know how he gets on."

"Thanks."

"Pretty chummy all of a sudden," Sir Joseph said as they walked from the building.

"It's the Army influence," he smiled. "But we've got a serious problem now."

"Yes?"

"That boy in there had been swimming all day. My hunch is he caught that anthrax from the pool. Why the hell the damn thing wasn't closed I don't know."

"Then that means—"

"Precisely. Every person in that pool could have been infected. Look, I think you'd better get onto the Army and police and get word around that anyone who's been in that pool better come in for a check-up. How you're going to do it without causing a panic is beyond me, but you've got no choice. If the anthrax has come from the water, you'll have an epidemic."

"We can have the police appeal over their loud-speakers. I'll see that the Army moves in and makes a door to door search. I'd better get onto Comcent straight away," Sir Joseph reached the car and leaned across the seat for the radiophone. This was going to cause one hell of a flap in London, he knew. Combs would have to find some troops and damned quick. And in the back of his mind was another problem. Things were beginning to get out of hand, even for him.

"Is he all right?" asked Trevor.

"The boy?" Thomas replied. "Yes, I think so."

"It's horrible, isn't it, Major? Why do people do it?"

"You mean experiment with these things?"

He nodded.

"I'm afraid I can't answer that, Trevor. It's just part of our world."

"But you do it. You should know why you do it."

"Yeah, I should. But I don't."

Trevor tried to understand and failed.

"Anyway," began Thomas, walking him away from the car, "when you grow up maybe you will see all this in a clear light. Maybe by then people will have stopped all this."

"You think so?"

He hesitated. "Maybe. Just maybe."

Trevor stopped and looked at the hospital buildings. His mind wandered far away, and perhaps he was thinking of home.

"They've had three more sightings—all within the perimeter," Sir Joseph was saying as the Bentley rumbled along towards Stoke Poges. "But that's not the worse. Combs has found out about your American Officers taking over tomorrow. He's threatening to resign."

"From the Army?"

"No—from the government. You know of course that he's the military adviser for all this."

"Judging from his reputation I'd say that's a nice quiet way of going."

Sir Joseph looked at him. "That's just it. If Combs resigns, he won't be quiet about it. He'll make it as public as the front lines of the Times. And he'll make sure everyone knows why he's resigned. It'll make us look rather foolish if it were known how much we're depending on you chaps, but worse than that it'll blow the lid off everything. The ruddy world will know it was you who invented this dust and not our men?"

"Where's Combs now?"

"Storming up and down the corridors of Whitehall last Chadwell saw of him. Murray tried his best to cool him off, but you know how he feels about Murray. No one dares go near him the way he is now."

Thomas was worried. This placed the whole operation in jeopardy and he knew if the Americans were at all suspicious that the truth might be revealed, they'd recall the dust and put a stop to everything. His stomach suddenly went queezy as he stared through the glass partition at Trevor and Randall. "Can't Lord Tenningly do anything?"

"The only person who can do anything is the PM and that's top secret."

"What's top secret?"

Sir Joseph hesitated. He had known that he would have to tell the Major at some time in the uncertain future, but he had held back. He wanted nothing to jeopardize the American offers of help. "There are only two people who know this, Glen—Lord Tenningly and myself. It must go no further. The Prime Minister is dead. They found his body last night. The whole railway carriage was crushed. He never had a chance. If this gets out on top of the anthrax scare, well, there'll never be an England again. Besides—in answer to your question —Combs hates Tenningly. Always has. Combs had been after a Cabinet position—Minister of Defense, but the most he got was an advisership. Tenningly got in ahead of him. Combs had made the mistake of telling everyone it was a sure thing—he was dead certain he would catch that job. When Tenningly moved in, Combs was made the laughing stock and he's always hated him for it. It's as if he blamed Tenningly. Christ, it wasn't his fault—it wasn't as if Tenningly did it intentionally. It was the PM's choice. Anyway, that's why Combs took over this operation so damned quick. It was his one chance of glory. If he could lick the anthrax, he'd walk over Tenningly. Now it's whipped out from under him—by the Americans of all people. No offense, Major, but you can see the implications."

"Can't Combs be replaced—I mean put another CO in his place and if Combs starts to bitch, deny whatever he says?"

"Too risky. Besides, the press would lap the scandal up. By the time Whitehall had finished denying everything, the damage would have been done."

"Transfer him to another country. Say Albania?"

"Still wouldn't work. We'd never get away with it."

"Then give him what he goddam wants. Tell him he's being taken off this job so he can be a Cabinet or whatever the hell it is. Bribe him if you have to. It's been done before."

"That's exactly what he *does* want."

"Then do it. Which do you want—Combs as a Minister or the withdrawal of American support troops? You know damn well what the conditions are and if Washington smells a rat, they'll recall the lot. Me included."

"If Combs gets in as Defense Minister, he'll have England out trying to regain the Empire. You'd have British warships cruising around Massachusetts Bay just like a couple of hundred years ago. Nobody'd be safe from him. That's why he's never been anything but an adviser—and most of his advice was ignored anyway."

"Then why the hell did you put him on this job in the first place?" He lit another cigarette. They were beginning to taste foul again.

"I didn't. It was his job—his position as Colonel. How the devil were we to know what this would turn into?"

"Let's be honest then. If this happened in America, the party would be dumped at the next election. They'd probably call for a referendum anyway. Nothing could save it. Not even a Jesus Combs. Something like this is going to crucify any government, right? Well, how long has this party got left? A year—two at the most?"

"And?"

"Stick the bastard in. Rome wasn't built in a day and it'll take a hell of a lot longer for Combs to stick the British Empire back together—even if he's enough of an idiot to try. Let him have his goddam post. The government will take months to recover from this disaster—they won't be ready for another."

"Try telling that to some of the Ministers. They still think they've got a chance at winning the election. At least some of them can stand on their own. They all know Combs too well to let him go meddling about in the Cabinet. They'd resign first. And don't tell me to let them resign, either. There's some damn fine men in the Cabinet, Lord Tenningly for one. He might not be all that good to you, Glen, but underneath he's what the country needs."

"There's only one alternative, then," Thomas said coldly.

"What's that?"

"Get rid of him for a while. All we need is a couple of weeks."

"I suppose in America—"

"Screw America," he snapped. "Doesn't matter one hill of beans what *we* do in America or anywhere else. We're in England now and however good and true your sense of fair play is, you're going to have to bend the rules a bit for this one. Sister Charlotte was right, though not the way she thought. It's not the people who should see cases like John in there—or Michael and Ralph or Trevor. It's your bastards who're running everything. Has Combs even put a foot out of Whitehall since this whole thing began? Has he seen anybody infected with this stuff—or killed by the nerve gas. Look how bad Chadwell was—a real pompous idiot of the first order. He refused to believe any of it could happen. And it took first hand experience to change his mind. He had to see the mess before he saw the light.

"As bad as the Yanks are—and I do admit we sometimes seem pretty bad—when there's trouble where our own people are concernd, we do everything to help them. Right now I'm sick and tired of all this petty bureaucracy and poo-pooing all over the damn place while your people are dying. I feel like pulling out of this thing and heading for home. Christ almighty, I stick my neck out to get this dust crap over here, I offer to put up with all this ridiculous playing about, and what do you do? The whole operation is jeopardized because you won't play ball with some meglomaniacal Colonel who's got his head screwed on the wrong way. What the hell *can* I do. Or can the American government do when they put their biggest secret up for open use in England and you risk the whole thing? Damn it, the only thing that keeps me here is seeing things like that little kid in there, half dead and suffering God knows what— and Trevor there who's lost his parents and Christ knows how bad he is underneath. It's not their fault, but by God they're suffering for it. It's our mistake which is killing these people off."

Trevor sensed something was wrong though he and Randall could hear nothing. He frowned and glanced up at Randall. Randall only smiled reassuringly and drew his attention to some cows and sheep in the fields alongside the road.

Thomas tried to relax. "Look, Sir Joseph, England won't be the first country to dump someone who's causing trouble. It's not like you're going to *kill* him—just keep him out of the way for awhile. Not long. Just long enough for us to dust the land and leave. I mean what else can you do? What exactly would you do if you were in my boots?"

"Probably pack up and leave, like you said. After all, it's not your fight. But I probably would have had the sense not to get involved in the first place—at least not to the extent to which you're involved. Whether you like it or not, you're up to your neck and over in this. You've got three planes arriving now and another lot tomorrow. You've put yourself right in the middle and you know exactly what would happen if you called the whole thing off—you'd be no better than old Combs. Combs is worried about one thing—himself. He's nursing an old grudge. And that's exactly what you're doing. You're fed up because nobody plays ball, as you call it. You won't get anything out of this except perhaps a clap on the back from our people and an honour from the Queen. What's that to an American? Nothing. But you haven't come through hell and back just so you can pack your bags and depart. Think of your new son up there and the responsibility you have to him. I agree with you, Glen—the whole thing smells—it's all wrong. But we've got to do something about it. You've come this far and you know ruddy well you won't quit. Save your steam for Combs—why don't you go down to Whitehall and tell *him* all this? It might do some good there."

Thomas drew in his lips and clenched his fists. He could feel the anger pulsing through every fibre of his muscles, and his ears sang with pounding blood. He gazed icily out upon the sodden countryside, and he heard the swishing of rain chasing the tires. The clouds were oppressive, and though the rain had taken a rest, the roads were soaked, the fields heavy with water and the air close enough to strangle him. The moisture and the cigarette smoke and the heated car stifled him, and he could think of nothing but the pounding tension. The lack of sleep and tense meetings had been building up. He had been expecting it. Someone had to pull out the plug so he could let go. Now he had to extricate himself from the predicament in which he was placed by his own anger. It was the Yanks against the Limies, and he knew *he* would have to step down from his horse and throw in his sword before the English would. He was one man against a government. His teeth clenched and his muscles rippled. A peal of thunder rolled in the distance, there was a flash, and Randall switched on the windscreen wipers in anticipation of the coming storm. He turned to Sir Joseph who was looking out the window, but who knew the Major's eyes were upon him.

"Well, Major . . . What is it to be?" he asked quietly.

"How do you use this thing?" he replied, picking up the handset of the radiophone.

Sir Joseph looked at him. He took the receiver. "Seven zero Juliet Whiskey here."

"Comcent clear down," replied a voice from London.

"Major Thomas wishes a word with you," and he passed the phone.

"Can you locate Mr. Chadwell for me? He is? Good. Yes, I'll wait."

In the silence that followed, Thomas kept his eyes fixed on the back of Trevor's neck, though he felt that he was being watched. He felt tricked, but he didn't mind. Sir Joseph played a mean game of chess, but he had done it to protect his country. "Hello? Chadwell? Thomas here. Listen, I've heard all about Combs latest and I want you to tell him something. Tell him it came from me on behalf of the Yanks. Tell him he can keep his job as C-in-C and that it was all a mistake. Say we realized how valuable having a man like him on our team would be. Tell him, tell him anything but make it believable. Just keep him happy for a while until we can sort something out."

"You know what this means, Major?" Chadwell asked.

"Yes, I know. Never mind. I've got a plan I think. You just do as I say and I'll see you when I'm in again."

"Right-O, Major. Good luck."

"Thanks, Chadwell, but you'll need the luck." He placed the receiver down and smiled faintly.

"And what exactly does all this mean?" Sir Joseph

asked. "What are you going to tell your people tomorrow?"

"Nothing. Combs can sit in Whitehall and think he's directing operations. But he won't be. I'm setting up shop at Ruislip. You can arrange for a carbon-copy of exactly what Combs has—a link-up with Comcent, maps —all the stuff we'll need to direct operations ourselves. As long as Combs sits tight in London, he won't have the slightest idea that he's being double-crossed. All his instructions will be received and acknowledged—and promptly ignored."

"But you can't just direct the Air Force to do one thing while Combs is telling them to do another. They'll pick it up on radar for one. He's sure to suspect."

"Your Air Force, Sir Joseph, will be doing what Combs tells them only they won't be dropping the dust. I'm getting our boys from Detrick over in the special dusters, and while Combs thinks the RAF is flying the dust, ours will be doing the job. If you want, your planes can do whatever the hell Combs tells them to so long as they don't mind wasting a lot of fuel."

"And you think you can pull it off—getting your own dust I mean?"

"You just watch. I'll pull it off. Leave it to me."

Sir Joseph left Thomas to his own thoughts until the car pulled into the long drive which led to his country residence just beyond Stoke Poges. Somehow he felt that things were returning to normal, that he could once again rely upon the American support. It has been a close call. He had sweated out the long minutes the Major took to make up his mind, somewhat confident that he would come to the right decision. And when he had made the call to Chadwell, Sir Joseph felt relief. Though the rain had come, the air was cleaner. The tension was gone.

Whitehall. 18:55 Hours

Combs' fist was thundering down on the table map when Chadwell entered. Admiral Downing-Wright was cowering in his chair beneath a tirade of derision aimed primarily at the Americans while Air Marshall Coff grinned to himself as the carefully plotted markers bounced across England.

"Message from Comcent—from Major Thomas, Sir," Chadwell offered meekly.

"Confound Major Thomas," Combs shouted. "No doubt he's behind all this. Never did like the man."

"He's made an apology, Sir. There was a mistake."

"Mistake—what mistake?"

"He apologizes for any information which you may have misconstrued to mean you were being relieved of your command of this operation," he replied as he had rehearsed it.

"Misconstrued? Me? Nonsense. I distinctly heard that the Americans were going to take command."

"Maybe they changed their minds, Colonel," the Air Marshall grinned. "Perhaps they feared the wrath of the British Army."

"Let me get this straight, Chadwell. You mean that I'm still in charge of this project—perimeter and all?"

"Not exactly, Sir. You direct the attack. We're still using the Americans' powder, but you will have command of the operation. The actual dispersal. After all, you know best where to drop it."

"Dust," he spouted, though somewhat more complacent. "That miserable powder instead of disinfectant. Never work. Never. How can a few tons of falling powder do more than ground to ground and air to ground disinfecting?"

"Never mind, Colonel," said the Air Marshall. "You

still have your command. That's all you wanted, wasn't it?"

"Now see here, Chadwell, you better not be pulling any fast ones. I've been in the service too long to be crossed, you know. I can smell a rat. Why should the Americans suddenly back down?"

"Perhaps there was nothing to back down from," he replied. "Perhaps they never meant to assume control in the first place. After all, Major Thomas did say—"

"Damn the Major. Anyone would think *he's* running the show. It's a British problem and the British should fight it—win or lose. Shouldn't have those bloody Yanks in England anyway. I was always against having colonials marching around our research plants getting all our ideas. No wonder they're so keen to help. You'd think they have enough what with Vietnam and all."

"That's precisely it," Chadwell began. "They do have enough. It's damned fine of them to offer to help. They don't have to, you know. And the Americans are not exactly foreigners. They have their finger in half the British pie already, or didn't that occur to you?"

"Of course that occurred to me," he snapped viciously. "And it's damned sickening. Why, we should kick them out once and for all. You act as if there's no England left. There is, damn it," he shouted, once again rendering a blow on the map and again rearranging the markers. "And there's enough of her left to stand on her own two feet. It's the British Army, man. And the Air Force and the Navy. You mean to say that our combined forces aren't good enough for the job?"

"It's not that at all, Combs," retorted the Admiral. "Of course we're up to it. It's just that we don't have the right method to fight this plague. It's not like war, you know. It's a disease, and the Americans have the means to deal with it."

"So do we. I say this disinfectant idea is as every bit as

good as that powder. Why shouldn't it be? Our people are developing it."

"Then where is it?" demanded Coff bluntly. "Last I knew they had formulated a disinfectant strong enough to dissolve half the country. Is that what you want to do?"

"Naturally not. Takes time, doesn't it? This powder wasn't developed in a fortnight, either, I bet. But it won't be long. I've got the best men on it."

"And how long are the people supposed to wait until your men come up with the right formula?"

"As long as they have to. Damn it, we sat through the last war all right, didn't we? They've been warned what to look out for, haven't they? They're not children, you know. If they do as they're told, well, then they have nothing to fear."

"What about the children, Combs?" Coff persisted. "What about that swimming pool in Slough? What's going to happen if Thomas is right and that water was infected?"

"They should have closed the pool. Bloody fools running that council."

"So how long, Combs? How long before we can drop this disinfectant? The Yanks can begin shooting tomorrow. Can you?"

"Well, if—"

"They may not begin tomorrow," Chadwell began carefully.

"There, you see," announced Combs happily. "Even the Americans are delaying."

"Not because they're delaying, Colonel," Chadwell continued. "They're ready to drop it now if they had the equipment here. It's just that Major Thomas sounded as if he might withdraw his support. He's rather cheesed off about all this, you know."

"About what—" Combs demanded indignantly.

"Withdraw?" the Admiral choked. "You mean pull out?"

"Yes, Sir. That's what I deducted from his tone."

Both the Air Marshall and the Admiral bolted up. "Look here, Colonel," started Coff. "If the Americans do pull out, we've had it. We need their support and you know it."

"What's the matter, Air Marshall," replied Combs coldly. "Think we can't handle it?"

"Goddam it, Combs, we all know you and your bloody Army can handle it only we need all the help we can get. This isn't a bloody war game, you know."

He looked disgusted. "That's the problem with the services today. No guts. No initiative. No one wants to take risks. Push them up against the wall and they run for cover. There're always risks. Look at you two—you sit there totally unconcerned with what's going on while your country is dying all around you. What have *you* done? Well, go on, tell me. What have you done?"

The Admiral drew himself up. "Combs have you gone mad?"

Coff flushed angrily. "Look here, you blind bastard. We've had enough of your high-mindedness. You haven't even given us a chance to do anything. You're the one who sits around on your fat ass and dictates everything. If the Yanks pull out because of you, they'll hang you by your, by your bloody great crotch. And I'll pull the bloody lever." He snatched his cap from the table and stormed out, slamming the door behind him.

The Admiral spoke softly, but he was fighting the repressed fury in his voice. "Combs, there are three services in England to-day. If we lose the Americans, I shall see to it personally that yours loses its C-in-C so bloody fast they won't have time to celebrate. You're nothing but a pompous naïve bungler with ideas that even Queen Victoria would have laughed at. You should be locked away in a pensioners' home." He made for the door. "I'm getting on to Thomas straight away. If what Chadwell here says is true, I'm finding out exactly what we have to do to keep him and his men and if it means dumping you in the nearest bog, by God, there'll be many who'll gladly help! You've lost this battle, Combs. You may as well surrender."

Chadwell didn't hang around long enough for the door to close behind the Admiral, and he followed after him as he headed for Comcent.

Combs stared at his map, at the rearranged perimeter markers, and the red flags which indicated his troops. He turned to look upon his machines which clattered hesitatingly in the corner as if awaiting his command. He walked to his desk and unlocked the bottom drawer. He knew he wasn't finished yet.

The Air Marshall was waiting outside Comcent when the Admiral arrived with Chadwell in hot pursuit.

"That blithering idiot's going to get us all screwed to a wall," he cried. "I don't mind playing his little power game for a while, but if we've lost the Americans, we might as well kiss this country good-bye. We haven't even gotten near the right formula for his bloody disinfectant."

The Admiral turned to Chadwell. "How bad did Thomas sound?"

"Not bad at all, actually," he replied, leaning casually against the wall. "I think he has every intention of carrying on as usual."

The Admiral thought he was losing his mind, too much pressure, poor fellow. "You—"

"I won't say that I got the impression Thomas wasn't damn close to pulling out, but he's not the type. No matter what happened here, he would have stuck it."

"Then what the blazes is all this about?" Coff demanded.

"It was a little plan that Murray figured out just before I left Comcent with the Major's message. He figured Combs would react the way he did and you played right into his hands. I doubt whether the Colonel will even want his command by morning—not after losing your support."

The Air Marshall smiled, then laughed. He glared at Chadwell. "You little two-timing bastard. You sneaky, underhanded bastard, Chadwell."

"Don't look at me—it was Murray's idea. He figured if he got you two worked up enough through Combs, you'd tell him exactly what to do. And you did. It worked perfectly."

Lt. Saunders pushed through the doors with a message clutched in her hand. She looked worried and angry. "Did you agree to this order? If you did, would you mind telling me what the devil is going on? Those men aren't exactly chess pieces, you know. It's—"

Coff snatched the message. "Hush up, woman. What's this order?"

"Combs has ordered the men to return to their camps. The perimeter line is to be abandoned."

The Admiral looked up incredulously. "He's done it. He's bloody well flipped his lid."

"Maybe he's surrendered," Coff said quietly. "But we'd better see what he's up to. Lieutenant, has this order gone out?"

She shook her head. "The men have just taken up new positions and there's a helicopter down that had to make an emergency landing. They're scattered all over the place. No one really knows what to do. The area commanders have given up deployment until someone makes up their mind."

"Then cancel the order. Tell the men to rest easy."

She nodded and returned to Comcent.

"Back into the lion's den," said Coff.

"He's really crazy," replied Chadwell. "He can't make an order like that. Not without Lord Tenningly and Sir Joseph knowing about it."

"It may be his final act of defiance, Chadwell. What do you think, Admiral?"

"I think the whole business is bloody sickening."

They pushed open the door to the Colonel's room. He stood by the window facing them with a revolver clutched in his hand. "I thought that would bring you running. Think I'm mad, do you? How mad does a man have to be to kill himself?"

The Air Marshall stepped forward. "For God's sake, Combs, put that thing down."

"You take one more step and I'll pull the trigger," he snapped, raising the gun to his head.

"You're going to pull it anyway, Combs, so why wait? Go ahead, get it over with. You've got your audience."

Chadwell thought he saw the Colonel grimace when the shot rang out, but he was distracted by the bits of bone and flesh that struck into the far wall. When he glanced back, the Colonel had collapsed in a pool of blood.

"He's done it," the Admiral gasped, stepping back. "The stupid bastard's done it."

"Get someone in here to clean up the mess, will you, Chadwell?" said the Air Marshall weakly. "And tell Comcent to get hold of Sir Joseph and Major Thomas."

Chadwell nodded slowly and left. He wanted to stop in the Gents before he did anything else.

The Vicarage. Stoke Poges. 19:20 Hours

"This is your room, Trevor," Mrs. Willetts said. "You and the Major can share. I'm afraid it's a small house, but you see we so rarely have need of a spare room."

He nodded shyly.

"Would you like to wash up before tea? Well, if you do, the bathroom's just down the passage on the right. I'll go downstairs and see if Sir Joseph and the Major are all right." She touched his shoulder gently and looked at him, feeling somehow the loneliness in his eyes. "Come down when you like. No rush. I can whip something up for you anytime."

"Ta," he replied without looking at her. He heard the door close softly behind him, and he walked to the window. He could see across the fields to the black ribbon in the distance which he knew was the Windsor Road, and beyond that more fields. He noticed cows grazing not far off, and from somewhere he heard children playing in the dim light of dusk. He rested his hand on the window pane and saw it trembling. He blinked. The tears were welling up inside him again, and he fought to keep them back. But the silence encouraged the memories of home, his mum and dad whom he would never see again. He felt the pangs of loneliness returning, surging up within, and a great emptiness inside surrounded and crushed him. He could think of nothing to cheer himself, only the grief and fear of the future, the unknown. He opened his eyes and he felt the warm trickle of tears run slowly over his cheeks to land on the window sill. He looked at them as they were joined by others and began to form a puddle. He felt himself crying harder, but he didn't resist. He thought of the Major's words, and searching for any comfort, he let the tears come: he let them pour out and surrendered to the shuddering sobs which wracked his body. He found the bed and buried his head deep within the pillow, hoping to find peace and happiness within its feathery walls.

"Would you like a glass of sherry, Major?" asked Mrs. Willets. "Or would you prefer something stronger?"

"Sherry would do nicely, thanks," he replied from the window. "It's quite pleasant up here, isn't it? Sort of away from it all."

"That's why I like it," said Sir Joseph. "Politics can become very oppressive. It's good to be able to get completely away from things. Like recharging one's batteries, don't you think?" He turned to his wife who was pouring the sherry from a small oaken bar. "What do you think Trevor would like, my dear?"

"I think he wants a good cry," she replied.

The Major turned from the window. "Shall I—"

"No, Major. I think he's best left alone. The poor child's been through so much. It's a wonder he's taken it so well."

"He's a remarkable boy," agreed Sir Joseph. "He's made of better stuff than most."

"You say he's lost all his family?" asked Mrs. Willets, handing the Major his sherry. "Do sit down."

He found a seat alongside Sir Joseph on the couch. "Thank you. Yes, it appears so."

"I feel so horrible when little children are involved in things like this. It's not right for them to have to suffer. Lord knows they have enough to suffer when they get older. I remember the Aberfan disaster. Terrible, wasn't it?"

"The avalanche," said Thomas. "We heard quite a bit about it in America. I believe Detrick sent some money."

"And will you adopt Trevor?" she continued.

"I guess so," he sighed. He's a fine boy. I've grown rather fond of him, though we see each other hardly at all."

"Yes, that's the right thing to do. He's very fond of you, Major. I can tell. Mothers can always tell these things. He needs someone now, and he's very lucky to have you."

237

He bowed politely. "I suppose I'm as lucky to have someone like him."

"You are," added Sir Joseph. "He'll be a fine young man soon. You can see it in him. Mind you, he's just a lad, of course, but you take good care of him and he'll be just the same as a son to you. You've very similar, you two. I can see that. And he's got a clever mind. Very little passes by him unnoticed. I could see it in the car." —He smiled. "If you don't adopt him, we shall."

"No, I'll take him with me all right. I'll get out of the service and find somewhere where he can grow up and have a good chance. Maybe in time he'll forget all of this."

"Of course he will. It'll be a struggle for a while— especially going to America and being so far from what was his home, but he'll forget the past and begin to look up to you as his father. You watch." He paused. "Do you think your friends will cure him completely?"

"He has a good chance," he said slowly. "They've cured harder cases."

"What will they do?" asked Mrs. Willets.

"You mean to treat him?"

She nodded.

He frowned as if trying to collect and collate what he remembered. "I'm afraid it's not very nice in the beginning. First they must give him a spinal tap to determine just how bad the nerve damage is—if his brain has been at all affected. If he's not too badly off, they'll inject stimulants into his vertebral column to speed up recovery of the injured nerve cells. Then he'll have hydrotherapy and physiotherapy which he shouldn't mind so much. It's his right arm that I'm worried about. It could be brain damage that's caused it in which case I doubt it'll ever fully recover." He stopped and stared into his drink. He was wondering if Trevor could stand up to the painful vertebral insertions which had pushed grown men past their limits of endurance. And the weeks after the insertions, the soul destroying headaches which not even morphine could dull as the brain struggled to replenish the cerebral-spinal fluid. He would grow thin and pale during those weeks and it would take more courage than he thought any normal boy possessed if he were to survive.

Mrs. Willets detected his sentiments. She was sorry she brought the subject up. "Forgive me, Major. It was thoughtless of me."

He smiled. "Not at all. I suppose I should be pretty used to all this by now."

"Too accustomed. That's why I brought you up here," replied Sir Joseph. "Let you have a fresh outlook on things."

The phone was ringing. Mrs. Willets made to answer it.

"I'll go," said her husband. "Pour Glen some more sherry."

"Tell me, Major, have you a family of your own?"

"Glen, please," he answered, handing her his glass. "I did have a wife. She was killed sometime ago. I live alone at the barracks at Detrick—sort of a sterile laboratory life." He gazed at her as she poured from the decanter. She was elderly like Sir Joseph, but kind. The wrinkles on her face, her greying hair and her love of children somehow endeared her to him. She was a remarkable person, but so was her husband. It was a pity that she had lost her only son.

"And this is what you plan to leave?"

"Now that I have Trevor, yes. I'll give all this up when I go back. I'd like to find a small town in New England and try again. Get a house and send Trevor to school—a day school where we can sort of grow old until he's ready for college."

"But can you—I mean, what will you do?"

"I really don't know," he replied pensively, accepting

the glass. "There's not much a retired Army Major can do in America. But I'll find something. Perhaps I'll teach chemistry and physics at a school and write or some such thing. I've saved up a bit of money—enough to get me started."

She hesitated. "Has, has what's happened changed your mind about this research?"

"Yes, I guess so," he admitted. "You don't really know what you're doing until you see it happen."

"Perhaps Sir Joseph has told you we had a son once?"

He nodded. "I'm very sorry about what happened."

"Thank you. You're very kind. He was a fine boy. Trevor is not unlike him. I can sense it—just like I could sense he wanted to cry. Mothers are like that—or have I said that already?"

He felt embarrassed.

She laughed. "I suppose I can say grandmothers are like that. Oh, it would be nice to have children, or at least some grandchildren. I get so much joy from watching them grow. My sister's children have all grown up. Now I see their children growing."

"You're very fond of kids, then."

"Isn't everybody?"

Somehow he couldn't think of Colonel Combs being very fond of children. He couldn't see Combs being very fond of anything except perhaps himself.

She finished her sherry. "I should give Trevor a few more minutes—then I'd go up. Don't say anything. Just sit there with him. It'll comfort him to know you're there."

He looked at her for what seemed a very long time.

"Glen," said Sir Joseph from the doorway. "Something horrible has happened. Chadwell has just been on to me. Colonel Combs has shot himself."

The Major stared at him, feeling relief, but feeling

shock as well. "It's a break for our side," he said at length.

"Yes," he admitted, leaning on the doorframe. "He went mad." He paused, trying to make some sense out of the terrors of the past few days. "You were right. He was a meglomaniac. He was crazy."

"Should we go back?"

"To Whitehall? No," he sighed, moving towards the couch. "No, there's no need for that—there's nothing we can do. Air Marshall Coff and Admiral Downing-Wright are handling things. Apparently Murray and Chadwell planned something that I suppose finally clinched it. They knew you were thinking of pulling out —Chadwell must have guessed it when you spoke to him—and they faced Combs with it. That forced his hand. When Coff and Downing-Wright walked out on him, well, he issued some insane order to break the perimeter line and then blew his brains out—in front of them all."

"My God," whispered Mrs. Willets. "Shocking."

"Very shocking, my dear. It won't do us any good when the press get onto it. How does it sound for the Commander-in-Chief of the operation to shoot himself? God, where's it going to end?"

The phone rang again. Sir Joseph looked up.

"I'll go," said Mrs. Willets, and when she answered she called the Major. "It's Manchester. It sounds like your men."

Thomas wasn't gone long, and when he returned, Sir Joseph had placed a whiskey on the table for him. "The first planes have landed. I asked for the dusters and they're putting the request through to Detrick now. The support transports are arriving tomorrow sometime and the dusters should reach Ruislip by afternoon if we're lucky. We should be ready to begin any time after that. And they've sent along someone for Trevor. Take care of him before we get home." He was wondering just exactly when they would reach home.

"You know," began Sir Joseph. "We're going to look pretty funny if your dust doesn't work. We'll end up using Combs' disinfectant and they'll bury the old goat in honors."

"It'll work. I know my men and I know they wouldn't even risk a try unless that dust was perfect. Wouldn't want to lose face in front of your government, would they?"

Sir Joseph nodded. Mrs. Willets excused herself to prepare tea, and for several minutes the two sat in silence until the Major glanced at his watch and decided it was time to see Trevor.

"I think I'll go upstairs now," he announced as if not wanting to disturb Sir Joseph's theoughts.

"Yes, do that. I hope he's all right."

Mrs. Willets met him in the hallway. "I'll call you when tea is ready—about half an hour. It'll give you time to do what you can."

As the Major climbed the stairs, he thought about New England, about school and a place to live. It seemed that somehow he was being cleansed of the filth which up to now had been part of his life. He smiled inwardly when he imagined the surprised expressions of his bosses when he handed in his resignation—he who had been such a devoted worker. But he forgot his work and his bosses when he pushed open the door and slipped quietly into Trevor's room. He could hear the end of what must have been a long and heart searching cry for the boy as he found a place on the edge of the bed, resting his hand on Trevor's trembling shoulders. He looked out the window and sighed softly.

Regents Park Zoo, like the rest of the places in London where people might gather, had been closed to the public. Only the staff remained active to ensure that the animals were fed and looked after. Even the bats in the bird enclosure received the same treatment as usual, though no doubt viewed by their keepers with greater respect. There was some fear among the staff that if contaminated bats were landing as near as Watford and Croydon, the zoo might easily hide one among it's cages and enclosures. Yet there was little they could do but make the occasional patrols and hope that when all this was over their animals were as healthy as before.

Their hopes were shortlived. But is was not an animal who first came down with the disease, but a park keeper. It was the more unfortunate that he failed to report his condition until it was too late for medical assistance—still more unfortunate because several of the larger animals soon collapsed in their cages and were beyond help within a few hours. All of the animals were highly susceptible. Having been in captivity all their life and perhaps for generations before, none had developed any kind of natural immunity to disease. Their body defenses were totally unable to deal with such a hostile invader. The Ministry refused to have the healthy animals shipped out should the contamination spread, and there was nowhere in the zoo to isolate them. The staff were reluctant to treat the disease should they themselves suffer, and in the end the zoo was left to its own. The disease took its course, and within six hours nearly every animal and bird had contracted anthrax and was either dead or dying.

Eventually the Army moved in to clear the corpses and treat the area. The zoo was empty, and the Ministry prayed the disease had stopped there. Around the park were some of the most populated areas in London.

Newsroom. Television Center. London. 21:00 Hours

"Rumors tonight that a high-ranking Army official committed suicide in Whitehall this afternoon have been confirmed. Colonel Reginald Combs, Commander-in-Chief of the Anti-Anthrax project and creator of the perimeter line idea, shot himself in his office at Whitehall. There is no comment from government sources, but it is believed that pressure from the intensely difficult work was the cause of his death. As Colonel Combs was the leader of the entire operation, it comes as a severe blow to those who must now take over from the Colonel. This could result in a further delay in the actual treatment of the country, but until an official statement is released, Wednesday is still the date set for disinfecting to begin.

"The situation on the Continent continues to worsen. France has reported eight outbreaks of anthrax infection, but these are believed to be mostly among cattle and have not spread. An Air France Boeing 707 which left Orly Airport on a flight to New York has crashed in the Atlantic Ocean three hundred miles off the coast of Newfoundland killing all aboard, and Air France has released a statement blaming anthrax for the cause of the crash.

"Germany has complained of three sightings, and Russia has warned England that if any bats were to come down within their territories, she would be forced to take a very serious view to the problem. "It would," said an Embassy spokesman, "no doubt have a strong effect on Anglo-Russian relations." Russia has also charged the United States of having to share the blame for this catastrophe because of her close alliance with English research in chemical and biological weapons.

"In Rome the Pope has asked for special prayers for those innocent people affected by the disaster, and he has called it a "warning for all men of peace to heed and learn from." He again reiterated his plea for a uni-lateral disarmament conference, and an end to the development of these weapons.

"In America the President issued a statement saying he sympathized with the plight of England and promised to provide whatever assistance is necessary to combat the outbreak of anthrax. He, too, expressed the view that there should be tighter controls on the research and development of chemical and biological weapons, and he has set up an inquiry into the research now being carried out in America. His previous cutback in the stockpiling of toxic weapons was a beginning, he said, but added that much, much more had to be done before the public would be safe from further accidents. "The American people must be protected at all costs, and the tragedy in Britain must be a warning to us all."

"What will the cost of this disaster be in terms of economics? Who will foot the bill and how long will it take the country to recover from the long-term effects? I put this question to Ian Fraser, Professor of Economics at London University."

In a taped interview Ian Fraser addressed his audience from a BBC stool facing his interviewer. "It is impossible to estimate what the cost of this operation will be, and it is equally difficult to estimate what compensation the government may be faced with paying. We have never had anything like this happen before so there is no precedent from which to work. In terms of pounds lost on shipping and air services alone, on imports and exports, well, it's going to run into the hundreds of millions. Even if everything were to return to normal within fourteen days, the backlog of work will set the shipping industry back several weeks at the least. Tourism will obviously be affected and no doubt next year will be the worst ever for this country. People would rather avoid the risk of possible contamination, especially to their families. I doubt trade in general would be affected once the country returns to normal, but foodstuffs may well be rejected by many countries until they are confident there is no possibility of infection. No, the cost in terms of trade and lost man hours will be something that the government will have to work very hard at to pay. I cannot see the next year as being anything but the blackest from an economical point of view."

"We have had many viewers asking us what are the long-term effects of anthrax. If the disinfectant program is successful, will there be any danger of contamination afterwards? Michael Billingsly talked with Dr. Roland Pierson from Porton Downs."

"Doctor, are there any long-term effects from anthrax infection—might a person be exposed to it and carry the disease with him for several days or weeks before becoming seriously ill?"

Dr. Pierson drew himself up and considered the question. "Firstly, one must realize that we are dealing not with an ordinary anthrax bacillus, but with a highly developed strain. Any exposure to this particular bacillus— no matter how brief—would result in death within a few hours. There is absolutely no question of becoming infected and suffering the effects a few weeks or even a few days later. Normal anthrax can kill within twenty-four hours. However, we are lucky in that the bacillus is influenced by any one of the common anti-biotics. Any person who becomes infected can be cured quite easily if he or she receives treatment more or less straight away. Even once the disease has taken hold, it can still be cured, though with a much less chance of complete recovery."

"Will the disinfecting program be one hundred per cent effective? Can the anthrax survive such an attack?"

"If the disinfecting is done properly with a formula particular to this variety of anthrax, there is no reason to suggest that the bacillus could survive. Because the anthrax is a type of bacteria, it is highly susceptible to common household disinfectant in theory, and as the major disinfectant companies are working on a highly specialized formula, I think that a thorough disinfecting would be very close to being one hundred percent effective."

"How long can the anthrax actually survive as a threat to life?"

"The common anthrax spore found in bone meal can last for years—the average is something like seven. The anthrax which has contaminated Gruinard Island off the coast of Scotland is reckoned to pose a threat to life for at least another hundred years. Whether this particular breed could survive that long or even longer is of course not known to us. There is no question of its virulence—it is extremely deadly—but whether this strength could last long, well, I'd rather not hazard a guess."

"When the disinfecting operation is over, what would you suggest the people should watch for—if anything?"

"Well, we must be very careful after the operation is complete—for a while, anyway. Quite naturally, there may be a few areas which will require a second disinfecting, but I think everyone would be able to resume their normal activities—provided, of course, that they still remain watchful to the signs of infection in themselves or their children."

"What about children, doctor? How hard will they be affected?"

"It is basically up to the parents to guard their children from possible exposure for as long as necessary. It is difficult to keep youngsters cooped up, as it were, but for the duration of this initial contamination period, it is important that they are watched carefully. Afterwards, provided they themselves are aware of the possible dangers, there is no reason why they can't return to school and so on. I think it is a shame that parents in Slough did not think to keep their children under closer observation or this terrible outbreak might never have happened."

"Do you feel, then, that the situation is safely under control?"

"I feel that everything is being done that can be done. It is an exceptionally difficult task to decontaminate half the country. We are fortunate in that nothing like this has happened before, but as a consequence it is difficult to know exactly what can be done to guarantee absolute safety. If the people take due care and heed the warnings of the authorities, I think we will all get through this disaster reasonably unscathed."

"What about yourself—have you been affected personally by what has happened?"

"If you mean have I changed my views on chemical and biological weapons research, no. What has happened is an exceptional accident—an occupational hazard you might say. But I would like to see more isolation given to these establishments. I think placing them where there exists the slightest chance of exposure to innocent citizens is asking for trouble. Undoubtedly, there will be a review of all this when the contamination period passes."

"Yes, undoubtedly. Thank you, Dr. Pierson."

The newscaster returned to the television screen. "One late report we have just received. A twelve year old boy has just died from exposure to anthrax, bringing the total fatalities to one hundred eighty five. The boy, John Rafferty, had been swimming in the Slough pool which has been responsible for a widespread contamination among children and has already claimed six youngsters.

Rafferty had been taken to Wexham Hospital where it is believed he was visited by Major Glen Thomas, the American Officer involved in the massive decontamination program.

"One final bit of news. The government has still remained silent over the whereabouts of the Prime Minister. Though a British Rail spokesman said that the PM was on the Edinburgh Express which crashed late Sunday night, this has not been confirmed by government sources.

"That's all from the BBC Television newsdesk at the moment. We advise you to stay tuned for further information on the anthrax crisis, and we will bring you reports of confirmed sightings as we receive them.

The Vicarage. Stoke Poges. 21:20 Hours

"Something wrong, Glen?" asked Sir Joseph.

"That boy they just mentioned—he was the kid I saw this afternoon. We thought he was going to make it."

Sir Joseph leaned forward and switched off the television. "I'm sorry Glen. It's rotten luck."

"Yes," he sighed, leaning back in the arm chair. "It's like sitting here and watching the country die. Bit by bit the people are succumbing to it, you know?"

"So it seems. But you must remember more people die in road deaths every month. As long as this thing doesn't get a foothold anywhere, we should make it."

"You were right about them getting hold of Combs— they didn't waste any time."

"Should have slapped a D-notice on the whole thing. At least they haven't found out about the PM yet."

"Well," he said after each had contemplated a few minutes silence, "I'm going to bed. We've got an early start in the morning I guess."

"Yes, I suppose we do."

He yawned. "First decent night's rest since Friday. I'm looking forward to it."

"I'll have Mrs. Willets bring you some tea around half seven—or would you prefer coffee?"

"Either, thanks," he replied, following him into the passage.

"Trevor doesn't stand a chance in there," he smiled as they walked towards the kitchen. "Mrs. Willets never loses. I think she's made it a goal in life."

"They certainly get on well together. She's a wonderful woman."

"I'm very lucky. She's stuck with me through thick and thin. And when you're in politics, it can get damned thick." He pushed open the kitchen door. "No money on the table, my dear? You're slipping a bit, aren't you?"

"Joseph," she cried indignantly. "I never bet with anyone younger than myself!"

He laughed. "That narrows down the opposition, doesn't it?" He winked at Trevor.

"Bed time, my boy," began the Major, standing so as to see his hand. "Unless you're losing."

"We're three games each," he replied eagerly. "Can't we play this hand out?"

"Sure. Let's see what you've got?"

Trevor pointed to his four, five, six, seven of spades and a pair of tens. "One card," he whispered.

Mrs. Willets discarded the eight of clubs. It matched his eight of diamonds, his odd card. Thomas signalled for him to take it. Trevor frowned. He pointed to one of his tens and the Major nodded. He discarded.

"Ah, gin," Mrs. Willets cried, laying open her hand. "I've been waiting for that card. Goodness me, whatever made you drop that ten?"

"He did," Trevor replied. "Made me go for that eight and give up my tens."

"Never mind, Trevor," began Sir Joseph. "I expect you'll have plenty of time to make up for it. If I know my wife, she'll have you playing rummy all day. She's fanatical about it."

"I'm not," she protested. "It's just a jolly good game for two people. Besides, tomorrow, we'll play for a penny a game. Make it more interesting."

"Shocking," said her husband. "You're teaching him all the wrong things."

"Well, I'm for bed," Thomas announced. "I'll meet you upstairs."

"Yes, some help you've been," he replied, pushing away from the table.

"I'll give Trevor some milk and biscuits to take up. You can manage that, can't you?" Mrs. Willets asked.

He nodded.

"Good night, Glen," she said.

"Good night, Mrs. Willets. See you in the morning."

Sir Joseph walked out with him and they climbed the narrow stairs. "It's just like old times in there. They used to play cards all the time when he was home."

"Your son?"

He nodded. "I'm glad you agreed to bring Trevor up. It's made Mrs. Willets very happy. And I'm glad Dr. Marsh had that serum—he looks much better."

"Thank you for having him. I think it's making a world of difference for him as well."

"Maybe help him get over his loss a bit quicker, eh?" They reached the Major's room.

"Have you got everything you want?"

"Yes, thanks. Everything's quite fine."

"Then I'll say good night. See you around a quarter to seven."

Thomas said good night and quietly closed the door. The sparsely furnished room looked comfortable in the dim light of the bedside lamp which Trevor had left on. There was quiet all around him, and even the partly carpeted wooden floor seemed reluctant to make more noise than necessary when he stepped across the room and sat on his bed. He hoisted his feet up and put his hands beneath his neck. Christ, it felt good. His body reacted to the rest immediately and his taut muscles collapsed. Sir Joseph had been right. This was the place to be.

Trevor's uncertain footsteps sounded outside. The door creaked slightly and he appeared juggling a tray on which precariously perched a pitcher of milk and plate of biscuits. He grinned as he kicked the door shut, and set the tray on the table between the beds. "She says she hopes you're hungry. She's nice, isn't she?" He began pulling his shirt off.

"Yes, very. Tell me, don't you believe in unbuttoning your shirt first?"

"Why? I only have to button it up again in the morning."

Thomas had never looked at it that way.

"I like it here," he continued, fiddling with an uncooperative belt buckle. "Is your place like this?"

"My place is about as big as this room—kitchen, bathroom, living room and study."

"Then where will I sleep if I go with you?" He still struggled with the clasp. "On the floor?"

"Come here," he said motioning to him. "I'm moving when you come. I want to go to an area called New England. It's in the East—New York, Massachusetts, Vermont and New Hampshire. It's very much like this country." He tugged at the stubborn buckle. "What have you done to this?"

"I pulled it too tight, I guess. You going to give up the Army then?"

"Yep. I've got some money saved up and maybe I'll open a shop—a big candy store. How would you like that?"

"You're fooling me, aren't you?" he grinned, looking down at the loosening buckle.

Thomas gave it one final jerk and it popped open. "Yeah, I'm fooling. I don't know exactly what I'll do—never really thought about it till now."

He stepped out of his trousers and held them up with one finger. "What'll I do with these?"

He took them, folded them in half and lay them under his bed. He looked up at Trevor who was standing naked save for his pants. He smiled at the pipe-stem arms and legs, at the slender ribs which pushed lightly against his skin and at the floppy hair which was too long and uncombed. Impulsively, he snatched him off the floor and rolled him onto the side of the bed. Trevor scrambled to break free, throwing mock punches wherever an opening appeared. The Major's strong hands gripped his arms and held him fast above him at arms length. He looked into the boy's eyes and for a moment he thought he saw something, something he was to see again many times. Trevor cocked his head and suddenly struggled to break free. Thomas let go, and he tumbled down on top of him. Trevor felt the Major's whiskers scratch his face and he laughed.

"You need a shave."

"And you need a hair cut."

Trevor rolled onto his side and propped his head up on his hand. He found a feather poking its way out of the pillow, and he plucked it, running it over the Major's face. He seemed disappointed. "Doesn't it tickle you?"

"Will power," he announced. "Here, let me try it on

you." He rolled over and took the feather. "Just keep telling yourself it doesn't tickle. That you don't feel it."

"But I do," he giggled. "Stop it."

"Ah, you're no good." He tossled his hair.

They were facing each other now, each had their heads propped on their hand, the Major in a borrowed service uniform and Trevor in only his pants and socks. Again Thomas saw that glint in the boy's eye, and he searched the corners of his mind to discover the answer.

"Are you leaving the Army because of all this?" Trevor asked at length.

"I suppose. I can't very well work at Detrick with a thirteen year old boy to support, though, can I?"

Trevor lay back and gazed at the ceiling. "When do we go?"

"You really want to go—you think you'll be happier staying with me than with your own people?"

"There's nothing for me to stay for, is there? And if I do stay, they'll only put me in a home."

Thomas couldn't reply.

"Then when will we be going?"

"As soon as this mess here is cleaned up. I should think we'll be back in Maryland by early November."

"That's me birthday, November."

"You'll be fourteen?"

"Not really," he grinned impishly. "I mean it's November—the tenth—but I won't be thirteen. You only thought I was thirteen 'cause everyone said I was."

"Then how old are you—twenty four?"

"Twelve."

"Twelve?"

"Nothing wrong in that, is there? I'll be thirteen soon enough."

The Major stretched out his arm. Trevor lifted his head to let him put it down. "Aren't you tired?"

"A little." He rolled onto his side and brought his

hands up under his head which rested on the Major's arm. He shut his eyes. "Only a little."

Thomas stroked his hair with his free hand. He looked upon his twelve year old and smiled. In America we grow them twice as big, he thought. He'll really be small for his age at school. And with the thought of school and of his own uncertain future, he closed his eyes and rested. Soon the tell-tale twitches of Trevor's body told him he was asleep, and he gently pulled him arm free. Hoping the mattress would co-operate, he lifted himself from the bed and, cradling Trevor, pulled back the covers until he could slide the boy inside the fresh, cold sheets and tuck him in. He looked down at him for a moment, smiled and sighed, and walked to the other bed. Lighting his last cigarette of the day, he poured himself a glass of milk and munched on a biscuit.

Outside the wind hurled drops of rain against the window, and he was once again reminded that this was England.

SECTION THREE: ATTACK

Tuesday, 13th October

III

He could see them as specks in the overcast sky, but they looked beautiful: three jumbo transports thundered through the brisk wind and porridge grey clouds, growing large and louder as they sank towards the roofs of the houses. He saw their undercarriages drop simultaneously, and a surge of relief pulsed through him. His own people were coming. The wind threatened to blow his Officer's cap away and made him shiver, but he hunched his back against the early chill and grinned broadly as the first transport touched down. It was followed by the second, and another after that. In perfect formation they swung their giant black noses towards the central control area and lumbered across the tarmac.

"Glen, how are you?" the Officer shouted, eagerly pumping his hand. "Christ, you look like hell—what have they been doing to you?"

"Hello, Ted," Thomas replied as eagerly. "Boy, it's good to see you fellows. I've been wondering whether I'd ever see you again."

Ted took him by the shoulder and walked him towards the tower. "Tell me, is it as bad as they say?"

"A hell of a lot worse. Half the country's affected."

"Hey, Sam," he called, stopping at the tower doors. "Check this stuff in for me, will you? I want a drink."

A Corporal who had been following them nodded. He looked about for a moment, clutching an armful of papers.

256

"It's over there," Thomas directed. "The green door." He turned to his friend. "The bar is this way."

"Where the hell is everybody? The place looks deserted."

"We've dispatched most of the men elsewhere—to the key areas. This crazy Colonel in London asked to do it. Then he blew his brains out."

"Did what?"

"Never mind. It's a long story."

"Say, you know you're famous now? We heard it on the news at Detrick. Old Huntley and Brinkley were really playing you up—"Major Glen Thomas, an Army scientist from Maryland, is the central figure in the emergency operations to save England from a dastardly end." Picture and all. Really something."

The Major pushed through a set of glass doors, walked down a barren green corridor and entered a small room. There was a bottle of whiskey on a formica trolley which stood in front of a cheap wooden desk. Two aging armchairs sat forlornly in one corner while several steel frame briefing chairs clustered around the other. Thomas walked to the trolley and poured out two glasses.

"Burr," Ted shivered. "They don't believe in heating in this country, do they?"

"You get used to it, Besides, it's their autumn. This'll warm you up."

"Thanks. Well, all the best."

"Yeah," He swigged the lot and continued in a voice Ted rarely knew him to use. "Look, Ted, it's bad. It's really bad. I've seen it—all of it. It's like nothing you've ever seen at home. I saw a whole village wiped out— people, kids, just lying about the streets. This anthrax has already killed nearly two hundred and a lot of them are youngsters. And it's going to get a lot worse if we don't sort things out pretty damned quick."

"Hey, you're really bugged by all this. That bad, huh?"

There was a map on the wall. He walked over to it and pointed. "We're here just outside London. There's a string of infected bats from here to the tip of Lands End. That's where the research plant was. Another string of bats is scattered around here in Wales and there's another lot of them along here up to Wolverhampton and Birmingham. The main concentration seems to fall around the cities. Maybe because there're more people to see them. We've had something like forty confirmed sightings and we're getting about one every two hours." He turned from the map. "These bats carry something more powerful than we've ever tried to develop ourselves. They've taken ordinary anthrax and mutated it again and again until it reached a potency where anything that gets near it is dead in a few hours. The effects seems pretty much the same, but the acceleration rate is tremendous."

Ted pushed himself onto a corner of the desk. It creaked disapprovingly under his weight, but resolved to hold him.

"The first case was in Beckington, here. A thirteen year old who caught it from his dog. He died inside of three hours—in a church of all places. He had a chum sitting next to him in the choir—he died soon after. I saw another kid last night who had been swimming when he caught the thing. Now he's dead and there are fifty odd kids in hospital who the Army managed to track down. And every time one of these cases is brought into the hospital, the chance of mass contagion increases." He walked to the trolley and refilled his glass. "I think I've hit onto something this morning. I got some information on each case and everytime a person survived the infection, he had to be injected with an antibiotic within ninety minutes of exposure. Anyone who hasn't, died.

258

There were a few exceptions, of course—like the boy, but it seems to be in the majority of cases. This particular bacillus is sensitive to antibiotics only in the initial incubation period. After that it's too strong to be affected by any treatment we know of. It's deadly all right. It's so bloody deadly that it scares hell out of me." He paused, and remembered why Ted had come in the first place. "And then there's this boy for you to see. Nice kid. And you'll never believe it, but Porton managed to snatch a sample of the cholinesterase stimulant. Lucky they did as the kid needed it, but that shows how good security is."

He laughed. "Leave it to the English to get through Tumlinson. How bad off is the kid?"

"Not too bad, I guess, but he's been under drugs all the time so how bad he really is no one seems to know. I'm bringing him to Detrick, but I was hoping you could sort of check things out now just to be safe."

"Where is he?"

"Should be over this afternoon. Have a look at him then. Meanwhile you can help me sort out this decontamination problem."

"Yeah, glad to. How old did you say he was?"

"Thir-no twelve. Got more guts than half of our kids."

He winced. "Twelve, huh? It's gonna be rough."

"I know."

"Have you thought of a chordotomy? At least for the moment?"

"Look, Ted. I haven't had time to think of anything since—"

The door opened and a timid Sergeant poked his head in. "Sir," he said, seeing the Major. "Am I glad I found you. I've been looking everywhere."

"Why didn't you look here?" Ted asked.

"Never mind," Thomas replied. "Come in. What is it?"

"Your boys from London have just arrived with the communications gear. They want to know where to rig up. Then a fellow named Murray phoned and asked why the hell you're having all this equipment set up here when you could use the one in Whitehall. Then Comcent phoned and said to tell you that Sir Joseph Willets will be contacting you to discuss this report." He handed him a slip of paper. "Then this Sir Joseph did ring a couple of minutes ago and he wants you to phone him back as soon as you can." He scratched his head. "I think that's all."

Thomas was unfolding the message. As his eyes skimmed the decoded script, a frown stole across his forehead. Without looking at either the Sergeant or Ted, he walked to the map and mentally noted several points.

"Begging your pardon, Sir, but they seemed awful impatient. They want you to call down as soon as you can."

"Tell communications to link up next door. And I want a small scale ordinance map on one wall and a large scale sectional on the other. And get me lots of markers—all different colors. Then get on to Murray and tell him to link up Combs' room with the one here so we can by-pass Comcent. God knows they have enough to do already. And tell him to mind his own damn business. See if you can't get him up here—I may need him. Then get me through to Sir Joseph. Do that first. Put the call through to me here. Got it?"

The Sergeant nodded hastily. "I think Mr. Murray is on his way up now, Sir."

"How's that?"

'He said he wanted to re-organize things a bit now that iron pants is out of the way."

"He would. Send him to me when he arrives."

The Sergeant turned sharply and left.

"Who's this Murray fellow—sounds like a live wire," said Ted, pushing himself further onto the desk.

"A mad Irishman who planned the suicide of our principle adversary. He's a good man to have around when things start hopping. He's Special Branch, whatever that is."

"And this Sir Joseph?"

"Probably the best friend I've got over here. He's in charge of all this from the government side. But listen to this." He took up the message. "Eleven more outbreaks since zero seven hundred. One's beyond the perimeter track they've set up—sort of an internal quarantine. In Wolverhampton—here—the hospitals and police stations are filling up with cases. It's what we've been scared silly even to mention. It's an epidemic. Now do you see what we're up against?"

He whistled. "Christ, it's a goddam nightmare." "What about this disinfectant idea we heard about? First I'm told to pick up a thousand back pumps, then halfway across the Atlantic we get a call through to dump them at Reykjavik. Then you say this Colonel has popped his cork. How exactly do you intend fighting this thing?"

"We've got the dust. I conned George into letting me have it yesterday. They're flying it in two hundred ton containers this afternoon if we're lucky. I've tried to rush them a bit." He knew the bomb had dropped.

"*Our* dust—from Detrick? The ZX-109?"

He nodded, grinning.

"My dust—my pet?"

"Your dust and your pet. It's our only hope."

Ted swung his head back and slammed his fist on the table. "Do you realize what this means? Do you know what'll happen if you-know-who-gets hold of it?"

"I know all of that. Sure it's a risk, but it's our money against the English people."

"But it's not our money—it's the taxpayers. Did anyone ask them before they gave it away?" He didn't feel anger so much as disbelief. "Do you know how much that stuff cost to develop?"

"A few years. A few million. And what good is it doing sitting around Detrick gathering more dust."

"Well," he replied slowly. "If you can swing it off, you've got more guts than me. They'll strip you for this if it doesn't work. You know that, don't you?"

"That's probably what'll happen. But I've got the British saying they created it and it was their idea. If we lose, they get the blame—not us."

"That won't matter a hill of beans in the States. Maybe nice and quiet, but they'll strip you clean. You'll never get within smelling distance of the Army again— not in this business, anyway."

"It doesn't matter. I'm quitting when all this is over."

"You're what?"

"That's another long story. Right now we've got a hell of a lot of work to do before those transports arrive. You're going to have to forget medicine for awhile and double as my Number Two. I want you to get onto Bomber Command or Strike Command—whatever the RAF calls it—and find me ten planes which can deliver this dust of yours from five hundred feet. We've got ten more planes on the way from Detrick and they're scheduled to arrive with the transports. But I want a back-up team just in case anything goes wrong. I want a meeting with everyone at fourteen hundred hours if our men are in, then after you've done that I want you to chase up that Sergeant if he isn't lost again and get that room next door ready as soon as you can."

Ted was shaking his head. "You're mad, Thomas. You're as nutty as that Colonel. You'll never do it. They'll strip you of everything you've got. That dust isn't even tried yet—did you know that? Sure, we let you fellows up there at the top think everything was hunky-dory, but we haven't even sprayed a bug let alone a few million people. And how do you know it's going to work against this particular bacillus?"

"I don't. We're going to use it straight as it comes and hope your life's work pays off."

"What happens if this stuff knocks off a few things it ain't supposed to, huh?"

"That's the gamble, Ted," he said slowly. "Either we let these people die from anthrax, or we give them a chance. It's better than nothing."

"What about those back-pumps? Detrick had to kick a dozen asses in the Forest Service to get those. What happened to whatever was going in them?"

"That was Combs' idea. He was nuts—fanatical. He set up this perimeter line and planned to spray all the area from the Midlands to Lands End with a specially formulated disinfectant—like you heard. That was where the pumps came in."

"So why not try that first?"

"Because the companies who were supposed to discover the magic formula for killing anthrax couldn't. The closest they got to it was a disinfectant which had the same properties as nitric acid—it ate through anything it touched. Try filling your back pumps with that, old buddy."

"So he blew his brains out over that, huh? No wonder they lost the Empire."

"He blew his brains out because he thought I was going to withdraw. That was Murray's idea."

"To withdraw?"

"To make Combs think I was withdrawing the American support. That way his colleagues turned against him. It's a lot more complicated than that—political under-

263

tones and so on, but anyway the plan worked better than anyone thought it would."

"That Combs sounds real popular. Well, it's your baby, Glen. I hope to God it works—not so much for your sake, but for my dust." He was at the door.

"Ted?" said the Major quietly.

He turned.

"You think it'll work?"

Ted stared at him and hesitated. He nodded. "I think it'll work, but I hope the country's got a hell of a lot of vacuum cleaners when all this is over."

Thomas grinned and threw his cap at him. "Get out of here. And get me that room fixed up."

"Aye, aye, Captain," he called as the door swung shut behind him and the phone began to jangle from within. "And get that boy of yours down here. I'll want to see him as soon as we get some free time."

Thomas walked to the desk and leant over to reach the phone. "Thomas here."

"Hello, Glen. Sir Joseph. Look, I want to know what your plans are for this Wolverhampton thing. It could get worse."

"You're darn right it could. I don't think we can wait any longer than necessary. I've had a check on our aircraft and they're due in around fourteen hundred if this wind doesn't blow them back out to sea. I figure we can brief our men in half an hour and deliver the first strike by three. We'll do a run on Wolverhampton first. It'll give us something to go on."

"As serious as that."

"Once this anthrax gets hold, it'll spread throughout the whole city by nightfall. There isn't enough antidote to go round without pulling it out of somewhere else which might need it next. And I doubt there's enough men to give it in time. Even if we could get enough. I've found out something else as well. I've figured that a person can survive an exposure so long as he's injected within ninety minutes from the time of contact. Anything over that and the bacillus is too resistant. That's what happened to that boy last night—the one at Wexham. It's just a theory, but all your reports seem to confirm it."

"I must get this to Tenningly. Should we inform the public?"

"It won't do much good. They'll come as fast as they can if they think they've caught it. It's the people in Wolverhampton that I'm worried about. You've got to prepare them for the air strike. Can you do it?"

"Let me know what to tell them and I'll pass it on to the television chaps. The police can handle the ones without telly."

"Tell them to inform the people to open ever door and window in their house, garage, office, factory, shop, car and so on. Put all their eating and cooking utensils away and cover sinks and cookers. Tell them to put away things they don't want to have to dust when it's over 'cause this stuff will penetrate anything. Now, is there a form of warning device—like an air raid siren?"

"There're the fire klaxons and police cars."

"Right. When our planes are about to strike—about ten minutes before—sound every siren in the city. Tell the people to get off the streets and lay on the floor—any floor out of direct hit from the dust. Have them cover their mouths with wet handkerchiefs and make sure they're wet. They must stay put for at least thirty minutes after the last attack. Then they should keep inside for an hour, then they can go back as they were. Got it?"

"I think so. I'll pass it on directly."

"Good. I just hope it works."

"So do I. Oh, and I'm sending Randall down to get Trevor around noon. He'll bring him down to you. I understand you've got one of your doctors there for him."

"Yeah, one of the best."

"Well, keep me informed on how things progress, and you'd better watch out for Murray—he left half an hour ago. I think he plans to take over."

"I'll stick him in the guardhouse—he can take over that."

"And Chadwell says to say hello. He really looks bad, you know. But he refuses to leave Comcent. Been at it three days now."

"Not as bad as when he began, huh?"

"He's doing good work, Glen. Anyway, I better get on with things here."

"Talk to you later. And let me know how this Slough thing develops. That's a weak spot for an outbreak."

The Major sat for some minutes staring at the phone. Somehow, in some miraculous way, this simple dust had better work. The epidemic at Wolverhampton would spread quickly. On birds, through cattle and wild animals, through people—everyone and everything would become a potential enemy. It would turn friend against friend, family against family, and finally brother against brother. He could see it happening. He could see it happening by morning. Then he thought of Ted, the Captain who had dedicated several years of his life to undoing what his colleagues could do. The man's devotion and time and brain had gone into every particle of that dust, and he had confidence in him. It had to work. He thought of Murray bursting in to take over. No doubt he would have his own ideas about the dusting just as he had about the perimeter. But at least his ideas were practical and well thought. He would come in handy. He liked Murray, and he now knew he liked and respected Chadwell. The poor fool had sprung from his shell into chaos, and he was trying hard to stay above the troubled waters. He could envision Chadwell dragging the reports back and forth from Comcent to the plotting room, pinning down every new sighting, watching the now obsolete perimeter track and waiting for news of the latest plan of attack. He was making up for his ignorance in Stumford, for his refusal to deny the blind faith he had in his superiors. He had been let down, and he was fighting back the best way he could. He grinned and shook his head. They were a good lot, these English. For the most part, anyway.

"What are you grinning like a Cheshire cat for?" Murray said flatly as he pushed open the door. "And what's the idea of having two link-ups—the government's going to have enough to pay without you lot around."

"Since when have you worried about how much this costs the government? And what gives you the right to come barging in here? This is American property, you know."

"Ah," he cried, jumping onto the edge of the desk. He glanced at it skeptically while it decided whether or not to hold him. "It's but lent to you, I'm afraid. So long as you prove valuable."

"And I hear you've been resting on your thorny laurels gleaned from Combs' scalp."

"I thought it worked damned nicely, didn't you? Still, I didn't expect the egotistical bastard to scatter his toupee all over the wall—but it's got him out of the way, hasn't it?"

"And what in hell does the Queen give you for that?"

"Twenty years if she knew. Killing people—or providing incentive for such—doesn't rank high on the New Year's Honors."

"So you've come to give us a hand? What's the matter, suddenly realized who's got the better team?"

"I heard Wolverhampton's got it pretty bad. I was interested to see how you're going to handle this one."

"It's handled already. I've got the dusters on the way and we're expecting a strike by fifteen hundred."

"Don't let the grass grow much, do you?"

"That's why we're the first on the moon. Come on," he said arising. "Pour yourself a drink and we'll see what our link-up looks like. Bet it's every bit as good as Combs'."

Perimeter Track. 11:00 Hours

The perimeter track was breaking up. Except for those occupying the larger towns and cities, troops returned to their vehicles and headed back to camp. It was a welcomed relief from the torrential rains and high winds of the previous night. Most had been soaked through as they huddled around their lorries to watch their tents blown away. Many hadn't eaten in eighteen hours or more and few had gotten much sleep. It was a typical Army exercise, most thought, chosen to tie in with the worst weather conditions in some of the wildest country. It was a farce. Bats, they laughed. A good excuse and so typically phoney. They had been through nuclear alert drills, flood, earthquake and avalanche drills, fire drills, but never anything like a plague of bats—diseased bats at that. But this was the Army, and it was a soldier's life they reasoned philosophically. And because security had been so intense, information about how serious the whole operation had been considered never reached most of the troops until they were home again.

Slowly the line fell to pieces as Colonel Combs' plans were burnt at Whitehall. The government in all its wisdom was staking everything on the dust—it was free, out of their hands to control and underneath it, everyone knew that the blame for failure would somehow find its way back to the Americans. Whitehall was breathing a deep sigh of relief, and they were hoping no one at Ruislip heard.

Wolverhampton. 11:30 Hours

For an hour police cars had been touring every street in the city, blaring instructions for everyone to switch on their tellies. Those who hadn't tellies were advised to turn on their radios, and those who had neither were advised to find someone who did. By half-eleven the city was one seething listening audience. Some thought it was a plan by the GPO to have a quick check on licenses, while others stopped police cars and postal workers to ask if it was all right to use their tellies and radios if they were unlicensed. The humor was not appreciated. Yet for the most part people clung to their screens hoping to hear what was going to be done about the outbreak. In some areas the fear was so great that families locked themselves indoors and refused to leave —or permit entrance to anyone. Many pubs and betting shops closed, hoping to avoid possible contamination through one of their customers. Other betting shops scrubbed down their floors hourly in an attempt to inhibit the spread of the dreaded disease. There was no doubt about it: it was the Great Plague all over again. Dogs and others pets were locked out of home—budgies hung precariously from window ledges while dogs scratched at hundreds of doors or cats mewed noisily in back gardens. It seemed strange how quickly the last war was forgotten when people stuck together to stick things out. But now no one wanted to have anything to do with even their best friends. There was no communing over the rear fence or front gate, no gathering in the local. No one popped in to see how Aunty Maud was, or what

Nan and Pop were up to. The city was shut up tight in a web of fear and every man's home had become his prison. For the War today was undetectable. Hitler, a physical object to be seen and hated, had been replaced by an unknown enemy far more insidious than the V-bombs of yesterday. It would be ironic, then, when the air raid klaxons sounded, they would herald not the proximity of danger, but the hope of salvation.

So a few hundred thousand people tuned in their tellies and transistors: the fortunate saw it in color, the less fortunate in black and white, and the poorer still had to settle for the radio. Through whatever means of communication they possessed, they listened.

Ashley Grove School for Boys. Epping, Surrey.
11:45 Hours

In the history of Great Britain there has been nothing disastrous enough to bring the ancient educational system to a grinding halt—at least not among private schools. Anthrax was no exception. Headmasters advised anxious parents that school was the safest place for their children. Lessons would continue uninterrupted, sports and games would remain unaffected, and Matron would just be a bit more vigilant.

Perhaps the headmasters were right. Only one school ever suffered from their decision.

When ten year old Eric first discovered a strangely diseased creature hiding among the bushes, he kept it to himself. It would have attracted little interest among the other boys. They dissected such things in the biology laboratory quite often and though this particular species looked fat and bloated, the white rats and frogs were much more interesting. Even when the headmaster called an assembly and very seriously warned them not to touch any unusual object they might find, and even when whispers of strange alien beings began to circulate, Eric kept his secret to himself. He hadn't touched it—he hadn't really got much nearer than a few feet so why risk a meeting with the headmaster when it would probably turn out to be a false alarm and he would only be laughed at?

"You know what it is, don't you?" announced Cecil over milk and biscuits at morning break.

Eric hated Cecil, but he listened. Sometimes Cecil managed to hear things that no one else did.

"*I* bet I know what all the flap is about," he continued proudly. "I've read about these things. I know why old foghorn won't tell us anything, too. He doesn't want to frighten us.

"So go on, brain-wave," demanded Terrence from across the table. "What *is* going on?"

"We're being attacked. We're being invaded by something from outer space. I bet it's because those dumb Yanks went poking about on the moon, too. Who can say that there's nobody living up there? Maybe they're too small to be seen, or maybe they can make themselves invisible. But that's what all the flap is about—I'm sure of it."

Eric plunked his biscuit into his milk and dribbled it across to his mouth. "Go away. Why'd they pick on us?"

"Maybe they're not picking on us. Maybe they just want to have a look around like the Yanks did."

"You think they'll attack us?" Terrence asked suspiciously.

"Maybe. Maybe they're all around us now and that's why the grounds are off-limits," began Cecil excitedly.

"What do they look like?" Eric asked slowly.

"How should I know?"

"You know everything else."

271

"They could be anything—big or maybe small. Maybe they flew down here all on their own."

The bell interrupted any further examination of the subject. But Eric now had his answer. He had been one of the first human beings to see a visitor from another planet. Maybe the very first. But he wasn't about to share his fame with anybody yet. Not until he was sure what he found was a visitor. He'd return to the bush after morning lessons and have a good look. Maybe the thing wasn't dead. Maybe it was sort of sleeping after its long journey. He would bring it to the science master and ask him. *He* would know. And then he could really show Cecil up. Of course he knew all along what the flap was about, but now he was sure. He had proof.

Ruislip. 12:00 Hours

Major Thomas was sticking red flags on the small scale ordinance survey map. Murray sat in the corner with his legs sprawled on the unsteady desk which had been brought protestingly into the link-up room. While he talked with Chadwell in London, the Captain sat at a smaller desk plotting his attack co-ordinates for Wolverhampton. In the background the teleprinters clattered away, pouring out rolls of paper in short, jerky bursts. When the Sergeant tried to approach Thomas with another message, he had to pick his way over several large cables, and through a maze of telephone wire.

"Sorry to trouble you, Sir," he managed. "But Sir Joseph asked me to give you this." He held up a bit of yellow paper.

The Major looked over his shoulder as he tried to push another marker in Bristol. "Read it, Sergeant. I'm rather busy at the moment."

"Yes, Sir. It says, 'Am sending Lieutenant Saunders up to assist. You will probably need the extra staff.'"

"Is that all—nothing more?"

"No, Sir. Shall I find out more?"

"No, Sergeant," he replied impatiently. "Just show the Lieutenant down here when he arrives. I just hope to God it's not another Murray."

Murray looked up from the telephone and crossed his legs. "You want me? Somebody call my name?"

"No, Murray. Get on with your conversation."

The Sergeant continued. "The message came through about forty minutes ago, Sir. I think the Lieutenant should be here anytime now."

"I am," said a voice from the door.

Thomas turned again from the map, but his pin missed Bristol and punctured one of the Admiral's ships off Calais. "*You're* Lt. Saunders?"

"Sir Joseph never mentioned my name to you? Surely you remember the face?"

The Captain had forsaken his co-ordinates. "Who wouldn't? I'm Captain Tarnoff, but you can call me Captain."

"And the Lieutenant knows exactly who I am—and that means Major. Won't you find a seat?"

Murray looked up again. "Hello, Lieutenant, Chadwell was saying you should be arriving soon."

"Well, why the hell didn't you tell me—what the devil are you on that thing for, anyway? Plotting another assassination or something?" the Major complained. "I can see why they sent you up here."

Lt. Saunders dropped her handbag on the desk and pushed Murray's feet away. "Sir Joseph said he wants you to ring him as soon as you hear from Manchester about your planes. He said they'll be marking the beacon there and they'll ring down to tell you they're here. And

Wolverhampton's been given the information you wanted—it's being broadcast now. And what can I do?"

"Help me plan the attack," said the Captain quickly. "It needs a woman's touch."

"Take these green flags," Thomas interrupted. "And stick them at these points on the big map over there. Then you can get the co-ordinates from Captain Tarnoff if he's managed to work them out."

"I'll help you do that," said Murray, hopping up from his desk.

"You finished that conversation damned quick," replied the Major.

Murray snatched a handful of markers from the box. "Ouch, damn it. These things have pins in them!"

"It helps them stick in," said Thomas. "It's an American idea no doubt." He finished with his flags and walked over to the teleprinters. He spent a moment reading the reports on each machine. "Three more sightings. And four more deaths. They figure there're about three hundred in the hospitals in Wolverhampton beyond help. The reports are coming in too fast for Comcent to handle." He took up another reel. "The outbreak in Slough's getting worse. It's spreading to the parents. They've closed off the Baylis Park Estate and're using the girls' school as a hospital. Somebody's found a bunch of Scouts in Wilshire—all dead." He looked at his watch. "I hope those planes are quick about it."

"It's getting worse in London, too," said the Lieutenant. "When I left, Comcent had picked up thirty eight cases in Westminster and that Regent's Park outbreak is spreading. Lord Tenningly's with Sir Joseph now trying to figure out what precautions to take. They've already sealed off all the roads."

"It looks as though to-day's the day," Thomas sighed. "We'll probably get the worst of the deaths this afternoon."

"When do we fly?" asked the Captain.

"Wolverhampton run at fifteen hundred. We'll strike the perimeter and the other bad areas as soon as we get the results."

"It'll mean night flying."

"We'll have to. We can have the planes fitted with spotlights or something."

"Flying as low as five hundred feet we're damned likely to smash into a dozen buildings, Glen."

"Well, we have to do it," he snapped. "Every goddam hour counts the way this anthrax is spreading."

"Do you think it'll work like you hope?" asked the Lieutenant.

"We'll know for certain after Wolverhampton. The effects are more or less instantaneous," Thomas replied. "Either there're no more cases after the dump or it's no good."

"Glen," began the Captain, twiddling his pencil over his plans. "We're eighty tons short."

"What?" he cried. "We're supposed to have fifty tons over."

"If the weather reports are correct, we're going to be short. There's supposed to be a high northwest wind blowing across the country all day tomorrow—that means we need another fifteen per cent concentrate. Can we get it?"

"Not a chance. It was hard enough squeezing out what we've got. You'll just have to make it stretch."

"Negative. You know we can't. Stretch it and you'll jeopardize the whole country. You'll just have to leave some areas out until you can get more."

"Can't do that, either. If this thing picks up again, it'll run into the clean areas."

"Then you better think of something. If that wind doesn't die down by at least ten knots, we just ain't gonna make it."

"What's your mixture?"

"I'm down to a minimum concentrate now—any more and it's a risk."

The Major paced the floor, stopped briefly to check his map, and paced again. He leafed through the Captain's workings, looked unsatisfied, and snatched the pencil. He was about to write some figures when he thought of something. "You say if we dilute the powder any more it'll be a risk?"

The Captain nodded slowly.

"But you're not sure whether or not a more diluted mixture would fail to have effect—you're not absolutely sure?"

He thought for a moment. "Well, we can't be sure of anything until we try it. But if we risk it and fail, there's no more dust around to try again."

"What about Wolverhampton—how much do you figure you'll need for them?"

He leafed through his calculations. "About three point five tons straight to twenty dilute."

"We can try it on Wolverhampton, then," he began excitedly. "The dusters will be here around fourteen hundred. We'll rush out two tons pure against the same twenty dilute. If it works, you can cut back your mixture for the rest of the country. If it doesn't, we can still fly another load up there and figure out another mix for tomorrow. Worth a try?"

"Anything's worth a try," Tarnoff replied. "But if this bacillis is as effective as it appears, I doubt if even the three-five mix would be enough. We've got nothing to work from. It's goddam guesswork."

"Yea, well you better pray your guesses are pretty good," he answered, grabbing his cap from the desk. "I'm going up to the tower to see if they've got anything on our transports."

Whitehall. 12:30 Hours

Sir Joseph rolled his Parker in front of his eyes. He was feeling much the same as Lord Tenningly who sat opposite him, and the Home Secretary who was peering out of the window. Parliament was in chaos. Few Members knew exactly what was going on, and the rest merely conjectured. Extremists swore the country would be reduced to a graveyard in forty eight hours, while others were still excited over the inoperable disinfectant idea. Rumors were circulating that the Americans were taking over everything, that their own government was powerless to act, and the entire decontamination program was in the hands of foreigners. The opposition censored every motion, while supporters of the party were cried down whenever they tried to speak. Reports relayed from Comcent were often themselves censored and the general picture grew bleaker and more confusing. No one person held all the facts, and as the terms under which the Americans agreed to assist were classified, no one person knew what was being done, now, when or where, or with what hope of success.

At the onset of the crisis everyone in Parliament had kept quiet about the Prime Minister, but the three days' absence in the middle of the conflict bred gossip—rumors about insanity, cowardice and death in the crash. Ugly thoughts spread quickly and there were those eager to back up their assertions with proof gleaned from inaccurate sources, from past times or from their own suspicious minds. Members were no longer afraid or hesitant to express their views, and the press were beginning to come round to the fact that something was amiss in Parliamentary circles. They were desperate for a lead to the PM, and they were pulling at straws handed out by panicky politicians, many of whom hoped to make a stand and rid themselves of any responsibility, any guilt. For the most part the press were sensibly reserved, not wanting to increase public alarm, but the scandal sheets of some newspapers went as far as prophecizing imminent doom, backed up by spurious facts and over-anxious journalists.

Under the pressure which was increasing by the hour, some Members began to crack and many couldn't be blamed for the vulgarity of the crisis; the revulsion of what was happening to their people was weighing heavily on their conscience. They had to find escape.

With the advice of the Home Secretary, Lord Tenningly had left Westminister and sought sanctuary with Sir Joseph for it was he who would be the first to hear of the success or failure of the Wolverhampton strike. Deep down inside each of them was the inadmissable shadow of confidence in the American project, but each was frightened to express any hope lest they were proved wrong; or by their very admission turned some unknown spirit against them who might jeopardize the success of the dust. It was far safer to think the worst—any improvement in the situation would come as greater relief. What made things worse, however, was that none of them could share their knowledge of the American attack with Parliament until the results of Wolverhampton were known. If it was a success, Lord Tenningly looked forward to crucifying the opposition and extremists who were at this time making the most of this horrid situation. He would brand them as cowards for their lack of confidence in their own government, and for being the source of ugly unfounded rumors. But if the project was a failure, he knew the party would be nailed before Parliament. Yet the idea of striding into the House and quietly announcing that indeed the crisis was under control, that through the brilliant political bargaining of the party, they had won—this he savoured. It would be the coup-de-grace for his, for the party's opponents, and by some slight touch of good fortune the country might rally forth to support the party once more. He thought of what the PM might do, what he might be thinking at this time had he not been laying in some deep freeze somewhere in the Midlands. "We have stuck together throughout this ordeal," he pictured him saying. "We have all suffered, but we have overcome the common enemy. We have proved ourself better than this insidious demon who dared threaten the British people." No doubt he would have given little thought to the fact that this demon came not by choice, but by being blown sky-high through some careless oversight. "But there will be harder times ahead. We must all work together to put England in her rightful position. The government has suffered disastrous financial losses, our trade has been severely handicapped, but we can and will make up for what we have lost. It has been proven by your very survival of the past few days that if we fight together, we can win, and I ask you once again to pitch in and give your all for the benefit of your families, and for England." No doubt the late PM's imagined stroke of verbal genius would be accompanied by waves of applause from the far reaches of his distorted mind. What he would have failed to realize was whether indeed the country wanted to fight on, or, war-weary and deflated, did the people want to sit back and let the government fight on for the betterment of England for a change. He shook his head to think that he had served under this man whom he knew would have once again made himself out to be a hopeless fool in the eyes of England and the world. England was gone, he admitted sorrowfully, and if the PM were still around, he would have been the type who was too busy telling everyone how safe the ship was as it sank beneath his feet. He would never notice the water rising above the funnel.

Sir Joseph glanced at his watch, and as he did so there was a gentle buzz from the telephone.

"Hello, Sir Joseph? It's Thomas. Look, I've got a report on the transports. They're over Manchester and we should have them in sight by fourteen fifteen hours. I figure we can still make Wolverhampton by fifteen hundred or maybe a little after."

"That's fine, Glen," he replied softly. "Let me know when you have a definite time for the strike."

"Any more news on your end? You sound pretty knocked out."

"Only bad news, I'm afraid. The government's in an uproar and no one really knows what's going on. No one wants to believe anyone who does, either."

"I suppose you'll be telling them something after the Wolverhampton show is over."

"I hope we can make it good news for a change. Lord knows what will happen if you fail."

"We won't fail. I've got my top men here and if anyone can do it, they can."

"I wish I could share your confidence, Glen, but I daren't think anything until all this is over."

"Well, we should know whether this stuff works by seventeen hundred. I'll get onto you as soon as we hear."

"Thanks, Glen. Speak to you later."

The others looked up at Sir Joseph, hopeful of reassurance. He stared back and shook his head. "Nothing yet, gentlemen. The American transports are over Manchester. We can expect the first air strike on Wolverhampton by mid-afternoon. Major Thomas hopes to have the result a couple of hours after that."

The Home Secretary pushed himself up and looked around for the sherry. "Is he confident?"

"He sounds confident enough—says he's got his best men with him." He lifted the decanter from the desk and pulled out the crystal stopper. "Lord Tenningly?"

He shook his head. "Have they any plans if this dust doesn't work?"

"If they do, they're known only to them. But they're a clever lot and I think if anyone can find a way out of this mess, Major Thomas can."

"And the English can't?" Lord Tenningly said curiously.

"If you'll forgive me for saying it, the English were making a pretty bad show of things under Colonel Combs. If it hadn't been for some pretty quick thinking by our Special Branch, he might still have been around. You know damn well what Combs was up to, and we all know we were powerless to act. It's too much for us to handle. We haven't got the time or money to invest in protection as well as creation of these wretched things. We spend too much already discovering those miserable creatures without developing neutralizers for each one—even if such things could be developed."

"I suppose you're right, Willets," he sighed. "We're not the country we used to be. I sometimes wonder who the devil I'm working for—the British or the Americans." He smiled. " 'There'll always be an England' "—I wish the soppy idiot who wrote that could be around to-day."

"It won't happen in your lifetime, so you needn't lose sleep over it," the Home Secretary decided. "Or in mine."

"And we should leave something behind like all good governments do."

"Oh, we'll leave something behind, but it's not what we like to be remembered for. If we lick this anthrax rubbish today, we'll have another fight tomorrow. We've got to fight like ruddy demons if we don't want the opposition down our throats. And what about the Continent—they'll be after us win or lose. Oh, no, this is only the beginning for us. Once that Pandora's box blew open, our life was cut short—politically anyway. And once we've got the lid back on, there's going to be sixty million people who want to be damn sure we keep it on." He rose stiffly. "Well, I'm going for lunch. You might just as well cry on your steak as dribble in your sherry, what?"

"That's what I find so refreshing about you," said Tenningly. "I've always admired your delicate touch. Coming Sir Joseph?"

"I think I'll have it sent up actually," he replied from the security of his desk. "I want to be near this phone if anything happens."

Tenningly nodded. "See you in about an hour then. And do let us know if anything happens."

"Only if it's good," advised the Home Secretary. "I don't want his dinner spoiled."

Sir Joseph stared after them. He watched the door close silently, and the gilt knob click into place.

The People

General reaction to the disorder, to the lack of information, to the mysterious disappearance of the PM and Combs' ill-timed suicide, and to the refusal of the government to commit themselves was varied among the classes as was the reaction to devaluation, the Torrey Canyon, the strikes, or indeed to the last War. Among the workers it gave them something to talk about, to lean over back fences and decide what was the best thing to do. It was an arguing point in pubs and while the workers downed their pints in boisterous dissertation in the public bars, their betters argued politely over gin and bitter lemon on the 'other side'. The cleverer ones preferred to speculate, and when a particular speculation struck an air of imminent danger or rang of clandestine overtones, it spread; and though emanating from no more an official source than a senior clerk or account executive, it circulated with fearful respectability. While the workers sighed of sabotage, revolution and the IRA, others feared a political coup, a take-over from one side or the other. Many just simply believed that somewhere a mistake had been made and where some swallowed their drinks in solemn fear of approaching doom, others were confident that the inconvenience of dodging anthrax-ridden bats would soon pass.

No doubt the crisis led to even greater speculation at Blades, or Simpsons. The word was out of economic disaster, and the stock market had remained shut. Investors and brokers dreaded the day when it would reopen, and shares were hastily traded and sold behind the market's back. At one point the highest off-market shares were those of the chemical companies when everyone thought the country's salvation lay in disinfectant, and ICI and Reckitt would produce more disinfectant in a day that it had in all its germ-killing life. Vast sums of money slipped out of the country and found their way into Swiss accounts, while others who were caught by the squeeze prayed that their particular bank branch was bat-proof. Executives in shipping, in imports and exports, cringed at the quarantine and awoke each morning with a stronger desire to wallow in the wretched anthrax and be done with it. While airline personnel enjoyed the holiday, the bosses of BOAC, BEA and the lesser airlines hung over the computers in masochistic terror, watching the minute by minute calculations of their losses. It seemed for once that the workers were better off, and if the crisis persisted much longer, the working class population would be joined by several thousand more and the waiting list for council accommodation would extend into an ominous unknown.

Among those who suffered most were the people to

acquire first hand knowledge of the bats. The public grew frightened of any flying object which resembled in the remotest manner an airborne mouse. Early that morning an elderly lady living alone in her Birmingham council house had just put the kettle on for tea and, waiting for the water to boil, occupied her time with the daily drudgery of cleaning the fire when she heard a scuffling in the chimney. Suddenly something flew at her and she stumbled backwards, covered in coal dust and soot. Contaminated or not, the bat fought with whatever strength it had left, and when she finally died after frantic attempts to rid her scalp of a clawing, chewing terrified bat, it was not from anthrax. When the neighbors found her some days later, her head was covered in dried blood and she was all but bald. There was no sign of the bat—it was the pathologist who determined the manner of death, but the official records demanded that her death should be recorded as one influenced by the disease, if not directly, otherwise.

Particular to suffer were the families of those who had been killed outright by anthrax, or those whose brothers and sisters, moms or dads lay critically ill in hospital, pumped to overflowing with antibiotics. Their grief and worry was nearly equalled by fear of themselves contracting the disease despite the assurances that once innoculated there was little chance of the infection taking hold. In one reported incident in Croydon a father threw himself over a bat which lay in the final throws of death rather than risk exposing his young daughter to the disease. Had it not bitten him several times, he might have survived the contamination.

One of the earlier cases was of a four year old girl in Watford. The little girl was happily occupying herself with a furry creature which had kindly dropped from the sky to play. She died two hours later while her mother lay seriously ill in hospital.

There were many such cases, some of selfless heroism, others of cowardice like the stranger who flung a young boy over an infected bat rather than expose himself, or the insanely terrified passengers at London Airport. Many people fought for each other rather than against; many stuck together as they had thirty years before. Younger families of the post-War generation seemed more neurotic as they fled in panic, heedless of the warnings. The greatest fear was not so much the discovery of a bat, but of what the bat carried. Because it was infectious and invisible, people feared each other, their children, their pets. More neurotic people feared the wind, the rain, insects and other possible carriers. It was as the Major and Sir Joseph had thought. Unknown, unseen, the disease lurked anywhere and could strike at any time. One's best friend could quite easily become one's murderer.

Youngsters regarded the whole thing as either deadly serious, or a marvelous game. They implemented a variation of "He": one child raced about the play area as an infected bat, and anyone he touched had to lie down dead. Others used the idea of death-by-anthrax as a threat to control younger brothers and sisters. The more suspect youngsters took great delight in scaring the life out of family and friends with rubber bats purchased at the local magic shop—or varying the humor slightly by laying down in the street with one of the toy beasts clinging to their necks until policemen and passers-by were successfully taken in. The police reciprocated. The youngsters were taken in.

As the government had ordered all state schools within the perimeter area closed and instead had set up specially supervised play and recreation areas, Scouts, Guides and youth organizations banded together to keep watch on the children and to make frequent calls on the old and sick. There was a great demand for babysitters as escorts to and from the play centers, or as supervisors. More adventuresome youngsters set up patrols, walking the streets or combing the park underbrush for bats. Frowned upon by police and troops, there was little they could do to stop the youthful guards. Their obvious fear that one of the patrollers might become infected in his wanderings was oftentimes realized, but fortunately it was usually discovered in time.

As news of the Wolverhampton air strike spread throughout the country, hopes began to rise, and the Nation's attention was focused on one city. People everywhere sat to await the news almost as anxiously as the distraught citizens of Wolverhampton.

Ruislip. 13:15 Hours

They had been standing on the tower platform staring out at the overcast sky for some time even though the transports weren't due for at least an hour. It was as if they saw something in the bubbling grey clouds which floated slowly but deliberately across the horizon in a timeless, endless search. Finally, the Major turned away and rested against the railing. "You know as well as I why Sir Joseph sent you up here."

Lt. Saunders smiled without turning around. She followed a bird sweeping across the runway. "He likes to run everything down there. He's not happy unless everyone else is." She watched the bird land before she pushed away from the rail and leaned against the tower wall. "He likes you a lot. I think he wishes you could stay and work with him."

"He's fond of you, as well—in a sort of paternal way. He says he'd like to see you get out more. Apparently you've developed that peculiar military disease called total absorption."

"I like what I'm doing—I like whom I'm doing it with." The wind crept through her hair and sent a shiver down her spine. She shook her head and ran her fingers through the tussled strands.

"Want to go inside—it's warmer in there?"

"No, I like it out here. It's open and free. It's a nice change from London."

"There, you see? You should be out more. The only light you ever see is from a bulb or a radar screen. It can turn you stale."

"And haven't those little creatures you spend your life examining under a microscope turned you stale?"

He hesitated. "They had, yes. But I'm getting away. I know when to call it quits. Besides, we'll be cut back to a skeleton staff when the President's cut in CBW work is made. Nope," he said determinedly, turning once again to gaze at the horizon. "I'm taking Trevor and I'm going to lose myself. I'm going to move away from it all and start something over. Maybe I'll teach—or write."

"What will you write about?"

"That's a good question. I've never written much before—just reports on what we discover. Maybe I'll write about this."

"This?"

"You know—everything that's happened here. Make lovely reading."

"I thought you wanted to get away from it all."

"It'll be my final gesture. I'll have said what I want to say and then everyone can take a running jump."

"The embittered soldier."

"Who's embittered? It's not our anthrax that's wiping out your people. I've just begun to realize the whole thing's ridiculous—pitiful. How much have the two of us —America and England—spent on CBW research? Say a few billion as a modest estimate. Then after we spend several years proving how horrible the little beasties we create are, the President decides he's going to save the world and cut back the stockpiles and so forth. We're gonna destroy all our creepy-crawlies in one fell swoop. Millions of them, all going bye-bye."

"Surely you're pleased—that's what you want after all this."

"Sure I'm pleased. I'm damned pleased. But I'm not pleased that all this money was simply wasted on messing about with dangerous biologicals. And how are we supposed to dispose of the stockpiles—flush them down the Whitehouse toilet? Look at your anthrax here. I can live for years and suppose some of that doesn't stick to the bottom of the ocean or wherever they dump it—then what? We'll have this all over again. You just can't spend years developing some highly resistant bug costing millions of dollars and simply say get rid of it. Some of it's bound to stick around. It's stupid, Joan. It's goddam stupid. All that time and money. All that risk—everyday, six and seven days a week, bending over some mutated monstrosity and hoping to God your rubber gloves don't pop a leak. Christ, no wonder kids today think we're crazy."

"Not if people like you try to show them you're not."

"Any suggestion how?"

"Write your book. Tell the world what you want them to hear. Prove you're right and they're wrong if you think you can."

"In other words get it off my chest."

"If that's where it is."

He made to answer, but the tower controller stuck his

head around the door. "Bravo Julliet's on approach.
She's due in any minute."

Thomas and Lt. Saunders scurried into the warmth
of the tower where he snatched the microphone. "Hello
Bravo Julliet. Command Delta. Over."

The speaker crackled. "Reading you Delta Command.
This is Bravo Julliet. Over."

"Thomas here. Have you got the payload? Over."

"Roger, Glen. I am ready anytime. Just let me bring
this thing in. Over."

"Is that Doug?"

"Roger. And I've been flying for eighteen hours so
keep out of my way. Bravo Julliet out."

He handed the microphone to the controller. "Get
him down safe, huh?"

"Yes, Sir. 'Bout five minutes."

"Well, this is it," Thomas said to the Lieutenant.
"Care to see how we do it?"

"I think someone else wants to see, too," she began,
looking out over the tower onto the tarmac. "Isn't that
your friend in Sir Joseph's car?"

The Major peered out of the windows. The Bentley
had parked just below them.

"That's Trevor—he's gone into the building with Randall."

"Thank God he's arrived. Ted's got just enough time
to examine him before everything starts hopping."

Thomas followed her down the winding stairs, along
the corridor and into the link-up room. Trevor was
standing next to Randall who was talking to Murray.

"What brings you out here?" Thomas asked, ruffling
his hair. "Sick of playing rummy?"

"Sir Joseph asked me to collect the lad, Sir," explained
Randall. "I'm on my way into London to get him now.
He said you wanted him for an examination."

"Why not?" Murray called out. "Have the whole family in. I mean this isn't a secret operation or anything."

"Well, find a chair somewhere and sit quiet, huh?" said the Major. "There's someone here who wants to have a look at you in a minute."

He nodded and found a chair next to Murray.

"Are you any good at figures? Murray asked hopefully.

"Not too good. Why?"

"These," he pronounced, thumbing his finger against a sheet of numbers. "Co-ordinates or something. I can't figure them out."

Captain Tarnoff appeared in the doorway. "Christ, looks like a family gathering in here. And you must be Trevor," he said, strolling towards the desk. "You look well enough—from what I've been hearing, I expected you to be laid out on a stretcher."

"It's those injections, I guess," he replied nervously, wondering why all Americans seemed so tall.

"Well, you can't live on injections for the rest of your life, can you?" He turned to Thomas. "Glen, you take the boy to sick bay and I'll get my bag. Shouldn't take too long."

"How's he look?" he asked quietly.

"Reasonable. I wouldn't like to say anything for sure."

"Well, come on, Trevor," called Thomas. "You don't want to miss the excitement later on."

"Naturally," snapped Murray. "Soon as I get some efficient help around here, he's dragged off to sick bay."

"He'll be back soon enough," the Major replied.

Lt. Saunders touched his arm as they passed. "You won't hurt him," she whispered.

Thomas looked at her. He tried to smile and nodded.

"At least it's warm in here," Captain Tarnoff announced as he pushed through the door: "Now all we need is a bed or something."

"In here," Thomas said, leading the way into a small examination room. He flicked a wall switch and the powerful overhead light filled the room with an unnatural glow.

"Now you sit up here," Tarnoff began, hoisting Trevor onto the table. "Let's have your shirt off. Say, I like that tie. Always said the English had better taste than us. Especially *him*."

Trevor glanced at the Major and smiled.

"Hand me the stethoscope, Glen. And while I'm doing this, lay out my instruments on that trolley, will you?"

"Christ," he swore, pulling open the case. "What have you got in here—an X-ray machine?"

"Well, when I got the call through about gas poisoning, I didn't know what the hell to expect."

Trevor winced at the frigid metal disc.

"Breathe in. Out. In. Out," he repeated. "Good, give me a cough, will you?"

Trevor coughed. He winced again.

"Hurt?"

"A little."

"Where?"

"Here." He pointed to his chest.

"Now take a deep breath—deep as you can. Another."

Thomas had finished laying out a score of instruments, realizing that he had long forgotten the names of many of them. He had been in administration too long.

"Can I help?"

The Major turned. He felt relieved when he saw the Lieutenant."

"I was in nursing once. I thought you might want an assistant."

"Sure I do," Tarnoff replied. "You don't mind, do you, Trevor?"

He shook his head.

"Hand me the opthalmoscope."

Thomas puzzled over the instruments.

"That one," she suggested.

He handed the optical device to Tarnoff.

"Look at my forehead. Now the ceiling. Look down. To the right. And to the left. Now, follow my finger."

Trevor's eyes chased after the wandering finger until he looked cross-eyed when it zeroed in on the bridge of his nose.

"Can one of you take down some notes?"

"I will," Lt. Saunders offered, pulling a note pad and pencil from her jacket.

"Suspected lesion in right bronchus. Slight impairment of periferral—probably temporary, OK?"

She nodded.

"Stick this under your tongue—all the way back."

Trevor frowned at the thermometer. The last time he had his temperature taken, he had bitten straight through the glass.

"Cardiovascular embarrassment of the chordae tendineae possible. Noticeable murmur." He returned the opthalmoscope. "Hand me the reflex hammer, Glen. That rubber thing." He tapped Trevor's knees, ankles and elbow joint, pausing to examine the still trembling right hand. "Loss of reflex at the olecranon process. Paling of skin on right forearm. Weak pulse." He grinned at Trevor. "Nothing to worry about, fellow. Now, off with your shoes and socks. Can you manage?"

Without answering he whipped the knots undone, kicked off his shoes and pulled off two brightly colored socks.

Captain Tarnoff looked startled. He pulled his sunglasses from his pocket and peered at the socks. "My God! Only Thomas could have chosen those."

"And what's wrong with them?" the Major retorted. "They're just for a boy."

"Wouldn't be caught dead in them myself," he replied. "Remind me to get you a decent pair when you get Stateside. Can't louse up a smart outfit like that with those."

"At least I can be seen," Trevor mumbled over the thermometer.

"Yea, but it's not your feet that's important, is it? Now, back you go." He eased Trevor onto his back and unbuckled the belt clasp, handing his trousers to the Lieutenant. In a moment he was naked save for a towel which Tarnoff had thrown over his waist. "Mustn't get the women excited," he grinned.

Trevor blushed.

"You're horrible," she replied.

The Captain pulled the trolley alongside the examination table so that he could reach his instruments. Thomas stood next to the Lieutenant who was waiting for more notes, and at the same time racking her brains for a diagnosis of what she had already heard. She glanced up at the Major in a frown.

Tarnoff worried over the right forearm which refused to cease its nervous twitch. The lack of circulation which left the hand pale and slightly chilled, the weak pulse and tremble were indicative of brain damage or damage to the central nervous system, the delicate chord that was protected in the spinal column. He thought that Trevor would indeed be in considerable discomfort were is not for the injection which anaesthetized the disrupted vertebral column and assisted the distraught nerve endings in producing acetycholinesterase. As his sensitive fingers wandered methodically along Trevor's body, probing the less responsive areas, he took various needle-like probes from the trolley and tried to excite sensation of one sort or another, usually without success. Trevor, he discovered, had also lost his ticklish nature: neither the sensitive underarms or calloused soles of his feet responded to touch. When he examined the thermometer, he found Trevor was running a slight fever. Reluctantly, he deduced that his nervous regulation was up the creek—though no serious damage appeared to impair the involuntary processes, there was much impairment to the superficial epidermal layers—the nerve endings immediately below the skin which were the first to be exposed to the gas, and the hardest to suffer. It was fortunate that the internal upset seemed slight, the body was functioning normally, but he felt nonetheless that the boy had a long way to go to complete recovery. It was a vicious illness.

At length Captain Tarnoff sat Trevor up and adjusted his towel to accommodate. He looked kindly but firmly into Trevor's eyes. "I want to do something to you now, but you will have to be very strong."

Lt. Saunders glanced at the Major. She gripped his hand.

"I am going to give you something to make you feel better and so you won't have to have any more injections. What I'm going to do is inject something into you which will, well, you see you have millions of tiny nerve endings going all through your body, and many of these have been bruised. The boss of all these endings lives here." He placed his hand on Trevor's backbone. "And if we give him something to make him feel and work better, he will share it with all the other nerves and make you feel better."

"What is it?" he asked cautiously.

"It's an injection—a shot—that puts the medication

exactly where it's needed most. This way your body will heal a lot more quickly."

"What do I have to do?"

"Nothing. If you promise to lie still and try to keep steady, it'll all be over before you know it."

"Does it hurt?"

"Tarnoff didn't hesitate. He had never worked with kids before, but he was sure the direct approach was better. "Yes, it will—a bit. But the Major here and Lt. Saunders will be right next to you and you just squeeze their hands whenever you feel pain. Now, first I'm going to give you something which will make you relax," he continued, drawing a cloudy fluid from a serum bottle. "Here, give me your arm. There. Now lay back and close your eyes for a few minutes."

Thomas faced him as he turned from Trevor.

"I have to, Glen," he said quietly. "He's lost most of the epidermal nerves and the circulation in that arm is dropping. His body temperature regulation has been impaired. He'll suffer a hell of a lot more if I don't. I'm putting xylocaine in the synthehomeostasis—when it's over, he won't feel a thing."

"What will you do?" asked the Lieutenant.

"He's going to make a puncture in the subarachnoid space in the lumbar vertebra and inject a fluid into the spinal cord." Thomas explained as he watched Tarnoff prepare his instruments. "It's when he pierces through the cartilege separation between the bones that it hurts. Once he's through that, he can find the cortex quickly."

"Right," the Captain announced. "If you'll stand on that side, Glen, and keep your hands on his shoulders, and you hold his hands, Lieutenant. Try not to let him move. OK, Trevor?"

"Yes," he replied sleepily.

"Now, you let me move you," he continued, laying him on his left side and bringing his knees upwards while bending his head forward in a kind of half fetal position. "Try to keep in this position the whole time."

The backbone fully bent, each vertebra pushed against the skin. It was easy to locate the exact spot where the two inch, 20 gauge needle would ease slowly but relentlessly through flesh and cartilege into the nervous cord. It was a rare operation, but it was rare that anybody survived a nerve gas attack. It was the only way the medical team at Detrick knew to arrest the nervous disintegration which would slowly take place as a result of the VX gas. It had saved men before from the slow, tortuous death, but for many it had come too late, and Tarnoff had watched as over the weeks their minds and bodies succumbed to the loss of nervous control.

Trevor glanced up at the Lieutenant from his awkward position. He grinned, and she smiled back, wiping his perspiring forehead with a strip of gauze. He tried to determine what was going on behind him, but all he felt was the moist, cold ether, and he wrinkled his nose at the pungent smell. He became aware of a sharp, stinging sensation. He winced. He felt the Lieutenant squeeze his hand. He responded and tightened his grasp. The pain intensified. He knew something was poking its way into his back. His muscles tensed and he closed his eyes. He shut out the world of his friends and was isolated in a dimension he had never known—a world of searing pain. He bit his lip. His hands were moist but he fought to keep his grip. Tears, more from the sharp stinging than from conscious crying, squeezed under his eyelids. He wanted to move, to unfold his legs, but he forced himself to lie still. There was something pushing deeper between the tissues and his body was mobilizing its defenses against the intruder. His muscles rippled beneath his skin, and sweat trickled from his forehead and beneath his arms. He wanted to cry out, not loudly, just a whimper, but something in his mind restrained him and he stifled a muffled groan. His hands were slippery and he could feel them turning in the Lieutenant's. Suddenly there was a blinding pain that bolted up his spine, spilled like an angry wave into his head, sped down his legs and crippled the strength in his arms. His eyes burnt a fiery red, his ears screamed and his muscles tightened on the verge of snapping. He had never known such intense pain—it seemed everywhere, and it refused to lessen its grasp. His head rolled from side to side and he lost conscious thought of anything but this sensation and his lips trembled uncontrollably. He felt powerless in its clutches—his muscles were resistant to any conscious direction. There was no breath in his lungs and he could barely whisper, "Stop. Please stop." And there was no reply. "Take it out," he persisted. "It hurts so. Please."

Then it was over. Nothing. No pain—no burning. Nothing. He froze, not daring to move lest it returned this formidable companion. He waited for someone to say something, to assure him it was all over. His eyes flickered open. He tried to focus, but all he could see was red. Then the red faded and the screaming passed. The grip on his hands was loosening and someone was stroking his hair and wiping his face. He heard the jangle of metal and he looked up. Dimly—like the house lights in a theater being turned up—the Lieutenant took form and shape. His vision cleared. He blinked. He forced a smile. He cocked his head a little and he could see tears in her eyes. She bent over him as she let him lay on his back, and rubbed her moist cheek against his.

Trevor and Murray pondered the indecipherable co-ordinates, the Major added several markers to his map. They heard the transports thunder in above them after a half hour delay when one of the landing gears stuck, and the giant aircraft were followed by ten dusters.

Thomas closed his eyes and sighed. It wouldn't be long now.

Captain Douglas Lloyd looked exhausted when he appeared at the door, flying gloves and cap dangling loosely from his hand. His face was drawn and pale as he stared about the room and until he spotted Tarnoff.

"*You*," he snapped, pointing threateningly. "You should be hung by your ..." and he noticed the Lieutenant. "Pardon me, Miss," he drawled slowly, touching his forehead. "By your darned neck. If your plane hadn't a pulled out so damned quick, I might be sleepin' right now instead of bucking these storms." He found a chair near the teleprinters and collapsed in a heap. "I've been up in those skies for goin' on twenty hours. I've been from Denver to Detrick and back to Denver," he sighed, waving his hand to illustrate. "And back to Detrick. Now I'm in England. My damn plane develops undercarriage problems and I can't even get down. Where do you want me to go next? Don't tell me." He pushed himself from the chair and walked to the maps. "Back to Detrick. And what in thunder are all these flags—someone havin' a celebration?"

The Major nodded to Ted. "Come on, Captain Scarlet," he replied, taking him by the arm. "We're having a conference next door and you're guest speaker."

"I ain't speakin' to nobody," he protested, winking at the Lieutenant. "Haven't you guys ever heard of battle fatigue?"

"Yeah, and we all got it so shut up," said Tarnoff. "You've got a lot more flying to do before your day is over."

"Oh yeah—says who?"

"Says me," Thomas replied, pushing open the door to the conference room. "Find a seat and shut up."

"Where?" he asked forlornly, noting that every seat was taken.

The Major and Captain Tarnoff walked to the front of the assemblage. Tarnoff sat in front of a large aerial map of Wolverhampton and its surrounds as Thomas began.

"For those of you who I haven't had the pleasure to meet, I am Major Thomas and my colleague here is Captain Ted Tarnoff. I know that some of you from the RAF never got much of a briefing before you were flown out here, so my job is to instruct you in the dissemination of the aureobacillus particles, affectionately referred to as the dust. In particular I want to get two teams off the ground by fifteen hundred whose task it will be to strike Wolverhampton where the greatest danger lies. I think Captain Tarnoff is the best man to explain the procedures and the properties of the dust, so I'll let him begin."

There was a scuffling from the rear of the room, and the Captain waited for the men who had just flown in to find somewhere to stand. Lloyd had sat on the floor. "The dust is not unlike any other finely ground powder. It disseminates quickly, but it has a specific gravity heavier than most powder and is less influenced by light winds. It is highly penetrative in its proper dilute form and will settle as easily indoors as out. What it is made of is still highly classified, and even if I could tell you, it would serve no useful purpose. It is harmless to humans and animals in proper dilution and perfectly safe to handle.

"Your job will be to fly parallel paths across the country on certain pre-determined co-ordinates and dump this stuff in strictly regulated amounts. Basically, it's as simple as that. But since your flight patterns and the amount you drop is governed by the wind, I cannot give you your co-ordinates and flight plans until immediately before take off. The first team will leave straight away and as soon as the results come through from Wolverhampton, you'll all be dispatched as quickly as possible. It will mean a lot of night flying, much of it over cities at low altitude, so each of your planes is being fitted with search lights now.

"The two aircraft which will form the Wolverhampton strike force will carry two tons pure concentrate each, but you will not dump this amount on the first runs. I shall be up there with one of you and I'll work out how much we should scatter when we're over the target." He paused clasped his hands together. "Gentlemen, I must tell you that this dust has never before been used in large scale attack such as the one in which you will be involved. It is therefore imperative that you make no mistakes. I cannot over-emphasize this enough. The amounts you drop must be strictly regulated. There is no room for errors." He looked to his side. "Major?"

Thomas stood up. "You all must realize by now that this is it. Either we succeed to-day or the whole thing is off. Every citizen in this country is depending on us so let's not let them down. As the Captain said, it is imperative that you follow your instructions to the letter. We haven't got enough dust here to make a clean sweep of the country, so we're having to cut the concentration down. If too much is dumped, we'll run short, and if too little goes down, it will have no effect. I leave it to you, gentlemen, and I know you'll carry this operation off the best you can. Now, I want Captain Lloyd to take one of the dusters on the Wolverhampton run, and I believe you boys from the RAF have decided on sending Flight Lieutenant Crowder."

"Yes, Sir," replied one of the Officers. "He's the best man for the job."

"Good, Captain Tarnoff will go with Captain Lloyd, and I'd like you, Flight Lieutenant, to take one of your navigators along with you. He'll be able to hold contact with Captain Tarnoff. Any questions? Then all I can say is good luck. No doubt you will all hear how it has gone as soon as I do."

The Major stepped down and as he did so Captain Lloyd pushed through the gathering who were making for the door. Cowder was talking with Tarnoff when Lloyd pulled the Major aside. "I've heard of no rest for the wicked," he protested, "but Christ almighty, I'm not that bad. Major, I'm bushed. I've had it. I saw three different runways when I came down on approach and I was sure there was an extra engine on my wing."

"You can do it, Doug. I'm depending on you. You can handle those dusters like your own hand and right now everything's hanging on an accurate drop. It's our only hope."

"Yeah, well, you're putting an awful lot of hope in an awful tired pilot."

"Never mind. Come on, we better get the flight plan." He looked towards Captain Tarnoff and signalled for him to follow with the Flight Lieutenant. They made their way past several Officers and flying crews who were standing about in the corridor, and headed up the stairs to the tower. Outside they could see two of the dusters being wheeled onto the tarmac, only just refuelled and filled with the precious cargo. Never had so much depended on so little.

Wolverhampton. 15:15 Hours

The announcement came. Throughout the city every fire alarm and police klaxon shrilled and reverberated, and the inhabitants headed for cover. Windows and doors stood open along every street, but there was no one in sight. Main streets usually packed with shoppers were deserted. There was no traffic, no lorries, no buses. Aside from the wailing of hundreds of sirens, the city was silent.

And when the sirens ceased, it was an unearthly quiet that was unbroken until the steady throbbing of two low-flying aircraft approached from the Southeast. Everywhere people instinctively turned their heads and looked up: from crowded bathrooms, corridors and drawing room floors, from beneath beds and tables, and even from wardrobes and under cars, people turned to hear the engines.

"Tango Charlie to Tango Delta. Over," said Captain Tarnoff.

"Tango Delta. Over."

"We'll make our first run from the Northwest. Plot your co-ordinates as three-one-five and zero-niner-seven. Over."

"Roger, Tango Charlie. How much of this stuff do we dump? Over."

"Set your counter to feed out one hundred pounds every fifteen seconds. Approach at five zero zero level and even off till your glide reads zero. Speed one five zero. Over."

"Roger. I'll run parallel to you all the way. Over."

"Roger. And be mighty careful with that dust. Check she feeds out clean, right? Over."

"Roger. Tango Delta over and out."

The two aircraft swung low over the city, lumbered slowly into the Northwest and banked sharply. Dropping down to five hundred feet, they decreased air speed. Captain Tarnoff checked his glide and gripped the dump lever securely. He leaned against the cockpit window to see the ground. Satisfied, he glanced towards Tango Delta, shaking his head. The plane dropped another twenty feet and slowed to what seemed a crawl. They were over the outskirts, still dropping. They reached four hundred and thirty feet. He looked again at Tango Delta, checked his glide, nodded vigorously, and pulled back his lever to mark one hundred pounds. Suddenly a fine sheet of white particles streamed away to the ground. Tarnoff looked quickly from side to side and grinned; it was a perfect dump. He had calculated wind velocity, airspeed and altitude precisely. Below, several hundred feet were being covered in each sweep and as they banked for another run back, he waved triumphantly to Tango Delta.

"Easy on," said Lloyd from the pilot's seat. "You're rocking the boat."

"Tango Delta to Tango Charlie. Over."

"Looking good, Tango Delta."

"Romeo One, here. How's it going?"

"Perfect, Glen. It was a perfect dissemination. We're covering about five hundred feet each per run. The powder's settling spot on. It looks beautiful from up here."

"How much more to go?"

"I estimate ten more runs. We'll have about three quarter ton each left over. It's sure to work."

"Roger, Tango Charlie. Let me know when you're on your way back."

"Wilco. Tango Charlie over and out."

Ruislip. 15:40 Hours

"He's done it," Thomas exclaimed. "By God, he's hit dead on!"

"Easy on, old man," said Murray quietly. "You don't know if the stuff works yet."

"Half it working depends on the dissemination," he countered jubilantly. "A good spread gives it every chance."

"When will you know for sure?" Trevor asked.

He looked at his watch. "It's nearly quarter to four

303

now. Figure they finish up in twenty minutes—we should have a confirmation by six. There's some fellows from Porton up there now with samples of the anthrax. If it knocks them off, we win."

"You better get on to Sir Joseph," Murray was saying as he dialled through. "Here."

"Hello? Yes, Sir. A perfect drop. I should know the results by six. I'll get onto you as soon as I hear anything. Yes, Sir. That I will." He rang off. "He says to congratulate everyone, especially the boys in the planes."

"I hope we can carry on celebrating tonight," Murray said sourly.

"Oh, don't be such a pessimist," said the Lieutenant. "It's got a good chance."

"I'll believe it when the confirmation comes through. Anyone want a drink?"

The Major picked up his cap and sidled over to the door. Silently he slipped out, walked down the corridor and pushed open the doors to the runway. The clouds which had been building up in the Northwest had moved over him and a chilly wind teased his windbreaker.

"Hello," called a voice from behind. "Can I come?"

He turned. "Hi," he grinned. "Didn't you want a drink?"

The Lieutenant shook her head

"I was just thinking. You know, wouldn't it be good if Tarnoff's dust worked and all this could be over in a few days?" He began walking towards the verge of the runway. "This whole nightmare would end and we could wake up and feel clean again."

"We?"

"Sure—all of us." He paused, and they walked on in silence. "Have you ever been to America?" he asked at length.

She laughed and tossed her head back? "On my

salary? Coming up here has been the furthest I've been from London since I can remember. They don't like you to be far away at Comcent." She thought. "I wonder how Trev will like it."

"Trev?"

"Trevor, silly."

"Oh, yeah. I guess he'll like it all right. It's a big country."

"So they say." She paused. "I've never seen a braver kid in my life. I could almost feel his pain when your Captain Tarnoff pushed that needle in. He never cried, you know. He hardly flinched. He just kept squeezing my hand tighter and tighter and biting his lip. It makes you think."

"Think?"

"His family and all. He must have had a remarkable home. He's taken everything so well. I mean first his parents, then this nerve gas thing and now that awful treatment. I wouldn't expect it from a kid, you know. And he's only what—thirteen?"

"Twelve."

"Twelve?"

"Yes, he told me last night. Everyone thought he was thirteen so he never said anything." He kicked a stone onto the tarmac.

"I just wish . . ." she began wistfully.

"Go on—wish what?"

"Oh, nothing. Just dreaming. I was just thinking that if ever I had kids I'd want them to be like Trev. But I guess he's one in a million."

"He had to be to survive that gas."

They found a grassy knoll on the edge of the runway and sat down. Thomas pulled a blade of grass and chewed it. He looked out at the barren tarmac and thought of nothing in particular, enjoying the first moments of peace of mind he had had in a long time.

SECTION FOUR: OUTCOME

Tuesday, 13th October

IV

Ruislip. 18:15 Hours

The desk had long since given up its threats to collapse: Murray was sitting on one edge, and Captain Tarnoff on the other. Major Thomas was in his chair while Flight Lieutenant Cowder and Lieutenant Saunders sat opposite. Trevor was leaning against one of the teleprinters and wondering how he had recovered so quickly. His hand had all but ceased its quivering and his muscles and whole insides felt relaxed. He wondered whether it was worth the pain of that needle. He watched the RAF Officers who hung back at the far end of the room waiting for any news. The only sound came from the teleprinters which even now refused to offer any respite from the monotony of their clatter.

Thomas looked up at Captain Tarnoff who shook his head. Suddenly the phone jangled and the Major pounced. "Hello?"

"Hello, Glen. Sir Joseph here. I take it there's no news yet."

"Nothing, Sir. I thought the men would have been through by now."

"Give them a bit longer. I hear the place is snowed under in your dust."

"Yea, it got covered all right. There's going to be one hell of a clean-up."

"It'll be worth it. We hope it will, anyway. Look, Glen, I'm leaving Whitehall now. When the news comes through, stick it on the teleprinters then ring me in the car."

"Will do. Are you coming by here?"

"Yes. I'll be picking you and the Lieutenant up with Trevor. I think she'll be a lot more comfortable with us than sleeping in the barracks, don't you?"

He grinned. "Yes, I'd think so. But it may be a long night if we're making the first attacks this evening. I'll let you know when you get here. With any luck the first planes will have left by then."

"Good enough. See you in an hour or so."

He rang off. The others looked at him. He nodded slowly and leaned back in his chair.

"What the hell are they doing up there?" the Captain snapped impatiently. "You'd think they all caught the goddam thing."

"Steady on," Cowder replied. "They want to be sure, you know."

"Yes, but how sure? Either that stuff works or it doesn't."

"You yourself told me it hasn't been used before. How can you be sure of its effects?"

"Aw, break it up," Murray cried. "It's bad enough waiting around here." He glanced about the room and spied the trolley. Hopping off the desk, he poured himself a drink, and though he was concerned that the dozen or so others in the room might share his interest, the pilots held up their hands to his offer. They still had hours of flying ahead of them. "Are any of you statues going to join me?" No one seemed interested. He corked the bottle and leaned against the wall.

"What are the plans if it fails?" Cowder asked.

"We give it another dusting as soon as we can," replied Thomas. "If that fails, we try something else."

"Like what?"

"Like I don't know. I suppose you'll have to go back to that disinfecting idea. It's about the only thing left."

"Not very prepared against this sort of thing, are we?"

"Never were. Everybody spends enough time developing it and never stops to think what's gonna cure it. Still," he sighed, pushing himself from the chair and walking to the map. "Learn the hard way." He stared at Wolverhampton and forgot about everything else.

There was a knock at the door and the Sergeant entered. "Latest reports, Sir. From Comcent."

The Major took them. The Sergeant looked around at everyone and wondered why the silence.

"Thank you, Sergeant. Let me know if you hear anything else."

Thomas spent several minutes going over the papers, and when he finished he made several plottings on his map. "One hundred and eleven killed to-day and six hundred people in the hospital. They're getting ten in hospital for every two dead every hour. The Army has cordoned off Marylebone and Croydon. There's a school in Surrey that's all been but wiped out and the Slough trouble is growing. So far there've been fifteen more confirmed sightings—all within the perimeter if that's any consolation." He let the papers fall onto his desk. "But no more cases in Wolverhampton. That's one thing in our favor."

"That's good then," Murray announced as happily as he dared. "Now will anybody join me in a drink?"

"Maybe it's good and maybe it isn't. Maybe everyone's just staying indoors. The worst of it is there'll be outbreaks everywhere by morning unless we can get off the ground pretty soon. By the time we've covered half the country, the other half will be running wild with anthrax." He closed his eyes. "Damn, if only we had been a day earlier."

"Relax, Glen, began the Captain. "You've done all you could."

"Here, here," said one of the RAF Officers.

"It's their worry now," he continued.

"It's our worry so long as we're still here. If it gets any worse even our government won't let us back in—not without quarantine." He laughed, but he wasn't feeling funny. "You know, we might not even make it out of here ourselves."

Trevor gripped his hands around the back of the Major's chair. He was frightened, and he chewed his lip nervously. He looked from the Captain to the Major and to Lieutenant Saunders. She saw his fear and tried to comfort him.

"Yes," repeated Thomas. "That would be funny."

"Hilarious," Murray retorted glumly. "I'll go pissed if I'm going anywhere. Sorry, Lieutenant, Trevor—slipped."

"I think I could use that drink now, Mr. Murray," said the Lieutenant. "Do you mind? But make it a weak one."

"Not at all. Anybody else change their minds yet?"

"In another five minutes I will," replied Tarnoff, leaning back against the wall. He hoisted his legs onto the desk top.

The Major looked at his watch. It had gone half six.

Woverhampton. 18:30 Hours

Down every street, on the pavements and rooftops, in shops, factories and homes, a thin white layer of fine powder had found its way into every nook and cranny, every crack and crevice. Nothing had escaped the particles: it had crept past windows and doors, through fences and gates, down chimneys and drains. Each of a million leaves on a thousand trees and countless blades of grass fluttered hesitantly in the breeze as if wondering what this strange film was that covered them so completely. The city shimmered in a strange opaque white while people everywhere emerged from cover to stand and marvel. It had really come. Housewives swore as thousands of hoovers roared and dust-cloths flew. Children ran about the streets and parks, kicking the dust into clouds. Cars and buses began rolling. The city was waking.

In the Government Research Office several scientists clad in heavy protective garments, masks and gloves stood around a table on which were four neatly arranged trays. Each tray contained a separate sample of anthrax: in one was anthrax taken from a contaminated bat; the next tray contained blood taken from a fifteen year old girl who had died from the infection; in number three tray was a live guinea pig who had been exposed to the first tray, and whose life depended upon the success of the dust. In the last tray was another guinea pig exposed to the second specimen. Each tray was covered in the same dust which had fallen from the sky. If the anthrax was neutralized, the bat's specimen would become harmless—the guinea pig would live, as would his comrade next door. But so far nothing had happened. Neither had the anthrax been neutralized, nor had the guinea pigs begun to show signs of exposure.

Then, at forty one minutes past the hour, the guinea pig in tray number four died. Suddenly and without symptoms, it lay on its side, twitched once or twice, and ceased to be part of the experiment. The remaining guinea pig continued to poke about its shelter, apparently as yet unaffected. At quarter to seven its breathing became erratic as it staggered from one side of the tray to the other. By ten to seven it lay on its side, not yet dead but not far from it. One of the scientists looked up and shook his head. Another walked to the telephone and dialed.

Ruislip. 18:52 Hours

Major Thomas was the first to reach the phone. "Yes? Speaking," he replied eagerly. "How did it go?"

"I regret to say it hasn't gone at all well. We lost the first guinea pig twenty minutes ago, and the other one is not far from death. The dust has failed to neutralize the anthrax specimens. It's had two hours' exposure with no other results but these."

"Oh," he choked. "Thanks. Thanks very much." Slowly his hand found the telephone as he replaced the receiver. Staring at the others, he shook his head. "It's not working. Not a chance. It hasn't had the slightest effect."

"But it had to," Tarnoff cried. "Damn it, it had to do *something*."

"Nothing. Not the least effective. It's just too strong a bacillus for the dust."

"What about a heavier dosage?" asked Cowder. "Or a second go?"

The Major shook his head. "It's not worth it. We might have had another try if it had some effect—you know—killed a little of the anthrax. But it hasn't done anything. A heavier dose might reduce the infection very slightly, but nowhere near a safe level."

"Well," Murray sighed as he held up the bottle to inpect what was left. "You'd better get on to the printers —and to Sir Joseph. I think there's just enough here for all of us."

The Major gazed at Lt. Saunders. She managed a smile and nodded slightly. "You did your best," she seemed to be saying. "You did all you could."

Murray pushed a glass in front of Thomas. "You drink this, Glen. You need it."

The Lieutenant arose. "I'll send the message. I know the codes."

"No," the Major snapped. "Not yet. I want to wait until that second pig is dead."

"Glen," said the Captain. "You're pulling at straws. There's not a hope anymore. Not a hope in heaven."

"There is that one chance," he pleaded, clenching his fist. "There's just that chance. It might be delayed—like the effect of the anthrax."

The Captain shook his head. He was about to speak when the door opened and Sir Joseph entered. Murray looked at the ceiling and downed his drink.

Sir Joseph glanced at each of them before he spoke. "I gather the worst has happened."

"Yep," Thomas replied. "It's had no effect."

"None at all?"

"Nothing."

"I see," he sighed, slipping out of his coat. "Well, we better think of something else, then. Have you notified London?"

"No," said Lt. Saunders. "I was just about to."

The Major stood up suddenly from the desk, looked abruptly from one person to the other, and pushed quickly out of the room. He headed for the doors, for the outside—anywhere but to be away from that room when the call was made.

Lt. Saunders began punching the code.

The phone rang. Sir Joseph leaned over the desk and answered it.

The Lieutenant hesitated. The code was through. Comcent would be waiting.

"Yes?" Sir Joseph began. "Yes, I believe so." He closed his eyes. "No, I haven't yet. You can send the report in the morning. Yes, I'll speak to you then. Good-

bye, and thank you." He turned slowly around and
looked at the Lieutenant. The others watched him curiously. Slowly, with an obvious effort to control his voice,
he said, "You can inform Comcent that Wolverhampton
is clean. The dust has worked."

"The Captain scrambled to his feet. "Worked?"

"The other guinea pig is alive and well. The specimens
of anthrax are neutral. The powder took three hours to
work, and it not only destroyed the anthrax, it somehow
cured the guinea pig. The men are trying to determine
how at this moment."

The Captain began laughing. "By God, it cured the
damned thing! It cured the guinea pig! It worked! It's
really worked!"

Sir Joseph collapsed in the chair and grinned. "You've
done it, chaps. By Jove, you've really done it!"

Murray blinked several times before he found the
bottle and poured himself another drink. "It's all too
bloody much for me. I've had enough!" He swallowed
his drink, looked approvingly at the bottle and made for
the door. "I'm going to get drunk. If you want me, start
looking somewhere in the hangars."

Sir Joseph looked at Lt. Saunders. "Don't you think
someone ought to tell the Major?"

She smiled. "Trevor, I think you should be the one.
Why don't you see if you can find him?"

"I think you both ought to go and find him," said Sir
Joseph.

She put her arm around the boy's shoulders and led
him past the Officers who parted a way for them. She
took him down the corridor and out through the doors
where she knew the Major would be. "There," she said,
pointing to an object in the distance. "On the other side
of the runway. Do you see?"

He looked up and nodded.

"Just tell him that everything's over. Tell him his powder's worked."

She watched him break into a run, hesitate slightly, and belt across the tarmac as fast as he could. She could see the Major bending down to listen to him—she could imagine what the boy was saying, and she knew he had said it when the Major picked Trevor up off the ground and whirled him around and around, shouting, "It worked! It worked!"

And when the echoes of the Major's words had faded away, she began walking towards them.

EPILOGUE

The bombardment of half of England and Wales began at twenty one hundred hours on the evening of Tuesday, 13th October—just four days after the Dwarf Hill Microbiological Establishment exploded, and lasted for two days. The powder worked. It was capable of destroying the anthrax bacillus, but more than this, it could destroy the disease even in those already exposed to it. By Saturday—exactly one week later—biologists from both the United States and Great Britain declared England safe. There was no further danger to man or beast, and on the Monday the quarantine was lifted. Once again ships steamed in and out of the harbors, and giant aircraft swooped into international and domestic airports. Road and rail transport returned to normal, and very slowly so did the people.

The casualty list was predictable long and tragic. When the final count was made official—including those killed in Stumford—two thousand four hundred and sixty adults and eight hundred and forty five children had died. Whole familes had been wiped out; parents lost their children, children lost their parents. Considering a population of sixty million, the actual loss of life was not as great as it easily could have been. As Sir Joseph had said, there are as many killed in automobile accidents. England had been lucky.

Parliament was in an uproar for a considerably longer time than were the people. The opposition was determined to remind the people of what they didn't need reminding—that the ruling party was responsible, and that *they* could have done better. It was an anthrax-ridden horse that was beaten month after month. Lord

Tenningly and his colleagues seemed up to it, however, and Tenningly gave his crucifixion speech just as he had planned it. He urged his fellow countrymen to stick together and help heal the wounds the disaster had inflicted. But it was England, he assured them, and so it would always be if they kept together; and as an extra measure of surety, kept his party in power.

France and Germany, the only two countries to complain of bats, got off lightly. There were ten sightings in France, all near Paris and Orly, and these, like the two in Germany, were quickly cleaned up with a disinfectant the French had managed to formulate in only forty-eight hours. Both demanded what they loosely termed "fair" compensation from Great Britain and an official apology —just for the record. They were quick to get the apology, but even today no money has yet changed hands. There just isn't any money around for disinfectant bills.

Perhaps the greatest tragedy during the four days of crisis was that of the Queen Elizabeth the Second who lay dying in the Channel. She had been hit by two bats, and though the first had been found soon after several passengers had been stricken with anthrax, the other never was. The ship was kept in the Channel by order of Coastal Command despite the Commander's pleas— and later demands—to enter the harbor for medical assistance. By the time Navy doctors and supplies of antidote arrived nearly thirty-six hours later, a quarter of the three thousand passengers were either dead or beyond help, and another hundred died before the outbreak was controlled. These figures were never entered on the official casualty list because the deaths did not occur on British soil; and as the Commander himself was among those killed and as it was only he who knew how much the authorities were to blame, little was made of the disaster and what publicity arose was ignored by the government. They denied any responsibility for with-

holding medical aid, and said that the ship was negligent
in reporting the outbreak soon enough. It didn't matter.
The government was under enough attack. Any more
fatalities for which the government could be blamed was
like adding buckets of water to Niagara Falls.

It was a couple of months later when the real figures
of loss were realized. Economically, England would have
been crippled had it not been for international—mainly
American—intervention. Vast loans were made to England both public and under the Parliamentary table.
Outstanding debts were ignored for another year, and
countries prepared themselves to wait for the back
orders of British exports. The stock market rose again
from the dead when it was felt that England was safe
enough for industry and commerce and no more bats
would find their way into the ticker. There were some
losses that Great Britain would never recover, however:
the millions lost in tourism—in air passengers alone; in
the produce which was refused by many countries for
months after; in the compensation of government ulti-
mately faced paying to thousands of families. Somehow,
though, the country managed to hobble along and many
thought she might actually recover.

Sir Joseph retired from Whitehall and politics a fortnight after the bombardment when he was sure things
were safe enough for the people. For his service he was
awarded a second knighthood. Murray and Chadwell
followed closely after him and each received, among
other things, the MBE. Chadwell resigned from the
government service and lost himself somewhere in London. Murray was promoted to a desk job in the Special
Branch where among the first items of furnishings he re-
quistioned for his office was a liquor locker—fully stocked.
Captain Harnoff was cited by Her Majesty, but in such
a way as to attract as little attention as possible. It was

still a closely guarded secret that the Americans were responsible for England's victory.

Trevor returned to America with me. We found a house in Simsbury, Connecticut, several miles from Hartford, and Trevor now goes to the public school in the village where I teach. He has adjusted very well to the American way of life and he has managed to forget much of the terrors which I was worried might scar him. Under Captain Tarnoff's care the treatment went smoothly and quickly. It was admittedly touch-and-go during the initial diagnostic and early treatment days, and Trevor seemed to totter on the edge of another world at times. But—says Captain Tarnoff—his courage and determination alone pulled him through. It seems strange to me how such a small boy could find so much strength and will to fight no matter how many times the doctors' methods appeared to hinder rather than help. It was brought home to me and to others at Detrick that this was chemical warfare.

The young lad from England won many hearts and many friends while he waited out the four months in the Intensive Care Unit. When he left Detrick in January and came home to Simsbury, there had been a going-away party that will no doubt be long remembered for the tears and happiness and American presents showered upon him. Yet out of all the fancy gifts and beautiful cards he received that night, there was one simple message he still returns to read today. "We are all very glad to hear of your recovery and someday you will have to come and see us again. Keep well and remember us." It was signed, Murray, Chadwell, Mr. and Mrs. Willets and Joan Saunders. It would warm them to know that he does remember them and often speaks of them. There is a hidden longing in him to return, and someday he will.

I have a surprise for Trevor which he does not yet

know about. I have asked Lieutenant Saunders to come to America and stay with us for a few months. Not that it was entirely my idea—Sir Joseph engineered much of it. But I am looking forward to seeing her again, and I know that Trevor has a deep affection for her, and now that he is over the worst of his loss, he will look to her as he did to his own mother.

This, then, is what happened when something that couldn't happen did, and even now no one knows exactly what caused the explosion at Dwarf Hill. Though much has been done to guard the public against a similar crisis, countries still explore the sinister realms of chemical and biological weapons. After what has happened to England, one would have thought that even the idea of experimenting with these weapons would be madness, but governments still intend to use chemicals and biologicals in a deliberate effort to destroy a enemy. Is any enemy, is any country and its people so great an adversary to merit total annihilation in so evil and cruel a way? Does not the picture of people writhing in death from gas poisoning, or ridden with anthrax or some other biological, mean anything to civilized governments?

Surely what has happened in England—what could happen anywhere at any time—is enough to destroy what in a few hours could destroy mankind.

Major Glen Thomas, U.S.A. (Ret.), O.B.E.

are you missing out on some great Pyramid books?

You can have any title in print at Pyramid delivered right to your door! To receive your Pyramid Paperback Catalog, fill in the label below (use a ball point pen please) and mail to Pyramid ...

PYRAMID PUBLICATIONS
Mail Order Department
9 Garden Street
Moonachie, New Jersey 07074

NAME_____

ADDRESS_____

CITY_____STATE_____

P-5   ZIP_____